Damned Rite

Melt

Signed by author

Janine-Langley Wood

J L Wood.

Published by Bad Day Books, an imprint of
Assent Publishing

For Shane and Jessie: making me the best I can be.

ACKNOWLEDGMENTS

Jim & Margaret
Many thanks to Marianne for the push.

PART ONE

A Beginner's End

CHAPTER ONE

Only the most skilled bikers scaled the avenue that cut up Rokerville's heart, and even they had to crank down to first gear midway. The estate crawled as far up the moor as was practical before the wind would whip off the roofs of the houses and deposited them around Beggars' Rock along with an array of crumpled beer-cans, spent hypodermics, and plastic bags snagged on the heather.

On one frost-peppered February night, setting out from a cul-de-sac at Rokerville's lower end, Callum Heslop took a stroll up that hill with a single purpose in mind. This was a school night, a week after the Heslop's old tomcat Percy had gone missing. Cal's gangly frame was conspicuous by the signature knee-length parka with the grubby looking hood strung in around his face. Within the furred canopy, his sallow bone structure supported the kind of glasses your mum has to get you if she's on benefits. Not a face you'd pick out of a line up; not for anything more drastic than a bout of hedge-hopping on mischievous night.

Odd members of the gang stationed at the Heslops' gate but lazy on weed, not expecting their target to drift absently past them, gave Callum minor hassle then drifted back to their sick-motor-based chat, resolving to "well-batter him" on the way back in. They were to be disappointed—Callum would not go back in. He walked along to the parade of shops with the Booze-Buster, the cut-price freezer store, then the rest just planked-up windows, before he began the incline of Rokerville Avenue. At the summit, he turned left to where the terraces had a view across to the moors; a bleak view only interrupted by the vast, dark structure of Saint Luke's Church, which, apart from the cordoned off grounds, was then still in use.

The only eyewitness who drove slowly by at the time—minding the *Skidding Hazard!* signs—would later state that they saw the young man trying the church doors. Callum did try the church doors but didn't persist. On finding the way barred, his mind quickly reverted to its original purpose. The *Keep Out* signs punctuated the high wire fencing that now separated the church pathways from what had once been a regular playground for the estate's Catholic kids. Behind the meshing, ancient stones and monuments earmarked for laying-down and reclamation still stood upright. Callum instinctively knew where the breech would be. Vehicle access gates had been installed in readiness for the scheduled demolition work. A padlocked chain ran through the central handles. Tonight the padlock hung unclipped—a detail that would later cost the current site manager his job. With bluing hands, Callum unthreaded the chain and entered the cemetery grounds. He trampled a path through the overgrowth to where he used to play as a child, ultimately to his favorite hiding place, the chest tomb. The heavy stone structure stood about a meter high and around two in length. The top tablet bore only the date *1537* and the inscription *Unknown.* At some point, the side panels had fallen outwards, leaving only the narrow end-stones to support the tablet's weight, while also allowing former hide-and-seekers access underneath.

Callum hesitated, reading and rereading the inscription, as if that limited information taken in often enough might tell a story. Through the snaked branches of the old oak tree that overshadowed the tomb, moonlight flecked the furrowed brow within the fur hood. Moving forward a step, Callum beat down hard on the slab with his bare fists. Small whimpers escaped him as blood trickled from his broken nails. The air around him seemed to stagnate. His expression darkened and he dropped to his knees, crawling inside the canopy of the tomb, where he turned over to lay on his back. Bunked between cold, hard stone he looked out from his hiding place to the world he had to hide from. Above the weeds, all he could see were the tops of the houses facing Saint Luke's. Lights were on in some upstairs rooms, an image that should have afforded the boy a sense of warmth, only everything in his rectangular view was now swamped in a murky green light; the full-moon's effect perhaps, blurring a mossy outlook, compounded by his breath-fogged glasses. An aerial view of his position, however, would have told him differently: that the bile-green fog he gazed out through, with its subdued luminous quality, hung only around the structure he'd entered.

Callum turned his face to the thick stone less than an arm's-length from his face. Nobody could say how long he laid there for. Not long enough to rethink things, it seemed. Had he stayed at home and simply downed the bottle of anti-depressants he knew his mother kept in the bathroom cabinet his story might have warranted a snippet around page five of The Evening Post, perhaps in comment on the steep rise in suicides on the Rokerville estate in recent years.

But slipping away quietly via the anti-depressant route would not have fairly reflected the sheer living torture the boy's life had become. So what Callum Heslop did that night, in that small, cold space, was he drew back his legs and kicked. *An examination of scuffing to the footstone showed that this first attempt had failed.* There would have been a creek, a giving, a smattering of stone-dust that, had he been himself, might have jolted the lad to his senses and seen him scrambling out of the tomb and home for supper. But Callum was not himself. Not the self he recognized anymore. And so once again, gathering all his strength, he drew back his legs and kicked violently forward. And with that blow, the weight that had stood near five hundred years of weathering came down and crushed the lad outright.

Callum made the front page.

The Heslops' thirteen-year-old ginger tom, Percy, strolled casually into their house early the next day. Mrs. Heslop, who had to identify her son without a face, was never seen at Saint Luke's Church again, and in the wake of the ensuing public scrutiny, the council finally had the decency to re-house the remaining Heslops into another area.

The doors of Saint Luke's Church had not been locked. Father Fionn Malloy might have turned prematurely grey doubting it, only he distinctly remembered going out through those doors to the cemetery when he'd heard the crash, though not realizing at that time what'd caused it. The doors had opened easily. He had stayed around later than usual that night, he explained to those investigating, way after vespers and evening prayer, to try to locate the mystery cat he'd heard yowling in the building for days. The night of Callum's tragic death was the last time he'd heard it.

The priest never did find a cat.

CHAPTER TWO

The last time Father Malloy had seen Callum alive was two weeks previous, when he'd done a stint out in the cold himself—colder then. The tent was make-shift: Two good sticks, a couple of blankets from charity shops—courtesy of a whip-round at Saint Luke's—lagged over outside and in with bin-liners, then all of it roughly moored down by blocks of Yorkshire stone Fionn had found dotted around his mate's allotment—the setting for the finale of his lonesome little mission. Behind him were the two bumper-sized nappy boxes that would serve as a bed. Nothing special. No middle-class hiker's comforts, just what you'd pull together if this was for real.

A small fire burned close by. Fionn sat huddled into a sleeping bag, a faux-fur deerstalker pulled down to his brow. Strands of wild black hair overshadowed his dark eyes and the oval of his face glowed pink from the fire's meager heat and exposure to the contrasting bite of iced wind. The stubble had progressed to a short beard. It was the thirty-first night of January. The last night. From his pitch on Ben Hunter's allotment, Fionn gazed out across the green to the sprawl of house-lights that rose in their organized clutter up the hillside, to finally meet Saint Luke's Church, a Gothic monument perched on top of it all, like the great goddess of all buildings appraising her humble subjects. It felt sad, looking up at his home of ten years now, knowing her days were numbered, that soon the moonlight would shine through a void left vacant of her eerie silhouette.

A faint crackle focused him back to his current dilemma. The fire was fading. It wasn't making much difference but the thought of it going out depressed him. If he made a dash for the wood-store by the shed, took a much-needed slash, then scooped up some logs, he could be back in the relative warmth of the bag within a couple of minutes. Instead, he just threw on the few remaining sticks, shuffled himself back and pulled the tent closed, securing the blanket-flaps with pegs. A Christmas bumper biscuit-tin holding a flask, a toothbrush, paste and a Penguin Biscuit sat open by his feet. He gobbled down the biscuit, then the last of the soup from the flask. Tight in the quilted bag, he then wormed his way through the open nappy boxes, forming a fetal ball within, any intention of using the toothbrush, like having that pee, put on ice. He could understand now why somebody in this situation might soil themselves. At least it would be warm when it happened.

"I'm struggling here, y'know, God," he muttered. "I'm wondering, what the hell are You doing about all this, eh? So much for bloody Armageddon. Fire and brimstone would be welcome in more ways than one, right now."

A scraping noise came from near the shed. Somebody was climbing in over the fence not so far away from his head. The iced fog of his blasphemous words still hung in the air like a signed confession. "Shit!" he said under his breath. A sudden attempt to sit up fast in wads of cardboard and quilting had him wriggling like a slug in salt before he could so much as free a hand to flick on the torch. When his human parcel finally gave with a crack, he lunged forward, grasping at pegs with clumsy, gloved hands.

"Who is that?" He called out, panning the light around the allotment but unable to see behind the tent.

The dark pole of a man's moonlit shadow stretched out toward him.

"Seriously, I'm not fucking about here—who is that?"

An "Ooof" sounded out and the shadow lurched forward. A young voice called, "Ouch, me knee. It's just me, Father Malloy. Me mum's sent you a full flask, that's all. I'm not gunner kill you or owt."

Fionn's heartbeat leveled. "Callum! *Shit*—sorry. Thought you were trouble." He leaned further out and caught a parker-clad Callum in the torch's beam, clambering to his feet. "You okay? Come in, lad. Get out of the wind for goodness' sake."

"Alright there, mate?" the lad said cheerily. "On me way."

"You needn't be out bothering about me, not at this time of night, anyways. I'm fine. Mind the fire there, Cal. Not much of a one, like."

Callum crouched by the flickering cinders, which warmed up the pallid complexion under the Parka hood, the same old coat he'd worn three winters. For a lad of seventeen, he just didn't seem aware of how these things did you no favors.

"Were you in bed already, Father?"

Fionn surveyed the tattered boxing behind him. "I *was*. Why, what time is it?"

"It was about nine-ish when I left our house."

"Holy crap. I thought it was a damned-sight later than

that. Anyways, come in for a bit."

Callum squeezed through the gap. "Ta, mate."

There was something a bit tragic about a teenager calling his thirty five year old priest mate. Fionn just didn't know what to do about it.

"They're cracking on with the new build," Callum said as he put down the flask of tea. "Your plush new pad, eh? Bet you can't wait to move in. All mod-cons and that. Won't be long now."

"You've never come through that building site, have you, Callum?"

"Aye. Why, what's up?"

"You shouldn't have. Not without a hard hat anyway. You're not even supposed to be able to get in there, it's dangerous."

"You can though. An' it's quicker from ours."

"All that scaffolding and what-have-you. Something'll drop on your head one of these days."

"Aye well, I'm good at ducking."

The two smiled at each other, but in a humorless way. Fionn balanced the lit torch in his boot while Callum poured steaming hot tea into the flask's screw-off cup.

"Good lad, Cal. That's nice of you. Can hardly feel me flamin' hands here."

"No probs. Clap 'em around this."

Fionn sipped slowly, his shivers sending small concentric ripples over the tea's surface. "Oh, that's nice, though."

"Have you done your film diary for tonight yet, Father Fionn?"

"No, I haven't done it yet, Cal. Didn't think I could hold the camera steady enough. I reckon this is the coldest one yet."

"Yeah, but the most important as well, as it's the last. I'll do it, mate, don't worry. You stop right there. Light's good. A bit spooky but good."

So with the torchlight ghouling up their faces, Callum aimed the lens at Fionn.

"January thirty-first," Callum announced in the deep, solemn growl of film-preview-type narrators. "Here, in the dead of night, on a lonely estate in the midst of Yorkshire, Father Fionn Malloy, our hero, sits out in the cold. And it is *deadly* cold, people, and no mistake.

"Say hello, Father."

Fionn lifted one hand for a little wave before returning it to the comfort of the cup. "Hi there."

Callum cleared his throat and coughed. "Ooh, I don't think I can keep that up, mind." He swung the camera back around to meet his own smiley face and in a regular tone continued. "Cal Heslop reporting, to all those whom it may concern." Then back at the priest. "So tell us, Father Malloy, where are we now in the whole sleep-out saga?"

"Well, as you say, Callum, it is now the thirty-first of January, so, this is the thirty-first night of the group and sometimes lone camp-out, as with tonight, in support of the homeless of our city. I know you've been there yourself a few nights on the Town Hall steps, Cal. Fair to say, we've had a lot of support and some media attention. Which helps, sometimes."

Callum swung the camera back at himself for a line. "That's true, folks. I *was* out there, and believe you-me, it is *bloody* cold."

"Yeah, so, it's the last night, then we're done for this year. The bad news is Tyler, one of the lads we all grew to know and love, has passed away; Telford Tyler, as we'd come to know him. Don't know if that's actually where he came from. We've been trying to track down relatives, if he has any. Trouble is, as with so many of the young homeless, we don't really know who he is, or was. Mental health problems meant he couldn't communicate very well.

"I *can* say, on a more positive note, just today I've heard back from two of the guys, Brian and Johnno, that they've since secured hostel places as a result of the campaign. That and some of our earlier contacts from around the city center, who we know are now in housing projects. Might have told you some of that before; losing track here. Yeah, still feels like there's so much more to do, so many more people who need help just getting a roof over their heads, a very basic human need. I can't lie, it'll be good to get back indoors, but I do feel bad giving up."

"You're not giving up, Father. Nobody thinks that."

"But I will be back in a warm bed come tomorrow. A lot of people out there won't have that; the simple luxury we all take for granted—just a warm bed, a roof to keep out the snow. So, if you're watching this on Saint Luke's website or via one of the links, please, go see, go look around your own town tonight. Those people sleeping in doorways are not out there because they want something from you. They're not professional beggars as some cynics would have you believe. They're just human beings without a home. Just people like you and me. And I can tell you, they feel the cold, just the same as you or I." He raised his cup to the camera. "So, to Tyler."

"To Tyler," Callum echoed.

Fionn swallowed hard. "Okay, Cal. We should wrap it up there."

"Okey-dokey," Callum said. "Signing off for the last time,

folks. Bye from Cal." That was a line that Fionn would replay too often, smarting at its horrible significance. It was followed by the lad leaning into the frame for a last grin with the two of them in-shot before finally switching the camera off.

There was a quiet pause as Fionn sipped his cup dry, thinking bitterly about the bishop's flat refusal to let homeless kids sleep in the church, one detail of the campaign that was never voiced on the website. Why hadn't he had the balls to just do it? Looking back at Callum, he noticed that the boy's mask of good-cheer had slipped, too; his face looked drawn, older than it should.

"You not sleeping well, Cal?"

Callum flinched a little. "Oh, not great, mate, no."

"What is it they say? 'Don't let the bastards grind you down.' A couple of years from now you'll have yourself a good job. The world'll be your new back yard. You've a good head on your shoulders, and a good heart to go with it; more than can be said for most around here."

"I know. I know." Cal smiled, but the expression failed to meet his eyes. "It'll be grand."

"Not very convincing, I'm afraid. There's something else, Callum. What's up?"

Absent-mindedly, Cal wiped a dribble from his nose along his sleeve. "Well. You know the Bible, right?"

That took Fionn by surprise and it showed. "Yes. Pretty well. I think."

"You know, like, it has prophesies, about the end of the world and stuff. Well, people say they're coming true, don't they?"

"Do they? Some might. But if we believed what everyone said, the world would've ended ten times over by now."

The boy shrugged. "Me dad, though, he showed us once, this ancient part of the Bible, from the Old Testament, which is like thousands of years old. It says in there, plain as day, that the world is round—a circle, and 'suspended on nothing'. Well, nobody could've possibly known that back then. The Babylonians thought it was a big slab balanced on a couple of camels…or was it elephants? Fair enough, the ancient Greeks were wise to it, but so many civilizations had crazy ideas. I'm talking three, four thousand years B.C. How could they know what the earth looked like from space? You have to admit, some stuff's just plain weird."

"You're a smart lad, Cal," Fionn laughed. "But why worry about all that? Okay, I'll grant you that, some stuff is weird, that one included, and can't be explained away scientifically, or rationally even. I just… don't grasp your point."

Out of the blue, Callum chuckled. "Speakin' of weird. When I came over the fence, you were laid there talkin' to yourself, weren't you? Sorry, or were you just prayin' out loud? You did say the G word."

Fionn smiled. "Oh, just my ramblings. It's stage one of a process I'm going through. Stage two involves a stiff white jacket with very long sleeves that tie round the back."

"Padded cell job?"

"Not far off, son."

Callum's solemness returned. "Well, I might be joinin' you in there before long."

"How's that?"

"I just keep havin' these weird, creepy dreams. Only it's like… they're real."

"That's not surprising, really, Cal. Certain people are making your life a nightmare."

"It's not them. Not this time, and it's not exactly

nightmares, it's even worse if that's possible because it feels kind of good—I want it back..."

For what seemed like no apparent reason, the boy's head shot around, his wide eyes fixed on the entrance of the fragile structure that housed them.

CHAPTER THREE

Something landed with a crack outside the front of the tent. Fionn and Callum both stared motionless for a second as the blankets sprung alight where the campfire had been smoldering. Panic twisted Callum's face. Fionn checked the tea flask—he'd drained it. He moved quickly, scrambling first out of his bag then the tent, and as the army of dark, hooded figures by the allotment's gate casually watched, Fionn turned aside, pulled out his dick and pissed on the flames. Splashback from the shriveling bin bags peppered his jog-bottoms. Fortunately, after all the backing up, there was a copious supply of fluid in his system, so the fire soon fizzed to a stop. The remnants of a beer bottle, a blackened rag sticking out of the neck, lay scattered around the stones that contained the fire.

After he'd tucked himself back in, Fionn turned, calling over, "Nice night?"

The usual tactic was employed: gang members turning to face each other, mumbling and dragging on cigarettes. The priest wasn't there to them, except to one, a girl by the sounds of it, who sneered, "Pervert." The others laughed, but not warmly, in fact their coldness rivaled the north wind. They might as well have been mercenaries in war-torn Angola.

Fionn smiled. "So, what can I do for you guys?"

One among the group—a chunky, cartoonish, box-chinned figure who Fionn knew to be the one nicknamed Xbox—turned brazenly to confront him. His pelvis jutted forward, as if to advertise his manly wares. He drew hard on a fag, its end reddening his jawline, and barked, "You can send out yer rent-boy, nonce."

In unison, the full number of them, a dozen or more, then turned forward to face the tent. Fionn quickly recognized odd figures—perhaps it was in the pose: next in line to Xbox was a weak, weasel-like character named Kelvin Goddard, the type who would naturally suck up to the top-dog; Xbox's younger brother Monkey flanked his other side. Fionn recalled the days when a bunch like this would have scattered the moment he emerged to challenge them. No such thing would happen here. Things had gone so much further than that.

Callum's labored breathing heaved behind the flimsy wall that separated him from his priest and the hostile mob beyond. Fionn could feel the boy's dread in his own bones. As the crow flies, Callum's house wasn't closer to the allotments via the new church foundations; he'd risked his neck sneaking through that way because he'd been followed, again. Like Callum's, the hoods the mob wore obscured their faces, but not for the same reasons. Cold nights or no, in this borough, kids wore hoods for one of two reasons: to cause menace or to hide from it. It seemed people like this lot were always hot on the trail of the Callums of this world. Fionn's own gang might well've been when he was young. Unlike

Callum, he hadn't been born good. Being good was something Fionn Malloy had worked at all his life, and would continue to work at till his dying day. On his deathbed there would remain to be done one last selfless deed to compensate for the wrong he'd inflicted, the hurt he'd caused others, and the anger that quietly stewed his guts whenever he looked out at the world, as he was looking out now.

"I'd offer you a drink, lads." He stooped, venturing a glance under the hoods. "And ladies?" One small figure beside Kelvin ducked her head. Fionn felt a surge of disappointment. "But I'm all out."

He was wasting his time. There'd be no charming them, no way he could punch it out either—he'd come unstuck that way before; winning a fight wasn't always the answer. All he could do was stand his ground and hope they'd give up and go.

"Heslop!" Xbox roared. "I've got summat for you. It's this cat we found." Laughter ran along the line. "I reckon it used to be ginger but it's kinda gone black now. Someone's microwaved it, y'see, so it's a bit busted open and sticky lookin'. But I reckon it can still catch me a *rat*."

Muffled sobbing bled out of the tent. *Don't*, Fionn thought. *Fucking don't give them the satisfaction.* "Fire and fucking brimstone," he spat under his breath. "Bring it on. I'm all out of sermons, God help me." Any pretence of good humor had abandoned his face.

Some among the line had stopped laughing. There were glances behind. Something was spreading through them, disabling their defenses like a virus. Fionn looked past them to a figure strolling casually across the green that separated the allotments from the crescent of houses at the foot of the estate. The huge man was carrying something bulky under one arm and a loaded carrier bag in the other. Fionn felt his anger subside. A nod from Xbox and the gang mobilized. Not rushing exactly, still flicking lit cigarette butts over the fence in defiance, but they were definitely on the move, and in the right direction—the fuck away. Fionn nodded over with a smile full of gratitude as the sandy haired giant reached the allotments. Under the streetlight, his hooked nose cast a beak-like shadow over his chin.

"Anywhere there's trouble," the big man said, "and there's you, Malloy."

"Hi, Hawk. Thanks for dropping by."

Ben Hunter, Hawk to his friends, hopped over the gate and threw the sleeping bag he'd been carrying for Fionn to catch. "I'll walk young Callum home," Ben said, "then we'll shell some of these, if you're up to it." He dropped the bag containing two four packs by the tent. "Out ye come, Cal. All's clear."

Callum shuffled out of the tent, chattering frantically into his cell phone, then listening intently, crying more with relief than anything else now—his cat, Percy, was safe at home. Fionn patted the lad on the shoulder as Ben led him away.

"Oh, and don't go putting my sleeping bag at the pissy end," Ben shouted back. "I saw that stunt."

Fionn nodded. "You and those damned binoculars." He watched the two walk away, suddenly aware, perhaps in contrast to Hunter's proud stature, of the wilt in Callum's, as if an unspeakable burden sat on his shoulders. Right then Fionn made a mental note to catch up with the lad, to get to the bottom of what was troubling him as soon as he next got a chance to, unaware that by the time that night's waxing moon was on the wane, his young friend would be dead.

CHAPTER FOUR

Afew weeks following Callum Heslop's death, Father Malloy stood looking out over the expanse of allotments from the steps of his new home, the new model Saint Luke's Church constructed at the foot of the estate.

Attendance for Mass at the new-build had trebled since the move from the old condemned site up the hill—working radiators being a big plus, for one. Fionn noted also that some newspapers were reviewing a similar uptrend nationwide, speculating that being hard up might be at the root of the formerly doubting populous pouring back into the churches en masse. The theory being: no longer able, realistically, to gain wealth in the material world, the need for a belief in Heaven comes back into play. One *Times* analyst declared that the whole credit crunch had in part been a symptom of ordinary people, who traditionally would have believed in reaping their rewards in Heaven, jumping in record time onto the capitalist bandwagon in an effort to grab all there was from an earthly existence. The failure of US-style capitalism and The National Lottery to deliver the goods— the latest recession plus all the subsequent years of hardship and recovery—had not only brought ordinary people back down to earth with a bang, but had retrained their sights to a higher plane, to the hope of a merciful God and rewards in Heaven.

But hereabouts, where The Lottery had failed more than most, Fionn was painfully aware of the main reason for the sharp rise in numbers. It was because of what Cal Heslop had done up there, up at the old church. Callum Heslop: the fairly forgettable, gangly youth, who would belt it out angelically above the throng at hymns; who somehow managed to get more delivered to the old folks come Harvest Festival than the rest of the volunteers put together; and who, by his final act, did more to drive the locals from Saint Luke's church than any amount of clunking radiators and ballast hurled through the windows.

Callum had made the heinous mistake, aged five, of soiling his pants in assembly in the presence of a largely unforgiving, unforgetting audience; that was a start, but the most heinous mistake came ten years later:

After spending the best part of his first four teenage years shut indoors perfecting his Xbox skills, best-scoring on the likes of Mortal Kombat and Hitman, Daryl Monk, a.k.a. Xbox—an honorary title—had resurfaced on the streets to viciously regenerate the image of Rokerville's gang; self-rule and open violence were to become its hallmarks. In the rewritten rulebook, name calling—Callum was a relatively tame "Specky-geek"—was for pussies. Xbox broadcast with gusto how Cal Heslop had "ratted him up" over an innocent, friendly punch at school—one which'd cost Callum a tooth. Monk had been suspended for a three-day reflective period, and this, he reflected bitterly, had been the start of the downturn for him. He might have stuck with school at least another year, learned more stuff, if he'd not had that taste of time out. After that, he'd rather burn the school down than show up another day. He didn't want to know. And all because Heslop couldn't take a joke.

So that was that. Overnight Callum went from forgettable to never forgotten.—he was the main job to do. Young gang members, ambitious of rank and drug related earning potential, were set business-like targets by older gang members, to be out of bed and at the Heslops' front gate by eight a.m. for bottle throwing and malicious threats. Older members targeted the whole family, blasting music outside the house into the early hours, bombarding the doors and windows with stones, dog turds, and spray paint that declared the place a "home for spastics"—that for the benefit of the wheelchair-bound Mr. Heslop. The garden was set alight, then the porch. Threats were leveled at anyone who dared to complain—usually Mrs. Heslop, who in her upset only ever managed to entertain and spur them on.

Mr. Heslop grew too stressed to get out of bed. Callum's siblings were hounded around school by younger boys who proudly viewed themselves as soldiers.

The council went so far as to install a fireproof letterbox. The police, for their part, failed at every turn, mostly even to turn up, and then to take effective action when they bothered. All of which strengthened the gang's resolve—they were invincible, beyond questioning. By the time Callum crushed the life out of himself, even his closest friends were avoiding contact.

Had Fionn Malloy ever been told he'd be glad to see the back of Saint Luke's Church on the moor, he wouldn't have believed it. Saint Luke's had been his home of ten years, where he'd found a little peace in his life, where some of the closest bonds of his life had been formed. But what emerged after Callum's suicide further soured the sight of the old place, not only for the priest but for his dwindling congregation. A local journalist and historian, Carl Wilson, published evidence from mountains of ongoing research, showing that a string of suicides and suspicious deaths had occurred in and around Saint Luke's grounds over several centuries, since records of the area had begun in fact. Twenty-five years ago—meaning some locals had their memories jogged—there'd been the hanging of a man from the ancient oak central to the grounds, then the strange suffocation of a young woman at almost the same spot ten years prior—it seemed she had gone to the trouble of burying herself alive. To his friend Ben Hunter's rage, the reporter had bundled his wife Anita's death into this trend, her parents' house, where she'd slashed her wrists five years ago, being on the terrace facing the moors and the churchyard. But, elsewhere or in the churchyard, the facts were there in black and white: suicide rates on Rokerville were high. Wilson had included an aerial map bearing semi-concentric rings panning out from the church to the foot of the estate, and a dot and date for each death. The closer the rings came to Saint Luke's, the more clustered the dots became. Wilson hadn't spelled it out, but the church seemed to act as a beacon for the sick of mind.

On release of Wilson's article, a sense of unease had infected Saint Luke's parish. The Bishop pulled strings and the new Saint Luke's was rushed to completion, the date for demolition of the old brought forward. Centuries of history would be stripped away internally and sold off, the graveyard cleared, down to the last stone.

CHAPTER FIVE

And yet up there in her Gothic tower, the bells are tolling, like an air-raid siren sent to shake the calm of night, a hollow clang more at-one with waking the dead than rousing the living. Cold sleet drifts down, clinging to the priest's bare skin. In his urgency to hush the bells he's set out half naked again, his wiry frame minus all but the half cut sweat-bottoms he sleeps in. Why didn't he put on his slippers? Just a second's job—slip on the slippers; between the new place and the summit of the hill the frozen pavement sinks its steely teeth into the soles of his feet.

The safety caging is split, punched outwards down one seam, as if by an almighty fist. The solid oak doors beyond, which had been boarded shut, now stand open, the space within their frame darkly unwelcoming; the blackness has a solidity to it. Having served their purpose, the bells cease clanging. The night air falls silent. He pauses, feeling a familiar apprehension. Vague ideas, not quite memories, are returning to him. It's been a while. Or has it? His eyes are drawn to the old bell tower, where the bell, considered to have been of some value, is conspicuously absent. Fionn attempts a retreat, but a force far more powerful than his own will drives him forward, through the ruptured fencing and onwards—as in a pursuing gale, he could fall backwards and remain standing. Soon he has passed through the black wall into the church.

Beyond the threshold, an ice-cold blanket envelops him. A crackling cold. His spinal hairs stand taught. The gloom inside the church is alive, shifting, revealing only what it wants you to see. A congregation of blurred shapes gathered in the pews reek of human desolation. As his eyes adjust to the gloom, the crowd gradually evaporates into nothingness. But somebody, or some*thing* remains, down by the altar. Something unnervingly silent, whose shape is confusing—wrong—wider at the top than at the bottom; a balloon-man.

"What do you want?" he demands. "You shouldn't be in here. It's a death trap. And what's more… you're trespassing." He's said it all before. His own voice mocks him in its frailty, like the rattle of a comedian dying a death onstage. Then suddenly, without having consciously moved, he is closer to the presence. How it glows.

"Oh my!" His spirits lift and he smiles with wonder. "Are you an angel?"

Her face softens. "Is it your wish that I should be such a thing?"

"Now, now. If you're going to grant wishes then you must be a genie. But look at your wings. Those look like angel wings to me. They're so lovely. But why are they black?"

Studying them, he sees that her luxuriant blaze of feathers is actually more silvery grey than black—flecked lighter underneath.

"What color do you think angel wings should be?"

"They should be white, like the rest of you."

"Because this is what you have witnessed in impressionist paintings and in the books of infants." She states this fact rather than asking it.

"Perhaps so."

As he watches unflinchingly, she becomes clearer. She is the most perfect being he has ever been blessed to look upon, her pale face softly luminous, candle-lit. The whole vision of her is glorious. She is a living Christmas card, but for those wings.

"I gather you have forgotten me again," she says. "What should I do to deserve your constant thoughts?"

The creatures, the squirming, scuttering things that have hijacked the old church in its emptiness, scurry lively around the priest's naked feet. He tries not to look down at their advancement, and wonders why she tolerates them.

"I refuse to remember you. You are my guilt—my nightmare. I know why you summon me. Because I doubt my sanity. Because I prayed for something to happen, for Armageddon, Fire and Brimstone, whatever it takes to end the atrocities in the world. Such things are wished for when the world gets too much for men. Had I wished for aliens to land in my back garden then, no doubt, that's what I'd be seeing now instead of you."

"But with such clarity?"

Strangely, as she says it, his eyes fall on her nipples, standing prominently against her flimsy gown—the definitive chapel-hat-pegs. "Angels aren't women. Angels of the Bible are men, but rather neutral…without gender." He is flustered.

"But if what you say is true, priest—that I am present merely by the indulgence of your imagination—then it is you who has made me as I am." Her tone has changed, taken on a cynical note. "So why not just make me as I should be?"

"Okay. So, let's say you *are* real; a real angel. What do you want? Why call me? If God knows all, then he knows me. I am not perfect. Far from it."

"What man is truly faithful to a power he cannot see? So many have been called. None have come this far. You want it so much more."

"What do I want, Angel?"

"It is what you want to be a part of. What you prayed for. What you wish for constantly. A solution."

"I also pray for a good night's sleep. To be left alone in peace."

"Then make me go away, if that is what you truly desire."

He struggles to think how he could make her go away, how he could make this stop.

"Okay. If I'm inventing you, as I truly believe I am—if, real as it seems, all of this is from me, from, I suspect, my conscience— then there's nothing you can say that I don't already know. If you truly are real and your wish is that I remember you, then tell me something I couldn't already know. Surprise me."

He is suddenly sure that if he touches her he'll snap free from the trance he's in. Rather than solid matter, she'll be the vapor of fantasies. So he catches her by the wrist, only to find that she is, indeed, solid. Her sweet face displays alarm then extreme offense at this audacity. He tries quickly to undo his action, to pull away from her, but finds he cannot let go, and is forced to watch, transfixed, as a grotesque transformation unfolds. Her cupid lips fatten and curl into a wet, malevolent sneer, her flesh reddens and bloats, her frame is diminishing in height but at the same time chunking out like some miniature Mr. Universe. Then the wings burst into flames, the heat from them searing his face. His angel is melting into something hideous—her neat teeth are mossy brow stumps; her withered scalp is surrendering its silvery locks to something like rusted wiring.

Panicked, Fionn cries out, "Release me. Please!" But his hand is welded to the arm he grips, by an escalating heat that soon has him screeching in agonized terror. His own arm is alight.

"Oops," it jeers in a Bronx-style twang from its gargoyle mouth. "Naughty, naughty. Look at what you've gone and made me into now, limp-dick. And there's you thinkin' tits was bad. Hey! Quit prancin' about like a ferret with a firecracker rammed up its pipe." Its guttural cackling congregates in the vaulted ceilings like a thunderstorm about to hail down rocks on humanity. "Ha-ha. You ain't seen nothing yet, boyo. Okay, mother-fucker—something you don't know already. Here goes: the one we really want carries the futures of four in a bag that leaks blood all over this whore's-gusset you call a town."

CHAPTER SIX

A nd that's when Fionn all but punched himself awake. So he hadn't escaped by switching rectories. Here she was again, infiltrating his nice, safe new-build, where he'd foolishly imagined he could tuck himself away under a ten-tog duvet in an IKEA pine-frame bed.

His body folded back against the pillows like a living corpse. It'd begun after Callum's death. Now it happened, he guessed, almost every night he managed to sleep. Something pricked his back. He reached under and pulled out a crumpled beer can. He flicked it away and tried to close his eyes again but his eyelids repelled each other like opposing magnets. After an hour of twisting himself into knots, he got up and headed for the fridge, resigned to seeing in another dawn with the BBC-24 news team.

Picking a cold four-pack out of the chiller-drawer, a nagging pain registered—one concentrated in the flesh of his right palm. He put down the beer and turned his hand over, oddly unsurprised to find a scorched puff of flesh there. The madness he feared had arrived, with bells on.

...well-known light entertainer, Adrian Adams, who was recently

commended by Her Majesty the Queen for his extensive charity work abroad, claims that what police describe as a "library" of pornography containing explicit images of children, some as young as six, is most likely the property of the tenant to whom he had been renting his Sudanese home in recent months. Mr. Adams stated at a press conference this morning that he had absolutely "No knowledge of such material being kept at his property" and that he is "appalled and disgusted" by the discovery. Police have so far had no success in locating the current tenant of the property, although local authorities have confirmed that on occasions the house has been sublet. We have just been informed, however, that both Mr. Adam's contracts with ITV have been suspended pending further investigations...

"Which will come to fuck-all. Give him a pay rise—dumb bastards. Or better still, give me a gun and I'll do the best thing for everyone."

Fionn had taken to shouting slurred abuse at the TV. He didn't rate himself highly at times like these, it was just an outlet for the frustration he felt, exactly with what he wasn't certain. Perhaps his impotency to right the world, or even his own small corner of it.

...West Yorkshire police are investigating the disappearance of seventeen-year-old, known sex worker, Kelly Atkins. Kelly was last seen around midday on the fourteenth of February after telling a friend she was going out shopping. Formerly a resident of the Rokerville Estate, Kelly had recently been living and working in the city center...

'Nooo!" Fionn snapped forward in his seat, staring at the photo on the screen. He knew that girl. "Not here! Why does it have to be here—again?"

He swigged back the dregs of Stella through tightened lips, closely observing the plain face of Kelly Atkins, absorbing each detail before she disappeared, until the next news bulletin that would probably announce the police's growing concerns of her whereabouts. Seventeen. Just a baby, and she looked so old, as if middle age had set in already. He tried to picture her at her sixteenth birthday party at the center of a crowd of wide smiles; was she using then? They nearly always were—supporting a habit, and kids soon enough, and alone. She wasn't Catholic, but he'd seen her around often enough, never smiling, sometimes scowling, sometimes at him. He tried to imagine a time when she would've smiled easily, maybe back when she was thirteen, fourteen. Her face would've been a bit rounder; there would've been a school photo, her grinning away, turning beetroot from her mates ripping the piss in the background. Then at six years old: a happy skinny girl in a shaky film her dad made in the garden, camcorder in one hand, swinging her around giggling in the other, before he fucked off and made a new family Kelly didn't quite fit in with. He remembered her clearly now, the girl, the child. Not a unique story by any stretch: Kelly's dad left when she ten; her mum turned alcoholic and progressed to heroin from there. Kelly was one of five. The mum died about two years ago. Overdose.

...Kelly is the mother of a ten-month-old daughter, who has been temporarily taken into care. Police are appealing for witnesses who may have seen Kelly that day, or since, to come forward. Saint Valentine's Day was subject to a particularly heavy thunderstorm, so it's believed Kelly may have taken shelter somewhere...

"A rainy day for you, Kelly, wasn't it, sweetheart? Let's not kid ourselves we'll be seeing you any time soon."

The screen was full of the football highlights by the time Fionn snapped back. The sight of men kicking a ball about for big bucks might not normally have irked him quite so much, but on the back of the ruined, abandoned, and probably dumped in a ditch Kelly, those bozos bothered him a great deal. And once again, he found himself slumped alone in an armchair at sunrise, plastered as green-stick fracture, growling his frustrations up to an indifferent ceiling.

CHAPTER SEVEN

Mid afternoon the same day, Ben Hunter sank his long-handled axe into the felled tree on his allotment before setting himself down for a quiet smoke. Last night's sleet had lifted away. A kind March sun beat down on his face, casting a shadow under the hooked nose that had earned him the nickname "Hawk" around the estate. His little niece, Lizzy, was gathering up the bramble clippings and blown down twigs from the February gales, plus any cheeky weeds he'd plucked out of the leek beds, and was stacking them haphazardly for burning.

"What a grafter, our Lizzy. I could do wi' ten like you."

He watched her grappling happily with the wheelbarrow she could only just see over, saying "oof" to herself at intervals. The orange wellies mirrored her curly red top, similar to his own coloring before the middle years'd kicked in. A sunny day like this, early spring, always felt somehow more satisfying to Ben than the best of summer days. A cycle had ended and it was in with the new. The surplus cabbages were boxed up ready for the short trip to the grocers, after judging of course. The tasters: chicory, endive, celeriac, celery and Jerusalem artichokes, would go in the shed overnight. All seed pots and trays were ready for off. Not much left to do. Get the fire cracking and they'd call it a day.

"Look at that sorry mess then, Ami."

"I can't look, babe—hurts me eyes to."

One pale, freckled face and one creamy brown intruded prettily from the next allotment. The two girls of about fourteen giggled loudly when Ben half turned to acknowledge them.

"Alright there, Amelia, Debbie?"

"She prefers Debs. An' it's Ami, dog. Less with the formalities. I see you got your best man on the project, eh, though?"

Lizzy bit into a huge grin. Two big girls with makeup on and shiny hair looking her way were well worth performing for. She worked that barrow.

"Steady on now, Lizzy. Your mum'll want you back in one piece."

"Where's your well-fit mate?" Debs giggled, her freckly skin turning pink.

Ben shook his head. "I hope you're not referring to Father Malloy, Deborah Smith. Eyeing up a man of the cloth, indeed."

"You helped him exercise any good demons lately?" Debs asked.

"Yeah, we raced one to the shops this morning."

"She said ex*or*cised," Ami rolled her eyes skywards, "don't you know."

"I heard what she said, madam. So, your dad managed to drag you out for the weeding, eh, Ami? What's in it for you?"

"A cut of the fifty we'll be stealin' off you, easy, man."

"Sure bet. *Not*. I'll throw a couple of quid over t'fence

your way when me and my storm trooper here clean up." An older head appeared over the fence. "Hey-up there, Louis."

"These two bothering you, Hawk? Cause they bloody-well are me."

Louis ushered the two by now hysterical girls off to their gardening duties then came back to the fence. Ben swiveled over the log to face him, slid a roll-up from his pack, and handed it to Louis. Both automatically hushed down their tone.

"Project's going well." Ben said, indicating the throng of people busy roundabout.

Louis hooked a thumb back Ami's way. "Trying to keep *her* out of trouble for two minutes is the biggest project I've got on right now. You alright though, Hawk?"

"Ticking over. Wasn't she knocking about with that one who fancies himself as Mr. Blond? A right f..k.n' waster, him. Nobhead. What they call him again?"

"Kelvin Goddard. Ashley Goddard's lad. Lives over from us."

"Is he really? Ashley's fallout? F..k. Pity that man."

"Couple of years back, I tell you, he was a sound kid. Never 'ad no problem with him. But he's lost it." Louis tapped his temple. "Any sense he had—out the window. All out to impress the big men now, as he sees it. That Xbox f..kin' cun'. Fascist. Used to have a BNP sticker in his window till he started dealing. Now he's everyone's buddy—everyone with a habit, like."

Ben kept one eye out for Lizzy listening in to the men's talk, dreading the day when his sister would come knocking with that look on her face, seeing as how little Lizzy had demanded a *f..kin'* lolly from the shop. But she'd lost interest since the big girls had vanished and was now back onto the business of gathering, tipping, and piling.

Ben scowled at the mention of Xbox, a.k.a. Daryl Monk. "Him. Don't know about fascist, but he's a right sm..khead, that f..ker. Waste o' space."

"Tell me about it. He wants dealers, runners—dun't care how young. Our Joe says him and that Rafiq tw.t—you know him, drives round in a Merc—they've had their orders to join forces, from some Mr. Big over the moor. Control all the shit on the estate."

"B.st..ds. Needs reining in does all that, sharpish."

"It's going t'other way, mate. Let's get real. You heard about young Kelly, Kelly Atkins?"

Hawk nodded solemnly. "Aye, 'fraid so. Do you reckon that's down to this lot, though?"

"I dunno this time. But, tell you what, they wanner chop the knackers off 'em anyway, just in case. That'll teach 'em, like no f..kin' amount of ASBOs, or whatever they're awarding 'em now."

"They can have a lend of my axe for that job, Lou. I'll sharpen her up."

"Pity about Kelly, though. Can't say I'd room for 'er when she were leading our Ami astray, but she was pulling it together from what Ami says: moved off of here, got hersen into college, was havin' nowt more to do wi' Kelvin, X and that lot, pimpin' her out. Most days she was down t' city library, swattin'. Poor lass, just tryin' to give her kiddy a better start than she'd had. And now what?"

"She might turn up."

Louis shrugged. "Happen so." His voice faltered. He cleared his throat. "I hear young Fionn's been round Ashley's again, tryin' to make him see some sense with their Kelvin."

"Well, Ashley Goddard was a big churchgoer at one time."

"No offense, I mean, I know Fionn's a good lad, an' all, but you should know when yer just pissin' into t' wind. Know what I mean?"

"Aye. I know exactly what you mean, Louis. But it's his job. No one else is trying to sort it out peaceably."

"True." Louis grinned, lighting another cig. "So how's about it then, Hawk? F.ck peaceably. Let's you and me join forces, eh? Get us an Uzi or two. Do us some drive-by-shootings."

"Ah, I dunno, Louis. Trouble with guns is they're like lollipops; if kids see us with one they'll all want one. And besides, I worry I'd go too far if I ever got started around here. Then there's no going back, is there, mate?" Ben glanced over his shoulder at Lizzy.

"I suppose. Just, they p.ss me off big-time, this gang-thing, as it's got, f..king running the show around here. Especially since they got to young Callum, y'know. Jesus. Can't believe they got away with that, man. It were like Brownie points to them, that. A right victory. They're still doing f.ckin' high fives over it, I tell you."

A flush of red ran up Ben's neck. "I don't doubt it."

"Swanking round in their woolly bonnets and baggy trackies. Thinkin' they're these swanky gangsters—they look more like toddlers that've shat in their pants."

"Aye. They do a bit. You're right. Well, shout that from yer car, Louis. A drive-by dissing. That'll piss 'em off more than a cap up the arse, that."

The two men shared a quiet laugh.

"So down to business. You thinking of winning this show-down are you then, Hawk?"

Ben stubbed out his cig, stood to his full height of six foot five and shook back his sandy blonde hair. "Thinking's all done, cowboy. I reckon this here's the best patch in town."

Louis ran an eye over the pristine stretch of Ben's allotment, chided, "Yeeer b.st..d," under his breath and disappeared.

CHAPTER EIGHT

Lizzy trundled over making tired noises. It was late in the afternoon for a tot. Ben picked her up.

"Your mum'll be round soon for you, Lizzy. Are you about beat?"

She shook her head. "Is Father Fionn giving us the prize for the bestest?"

"It's up to a whole panel of judges, pet. But he's the founder of the allotment society. It's his job to give out the prizes. So he'd better, or else."

"Can I see Father Fionn tomorrow?"

"I think yer mum and dad've got plans for tomorrow." He kissed her cheek. "But thanks for all your help. I couldn't 've done it without you. And there's a slush-puppy coming your way if we win."

"Daddy doesn't like me getting a blue tongue."

"Blue tongue or no, there's slush-puppies due."

"Uncle Ben?"

"What, love?"

Lizzy's bottom lip stretched out. Her eyes focused down on the stick she was twisting in her hands.

"If Anita wasn't gone to Jesus would *you* have a little girl?"

"Like I said, Lizzy, I'd have ten like you, tomorrow."

"And will you come and live with us then?"

"What, when I have lots of little girls of my own? Oh, I don't know, Liz. I think I'll need them to stick around here and look after the allotment. You can be the boss, of course; my little foreman."

"I want you to come and live in Ilkley, though. Mummy does as well."

"What's wrong with living here?"

"It's a shit-'ole."

"A what, sorry, Lizzy?"

"A shit *hole,*" she corrected.

"Who says that, like?"

"Mummy does."

"Aye, well, I'll be having a few stern words with your mummy." He put her down and squeezed her hand. "Come on, let's light the fire then. Have you made sure and put the dry bits at the base, Lizzy?"

"They're on the bottom."

"Okay."

"Not the base." Lizzy twisted her hand awkwardly out of Ben's. The pout-lip was coming out again. "I've got a spell."

Ben crouched. "Aw. Let's have a quick look then."

She held out her hand. He could see why she'd kept it hidden as long as she could. It was a monster, and lodged well in, the dull end of it standing proud like a black bug from the tip of her index finger. Without a word, he took the finger and sucked until he tasted the soft metal of her blood and felt the dull end of the splinter give against his tongue, then pinching the end with his teeth he pulled gently until he'd eased it out. He spat the culprit into the palm of his hand, displaying it to Lizzy. She smiled, despite the sight of her own blood.

"There," he said. "All out. Shall I give it a whack for being naughty?"

"Yes!" She didn't have to think hard about that. Her eyes went wide with gleeful anticipation and she almost fell over laughing when Ben slapped himself hard where the splinter sat. She made him find it and do the same thing several times more before he could get her to calm down.

"Can we light the fire now?" she asked finally.

"Okay. We'd better make tracks, eh?"

Up behind the old Saint Luke's church the sun was sinking, casting a red cap over the horizon. In the glow, he could've sworn for a moment that he saw a familiar figure standing in the open bell tower, looking down. Someone he'd seen in a dream. He blinked and the illusion broke. There was the bell tower, boarded up just as it should be.

Once the flames took hold, Ben stood Lizzy back from the smoke. He straightened up a while, admiring the best sunset of the year, scanning around over the hurdle of fences, at the expanse of plots with everybody hard at work ready for the judging, but mostly just ready for the new season—young and old alike. He felt proud. "Shit-hole," some might say, but this estate still had a heart, and this is where it beat hardest.

Still immersed in uplifting thoughts, Ben was physically jolted when, looking back at the fire, he was met by a strange and unwelcome anomaly in his frame of vision. Through the rising smoke he locked eyes with somebody extremely odd, who was suddenly standing right opposite him, so close to the fire as to be in it—or was he in it? From beneath the canopy of a grey cowled hood, the little man grinned brazenly, knowingly, at Ben, as if having access to his deepest fault. A hideously ugly fellow to boot, short and stocky, like a living boulder. And something even more troubling: as their face-off persisted, the little man stepped away, reaching back to where Ben's axe sat lodged in the tree-stump, and wrapped a meaty fist around the handle, flexing out one finger at a time. Then, raising the other hand, he kissed the palm and blew.

Bitter smoke billowed toward Ben and Lizzy, sending them ducking away, coughing hard. When Ben looked back again, the figure had disappeared and, to his relief, the axe remained there in the stump. He had seen someone there, he was sure of it, standing only feet away: dressed in a dowdy old robe; the kind of goblin-featured, background freak featured in the bar-scenes of Star Wars movies. He gripped Lizzy's hand, feeling an involuntary shudder as he scanned the area.

Nothing untoward. Surely, nobody could move that fast.

Ben told himself he must have been working too hard, getting too little sleep. If his house—his parent's old house— hadn't stood so close to here, overlooking the green and the allotments, he might be able to relax a bit more at the end of his working days. But lately he'd found himself just sitting in the front, where he'd added the little sun-room for his mum before she died—just sitting there for hours, staring piss'out, oblivious of the dark closing in. And the binoculars were no joke. This project, not just for him and Fionn, but for the whole community, was everything now. No smacked-up fucker would mess it up.

When he turned back to Lizzy, his brow was set in a frown.

Lizzy frowned back. "What's the matter, Uncle Ben?"

"Ah, nowt. Time to clear up, our Liz," he said quietly. "Be our bedtimes soon."

Lizzy rubbed her eyes.

"I'm not tired yet," she insisted, as tots do mid-yawn.

Last job: Ben yanked his long-handled axe out of the log, to be put away safe and sound behind the padlocked shed door. Not the sort of thing you wanted falling into the wrong hands. Not on Rokerville.

CHAPTER NINE

Mr. and Mrs. Sutherby were late leaving the rectory. About twice a week, they called in for a heart-to-heart. They'd lost a son to cancer two years before; he'd been forty-two. They'd been offered counseling through their GP but both said they didn't see the sense in talking to somebody they didn't know about something so very personal. Talking to your priest at times like this was the practice they'd been brought up with, so that's what they did. Fionn liked them a lot and relished the chance to cook for more than just himself. Tonight he'd made the traditional stew and dumplings recipe his mother had passed on, with a cup of good stout to tenderize the beef. That'd gone down well, that and the home-brew wine the Sutherbies had brought along. It was after ten when they eventually said their good-byes.

The phone rang as Fionn was filling the dishwasher. He just made it before voicemail kicked in"

"Hello." No response. "Hello."

"Fionn, it's me."

"Hawk. How are you doing? I heard little Lizzy was helping out today. Sorry I didn't get a chance to pop down and say hi. Is everything okay?"

"Fine. Yep. What you up to?"

"Oh, just clearing up a bit, y'know. You're not yourself, Ben. What's up?"

"Nothing. Well, it's funny actually. I've got a question for you. And don't laugh."

"Your penis is fine. I've told you. It's twice as big as everybody else's."

"There you go. Can you just stop and be serious for one minute?"

Ben's tone worried him. "Where are you, at home? Shall I come round? I've got some of the Sutherbies' natural sleep remedy left over. I could certainly do with a drop more myself."

"Nah, you're alright, Fionn. It's been a long day." Ben paused, stretching and groaning in response to his own comment. "What I really need is some shut-eye. I'm just being fuckin' daft here anyway. Just something's addling my brain. It's like I can't think straight anymore."

"Okay. Just spit it out. Say it. How stupid can it be?"

"Stupider than most things, maybe." Ben paused again, then asked, "Do you think there's such a thing as angels?"

Fionn didn't know how long his silence went on or what it said in response to Ben's question. On some level, he hoped it said everything, so *he* wouldn't have to. Easier than in the mundane routines of a normal day, trying to realize the sleeping mind's deepest traumas. All of a sudden, he felt trapped in some strange limbo between dreams and reality. Ben surely wasn't talking about *his* angel?

'I…er…they're certainly there in the scriptures, Ben. More the Old Testament. They'd take on human form for one reason or another. Like to get Lott and his family away from Sodom and Gomorrah before God nuked the place. And then there were the wicked ones, who basically wanted to shag women; many refute that, though. Some in Revelation are named, I think. The ones with big swords waiting to come down and pummel the lot of us for our sins. Others were warriors before that, raining down punishments on the Israelites. Not always nice guys anyways—" Fionn cut himself short. He was waffling on. "Does that help?"

"Nah. That was back then, though. What about now? These days, y'know. Do you think there's such a thing as angels around now? Watchin' us?"

Fionn found it hard to think straight himself. This was a strange one coming from Ben. Very strange. And the coincidence was undoubtedly there. Could people maybe share dreams in times of stress? Transmit them? Pass them on like a virus? The human mind was strange, untapped in more ways than Fionn could guess, or articulate at that moment.

"I believe there are forces greater than just us. I mean, just watching telly, or hearing your voice there on the phone, Ben, like you're in the room with me. How does that work? We don't question the miracle of technology any more—well I don't—we just accept it, utilize it. Yet if somebody claims to 've seen an apparition, or say has projected a thought to another person—and people do make such claims all the time—they're passed off by and large as crackpots. All I'll say is it's at the moment when you most need to bare your soul that you begin to doubt your sanity. Or worse, fear that others will doubt it. Are you sure you don't want me to come round, Ben? I'm all done here for the night. I think we need to talk, face to face."

Ben laughed, recovering the side of him more familiar to

Fionn. "That's why you moved down the hill, isn't it? So you can get round quicker to drink my beer."

"That and a look through those binoculars of yours."

Ben paused. "Look, forget what I said. I'm knackered, that's all. Practically seein' goblins in the garden, here. Not sleeping too well, that's all it is."

"I know what you mean, there. Really. You're shattered now, I can hear it. We'll talk more tomorrow, about all this. Seriously, I'd like to."

Ben sighed. "Okay, if you want. I'll be off then. The weather's set to be fine for tomorrow afternoon, any road. Are we down The Crown after judging? I'll get t' first one in."

"Now you wouldn't be attempting to bribe a member of the committee there, would you, Hawk? 'Cause the price of a bribe is a bottle of Jack Daniels."

With that, the mood shifted, and the relief on both ends of the line was audible. Even so, Fionn promised himself not to let this one go by. He looked again at the scorched patch in his right hand. Tomorrow he'd find the words to be honest with his friend, to talk about his own dreams, and increasing fears for his sanity.

PART TWO

Nightmare

CHAPTER TEN

"Run around in church and the devil himself 'll catch up with you." Advice doled out on the back of a sharp clip around the lughole, courtesy of Fionn Malloy's dad the last time he'd tried it. Yet here he was again, a grown man, a priest no less, charging hell-for-leather through the pews. Because there was something about that battering on the doors that froze him to the marrow.

Sirens had been going off all over the place, but then sirens weren't that unusual around here. Only now came that battering on the doors that rattled through the apses. Urgent. Panicked. When the assailant's knuckles bruised themselves out, a flattened palm took over the task, slapping out a dull boom.

It was approaching eight in the morning.

Outside, Fionn could hear the heaving breath of someone in distress. He wasn't sure how he knew it was Mrs. Chuk. Perhaps crying held the same tones as singing. Mrs. Chuk, also dubbed "Super-Seminarian" by the congregation, who wore the many and varied hats of receptionist, cleaner, typist—because Fionn avoided using computers and couldn't read his own scribblings—also flower arranger, assistant event organizer and website manager—even adding a "Pray-as-you-go" link for parishioners with iPods.

He opened the doors, catching her by the arm as she stumbled in.

"Lin? What on earth is it? Where's your key?"

"I can't think. Sorry, Father. Oh, God, Fionn!" She never used his first name, or profaned. This was bad then. "I need to sit down."

"Tell me what's wrong, Lin."

"Sorry…I can't…" She gasped. He guessed the end to that was "speak."

Fionn led her into the vestry and made strong tea. Out of the back windows, he could see people, uniformed and otherwise, dashing about around the green. "Oh, Jesus help us," he sighed. "What now?"

Lin somehow made the TV come onto the computer—the kind of technology he'd never explored—and was flicking through the channels, quietly sobbing into a huge handkerchief bearing her husband's initials. When she couldn't find what she was searching for she hit the guide button and found a local radio station, then with trembling hands, sipped at the tea he'd made until, at eight a.m. the news was announced.

It was the first item.

…Two girls aged thirteen and fourteen are recovering in hospital following a vicious gang attack…Severely beaten… sexually assaulted…one girl is said to be in critical condition… Residents of the Rokerville housing estate, well known to police as a black-spot of the city, are so far said to be reluctant to come forward for fear of reprisals… gang violence… a growing problem in the area… As yet, no suspects have been arrested or charged…police are appealing for witnesses…

Fionn sat down heavily. He took the teacup from Mrs. Chuk and wrapped his hands around hers. Outwardly, his brown-eyed expression was softly concerned; inside, his blood boiled. "Who is it, Lin? Who'd they get this time?"

It was clear by her hesitation that she was reluctant to say.

"Come on," he urged calmly. "I can't do anything if I don't know the facts."

"Louis…Louis's girl."

"Amelia?" Something like a marble had lodged itself in his throat.

"Yes. And that little mate of hers. The fair one."

"Deborah." He continued, but hoarsely. "Does… does anybody know who did it? Who assaulted them?"

She shook her head.

"From what was said there on the radio, it's obvious that people do know. We have to pull together this time, Lin." Doubt burdened him even as he said it. "All of us. We can't let these… We can't let them get away with it again. Not after something like this. Tell me anything you've heard. Who might have seen something, Lin?"

"Hawk…" she sobbed it out. "Ben turned up. I heard— well, everyone is saying, because he wasn't the only one heard the racket, the screaming—it was Ben Hunter stopped them all in the midst of it, who had the guts to break it up, but I don't know what else. I just don't know anything after that, Fionn. You'll have to go talk to him." She patted his hand, a little calmer. "You go talk to the police, love, as well. They're all down there."

"Where?"

Again, it was clear she did not want to say.

CHAPTER ELEVEN

Fionn stepped out onto the terrace at the front doors of the church. From this raised position, he could survey, to some degree, the devastation. It seemed Armageddon had come to Rokerville, just as he'd asked for it to.

The allotment's "New Season" judging was scheduled for two p.m. Now, at approaching eight thirty in the morning, Fionn stumbled dazed toward what was left of the project. What struck him first was the blackness that had swallowed up vast expanses of green, and, as he walked toward it, the acrid smell: a cocktail of charred vegetation mingled with a heavy drenching of the vandals' old favorite—petrol fumes. Louis Johnston's plot was razed to the ground: shed, fruit trees, and all. The surrounding allotments had suffered extensive scorching, plus the aftermath of the collective rage that had sparked this off. Ben Hunter's shed had been kicked through in places, the windows shattered, his stored crops mashed into the ground. The whole area was ribboned off and swarming with police officers. More ominously, Fionn noted, a forensics' tent had been erected on Ben Hunter's plot.

Abhik Ali, the local community officer, stood stiffly by the gate. Abhik was the type who could always muster up a smile, even in the tensest of situations—a good local bobby, a peacekeeper—but mustering a smile today was far from his remit. He had adopted a more official stance—his way of coping, no doubt.

"Abhik."

"Father Malloy. You can't come any further than this. Sorry." His hand was out. He was a sentry. A warning that today, nothing could be as it normally would be.

"It's okay, Abhik. I just came to talk to you, to see what I can do. Mrs. Chuk told me a bit, then it came on the radio. It's terrible. I know things 've been getting worse, but this… Where's Ben? Has he spoken to you about what happened? Is he alright?" Fionn's heart thudded with deep dread as he gauged Abhik's reaction to that.

"Who knows? I was hoping you might be able to help us with that one, Father. He was here alright, we heard that as well, but nobody's seen him since."

"Really? I haven't either. We spoke last night. On the phone." Fionn was fading inside. "Not since." He suddenly felt as if he had half the blood he needed to remain upright. He placed a heavy hand on Ben's fence but managed to remain standing. "I should 've gone round. I knew it. Fuck!"

"Take some deep breaths, Father. What did you know?"

"Just a feeling. Nothing concrete. I really don't know anything, Abhik. I hope you don't think I'd lie."

"'Course I don't. I just have to ask. What time did you speak with Ben?"

Abhik was now officially PC Ali. The notepad was out and another officer, a young woman, had quietly joined him.

"It was about ten-ish."

Abhik was talking, but Fionn drifted back to last night: *Do you believe in angels?*

"When you spoke to him, did it *sound* like anything was wrong?" Abhik said loudly, as if he'd said it once already.

"Sorry. Sort of. He was very tired. He's been working full days—he's a gardener, then evenings and weekends grafting here."

"Grafting?"

"Sorry." Fionn shook his head. "I forget that means something else nowadays. Working hard's all I mean, helping everybody else out with the project as well as doing the day job. That's Ben for you. We were just talking about today, about the show and all."

"That's it? Nothing else?"

"No." Fionn looked him in the eye. "Is it true he broke things up here?"

"We're pretty sure he did, but who can say for sure? You know what it's like round here, Father, nobody's saying enough. There's rumors of course. From Ben's house over there, he would have seen the fire or smelled it once it got raging. Lots of people would—it took three fire engines to kill it. In fact..." He checked his notes. "It was his next door neighbor called the fire brigade." He shrugged. "Better if we could talk to Ben, like, find out first hand."

Fionn's eyes fell on the tent pitched on Ben's allotment—about the same spot where his own patchwork effort had stood a couple of months before; before Callum, before Kelly, before all this—its bleached sterility making the blackness around it that much filthier.

"Lin said it was Amelia and her friend who were attacked. That right, Abhik?"

"Yeah. Little Ami."

"How bad?"

"About as bad as it gets if you're still alive. You know, as bad as it gets for a girl."

Abhik's hands were shaking. He put his notebook away and drove his hands down into his trouser pockets. "You just talk to us, Father, about owt you find out, okay? People will talk eventually, and it might be to you. You're trusted round here. And no reporters."

"You can trust me on that."

The female officer stepped forward. "Father Malloy? It's Judith. Nice to meet you." She offered a hand, which he shook. "Look, something's going on."

Abhik nodded his agreement.

"It's not just the usual them-and-us crap, Father. It's something else, and it's spreading through the estate. You won't be able to talk to Ami, but Louis's Catholic, isn't he? Try talking to him, would you? He's certainly not playing ball with us. Nobody is."

CHAPTER TWELVE

Amelia was Louis's youngest, the only girl. The baby. Her
hospital bed was in a private room off the children's
ward. Hospital staff kept a close eye on her. Louis sat outside
Ami's open door, next to a Woman Police Constable. What
struck Fionn initially was how wide the man's eyes looked in
his head and how pale his skin, gone from the Caribbean
sheen of his forefathers to a sickly grey. Two plain-clothed
officers stood talking along the corridor that led to the exit: a
man of about thirty Fionn thought he recognized, and a
woman, maybe late thirties, treacle skinned, with short, dark,
spiky hair and dramatic blue eyes—hard to look away from at
first glance. She acknowledged Fionn with a nod, then
listened closely to something the man with her was saying.
Fionn all of a sudden felt paranoid, sure, despite all that was
going on, that he was the subject of their conversation.

"Father, thank God." Louis seemed drunk on a mix of
grief and gratitude, as if his priest could undo all of this in
some way. He clutched at Fionn's sleeve, struggling to rise
from his chair.

Fionn eased him back. "Don't try to get up, Louis,

please."

Fionn got another chair and sat down beside Louis. The WPC on his other side watched slyly, her ears fairly panning round like radar receptors.

"Louis. I'm so sorry. I just came to see if there's anything I can do. Anything at all?" He gripped the man's hand.

"Nowt much anybody can do, Father. But it's good of you to come." Louis started rocking, swallowing air in lumps, as if air had become a solid object to contend with.

"Poor Ami. Has she spoken at all, Louis?"

"She…can't."

"Are you a close friend of the family?" the WPC cut in, anti-Catholicism searing through every syllable. "Because Amelia's really not up to talking to just anybody. It's best she just rests till she's ready to talk to us."

Fionn glared at her. "I wasn't suggesting I go in there." That sounded bad. As if he was afraid to. He was afraid to though.

"Fucking bastards. This is all my fault. I was taking the piss, 'cause I'm sick of 'em. That fucking lot—you know who I mean. The girls were in the car with me, laughing at 'em." Louis's sudden cries clattered around the high corridor like unwelcome visitors after hours. He steadied himself enough to continue. "They came in and took her from her bed, right from under me nose. I didn't even know. Christ Almighty, she's just a baby. Fourteen, and they've stamped her out. Ruined her for life." He fell forward into his hands, heaving out tears that seeped through the cracks between his fingers.

Fionn wrapped an arm over his shoulders. "You're not to blame, Louis, no matter what you think you did. I know it's hard, but you have to be strong for her now. You have to believe she'll recover. She's better than anything some scumbag can do to her. She'll come through this. She's a tough one. She'll survive this and have the life she deserves, the life you always wanted for her."

He'd stopped believing it himself even before he'd finished. This wasn't the first time he'd seen something like this; he'd hoped he would never have to again. There'd been Anita, Ben's young wife, who'd suffered a similar trauma, and he knew too well how that one had ended: with a bottle of whiskey and a bath full of warm, watery blood. He got up angrily and forced himself to the doorway of the girl's room. Only glimpses of Amelia were visible through the wads of bandaging. One fractured arm was in plaster, one eye heavily dressed, the other just a slit in a purple egg. Dressings covered burns. She'd been punched apart and stitched back together. Her breathing was shallow—drugged. Sure, at some point she'd tidy all this away into a safe little place at the back of her mind, where other comparatively lesser ordeals than this had been stored over the years: her mum going back to live with her family in Birmingham and not bothering to take Amelia, the phone calls stopping after two weeks, the fights at school, hurtful things boys said to get to her; all that stuff. Something this big, though, turned that safe place into one of those cupboards where nothing fits in tidily anymore, so she'll go there someday with some fairly trivial problem she needs to put away and it just won't go in, and pushing 'll bring the whole lot crashing down on her head.

Fionn turned away. "Louis. Is it true that Ben broke things up?"

Louis's face showed a little more clarity. Fionn went back and sat with him. He sat more heavily than he'd planned to.

"He did break them up." Louis lowered his voice, cautiously eyeing the WPC at his other side. "He brought our girls home to us. Jesus Christ, like I say, I didn't even know she was out, till he turned up at the front door with her in his arms, all smashed up." His lip quivered. "He carried Amelia all the way. Debs was walking, with some help; walking wounded. She's hurt, like, as well, poor darling, but not.... Amelia got the worst. That was the plan, obviously. Fuckin evil..."

"I'm so sorry."

"Thank God for Ben, eh? She'd be dead otherwise. His neighbor, Ben's neighbor, Gordon, says he chucked one of 'em clean over the fence, then they all scarpered. Fuckin' cowards."

"Was he alright, Ben, when you saw him? It's just, Louis, I can't find him. I've tried everywhere..."

For a moment, Fionn swore he detected a smile creeping across Louis's face. That wasn't right. Then his attention was diverted by the smart suited young man, the likely detective who'd been talking with the woman in the corridor, who was now heading their way.

"I've never seen Hawk like he was, let's put it that way." Louis's look was different again, in another world.

"Like what?"

"I don't know. He kind of looked...bigger, if that's possible, driven, like a machine. He's done us proud, I'll say that. I love that man—I'd do owt for him." Louis clenched his fists. "I can't tell you what I'd do to them cowardly bastards myself if I could get a hold of just one of 'em."

"Louis, I know you're suffering, but we have to trust the law to deal with this now."

Louis gave him a look he'd never had to suffer from the man before—utter cynicism.

"The law? Don't you know them evil cunts are already

cookin' up alibis for each other? That their mummies and daddies 'll back up? Like they do every fuckin' time? Anyone'd think you'd not been around to see what happened to young Callum and his family."

The WPC cut in again. "We've upped our game since then, Mr. Johnston, I can assure you."

The young male detective had stopped short of them and was beckoning Fionn over.

"Sorry, Louis," he said. "I'll be back in a minute."

"I know you, don't I? Detective James Gaunt." The narrow-eyed young man offered his name minus a hand to shake. "That was you who was priest over at Saint Mathews about ten years ago, wasn't it? They moved you on, did they?"

Fionn's face hardened. He remembered Gaunt now. "I'm here for Louis and Amelia. What do you want?"

Gaunt's face slipped into a sneer. "They look after their own, don't they, the Catholic Church? Bury the dirt. All boys together."

"Like the police, you mean?"

The blue-eyed female detective joined them toward the end of that.

"Detective Inspector Beena Ryan. Pleased to meet you."

She held out a hand, which Fionn shook. Gaunt dropped back a little, watching.

"Father Fionn Malloy, of Saint Luke's Parish." His voice was still agitated. He tried to get a rein on it. "Sorry, Ms Ryan. Bad day."

"I know. I've heard. I've also heard good things about you, Father. You organized this 'Seasons Project', didn't you? Converting wasteland into allotments?"

"Well, myself and Ben Hunter, yes."

"I thought it was a really good idea. A real positive for the area." Her stare had an unrelenting edge to it. "What can you tell me about Ben Hunter, Father? I hear you two are close friends. Have you seen or heard from him this morning?"

"No. I was hoping you had. I'm really worried about him. You know the estate? The types who've, well, taken over, I suppose you could say."

"Yes I do. He's disappeared, I'm afraid. We've been unable to ascertain his whereabouts, as yet."

"Ascertain his whereabouts?" Fionn echoed. "That sounds bad, even in the jargon."

"Sorry." She was consulting her notes. "He has a sister, I believe. Where might we find her?"

"Ilkley. I could give you the number but she already rang me this morning trying to find him herself, after she saw the news. They have a little girl, Elizabeth—Lizzy. She's about five. Ben's really close to her."

"Okay. Good." She shut her book abruptly, as if to place a full stop on their conversation. "Well, if you hear anything, call me. I take it you pick up a lot in your line of work?"

"The people who did this aren't about to pour into confession, Ms. Ryan."

"You're at the heart of the community, Father, is what I mean. People trust you. It's important we wrap this up quickly. I've seen this sort of situation escalate before. We wouldn't want this to be left to local justice, if you know what I mean. Would we?"

He laughed bitterly. "And what 'justice' will Amelia and Deborah get, Detective Inspector Ryan? These filthy animals living back on the same streets as them in two to five years? Is that the 'justice' we're to expect?"

Her attitude was strictly no-nonsense but he wasn't backing down. Lack of sleep only added to the intensity in his glare.

"Call me then," she said. "Whatever you hear, whenever you here it."

She handed him a card before rejoining her colleague. Fionn was staring absently at the floor when she turned back to him, and he hoped she didn't think he'd been sizing up her legs, which happened to be very nice legs, but still, he hadn't been. On seeing his caught-in-the-act expression, her face almost relaxed into a smile.

"Oh, I meant to say, Father, I am really sorry about the allotment project. I'm sure you'll pull it back together at some point."

Fionn nodded blankly. All of that seemed pointless right now. When he turned around, he saw Louis had moved away from the WPC and was standing talking quietly to his eldest son, Joe, who'd turned up in the last few minutes. Louis's eyes had suddenly come alive. He seemed wild, excited, like an athlete about to best his own record. But when Fionn approached them, Louis trained his sights down at the blandly tiled floor, clearly saying nothing to a man who trusted in the dealings of the law.

And so there the priest stood, alone, between the two parties, having said just enough to be trusted on neither side.

CHAPTER THIRTEEN

Shortly after his return from the hospital, Fionn dragged himself out of a short, troubled sleep. He'd been up to the old church to ask the angel if she would grant him the power to avenge Amelia and Deborah, and to ask her where Hawk had got to. But when Fionn had looked closely, into the depths of the aura cast by the angel's presence, Ben'd been standing right there behind her like a great dark shadow all along. Others were there too, a mass of them further into the dark behind Ben, one of them a tall, gangly boy with no discernible face beneath the hood of his parka.

"What do you want me to do, God?" Fionn groaned, exhausted. "Tell me straight or let me be. I've had it up to here." He raised a hand to draw a line just under his chin. He got up and drank two cups of strong coffee, needing to focus, to be there as a priest for his community. He couldn't find Ben, he'd tried everywhere, even The Crown. *Ben's too big to be dead*, was all he could think.

His mind cast back to that bad old time after Anita's suicide. He'd known the couple a few years, and feared that when she went, there was a chance Ben might follow; they'd been so close. He'd been wrong about that. There was something else about Ben: a strength, a concern for the world outside of himself. About a year after his wife's death, he and Fionn were coming out of the city. They just ended a meeting with the council about obtaining a grant for the allotment project. Things were looking good. They had a couple of pints to celebrate, and Ben reluctantly paid a visit to the toilet on the train back home. While he was gone, a young couple seated in the same crowded carriage where Fionn stood, began bickering loudly between themselves. A baby boy of about eighteen months sat in a buggy facing toward them. As if testing the dad, the baby began reaching up, grabbing for the pasty the dad was stuffing into his face through the argument. When the father said, "No!" with unnecessary aggression, the baby started to cry. The whole trainload of passengers in view of the small, troubled family fell silent, watching with collective dread. As the dad continued eating more and more angrily, the young mum, clearly wise to such situations, started giving frantic instructions for the baby to "quiet down" and "be good, now", but this just spurred the kid along to shriller protests, until the dad, radish-cheeked, leaned down to within a fraction of the kid's head and bawled, "Fuckin'! Shut! Up! Now!"

Wet pastry splattered and stuck to the child's now frenzied face.

Like everybody else around him, Fionn was momentarily frozen in shock. But one person in the carriage was moving at speed. Fionn hadn't noticed Ben pass him, hadn't even known he was back, until Ben had the startled young daddy hauled up by the scruff of his neckwear and slammed against the train doors. A sludge of cheap mince and carrots dribbled down the young man's chin as his eyes darted between Ben and the doors behind, that he clearly feared might spring open at any second. His feet dangled high off the carriage floor as Ben leaned in as close to his face as he'd been to his baby's. "You shut uuup!" Ben bellowed, with a force that almost knocked the cap off the lad. "Remember what it feels like? Eh? Just because your dad did it to you!" he yelled. "Doesn't mean *you* have to be so fuckin' stupid!" Ben let go. The young man, his legs jellified, piled down like a shot deer. The silenced baby stared sideways around his buggy in wide-eyed awe. His young mum grinned uncontrollably into her sleeve. There came a short burst of applause.

A dull pounding sound echoing in the distance brought Fionn back to the present. He'd been hearing it all morning. He went to the rectory's back window, which had a view up the hill. Work continued as scheduled up at the old church. Diggers and cranes were mobile. Looked like they were hacking out the pews. It pained him to see how roughly they dealt with the place. Something caught Fionn's attention: a fire had started round in the graveyard, that looked to be out of control and that the workmen on site seemed oblivious to. The great oak that had stood in the cemetery for centuries was on fire.

Fionn was no tea and buns priest. He kept as fit as time allowed. He was up there in a dash, still in the vest and joggers he'd napped in. The closer he got, the more evident it became that the fire couldn't be tackled by himself and a few Saturday-minded workmen. Smoke billowed out at him as he passed the wire fencing. He coughed violently, wafting his way ahead.

"You have to stop," he shouted, reaching the front doors. "There's a fire round there. Round the side of the church!"

Two workmen who'd been loading a pickup turned and

looked dumbfounded at him. Others came from inside. Seeing them all stop working the one riding the crane did likewise.

"There's a fire round in the graveyard." Fionn took his dead mobile out of his pants' pocket, shaking it frantically. "I'm all out of battery—we'll need to get the fire brigade quickly! His outburst was met with silence. "I'm Father Malloy. I was priest here. Please, do something. The old tree! It's protected. You can't just let it burn!"

It seemed the wind had turned, diverting the smoke away so there was nothing to back up his rant. The builders continued to stare at him nonplussed.

"Oh, Father Malloy," a bearded man laughed, as if he'd just woken from a deep sleep. "Sorry. Yes, I seen you here when the bell got hauled down. It's the outfit. I thought you was a mad hippy jogger there or summat. What's all this? A fire, you say?"

They all traipsed lazily around the side of the church after Fionn, then stopped, adopting the same blank looks that'd greeted him. The only evidence of there ever having been a fire was one feeble trail of smoke rising from beneath the old oak tree, which in itself appeared unblemished.

"Okay, get back to work, you lot. Show's over," the bearded man shouted. Then discreetly asked, "Are you alright, Father? I know it's been one bloody hell of a night."

"Sorry. I thought…"

The other men drifted away with acid banter kicking off between them. One sniped, "Keep your cassocks on, love." Which led to laughs all round and another to enquire, "Hey, how do you get a priest to swim the Channel?" Then to answer himself, "Tell him for every mile he swims he can grab a-hold of a buoy."

The bearded man, who Fionn recalled was the site manager, gave the men a stern look. "Well, no panic, Father, but we'd best go have a check, eh? Go see what's what."

He was clearly humoring Fionn, the way one might humor a small child who's claimed to 've seen pixies at the bottom of the garden. Fionn followed him through the jungle of weeds, silenced by confusion.

"Be bloody kids, I bet. As if they haven't done enough damage for one day."

The two men stood over a charred rectangle of earth, where smoke was rising in faltering ribbons.

"We only moved those stones this morning," the manager said. "Don't know what the Lucy-Lu the buggers found to burn. It's just muck."

"The stones from the chest tombs? Is that what you've cleared today?"

The site manager nodded. "Earlier, aye. They'll fetch a bit, them. This was the one that'd come down…where the young lad…you know, topped himself. So we only had the base stone left to shift." He sighed, straightening up and looking around. "This'll all be churned over by end of next week anyway, so less for the little vandals to piss about with, eh? Anyway, I wouldn't worry, Father, looks like it's about out, that." He checked his watch. "Nearly knock off time. We only do half day Saturdays. So I'd best be off. Get that load of slackers organized. No point bothering the fire brigade, I don't think. They'll be needing a kip after all that commotion down the allotments."

"No. Of course not. Silly me. Thanks for your help anyway."

"No sweat, Father." The site manager scratched his head, saying, "That lad who was with you before. Where's he got to?"

"Sorry, who?"

"That lad as followed you in—him in the parka? Doesn't matter. If you could just make sure he's not still about before you go. This place is no playground. Not no more. Summat'll come down on his head."

Any possible words died in Fionn's throat as the site manager left him there, rooted to the spot, scanning every inch of the rugged grounds around him. Nobody else was there. He was alone. His heart lurched horribly, then his attention returned to the perfect black rectangle of ground before him, and he wondered how many mysteries would unfold before the day was out. What the other man had failed to notice was that the smoke, now thinning away to curling wisps, was not simply rising from the ground, but seeping out from underneath it.

And, once more, his attention was split in two. Around the estate, the sirens blared again.

CHAPTER FOURTEEN

The weird thing about the sirens was they didn't seem to be heading in any one direction, more darting around as if involved in a motorized game of hide-and-seek. Coming back down the avenue, Fionn witnessed the chaos first hand. People were on the move too, an aura of giddy hysteria apparent all around. No one stopped to talk to him, and by then he felt an urgency to get back to business.

Morning confession had been cancelled. Mrs. Chuk had posted apologies on the website, but with the Seasons event well and truly terminated, there might well be takers for the four o'clock stint. Fionn gauged that somebody, by this time, must have something to say, something concrete about the perpetrators of the assault, and where the hell Ben might have got to.

And concrete's what the priest got.

At around three o'clock, the new church doors clattered open and a short, stocky lad of about fifteen, wearing a tracksuit and a neck-load of hand-penned tattoos, came flailing in like Bambi on ice. Heavy sweat gave his acne a scarlet sheen, but there was another redness about his person—what looked like blood was splattered around his face and drenched his clothes. Collapsing partway in, he began crawling frantically away from the open doors behind, reeking like he might be about to drop a load on the spot. In stark contrast to the nonplussed, monotone gangster-speak obligatory to the uniform, Kelvin Goddard—Fionn realized—while trying to scramble back to his feet, took on the tone of a yodeling lunatic. "Lock that door, priest! Lock it! Don't let him in!" he screamed. "You're not allowed. You have to protect us. It's your fucking job! Sanctity!" *He meant sanctuary.*

Fionn took hold of the boy by the slack of the shoulders and dragged him to his feet. "Okay, Kelvin, calm down. Make some sense. Tell me what's going on. Who's after you? The police? Whose blood is on you?" Fionn could see no obvious wounds on Kelvin himself. "Talk to me, or the doors stay open."

"It was their own stupid, fucking fault." Kelvin spat the words through globules of saliva and mingled blood. He'd clearly taken a swipe to the face. "I'd told 'em—warned 'em to quit taking the fucking piss out of us, but she just wouldn't listen. I told her a thousand times, *"Can't you just shut the fuck up, bitch?"* Then there's her and her fucking dad an' all, dissin' us out of the car, fucking doin' us down…idiot! Bitch!"

"Ami? You mean Ami?" Fionn shook him violently till the boy dropped back to his knees with his clothes rucked up around his chest, exposing a band of doughy midriff. "What did you do?" Fionn ranted. "What have you done? Tell me right now or I'll fucking land you one myself."

Kelvin knelt there shaking, glancing anxiously back at the open doors. His voice cracked, "Please, man. It wasn't me. I'm not that bad. I'm no rapist, me. I just whacked her one, just once is all, 'cause I was pissed off, 'cause I'd warned her loads. So don't you let him in! You're not allowed to. I didn't do owt. I was just there. Loads of us was. I wanted it to stop, me, I was just scared of X."

Kelvin reached into his pocket and pulled out a mobile phone, which he held up, pitifully—a peace offering—then clicked *play-film*.

"See, look... it weren't me."

Instantly, Fionn was subjected to the jittery image of the previous night's attack flashing before him on the screen; was hearing the screams and pleas of the two girls drowned out by the jeers and laughter of the pack bearing down on them like scavengers on the plain, their laughter cold, mocking. One voice—that Fionn recognized as Xbox—ranted out the same threats over and over as his elbow rose and his fist drove down. "You're going to die, bitch! When we've done with you, slut! You're dead meat." And he'd meant it. And now here knelt Kelvin, all but spilling his bowels in fear and self pity, having stood by and filmed it all, no doubt to play back in the privacy of his grubby little room. Fionn drew back his free arm and swiped Kelvin to the floor with a back-hander sharp enough to numb his own fingers.

"You can dole it out but you can't take it, can you? You'll get what's coming to you, you yellow-bellied little bastard! I'd have your eyes for watching them suffer that evil, if you were mine to deal with; and filming it! How dare you come into this place expecting pity? Get the fuck out of my sight!"

The pound of footfall heading up the steps outside saw Kelvin Goddard's sphincter finally let loose with gusto. He screamed fit to die, curling down into a fetal ball, arms clasped over his head, a rancid brown stain spreading out around the seat of his pants. His mobile phone, still blaring out the scene he'd recorded, went skittering across the parquet flooring, coming to a stop by the foot of Detective Inspector Beena Ryan, who was now standing with her colleague Detective Gaunt in the frame of the open church doors.

CHAPTER FIFTEEN

Penetrating blue eyes were not Beena Ryan's only asset, she had a way of looking at you that made you feel at ease while at the same time certain you had done something wrong; something she already knew but just wanted you to admit to. Fionn ignored the cup of tea she'd brought into the interview room. Apart from feeling loaded with the day's overdose of coffee, he still felt physically sickened by the images he'd seen on Kelvin Goddard's mobile phone. Detective James Gaunt, who'd remembered Fionn from his last parish, also sat quietly across the desk from him. Detective Inspector Ryan placed a red folder between Fionn and herself and drummed her fingers on it. He was instantly certain he didn't want to see what was in it.

"Tell me about Brian Askwith, Father Malloy."

"Is that it? That's why you brought me here? You've read the file, surely, if you're interested in history."

"I want you to tell me," she pressed.

"Of course you do." Fionn shifted uneasily in his seat but was relieved in a way. This had to be easier than facing whatever it was he'd really been brought here for—whatever it was in that folder. When he spoke, though, his voice was quietly strained. "Well. A lot of women, wives of parishioners, when they come to confession, confess of ill feeling toward their husbands. It's nothing new, as you can imagine. And if you've moved from somewhere else and not made new friends yet, and you feel the need to talk, the church is sometimes the first port of call. Well, with Mr. Askwith's wife…"

"Maria?"

"Yes. With Maria, it was clear she needed quite desperately to talk. After a while I suppose I got too interested in the reasons why she had so much ill feeling towards Brian, who I'd also come to know by then."

"And things got out of hand?"

"Not the way you're thinking. I was trying to be a friend to her, to get her to open up. I won't even say it was a mistake, not that part—she did need a friend; there was violence, behind closed doors, that needed addressing. But, of course everybody thought the same things you're thinking now. There was the predictable gossip. Her husband picked up on some of it—I don't know what exactly—and the fact that she was out a bit more than usual. I'd put her onto a help-group. She'd started to attend. I was proud of her."

"And then he came round to confront you, is that right?"

"No. No he didn't. He came to confession, as he always had since they'd moved, but not with the usual petty sort of things this time. He said he suspected his wife was seeing another man; he'd heard rumors. He didn't know who, but that she wasn't going to get away with it. He'd already seen to that. See, what he'd come to confess to, was having beaten Maria to within an inch of her life. He'd cracked her damned skull open. Still had the fucking blood on his hands."

"So you returned the favor?"

Fionn lowered his eyes, feeling too tired and emotionally ragged to face the penetrating gaze of Ms. Ryan. "What does any of this matter now?"

She leaned forward, arms on the table. "You've been protected, Father. You committed an extreme act of violence. No charges were brought. You kept your job, and a mere bus ride away from the scene of the crime, at that. You got away with it. And now, here we are."

"There was a price to pay."

"Giving her up?"

"That doesn't seem like much to you, does it? Relinquishing a friendship? Swearing to never see her again. But I had to. People would have just kept on talking. People always believe what they want to believe. I had to think of her—of her recovery."

Detective Gaunt was smiling smugly to himself.

Fionn let out a long breath. "Look, I really don't care if you believe this or not. God is my witness."

"Since your *attack* on Mr. Askwith, have you been involved in any further acts of violence, Father Malloy?" Gaunt said coolly.

Fionn looked genuinely confused. "No. It was an extreme case. A one-off. I could say I was young, but that's no excuse. I let it get personal. I've learned from it, believe it or not."

"Have you recently collaborated in any acts of violence or harbored or assisted a person who has committed such an act?"

"No."

"What about Kelvin Goddard?"

"Well, yes, you saw all that. Do you need to ask? You've also seen what that little shit had stored on his phone. No doubt if you hadn't got a hold of it first, it would've been uploaded onto some sick fucking pervert website by now. Sorry, Ms. Ryan. I've sworn more today than I have in ten years."

DI Ryan gave Gaunt a look, then stepped back in.

"Is it fair to say that you're skeptical about how the law will deal with the likes of Kelvin and his mates, Father Malloy?"

"What?"

"What you said to me at the hospital." Her look was cold steel. "You don't trust in the law to adequately deal with this kind of crime, do you, Father?"

"I was angry. Seeing Amelia. And Louis in that state. I'll be angry for a long time to come if I'm honest, but my only intention is to be there for the families, to offer support. I really don't know what more you're expecting me to say, here."

"What was it you said to Kelvin Goddard, Father? I'm curious about that."

Fionn bowed his head. "Ami was just a tot when I first met the family. Part of me still thinks of her that way. I wanted to hurt him badly. I can't lie. But I wouldn't follow through."

"You said you'd 'have his eyes'. Is that right?"

"Yes, I did."

"Besides striking Kelvin Goddard, Father, have you been involved in any acts of violence in the last twenty-four hours?"

"What? No. You saw me at the hospital. I was asleep after that, not for long, but my P.A., Lin, was around most of the day. Won't you just tell me what this is about? Please." His face began to collapse against his will. "If that's Ben Hunter in there…" He glanced at the photo protruding from the file on the desk between them—a bloodstained white T-shirt. "Then please, don't show me what's in there. Just tell me. I have to know."

Watching him closely, she opened the file.

"I'm sorry," she said, "but I *will* need you to look at these."

She turned and carefully arranged the four photographs so that he could clearly see them. In an obscene way, they all looked the same: four people, men…boys he vaguely recognized though they would be unrecognizable to most—men he'd known if not in person, certainly by reputation. They were all splayed out in the same manner: one hanging out of an old Mercedes, two others on beds that were likely their own, the fourth left in the middle of a road in broad daylight, for all to see; a Rokerville road, he was sure. Each of their bloodied faces was fixed in a visage of semi-conscious agony. Their sunken, gluey eyes had been punched through with a sharp implement, an act which no doubt served to disarm them for what was to follow; each victim's pants was bunched down about his ankles, leaving openly displayed the gory cavern from where his genitals had been hacked out at the root.

The backdrop of every picture was the same—drenched scarlet. So much blood.

DI Ryan placed a finger on each of the four in turn, stating their names. "*Steven Briggs*, sixteen years old—our friend Kelvin Goddard's best mate, I believe. *Amjad Rafiq*, eighteen, known drug dealer. *Daryl Monk*, seventeen, similarly occupied, also known as Xbox. His younger brother, *Gervais Monk*, nickname Monkey, fifteen…"

Fionn spun away to hurl coffee colored vomit across the grey linoleum.

CHAPTER SIXTEEN

Raz and Mumpy grabbed turns with the remote. Raz got a firm grip and held on. The high-ceilinged room they languished in, with the two Georgian sash-windows overlooking the moors toward the bad-old town, was sparsely furnished. A couple of sofas that would double up as beds for the night, a fridge stocked with beer, milk, party sausages and pre-bought sandwiches, and opposite the couches, and most importantly, the wall-mounted fifty-incher that was the focus of the two's attention.

"Wants to watch the game then, Raz-man? Come on—give."

"No, Mumps. Told you. Shut the fuck up."

Mumpy was called Mumpy—Mumps for short—on account of the big bulbous neck he'd grown through puberty. He'd tried to subvert it loads of times to other, cooler nicknames—a year or so back, after a two-stretch in Y.O.s, it'd been third person references to "The Cutter" whilst openly brandishing his trusty blade—but no one was buying that. Mumpy stuck like a dog turd in a trainer-tread.

Raz surfed the TV guide. "I already said *no*. No fuckin'

football. Gay boys all of them. Overpaid ballet boys and supreme divers—and I don't mean of the muff."

"Well, now yous mentions it, muff's a mint idea. Scan v porn channels, mish."

"Later maybe. Too early for pussy."

Mumpy howled. "How is it ever too early for pussy, limp dick? Pussy's like v all day breakfast, mush. It's for all v day. Oy, or that Sexettera, there, you gone past it; it ain't straight-up porn but it ain't bad. Migs telled us all about, like, how it teaches you fings. Tricks and that."

"'Tain't on yet, Mump. Sounds shite anyway."

"It teaches you techniques, though, dunnit? Like, treats for the bewer, getting her well-bucking—caressing her in the vulvo and fings."

Raz side-eyed him. "You tickling this bewer in her cunt or her car?"

"She ain't got no car, man. It's a chav, my main-squeeze, innit?"

"I swear down, Mumps. You learn to talk proper or I ain't taking you no place no more. You proper make spectacles of us both, you do. It ain't cool."

"Man, I ain't hearing this." Mumpy swigged off the dregs of a beer bottle and belched loudly. "I suppose now I has to say *pardon me,* innit?"

"No. That's all wrong."

"What, I can'ts blow out a beer ghost now?"

"My old lady says, 'It's excuse me for a burp, pardon me for a fart.'"

Mumpy lifted one cheek and let one rip. "*Pardon me,* then. Happy?" He slammed his arms into a fold. "Look, fuck all that. If we can't comes to an agreed arrangement on the footy, just let's get back on my PlayStation. This is fucked.

I'm bored, man. I had plans for tonight. What's your man need us on-site for anyway, like babysittin'?"

Raz continued to surf, poker-faced. Sometimes people would ask him, "How comes you never smile?" To which he'd reply, "Coz it hurts my face." And wouldn't even smile saying it.

"You don't ask about the man what the man want, what the man think. And no more talk of PlayStations. PlayStations are for little boys, little boy."

"A film then. What about that one, Raz, there, a sci-fi movie? I don't minds vem oysters. If I has to watch a stupid film, a sci-fi will do for me. So move on up, man. Surf back."

"What film?"

"There. That *Tunnel of Air*, or somefink. Look, you've gone past it again, man. Be about a vortex you can go frew maybe, and like, go frew time. Scan back up, bro. Back up one. There, right, *Chanel of Air* on v strip fing wiv words on." He snuggled down to near-horizontal. "Yeah, man. Movie time."

"*Channel off air. Off*, you dufus. Don't you have a fuckin' telly at home? It means that that channel's not got noffing on it. Cunt."

"I've got my PlayStation, me. Why do I needs TV? TV's shite, man. Full of soaps and all your fly-on-v-wall crap. Telly's for girls, innit. And anyway, it's v same fing, all that *ov* and *off* shit. How am I supposed to know which is which when it all means v same fing?"

"No it don't."

"Trust me, mush, it do. Swear on my baby's life."

"How does it mean the same? Why would there be more than one spelling of it?" Raz flicked on to the soccer, hoping that'd shut him up for a bit. "There. Happy?"

"It makes no difference," Mumpy griped on. "It all means v same fing. They is too much words in this land we don't need, bro."

"Why is there, if we don't need them?"

Mumpy shrugged. "For v politics-boys to mess wiv—get us all wound up about learning stuff—and to keep v dictionary moguls in Jacuzzis, innit? Now shut up. Lets me watch v footy in peace."

"I swear down, Mumps, you needs to get yourself back to school, man. Or like, do a sci-fi and go back in time and like, go there in the first place."

"Eh? Fuck off out. There's noffin' school can teach this boy I ain't best learned from life. Life is what teaches you v fings you needs to be knowing how to survive out in v wild."

"You're only saying that 'cause they wouldn't take you back anyways."

"Not so, Raz. Like, straight up, in school I wasn't so bad at all fings academia. Like, history, for starters, I hated vat less than v rest of classes. But even so, what does it benefit me to know that Henry v sixth lopped v heads off of Kafleen of Oregon and some uva bewer? Noffin' is what. The man was a Section-eighteen, simple as. So now lets me watch v footy! *If* you don't mind."

The mobile in Raz's jacket pocket that Mumpy was wearing buzzed, making him jump up and rummage. He flicked it on.

"Boss?" Only one number rang that phone. Mumpy immediately passed the phone to Raz. "He wants to talk to you, bro."

Raz listened closely. "Yeah? Okay." He gave Mumpy a shove and they were up, walking to the door. "We're on our way, boss. No, it's no problem. No problem at all." They were out of the room and up a short stretch of corridor on the first floor. "Just some daft footy game. Wasn't even into it. What? No, no porn, it's too early in the day... eh? Yeah, sweet, that's what Mumps says. Ha." Up three bare wooden stairs and knocking on a door. It opened. "Here we are, boss. At your service."

A man of about fifty with wild grey hair and eyes popping out like a pug-dog's stood at the open door. He clicked his phone off, his unblinking stare settling on the two young men a step beneath him. His smile was crazy. Running around his feet were two pug dogs.

"My boys. The rather dashing Mr. Razool, good evening to you, young sire, and...somebody pale and spotty whose name escapes me. Good evening nevertheless."

Raz snapped his phone off, too. "Boss. What can we do for you?"

"You can call me Stanley this evening, if you so wish. But do come in, boys. Rude me. Come into my humble little boudoir. Sorry to inconvenience you at such short notice, but there's been a little glitch in our operations, as I so feared, a minor pube in the teeth that will require some swift flossing."

He stepped back, letting the two inside. Another vast room opened up before them, but one far more plushly upholstered than what they'd left, mostly in white muslin and leather. Like the whole exterior of the mansion, even the floorboards were whitewashed—an overall madhouse effect. The ceiling-space had twice the height, having been knocked open to the roof beams and vaulted.

There was a smell of dog wee.

"It seems we're two down, mid-rank, and at short notice, so I'm afraid I'll have to pool your services for the evening, gents. Relocate them, as it were, back to the streets of our lovely township. Yes? Our clientele can't wait, now."

Mumpy turned his head to Raz, who was looking only slightly less bemused.

Stanley took Mumpy firmly by the chin. "Look at Stanley," he said.

Mumpy and Raz kept their eyes dead ahead.

"Ok. En-ga-lish. Go to the business premises of our dear friend Mrs. Copeland, and pick up the shit that that nonce Rafiq was supposed to pick up at five o'bloody-clock. Mrs. Copeland has been kind enough to make it known that all business this week will be conducted from the snug at The Crown on Green Street, rather than our usual haunt. Our contact is already there awaiting your delivery. Are you listening? Yes? Good. Oversee operations. Keep our lovely customers at ease. There has been trouble, lots of extra Bobbies on the beat—*police men and ladies to you*—and our regular consumers may have concerns that the rattles are but a short nap away. Offer our reassurances. It's business as usual. Understood?"

"Yes, boss."

"Yes, boss."

He scooped up a pug and kissed its flat face. "I say Stanley. Please."

CHAPTER SEVENTEEN

The café opposite the city library stayed open on Saturdays until the bars commandeered any passing trade. That was a different crowd, one Donald had no wish to consort with.

Having finished his duties mid-morning, he had stayed on to use one of the library's computers, a device he felt no need of at home. It wasn't a money thing. There was more than enough of that. Donald had found the search engine a useful tool when it came to researching the region's parks, and was amazed that as well as detailed layouts, you could now get an aerial view of just about anywhere. He was particularly interested in those parks that backed onto green-belt or other less-frequented lands. Only once, late afternoon, with the place almost deserted, had he given into temptation and searched for the quarry, had a sneak peek. The overhead view was quite spectacular, utterly tranquil, as described in the detail: a peaceful spot for ramblers and dog-walkers; home to an array of wildlife. And as he'd assured himself, so vast an area that not a trace of his activities would be apparent. And if they were to become apparent, so what? The region's park search showed so much other potential.

The pretty brunette waitress with the blonde streak through the fringe came over to Donald's table carrying his order. "Tea and a toasted teacake?" she checked.

Donald nodded, smiling, moving aside his book, *Great Yorkshire Roads*. He looked closely now at the waitress, finding her not that pretty after all. So few faces were perfect when closely observed. There was a general over-application of an ill-selected concoction of cosmetic shades, mainly, he deduced, to mask the acne scarring—this one had left the spots to their evil—and there was too much mascara to enlarge her piggy little eyes, one of which had a slight sag to the upper lid. Symmetry was so important. Also, her belt cut into the kind of midriff bulge one associates with middle age, or the telly-bound idle. And the last cannon hole to sink the boat: a small jagged scar under the chin, a biking accident perhaps. Shame.

"Will that be all?" she asked curtly, in that semi-hostile tone they all adopt eventually.

Donald nodded again. "Thank you."

As he sipped his tea, he gazed out of the window, through his tidy, quite handsome reflection, at the lazy pace of the evening's incoming crowd, largely under-dressed in response to an unnaturally sunny March day. They'd be shivering within the hour he predicted. For his part, Donald liked rain. With rain came new opportunities, the unique privilege of being a port in a storm. Since that doorway had opened for him, Donald had familiarized himself with another useful website, the Met-Office weather forecaster; though it wasn't time yet to take such note of it. He'd know when the time was right.

While Donald finished the buttered teacake, his attention

returned to the rather homely waitress who had served him. She was standing at the counter, arms folded, glaring in his direction, exchanging unpleasantries no doubt to an even less attractive, older waitress at the till—one of the un-plucked chin brigade. Donald placed his cup on its saucer, smiled pleasantly, and with a beckoning finger summoned the younger lady back over. Her cheeks blazed as she approached him.

"We're closing," she said.

"Yes, I know," he responded. "But just one more thing, young lady, before we settle up. He pulled a silver flask out from a sports bag by his feet, placing it on the table's edge. "Could you fill this for me, please. Two sugars. There's a dear."

CHAPTER EIGHTEEN

Detective Gaunt went outside for a smoke, leaving the two of them alone. Fionn felt easier without him around. They'd moved to the next room; vomit-free. A fresh cup of tea sat waiting on the table. Fionn stared at it as if it were arsenic. A quick glance at the wall-mounted clock told him it was six p.m. The longest day of his life wasn't over yet.

Detective Ryan caught and held his eye. "I needed to know that you weren't involved."

"In that massacre? Why would you jump to that conclusion? Of course, I'm angry for the Johnstons. These people are my life. My family. Can't you understand that? Sure, I'm no saint."

"So I've observed." She smiled. "And frankly, you must know you're not the first priest to have given an overzealous husband a hard preaching to. Don't quote me on it, but it has been known to be an effective antidote."

"Would you've said that with him in the room?"

"Detective Gaunt's standoffish with everyone. Don't let him get to you. The thing is, there's another reason I wanted you here for a talk. I need—we need, an ally in the camp, if you like. At a time like this, it's far better to keep the lines of communication *open*. That's why I need to know that I can trust you. You must have considered how all this could end, that it could be all out war if the violence keeps rolling. Reprisals…lead to reprisals. You're Irish?"

"Yes. But I've never seen a bomb go off, if that's what you mean. Most of us haven't. My parents moved from County Down to Galway—we'd family there—when I was three or so. That's the life I remember. A simple, wonderful life. There were fights in school, like any, but the last few years around here, it's the closest thing I've ever seen first-hand to war."

There was no desk between them. She leaned forward, hands on knees.

"You're not telling me what I want to hear, Father. You're hesitant. Why?"

"Fionn. Don't call me Father." He smiled. "You're older than me."

She almost smiled back but held onto it. He looked her in the eye. His own eyes wore the dark circles earned by countless troubled nights. His black hair cut through them in ragged strands. Then she did that thing women sometimes do without warning; glanced from his eyes to his mouth and back again—an inadvertent gesture perhaps—which seemed odd under the circumstances. He still got a mild rush from it.

"You can trust me," he told her. "Is that what you want me to say?"

"Only if you mean it, Fionn."

As she spoke, an almighty commotion kicked off in the foyer beyond the closed door of the interview room. Panicked voices were shouting, screaming in some cases, for whoever had walked into the station to, "Put it down! Put the weapon down! Just put it right down on the floor. Now!"

DI Ryan was instantly up and out of the room. Fionn followed despite being warned not to by an officer standing outside the door. He'd been unable to admit it to himself, to let the thought take shape; the thought that had surfaced the moment he'd been confronted with those pictures of the butchered gang members. The truth was, he knew exactly what was going on, just like he knew the tree fire had been to get him out of the way, likewise, he knew what was happening here—who he was about to see.

In the center of the foyer, surrounded by a host of very jittery police officers, stood the gigantic frame of Ben Hunter, his eyes distant, fixed ahead, as if he'd sleepwalked in from another world—a crime scene judging by the looks of him. Ben was caked in blood. Only from a rear view of him could you have guessed his T-shirt had started out white. His big garden boots were beetroot purple, as if soaked overnight in gore. The smell was cloying, but then it was coming from more than just Ben and his car-crash clothing. A trail of blood ran from outside the station doors to where he stood. Sticky droplets still oozed out of the punch-holes in the carrier bag Ben held in his hand. His other hand held a long-handled axe. A screwdriver honed to a sharp point was lodged through his belt.

"Ben!" Fionn almost ran, but was halted by a web of uniformed arms. "Let me past."

"Be careful, Father!" DI Ryan shouted, signaling to those preventing his progress to pull back. "Fionn! I mean it. Be careful."

Fionn walked slowly forward until he stood, a head smaller, before the man he'd come to know as Hawk.

"Ben? Look at me. You're here now. It's over."

Ben first looked at his friend as if seeing him from some distance away, then his focus seemed to tune-in and he nodded calmly, throwing the carrier bag forward, away from the two of them. There was a sickening squelch. Giblet-like chunks of groin-flesh complete with short wiry hairs oozed out across the floor. A young PC threw up in that direction and was dragged hand-on-mouth away from the evidence by another who'd been unwittingly nursing his crotch. Fionn kept his eyes fixed on Ben's. "Come on, mate," he urged shakily. "And the rest." The screwdriver was pulled free and dropped. The axe went down next, the blade clattered against the tiled floor, sounding off a piercing echo that seemed to spring the duty officers into action. Ben Hunter was seized and tussled to the ground.

He didn't fight it for a second.

CHAPTER NINETEEN

It begins with a whisper. "Father Fionn. Father Fionn, wake up."

"Eh?"

"I've been tryin' to find you, but I can't hardly see. And I'm so tired. They're sucking me dry, mate."

"Callum? What? Where are you?"

"I've been waiting for you to come back, before they round us up again, like animals. We need…" He pauses, as if listening intently. "Oh no. They're coming…"

Fionn senses panic in the voice, feels a dark void opening at its source.

His vision is adjusting to the semi-dark surroundings. Though he has no true sense of time, a conscious thread of his insight tells him that several days have passed since he stood facing Ben Hunter, fresh out of a blood-storm, his boots pickled in its flood. Now he stares down at his own black brogues with the comic swagger of a drunk who catches sight of himself in a chance mirror. He doesn't remember walking up here in those. Funny that. He just opened his eyes and here he was sitting, all alone in the dark on one of the few remaining pews that haven't yet been ripped out yet. The crawling masses have taken their leave; even bugs know a sinking ship once the tilt sets in. All is still. The presence he felt and heard on waking has fled and he fears he has missed a chance there. He studies himself further. He has on full vestments. Why?

It's so cold in here. Like the collective breath of its deceased congregations. Hairs stand taut on the back of his neck where he feels the sudden sensation of her warm breath as she rises from the seats behind. Even angel breath is sexy when it hits you there. The scents of lavender, bergamot, and intense spices surround him. Yet he's afraid. His head feels locked in a vice. The breathing draws closer, feels hotter. Something that has wheedled beneath his robes nudges him above the shoulder blades, something blunt and flicking, like a wet tongue. It knows the nerves that tick and where to find them. He struggles against its pressure, reaching back, but the deed is attached to nothing physical that he can grab or push away, and the sensation only intensifies, moves lower, all around him, intent on exploring his senses, on tasting him, eagerly. With it, the scent of his approaching angel has been swamped out by something like stagnant pond weed; a dull radiance of that color hangs in the air: a bile green haze.

"Don't," he demands, pulling, twisting away, but weakly, somehow drugged, locked in its grip. "Stop it. Stop!"

It does so suddenly, and at that moment, the angel is standing there before him, having switched herself on like a light. Instantly he feels his strength return. He wipes the cloth of his robes against the flesh the demon tongue has dampened, feeling contaminated, corrupted.

"Why did you let that happen?" he asks. "What is that? Why is it with you?"

"Not with me, but close at hand," the angel says. "You must know, Priest, that good and evil stand in close proximity, even walk the same pathways. We are a magnet for their desires, a target for temptation. You must be strong, vigilant."

"Callum was here. I heard him. He's terribly afraid."

"Is this not the guilt you spoke of, Priest?"

"Maybe. I don't know any more. What about that thing that took over when I last saw *you*. The thing you became—is that monstrosity good or evil?"

"My Zwerg is fearsome but a necessary aspect of my being. Men see my fragility. They must equally fear my protector. Now, holy man, I must ask the thing of you that is your purpose."

"Tell me first, your name—not Zwerg—your name."

"I am Appolyn."

"Thank you. Tell me, Appolyn, what am I, that God's own messenger should ask my help?"

"You now believe this to be so?"

"Yes... I don't know. You certainly did what I asked you to do. You—your Zwerg—told me something I didn't already know. It's Ben who carries the bag—the futures of four men; their seed, though I wish now I'd never had to realize it."

"More wishes?" She steps closer—her scent is heady. "Be careful what you wish for, Priest. Words spoken in earnest cannot always be taken back."

He feels vile in the face of her utter beauty. Her wings stand open, emitting light all around. The sweet scent is overwhelming, intoxicating. He notices in the intensified light that his garden spade is standing close by—strange. But he did bring that along with him. He remembers now.

"So Ben is the one you wanted—for what? And what is it

you want with me?"

"I can reveal little of his purpose, only yours."

"Confidentiality, eh?"

"You are our thoughts, Fionn. Our eye on the world. Our conscience. A good servant. And for this, in beginning our mission, we will grant you a wish: of those many you watch with disdain, whose guilt is transparent to a world that fails to issue retribution—one such miscreant will be dealt with swiftly. Others will follow."

"I see." Fionn pictures himself shouting at the TV, at the news, and wonders how long she has been standing behind him, watching, listening. "How will I know it's divine retribution in progress, not just the law, or some crazed vigilante?"

"You will know. So much lies in your hands now, Priest. Time is short and you must act fast."

"And if I don't?"

"Men who wish for Armageddon must surely untether the horse of the angel of death. No, you cannot hide your thoughts from us, Priest." The angel smiles. "Your task is simple. In these grounds, lies buried the ashes of a saint, namely *Agnes*, whose church stood here in distant times. Her sanctity must not be defiled by the unholy who pillage this place. Her ashes must reside with the chosen disciple. In turn, her spirit will endow him with the strength to live on. To play his part."

"Saint Agnes. Yes, her church stood here. But buried where?"

"You know where. Come."

She offers a hand, which he takes apprehensively but finds to be warm, comforting. He stands, picking up his spade, and is led outside. He feels like a little boy at the beach.

"So many things have been bothering me, Angel," he admits, on the verge of tears. "I know the world has to change, but I'm afraid."

"We know. Please be strong. Nothing begins without you." She guides him to the scorched patch of ground in the cemetery, where, without further instruction, he begins to dig. "And it must begin here and now. It is our time. A time for change. It is what you wished for."

CHAPTER TWENTY

Gervais Monk, a.k.a. Monkey, died from his injuries within twenty-four hours of receipt. Once the other three gang members survived beyond that point, it was presumed they would just carry on surviving, perhaps a worse fate, *The Evening Post* speculated, than that of the youngest of their number. The events made national press. The tabloids went wild and, in light of a rise in similar gang-attacks, spared no mercy for Rokerville's mutilated offenders, marrying phrases like "rapist scumbags" and "cowardly thugs" with others like "apt retribution" and even "come-uppance". And though the broad-sheets inevitably expressed concern at the prospect of copy-cat vigilantism, Ben Hunter's portrait was generally drawn on the lines of a local man of good social conscience, who finally snapped in the face of his neighborhood's decline under gang violence.

For his own part, Father Malloy ignored several messages from the local reporter, Carl Wilson, requesting a meeting. Fionn couldn't say why exactly he was so strongly against such a meeting, only that he did feel strongly against it.

*

Three weeks after his closest friend of ten years had walked into City Central police station with a Morrison's bag full of castrated genitalia, Father Fionn Malloy set off up through the estate to see the real victims in all of this.

It was early April and summer was already pushing through, as if it knew Rokerville was due a respite. Birdsong rang out of every privet hedge, but more markedly came the sounds of children out playing—a dwindling normality in recent years—the *nee-naw nee-naw* of toy police cars and fire engines finally usurping the harsh sirens of unrest. Further convictions of other gang members present at Debbie and Amelia's attack had followed Kelvin Goddard's arrest. On top of the evidence police took from his phone, Kelvin had obliged them further by singing louder than Tweetie Pie at Sylvester's funeral; not so much due to a change of heart but rather in abject terror that he might be next on Ben Hunter's list of jobs to do. And so, the darkness lifted. Makeshift goalposts were set up on the greens. The footballs were flying, the bicycles out and racing, the park glass-free and heaving with the squeals of toddler exuberance.

Deborah Smith's parents thanked their priest politely for calling by, but Debs, they said, was staying with cousins over in York. She didn't want to be around the estate, probably not for a long time yet. Your home should feel like a safe place, and it no longer felt that way for Deborah. They were thinking about moving altogether, her mum added bitterly, making a fresh start, what with all the publicity. The girls' identities might be protected by law, but they'd never be allowed to forget it in these streets.

At the Johnstons', Louis answered the door. The look on

his face was severe yet expectant, as though he'd been waiting for Fionn to knock for a long time.

"Come in, Father," he said. "Amelia's in the front room. Just go through."

She was sitting on the floor hugging her knees in front of the TV. He could tell, even from a side view, that her facial swelling had eased considerably, though the eye he could see bore stitch marks running proud from the lid and up through her brow. The TV was blasting. There was a music station on playing a Rap track Fionn had never heard before by somebody he wouldn't know if they knelt before him for Holy Communion, which was unlikely. She turned her head slightly and they said their hellos.

"What's on?" he asked.

"Usual crap." She picked up the remote and flicked a couple of stations along. "This more your thing, is it?"

"Who is it, Elvis Presley?"

She rolled her eyes and snorted. "Kasabian, man. Jees."

"I'm joking. Just, I lost interest in it all the last time Oasis broke up."

"Can't help you then." She switched off and got up. "You want a cup of tea, Father?"

"I'd love one, ta. Can you manage okay with that?" He nodded at her plastered arm but didn't go overboard on the point.

"Yeah, fine. You take sugar, yeah?"

"Yeah, Ami, just the one, ta very much."

She remembered, bless her.

When she returned, she was carrying two hot cups in one hand. He took them both, handing her back the one with the picture of the bunny rabbit on.

"That one's yours," she said and swapped.

"Oh, right, thanks."

They both sat down in easy chairs that didn't quite face each other. After a long pause, Amelia said, "You've not come to hear my confession, have you?"

"Hell, no." He almost spilled his tea. "You've nothing to confess, Amelia, especially not to me." He hadn't meant to sound so emphatic on the *to me* part of that statement. But this last few weeks, even though he still wore the collar, it felt bad playing preacher. "I'm sorry," he said. "I didn't mean to sound mad. That's the last thing you need."

Amelia's expression came as close to a smile as she could possibly have managed. "That's okay. That's like, what they call you."

"What?"

"Mad-Malloy, and Raspa; like, there's this old song, Ra Ra Rasputin…" she sang it.

"Oh, yeah. I heard that. Boney-M. Even before my time, that."

"I had to Google him 'cause I didn't get it at first, but when I did, I sees it. Yep. The black hair, all wild an' that."

"My granddaddy had a farm up on the moors in Ireland. Ten generations of gale-force winds blowing at your ancestors will get you born looking like this."

She was thoughtful for a while. "There's this reporter. He seems really nice. Carl Wilson. You heard of him?"

"Yes, I have."

"He wrote stuff about all the suicides and stuff round here, like, in the graveyard up top?"

"Yes I know. Mr. Wilson didn't do Saint Luke's any favors, I have to say. I'd be careful who you talk to, Ami."

"Sometimes I really feel like talkin', though. It's just…I know who's responsible for all the shit round here, you know.

There's this geezer—Coxer he's called, has that big white mansion over on Millionaires' Hill, near the golf course. If you go up Beggars' Rock you can see it, sittin' there all proud, sneering back at the likes of us."

"Yeah, I know the house. Big money."

"He's an ex racing-driver or some shit like that. Like, he brings in boatloads of drugs from, I don't know, all the countries we're at war wiv half the time, brings 'em in through Russia and Amsterdam, all those places. Kelvin used to tell me everything. He couldn't stop himself. That's how comes he got so scared of me when we parted ways." She looked Fionn in the eye. "They keep us all down, y'know, people like that Coxer. Keep us all nobodies fighting over nothing. Nothing that matters."

"I know, Ami. It pisses me off royally. Just be careful who you talk to, is all I'm saying. There's obvious reasons why people don't discuss the goings-on of the Coxers of this world, especially not with reporters."

"I know *that*." She was thinking hard. "Father, I do want to confess something," she said. "Something that's been eating me up."

"Please, you really don't have to, Ami."

"I know. But I'm goin' to. That night when you was camping out a couple of months ago, and Callum was wiv you, and the boys, like, lined up and taunted you…"

"Yeah, I remember."

She shrugged, not happy to say it. "I was there. Like, in the line-up."

"I know, Ami. It doesn't matter."

"But it wasn't me called you 'pervert'. That was Kelly—you've heard about Kelly?"

"Yes, 'fraid so."

"Anyways, it was that night tipped things over for me, and Kelly as well, I reckon, hearing Cal sobbing like that, an' them carrying on regardless, as if he hadn't had enough. Bunch of dicks."

"You changed, Ami. Kelly, too. Some people can. Others just don't want to."

"Why did you want to be a priest?" she asked him out of the blue.

He took a long drink of the tea, hot though it was, his mouth suddenly feeling dry. "I can't always put a finger on it," he said. "I truly believed in God all the time I was growing up. And I suppose, I didn't want to be a social worker or anything like that, but still I had all these trumped up ideas about solving the world's problems. I always dwelt on the negative stuff, even as a kid. As long as I can remember. Not that I was a good kid. We—me and my mates—we used to fight in lumps like anybody. I dunno, maybe I thought I could make a difference to the world. Save people."

"Like Superman?"

"I suppose, kind of, but without the super powers. Or the red cape. Which is a bit of a raw deal, really."

Her smile faltered; she began to crumble. "Do you think Hawk believed something like that?" That he could change the world for the better? D'you think that's why he did what he did?"

Fionn suffered a saddening flashback of his first home visit here, when the mum was still around, the Beyonce of the estate, all dressed up to suit, and Amelia a tot of about four, playing with Lego on the rug by the fire, shouting building instructions at her big brothers. The mother was constantly texting or talking on her mobile, never looked at the kids once all the while he was there, or responded to Louis with more than a shrug. "She's got bigger plans," Fionn thought to himself at the time, and hated himself for being right.

"I think Ben was very angry at first, that he lost control. But to keep going, I suppose he had to believe what he was doing could change things for the better." He paused. "But how do you feel about it, Ami? What happened to those boys? They really hurt you and your friend, near killed you."

Ami hung her head. "I wasn't the first Xbox'd done that to. Kelly was. That baby…it's his." Ami's eyes turned wet. "They say, after the massacre at the Monk's house, that everybody knew. X was just left out in the street, like an example. People were tracking Ben, making calls to and fro. People knew where he was headed each time. Nobody stood in his way, tried to stop him. Everyone just stood back and let him get on with it. Except for X and Monkey's mum charging round the streets screaming like a nutter. They say Ben even got a tip-off, y'know, tellin' him where Rafiq's car was sittin'—him in it. There was like this euphoria, like the people were ready for it, like it'd been waiting to happen."

"Does that shock you, Ami?"

She swiped angry tears from her cheeks. "Like, I don't care, right, how much those bastards suffer. When I'm laying awake of a night, scared to sleep in my own bed, I wish he'd got the ones who were watching and laughing as well, and saying "do it, man" and goading them on; fuckin' loving it, weren't they? But then I wish as well…I wish Ben hadn't done so much about it, so things could be the same again— some day. But now, he ain't gunner ever see the light of day, is he? Not as long as he lives. It's all just crap, man. Nothing can ever be normal now."

Fionn couldn't console her from there. After a while, her

brother Joe came in and took over, reassuring Fionn that she needed to cry; the counselor had said so. It was eerie, seeing Joe acting so calmly. Fionn had a good idea now what it was he'd been whispering to Louis at the hospital that day. A great deal of time had elapsed between Ben rescuing the girls and then going on his axe rampage. He'd been laying low somewhere between times, thinking, deciding what to do. Maybe it had been here. Maybe, in the absence of Louis, it'd been Joe who gave Ben the family's blessing to do what he planned to do.

Fionn had to remind himself that untold forces were at work here, that Ben may not have acted on the blessing of mortals alone.

Louis was sitting at the kitchen table smoking when Fionn went to say his good-byes. He gave his priest a sour look.

"Draggin' our feet a bit, aren't we, Father?"

"Am I? In what sense, Louis?"

"In the sense that Hawk's waiting for a visit. I take it you've not been yet?"

Fionn shook his head. "I haven't. I plan to."

"Good. Seeing as you're his priest, so about the only one who *can* see him right now, him being on t'seg-block and that. And summat else you should know, that they're keeping schtum about in t'nick. An' just so you know how much time you've got left to lag about, Hawk's been on hunger strike since he gave himself up. Hasn't touched a bite. He's planning on dying, Father, if nothing's doing. So if there's something you're planning on doing, you'd best get your arse in gear. Don't go thinking you've got forever."

CHAPTER TWENTY-ONE

Through that night, Fionn blitzed the paperwork, watched the news on and off—*no sign of Kelly Atkins, dead or alive*—and prayed to a God he felt somehow more and more distanced from; anything to avoid picturing Ben laying there alone in a cell, wasting away. A body that size: how long could it survive without sustenance?

At approaching three in the morning, staring out of his rear window to the shell of the old church on the moor's edge, he whispered, "Tell him I'm coming. I'm sorry."

The door to the storeroom at the back of the rectory was firmly locked; he'd made sure, even slipped the spare key off of Mrs. Chuk's set while she'd been busy online. He unlocked the door and went inside. His dirt-logged brogues still lay discarded by the wall, as they had since the night he'd dug something strange and mystical out of the depths of his old graveyard, something that now glowed emerald-like in his humble hands. Why, he asked himself, had he not delivered the ashes to God's disciple, as promised? Because this one question remained: *why had so many people chosen that spot, a saint's burial site, to take their lives? Had they gone there for help?*

Perhaps countless more people had gone there and found their prayers answered; people *were* drawn to such places. Perhaps only the weak failed and died.

But, Callum, his mind protested.

Through the small window beyond the workbench, the old Gothic Saint Luke's looked down, continuing to watch his every move, seeming, like Louis Johnston, to judge his inactivity as the act of a coward. He was the one, after all, who had demanded that something should happen—*fire and brimstone!*—and here he was, holding up the the show.

From an iron casket buried deep within the twining roots of the old oak, he'd prized out the silver urn he now held in his hands. The urn's lid had been sealed so tightly he'd cut his hands forcing it that first night. Inside, there certainly were ashes that glowed like fairy dust—of Saint Agnes? Certainly somebody of note. Fionn peered inside at the fine, glinting powders. Not much there to speak of. Whoever it was had been virtually incinerated.

Returning to the church, Fionn again knelt and prayed, hoping for some line of guidance that might lead him down an alternative route. He got nothing. At around five in the morning, he took the silver chain his mother had given him for his twenty-first birthday, with the phial containing holy water from Lourdes. He kissed the phial before pouring the water into a pot-plant. "Good health", he said, then left the phial up-ended on the radiator to dry.

*

There had been other visits to the prison; he could hardly call his flock white-woolen. Some inmates referred to the place as "The Disney Castle". If so, it had to be one the wicked witch hoarded her minions in; those blackened stone walls could hardly tempt a princess. The add-ons, the later extensions, were somehow worse, being the mid-twentieth century's block-of-concrete answer to everything building-wise. One feature that had previously escaped Father Malloy's notice, that now glared back at him with sickening irony as he walked toward the main gate, was the moldings that capped the rungs of the iron fencing along the way: a motif of an executioner's axe.

The Chaplaincy's Roman Catholic rep was off on long-term sick leave. Ben'd registered Catholic on arrival, so it wasn't hard to set up a meeting from his home parish. At security, Fionn was questioned about the phial on the chain. He explained that they held the ashes of Saint Agnes. He got the loopy look. A dog walked around him, but clearly smelled nothing suspect. Louis had said nobody would stop him. "Hawk's the man," he'd assured Fionn. "You'll see no trouble."

To one side of a small chapel off the multi-faith center, tables were set out for such meetings. Ben was sitting at one, waiting. He was only a few years older than Fionn, had not long since seen his fortieth birthday in, but had somehow grown younger over the past weeks. There was a glow about him. He was thinner, yes, making his hooked nose all the more prominent, but he sat upright, bearing all the dignity and grace of the God-like beings in Italian renaissance paintings.

They said hello with unusual formality, then Fionn sat down. A tall, bearded man in a tweed jacket brought in two plastic blue cups half full of tea, urging Ben to drink his "this time", then left them alone. An officer remained by the door. Fionn glanced back, not sure if in this tall, echoing room they'd be overheard.

"Do you wish to confess, my friend?" he began.

"He won't hear us," Ben said calmly. "And no, Father. Should I confess a sin I'd repeat tenfold?"

"No, Ben. You should not." Fionn paused, overwhelmed by conflicting feelings for the man sitting opposite: love, wariness, wholehearted respect, and a deep inexplicable dread. "You look strangely great, by the way," he smiled. "But you're dying. Anyone can see that."

Ben's eyes drifted down to the phial at Fionn's chest. "They bring me tea the same time every day. Will I drink it today, Father?" Through the warmth of Ben's smile there was a cold clarity.

"Before we talk about this," Fionn wrapped a hand round the phial, "I need a promise from you. The other gang members... the ones here from Rokerville. I don't want anything more to happen to them. Any of them."

Ben shook his head. "She said you're weak, you know that?"

"Maybe so, but all the publicity is bad for the girls. People on Rokerville need a chance to recover, Ben, to get back to some sense of normalcy."

Ben nodded. "Point taken. You're right. Nothing good's comin' to that lot in here anyway. Nonces, rapists, granny-bashers, might think they're tough out there; in here they're just the arse that needs a good kickin' as far as everyone else is concerned. Any regular lad in here would bring hanging back for that lot."

"Yeah? Then what next? Chop the hands off thieves? How would 'everyone else' like the sound of that?" Fionn clutched the phial but didn't remove it. "Look, Ben, I don't know what's going to happen next, but I do feel certain there'll be no going back. This force we've encountered—it's too powerful. Ben, you know you have a choice…"

"Between God's will and what?"

"Do we know that's what this is, Ben? So much violence. Yes, I've seen the same evidence as you have. There's no denying her, but have you ever heard her speak of God? Of prayer? There's talk of wishes…"

"What else could she be? Why would she, *it*, bother with the likes of us?"

"I don't know, but I've seen something else, too, when I've been close to her, something…vile, ugly."

Ben laughed. "Fionn, you've read the Bible. Angels aren't always pretty. They're what they need to be to get the job done. And violence—so be it. What about the flood, Sodom and Gomorrah, the Egyptians, Jericho? Real change comes at a price. You've wished for it, too."

Fionn gripped his friend's hand. "Then let me do this."

Ben wrapped both his hands around Fionn's. "You know you can't, Fionn."

Tears welled in the priest's eyes. "Ben, something's not right about all this. I've felt it. There's something malevolent just hovering on the outskirts of it all. So many people have died around that church. Why? I want justice, yes. I want change like you do, but I don't understand what's happening here."

Ben shook the hands in his. "I have to trust her. It's the only way forward for me now. I won't live on in this." He looked around at the barred windows. "I won't. Things happen for a reason. All this is happening for a reason. Now help me, mate. Please."

Fionn wept quietly. "I'm sorry, Ben. I took too long to act. I'm a fucking coward, you know that?"

"This isn't about you and me. You're doing your best. I love you, mate. Hey. Come on."

Fionn shook his head. "Ben. Can't you just live? Just carry on?

"People talk about crossing lines, as if they're not really sure where the line is or what'll happen if they cross it. You've seen what I did. It was no moment's madness. I had plenty of time to think about it. I planned and executed my actions. You must see there's no going back for me after that, Fionn." Ben looked again at the phial on the chain. Slowly he let go of his friend's hands and sat back. "So. Will I drink the tea today, Father?"

Fionn wiped his face on his sleeve. "I could just go. Walk away and never come back. I can stop this happening."

"Right now you can. You can leave me here. I'll die. And things'll stay quiet for a bit, then it'll all start over again. Ten—twenty years from now, all this shit'll have kicked off again. And it'll go on happening till someone acts." Ben pushed his cup toward Fionn. "So. Will I drink it? Or will I die?"

Fionn turned his head to check the officer by the door, but the man was staring dream-like off into space.

"He can't see anything," Ben told him. "Now, Fionn. It's time."

Fionn smiled weakly and removed the chain from around his neck. He could barely work the cap on the phial for his hands trembling. Once it was off, he poured the gleaming powders into Ben's tea. The liquid quaked furiously—like something alive was thrashing about in it—then settled to a quiver, and both men leaned forward, staring with wonder, as Ben's tea lit up like lava.

CHAPTER TWENTY-TWO

Social, religious, and educational staff had wound up and left for the evening. There was the usual cacophony of sounds on the wings: the clatter of inmates cleaning out the kitchen, trance blasting out the barred windows, the garbled clash of TV stations and settled-down banter behind cell doors.

Association never happened on the segregation block, leaving the atmosphere overall more subdued. Lockdown was permanent unless an emergency situation arose. Ben Hunter lay in his solitary shoebox of a pad. He finished off Deuteronomy then put the bible down. Gently. The book had been a true friend over these past weeks. And it confirmed what Fionn had said on the phone the night the troubles'd kicked off. Angels would take on human form and appear on earth, usually prior to some catastrophic or miraculous event; one that would return a degree of balance to humanity. There was in each case an earthly contact: Abraham, Lott, Moses, and of course Mary. It had been easier to think he was crazy at first, rather than accept what was happening, that an ordinary bloke like him could ever be the one "chosen" for such a grand call of duty. After Anita, he'd come as close to stopping believing as possible without actually declaring himself an atheist. Fionn'd seen him through that phase. So it was right that he'd been the one to see him off today, to open the gate to a pathway back to God.

That last night on the estate, when the angel had appeared to him in the flesh, her wings unfurled like heavenly banners, and woke him from his untimely doze, alerted him to the evil in progress, that's when he'd known. From that moment, there was no room left for doubt. From a small speck in the universe, he was to become part of a larger purpose. What it would amount to, he didn't know yet. There would be pain—no doubt about that. But whatever it was he was ready to face it. He wouldn't be alone.

His gut felt pleasantly warm. He'd even accepted an evening meal. He'd need his strength for what was to come. It'd been hard seeing Fionn crumble like that, one of the hardest things he'd ever had to watch. But he'd needed to keep the both of them focused. After Anita's suicide, Fionn had been the one who helped him carry on living, given him some purpose in his life. But compared to this, now, his former life was dust in the wind. Things had to change. The world needed a shake up. It had happened before and now, it was time again. The spirits needed a vehicle in which to rage their justice through the world, and after what he'd seen over the past few years, Ben was more than happy to be it.

There was a sudden blinding pain in his stomach, like trapped wind but searing hot. With its intensity came something he hadn't expected and didn't welcome for a second—heavy regret tugged at his heart; it hit him that he could never again be with the people he loved, not under normal circumstances. He'd felt sure he'd come to terms with all this, yet here they were again, the faces he craved to hold in his hands: his sister Annette, Fionn, Louis, Ami. And Lizzy... not little Lizzy—he had to stop thinking. It would all be over soon.

Chaos suddenly rang out from the far end of the block. An alarm sounded. Keys rattled and heavy footfall pounded in that direction, away from Ben's pad.

He began to feel extremely odd, like he was drifting out of himself. The warmth in his belly was rising, shifting thickly like butter in a churn, steadily coming to a boil. The agony was growing unbearable. He threw off his clothes and lay naked, panting hard, doing what he could to prepare himself, but it hurt like fuck. She, Appolyn, had warned him that it would be worse the first time, but that it would become easier; knowing the outcome, he would even grow to embrace it.

He tried to think of other things, any distraction, otherwise he'd be screeching like a seagull pretty soon, and then the footfall would be heading back his way. It was Lizzy who popped into his head, as she was prone to—bright, giggling, curly topped Lizzy, tramping clumsily around the allotment in her best orange Wellies. But that was the last thing he wanted, her in his head right now.

He struggled mentally to block her out, even replaying the looks on the faces of those four boys as he'd pressed them down by the neck and raised the screwdriver. But that only made it worse when she came skipping back in. He'd committed irreversible acts, changed the course of his life forever—no going back now, no matter what. Regret was useless. "Lizzy," he whispered. "I'll miss you, pet." And he fell into fits of sobbing. He had to clamp a hand over his mouth to contain the approaching hysteria. It wouldn't be a good idea to draw attention to himself right now, not the way he was, lighting up like a Royal Navy flare.

Thoughts that are not his own flood into his mind's eye without invite, like old films replaying in fast motion: Tethered horses, a baying crowd in Tudor apparel, all viewed through the living flames that consume the writhing body he looks out from. The jeering crowd are stilled, their smugness obliterated, replaced by terror as the mood changes; the power that was sought has arrived. Slower now, a vision is taking him backwards from that time: three freshly hung corpses wearing church-robes, one face he has come to know, swaying dead and limp in the moonlight, roped up from a young oak: he couldn't help her. Then once again, he is speeding forward in time, weightless as an eagle in flight, away from that death-scene on the hilltop, out over a dark, barren landscape—the shape of the land and the rock formation one he knows as he comes to land. Now he winds like a snake through the dust of a cave, toward a greenish light that seems not to be from any source, that just hangs there like air-spill from toxic waste. Deep in the cave, a fire crackles. Somebody is sitting there by it, shrouded by the hood of a robe, chanting hoarsely, raising the axe to hack open the chest of her corpse.

"No." Ben half closed his eyes but the lids almost welded to his eyeballs. "What are you?"

He began to sink, to flatten. Thinking became harder. Except there was the horrible knowledge that he was no longer in charge. Lizzy popped in again, only in front of him, as if she were right there in his cell—come to say bye-byes. "Leave her out of it," he groaned. "Not Lizzy."

The bed was smoldering and would soon be alight. What

remained of his vision strained to focus through rippling rivers of scorched air. He could still make her out though— his little Lizzy, holding her hand out to him, her little face pained, blood on her fingertip. They were recalling the taste of it on his tongue, tapping into the memory, recovering the code. Ben honed all his energy into blocking out her face, so at least they couldn't get that. Then bracing himself as much as was humanly possible under the circumstances, he trained his blurring vision on the gap at the foot of the cell door.

PART THREE

Frustration

CHAPTER TWENTY-THREE

"Which would yous rather have, wings or arms?"

"Wings with hands on."

"You don't get hands on va wings, bro. We is not back in va historical times of v Angallos and Saxons and Jews, wiv all they weird lookin' dinosaurs flyin' around their heads and shit—you has to choose."

Raz rolled his eyes. "Arms then."

"I'd have wings, me. Cushty."

Cruising out of town, Raz kept one eye on the rearview mirror; such tasks were always down to him. They'd had to switch venues twice in the past few weeks, still Mumpy was about as alert as a stoned puppy in a bed full of candy floss. Of late, it seemed every cunt was out to get them. The fact was, if *they* didn't deal, somebody else would. The market was ripe.

A twin-set of lights that'd been worrying Raz for a mile or two steered off toward the suburbs. He eased up some. Mumpy lit two fags side by side and handed him one.

"What are you, my wife? Did we just make a baby?" Raz scolded, accepting the fag regardless. "Don't pull that shit with men."

Mumpy shrugged. "Speakin' of which, we ain't gunner have to stay at your man's again tonight, is we?"

"What, your mum's house better, is it? She slipping a nice hot water bottle in your four-poster as we speak? Anyhow, not to my knowledge. But we has to keep it open-minded, do what the fuck we're told. These are times of trouble, Mump. Make no mistake."

"I don't like stayin' there, though. "Cause, like, he makes me dead nervous, innit. What's wiv those eyes? And those yippy little dogs? Why has he gots those gay little doggies, eh, mush? Not a man's dog vat, is it, like your Pekinese, Chihuahua types? Them's a aeroplane blonde's dog. Your demestos blonde but wiv the black-box intact—it's her type innit?"

"Well you tell him, Mumps. Like, 'Go get yourself a Rottweiler, you gay, ponsy-pup totin' mother-fucker'. Get the man told, bro. Down the line. I'll watch with popcorn."

"Yeah, I bet. Ha! 'Cause he's mad though, in' he? Well-barkin', like them weenie doggies. Has you heard them, like, let rip an air-biscuit? I mean what size is they sphinctusses? They's well loose, man. They's like horse farts echoing off va walls. And them floors being, like, white an' all. Leaving all they little brown splotches where they ripped one out. *Proper* disgustin', mish."

"They leave more than splotches, Mump. Check you treads. Yeah. I tell you—arsenuts."

Mumpy checked his treads there and then. Raz gave the gas some boot once they got out on the dual carriageway. They were running late, which wasn't smart given the current climate.

"Fuck, man. Give me a cat, right, any day. My mum has

cats. They's cool is cats, they is like, 'I'm the main man'. They's out there looking out for vemselves. Not like your dogs, like you has to be babysitting vem twenty-four-ten."

"Seven, Mumps."

"Seven what?"

"Twenty-four-seven, as in seven days of a week. As in twenty-four hours of a day."

Mumpy swung a loop with his head, well put out. "Not necessarily, bro. It's just a saying.

Tain't necessarily about days and weeks an' hours and shit. A saying is a saying and you can say it however the fuck you wants. But like *I* was saying, cats is the man, mish. Like, you won't never hear a cat fart like dem doggies do."

"Every living thing farts."

"Not fruit."

"Maybe not fruit. Every livin' breathin' thing does, though. It's a fact of nature, Mump."

"They might, right? But what I'm sayin', Raz, izzz, you won't never hear no anal-blowage from yours feline friends. 'Cause they eases them out, subtle like."

"What, to be polite? Fuck off, Mump. Jesus, what it's like being trapped in a motor with you. Of course, cats fart. They eat smelly food. And for sure when they're heaving out the Havanas they has to let a stray one go like anyfink else. Jeees."

"Not so. Not even launching a scud. I swear, as long as you *exist,* man, you won't never hear v sound of a cat-fart. I swear *down* on my baby's *life.* Respect v knowledge, Raz, man."

Raz skidded to an abrupt stop outside the Copelands' warehouse, then paused, eyeing the place over. Mrs. Copeland usually made her presence known, gave the all-clear. But tonight, nothing. Things seemed way too quiet.

"We'd best get in. You got the money, Mumps? Get the bag. Let's make this a quick drop. I'm getting fuckin' paranoid already, here."

"That's v weed workin' its evil on your brain, bro. Too much of v good stuff."

"Okay. Shut it."

The warehouse was on a largely deserted industrial estate west of the city. Raz and Mumpy entered by the reception door. No lights appeared to be on until they came through to the holding area, where high shelving units running almost the length of the warehouse blocked their immediate view. Alarm bells went off when Raz spotted Stanley Coxer's two pugs playing tag under them. The dogs yapped at their intrusion.

The two lads stood quietly, waiting. Mrs. Copeland, a heavy smoker that looked ten years older than her forty-five years, usually did any talking when necessary. Copeland and her cronies—she had been widowed under suspicious circumstances—kept stock of the kind of trash-wares that littered the floors of pound shops. She was making good money peddling the kind of shit people didn't need to invest in, the kind of shit others grew to need badly. Tonight she was mooching in the background, minding her business. It was Stanley who came forward, with a wide smile that failed to reach his eyes, while his eyebrows invaded his hairline.

His initial query was a melody. "Boys. Boys! Where have you been? Have you been to London to see the Queen?"

"No, boss," the two responded in tuneless unison. Coxer was the kind of boss who, right or wrong, made you feel you'd done badly wrong—their expressions told as much.

Raz stepped up. "We got followed again. I mean, I wasn't

sure, not one hundred percent, but…"

"But you made sure," Stanley finished on his behalf. "Good-ho." He whistled. "Wilby! Booboo! Come to daddy!" The dogs came scampering and were rewarded with cuddles and chocolate. "Now I've got my two doggy boys, you two… biggy boys, come along with me. Oh, give our friend Mrs. Copeland your bag; let her relieve you of that. Thank you, Iris." Iris gave him her sexy wink and took the bag. "Come along," Stanley continued. "I want you to meet a much traveled and adventurous entrepreneur. A dear old chum. He's jetted all the way from Amsterdam today, but is originally from Russia. Quite the ladies' man; likes to ship them in on the quiet, ten at a time, from Eastern ghettos— right onto my patch, would you believe? So, I've decided our Russian friend should take early retirement, as from today. Come say hello, boys."

Raz and Mumpy dutifully followed Stanley around the shelving units into the concrete central area, where there sat a conspicuously placed tin bath. In it was a man—just his pale grey head and one hand protruding over the rim. It was hard to guess the man's age, battered as he was, his nose pummeled flat to his face like a mashed red pepper. His glazed eyes, however, still displayed enough awareness of his predicament for him to be suffering intolerably. His throat had been cut.

"May I introduce you to… let's call him Jerkoff Onabitch, like his hobby. Say hello to Mr. Onabitch, boys."

Raz offered an awkward, "Wazup?"

"Hello, Mr. Honabitch."

The dogs were wriggling to be freed. Stanley put them down.

"How very polite. You may shake hands if you wish."

Mumpy stepped forward. In his head Raz screamed, *Don't do it, dick-splash!* but Mumpy didn't catch that. Moving to the side of the tin bath, he picked up the limp hand resting on its side and shook it. "How do you do," he said.

Stanley bent, slapped his knees, and squealed with delight. The pugs took that as a green light and scurried giddily around the base of the tub. A trail of blood from the Russian's slashed jugular was seeping over the side to form a sticky puddle on the floor. The dogs lapped away, nudging each other competitively for ownership.

"Wilberforce! Boobies! Naughty, naughty," Stanley scolded, wagging a finger. "You'll be sick. There'll be *no* din-dins." Hitching up an Armani suit-sleeve, he pushed the tub's occupant roughly down by the head into the rising pool of his own blood. "Enough of you," he said. "Stuck little piggy, hogging all the limelight. Let's go talk in my office, young fellow-me-lads."

Mrs. Copeland was hovering around pretending to be busy but obviously under orders to just stick around. Raz's innards were turning like a pig on a spit. He hadn't signed up for this.

The three men sat down in the back office with the pugs, smelling of fart-gas and fresh blood, plonked on the desk between them.

Stanley fanned a hand. "Woofy-woos. No more chockies for you twos."

Mrs. Copeland came in carrying a cup and saucer with two sugar lumps on the side and placed it before Stanley, patting him on the shoulder. "There you go, lovey, nice cup of tea for you."

"You spoil me, Iris."

"Don't be daft." She offered him a wrinkly-nosed smile. "You've been working 'ard." She slung a thumb toward the warehouse door. "Do you want me to clean that lot up for you, petal? Our Phil's got a good chain saw I could have a lend of." She laughed like a chain saw starting up.

"Don't you worry yourself, Mrs. Copeland," Stanley said, sipping the tea. "We'll see to the mess."

Iris gave the two young men a look that said *you'd better* and left the office.

Mumpy allowed his eye to wander over to the bloodstained cricket bat leaning up against the wall close to Stanley's plush executive chair. Stanley clocked his sight line.

"Admiring my willow, young man? Well." He waved. "I know baseball bats are all the rage but I do think those of us who still care, need to preserve our Great British traditions. Don't you?"

Mumpy nodded. "Sure fing."

Stanley pushed the tea aside. "Everything okay, boys?"

"Yeah," Raz struggled to say.

"It's just, I detect a hint of uneasiness, may I say, gentlemen, in that you are perhaps not quite at one with some of the harsher realities of our trade. Perhaps we fail, sometimes, to associate the meat we eat with the slaughter that is necessary."

"Ver is no problems, boss," Mumpy managed, gulping hard.

"No, boss. It's cool." Raz tried, cutting through the tension. "Are you wanting us to be staying at yours tonight, boss?" he asked, as if staying at Stanley Coxer's place was a treat. "We're all set if you need us on call."

"That depends." Stanley leaned forward, one eye twitching ominously, his boney elbows crunching on the desk. "You see, lately, I am overwhelmed by a sense of foreboding. Let's just say, I'm getting a little…paranoid."

Don't go there, Raz thought, glancing at Mumpy. But he wasn't that stupid.

"We're all feeling like that, boss," Raz said. "Some shit's going down hard. You know, a month back, we was the man. The friend of the people. We have the gear, right? And everybody wants the gear. And now it's all, you know, some vigilante fucker is the man. And now, suddenly everybody's of that mind-set, like, anti-us, and every no-nuts cunt's out to get you. I understand how it is. It's a pain in the butt-crack is what. That fucker should be strung up for what he did to our boys. We'd get away with no shit like that. All said, it's hard to tell who's your friend anymore."

"And are *you* my friends, boys?" Stanley asked, reaching out to them.

Each awkwardly offered a hand, which Stanley gripped.

"We are all friends here," Raz assured. "No mistake."

"We're your friends, boss."

"Do you swear?"

"I swear down," Raz said.

"I swear, boss," Mumpy said.

Stanley's eyes went wide with glee. "But do you swear on your baby's life, Mumpetty?"

Mumpy's lids closed momentarily. When they slid back open, he was giving Raz the look. He only talked that shit to Raz.

"I swear—on my baby's life, boss," Mumpy affirmed.

For an agonizing moment, Stanley stared from one to the other, then dropped their hands abruptly and slapped the desk in a fit of decision. The dogs jumped up and yapped. "Good!" he bellowed. "Fabulous! Friends forever! Now go load that fucked Russian dollop into your boot and dump in the Aire."

CHAPTER TWENTY-FOUR

Donald had a feeling about today, so made good and sure to take along a fresh change of clothes.

The van did sixty uphill at best, but he was in no rush to get anywhere. Certainly, some young buck with TMT—Too Much Testosterone—in his blood, would have the *Complete Works of Shakespeare* sailing like debris in a hurricane at the turn of a corner. No, this was more a job for a fellow with the right manners and a little maturity. And, the finest things came to he who conducted himself with patience. His great-aunt Sophia, that very morning, had once again reminded him that there was no necessity for him to work at all. Since his sister's tragic accident, the estate, soon enough, would fall to him alone. He could retire to the Dordogne today for that matter, if he so wished. After all, the villa at Castelnaud-la-Chapelle was only let due to lack of use—but, she had conceded, it was nice for a man to have a hobby, to keep himself busy. But for Donald, the job was so much more than that.

Epshot was one of the smaller spots on Donald's rounds, but no less important. At ten o'clock sharp, he parked in his usual spot aside the village green by the Post Office and opened the side door, solidly positioning the pullout steps. Soon enough, several of his regulars were aboard, happily browsing. As always, Mrs. Carter, hobbling along, stick in hand, carried Donald's fortnightly treat, a hot, sweet cup of cocoa. On summer days, it was iced tea but today was a cloudy one, dismal in a way that made Donald quite giddy.

"Thank you, Mrs. Carter," he said warmly, accepting the cup. "Very kind." Then he supported her arm, guiding her up the two steps. A younger woman of about forty, whom he guessed was likely a visiting daughter, followed Mrs. Carter inside, commenting with loud intent, "Hey, he's a bit of alright, isn't he, eh? Very smooth. He can stamp my book any time." Old Mrs. Carter's chuckles shook the van. Donald went to the front passenger seat where he could sip his cocoa and keep an eye on things behind, but also outside. After a few minutes, a young woman wearing a denim skirt, tight top, and suede, tasseled boots came out of the Post Office tucking her purse into her bag. This was the one he watched out for, who, apart from Mr. Tompkinson's prize-winning rose garden, was the only thing worth perusing here. Her name was Jo; he'd heard somebody call hello to her from the van on a previous occasion. Jo was twenty-five or -six, with long dark hair, no dye, just wonderfully glossy hair, above average height, slim, with a small waistline, a form more reminiscent of Busby Berkeley's flappers than today's female. If he had to compare her facial features to any starlet of stage and screen, it would be a young Elizabeth Taylor. Almost criminally wasteful that she should be languishing here, in the backyard of nowhere.

Jo noticed Donald staring and smiled. Not the usual reaction. He nodded, smiling in return. She began to walk over, for what he could but wonder; hardly a big reader by the looks of her and from the idle twang he'd observed in overheard exchanges. Still, Donald's heart beat a little faster and he turned in his seat to face her approach.

"What you got in there?" she asked.

"Books."

"Get out." Her smile progressed to one showing teeth, a little yellowy. "Got anything saucy?"

Donald considered this question. "I believe I could acquire a copy of *The Flavor Bible* by Karen Page and Andrew Dorenburg, or alternatively there is a most informative hardback by James Peterson on *Classical and Contemporary Sauce Making*."

"You're a peculiar one, aren't you?" Jo mused, looking him over steadily.

Donald simply smiled and continued to sip at his cocoa, waiting to see what her next stupid question might be. Jo swayed a little from side to side, clearly enjoying her little flirt, then rummaged in her bag for cigarettes. She lit one.

"Dirty habit," he said.

Jo's eyes narrowed, not unkindly. "And what's wrong with dirty habits, might I ask?"

Donald felt something very unpleasant happening in his trousers. An untimely twitching. By good fortune, at that same moment, Mrs. Carter called out, "Donald! Could you give us a hand, lovey?" His ardor plummeted as he rushed around the outside of the van to the old woman's aid. She was practically wedged inside the doorway. To compound the problem, her fleecy jacket was snagged on the latch. Donald unhooked her and with his thin, sinewy arms, hoisted her down. The daughter behind, laden with the typical paperbacks, was practically swooning, but Donald wasn't listening anymore. He was checking the position of young Jo, who he now saw was slouching against the hood of the van, practically eviscerating her cigarette.

Mrs. Carter straightened herself. "He's a good lad," she told the daughter. "Aren't you, Don?"

Returning the empty cocoa cup to her hand, Donald eyed the old lady with polite confusion, struggling to recall at what point he had given this simpleton permission to call him "Don".

Once they'd cleared off he returned to the front passenger seat close to where Jo remained standing. "I'm about finished here," he said. "Would you like a lift anywhere? It looks like rain."

With his words, thunder rumbled overhead. He smirked inwardly, interpreting this as a favorable sign. But before Jo had a chance to respond to his offer, an old Astra with a rough looking, shaven-haired man practically hanging out of the front driver's-side window, screeched to a halt outside the Post Office. "Get the fuck in 'ere, now!" the man bawled at her. Jo's smile never faltered. She dropped the now spent tab in the road, ground it down with a soft boot, then strolled lazily over to the fume-spewing wreck containing the amazing human-bulldog, whose face softened a tad with each dainty step Jo took his way. "You said fifteen minutes! You've been nearly a fuckin' hour!" he ranted as she climbed inside. The two leaned an equal distance toward each other and kissed. "Keep yer fuckin' hair on, baldy." She laughed. "I had stuff to do."

"Aye, I bloody bet." The boyfriend, husband perhaps, shot Donald a sour-grapes look. Jo leant forward to offer Donald a good-bye wave. Donald heard them happily bickering into the distance as the car roared away.

His hands trembled violently as he meticulously filed away the returns. Sweat prickled his neat scalp and stung his eyes. She would have been no good for you anyway, he told himself, not the right type. Too connected for a start. Too closely observed. Too dirty. Too cock-sure of herself. If he wasn't careful, all of this, his goal, his purpose in life, his dream and his mission, could end in its infancy, and so soon after realization. That would be a crime too dastardly to contemplate. Again, he reminded himself that he would know when the time was right.

Even so, as he drove toward his next destination, Donald imagined her as she should be: in dire need of comfort, weeping quietly on his shoulder, growing sleepy, his soothing words a trinket to store in her heart for an eternity. His body broke into small spasms, so that he almost lost his grip on the steering wheel before he managed to pull over at the roadside. The lane was quiet, but lunchtime traffic created something of an audience.

Still, a well deserved interlude was due, one that called for some modicum of relief. The *Britannica Concise Encyclopedia*, God bless her, would do the trick. Donald reached back, easing the sizeable hardback from its handy spot on the shelf nearby. He stood its opened covers against the steering wheel, each side resting on a taut thigh. One corner of his mouth twitched uncontrollably; the sweat had progressed to rivulets that soaked the collar of his freshly pressed shirt. He noted, unzipping and freeing himself, that the pages had parted fittingly on the "G" listed "Gagra choli", the traditional garments of women in Rajasthan, India; those most tantalisingly displaying the mid-riff portion of flesh, as depicted on the slender model alongside the text: a consolation for his former restraint. It was such little signs that reassured Donald he was on the right track. No, Jo had not been right. He would know the one. The coming one. And she would be worth the wait. The best things in life were never rushed, as he reminded his hand in the stroke.

The stiff, perspiring man so ardently engrossed in his book drew quizzical glances from the occupants of approaching cars; but soon enough they had passed him by, to continue another mundane day in their utterly mundane little lives.

CHAPTER TWENTY-FIVE

Superintendent Osbourne burst in on Detectives Ryan and Gaunt mid-conversation. Both shrunk inwardly at the sight of her hardened face. A hundred phone calls back and forth and they had nothing new to tell her, at least nothing that made any sense.

"It has to go public sooner than later," she ranted. "What have we got? Besides a fucking mess to mop up? Christ almighty, Joe Public has hailed this bloody axe-man a hero. Let's see how they feel about him when he pops out from behind their sofas any time now. Well, they'd better be on their best behavior, hadn't they, if their blessed *hero* drops round for a cupper?"

"Every inch of the prison's been turned over, Ma'am." Gaunt reiterated, as if his superior didn't know that already. "There's no trace of Hunter. And, as we've been told in the last few minutes, no human remains were found in the remnants of the fire in his pad. Not so much as a finger nail. With all the kafuffle, word's got out in the nick. The governor's requested a meeting before it goes to press."

"Dandy. A good old face-off before the murder of crows

lands to feast on this car crash of a case. What's that you've got, Ryan?"

DI Ryan had a finger on a black and white photo, which she reluctantly pushed forward for the superintendent to look at.

Osbourne placed her hands on the desk, scrutinizing the shot. "Where's this from?"

"Prison security camera, Ma'am. It's looking through from central into the seg unit," Ryan said. "Hence the bars between. So it's hard to say for sure what it is we're looking at. But that...movement is right outside of Hunter's pad, just minutes before the fire inside got raging and set the alarms off; when he was discovered to be missing. Apparently there was an attempted suicide up the other end of the block."

"Convenient."

"So nobody saw, in person, what we're seeing here, what the camera picked up. We've already checked."

"What the fuck? Who is that?"

Gaunt put his face in his hands, rubbing his temples, having obviously looked at it for long enough.

"Well," Ryan said. "It looks like a child."

The still black-and-white picture from the security camera wasn't a hundred percent clear, quite grainy, but even through thick bars the figure, not quite facing away—rising awkwardly, bottom first, from its hands and knees—was undeniably a little girl, one dressed in a jumper, tiny kilt, and Wellington boots. Though the best part of her head was obscured, her hair looked to be curly. Looking closer, Superintendent Osbourne visibly recoiled, as had the two detectives shortly before she came into the office. The child's head was wrong: far too big, and sprouting—around the section of jawline that could be seen—what looked like coarse, dark hair.

Osbourne picked up the photo, staring hard enough to x-ray the thing.

"That camera in central automatically takes shots at intervals of every thirty seconds," Ryan said. "There's two more after that, then nothing." She took out the second photograph from where it had been placed, face down in a file marked *HMP—Security*. The very act of turning it over seemed to sap her spirits. She sat back, just leaving it there at the edge of the desk, face up.

"How is this possible?" Osbourne asked, looking bewildered at it, clearly not expecting an answer.

In the second still, the child had reached the gate. The thin little figure was again obscured in part by the thick bars she gripped with her tiny hands, but more than half of the face, this time, was observable. The child's body, with its delicate limbs, appeared to support the head of what looked to be an adult male. And no film star at that. The pretty curls crowned a heavy black brow; the broad jaw was stubbled, the nose a broad hook that overshadowed its grin full of rotten teeth. The cold black button of its one visible eye glinted defiantly up at the camera. Just as Osbourne thought she'd seen it all, she detected possibly the worst, most perplexing aspect of all: the skin, not only on that glimpse of face but on the hands and expanse of bare leg above the Wellington boots, appeared to be wilting into miniscule rivulets, to be folding over itself, as if in the process of melting.

"Jesus wept. You'd better just show me the last one," she said. "Get it over with."

The third still was placed before her.

"What am I looking at here? There's nothing in it." Osbourne frowned.

Whatever had stood at the gate had completely vanished.

"Look at the section of floor this side of the gate now, Ma'am," DI Ryan advised, pointing to the tail end of a long object whose front curved beneath and out of the camera's range.

"A tail? What of?"

"Look closely, Ma'am, the pattern, the scales. I'd say that's a snake."

CHAPTER TWENTY-SIX

Vince Fontaine in a small-time production of *Grease*. As if that wasn't the pits. But by next Christmas it could be Dame in a panto at best. *"He's be*hind you*"*. So this is what it had come to.

Adrian Adams stared critically at his reflection through the thick layers of pan-stick and tart's-measure of black eyeliner. The wrinkles were winning and the hairline had ebbed to low tide. The hundred-watt-bulb-lined mirror didn't help, neither had long doses of glorious Sudanese sunshine, which, in all the fun and frolicking, he'd failed to adequately protect himself against. At least he'd stayed thin, although some might say scrawny. He sighed and began the laborious process of removing the grease paint. Last show of the day— his skin could breathe; he could breath. On the bright side, if ITV's Head of Family Entertainment held true, pending a total acquittal, he could ditch this heap-of-crap excuse for a living once and for all. If he sang "Beauty School Dropout" one more time this side of next week he'd go ape. But, as his agent, Rod Thurlow, kept reminding him, the best strategy was to remain optimistic, take the blows as they landed face-on, get-up, dust-off, and plod on. He was a tough old bird and his carcass had been flayed harder than this. Fortunately, those Sudanese pigs had their heads so far up their arses half the time that the most damning evidence had been torched long before they'd even raided the house.

Adams unscrewed the cap off the Glenmorangie Rod had sent him in a slim gold bag complete with oversized show-biz bow, and poured his third. The show was a sellout—albeit more due to the press coverage and Joe Public's warped curiosity than any professionalism in the production; the producer was a prize ham. But, scraping the barrel-base as it was, at least this show meant they were signed up and safe for as long as the scandal would take to blow over. He studied the bottle as he downed the contents of the glass. A nice enough pressie, Rod, but hardly the big congrats he'd expected, what with the extended contract on the show and such a fucking storm of a success of a meeting with ITV. The new quiz show idea had them buzzing. Typical Rod. Tight-arsed queen.

From outside his dressing room came the clattering of heals of the chorus line taking off for the clubs. Nobody invited him any more—playing judge, jury, and executioner as the weak-minded do—but things would swing back his way. They always did. He was managing the publicity well enough; the many close friends that ceaselessly stuck by him perused the press daily, something he couldn't be fagged to do, and kept him posted. Just tonight, there'd been a photo op with the family of two down's-syndrome kids—*who the fuck would go for that deal twice?*—hardly petite little petals. He'd been crushed out like whipped cream in a cheap sponge. Then there were negotiations for the next *HI!* spread, at home with the wife of course, if he could drag her out of rehab and keep her latest boy at bay for long enough. She'd do it. She needed the cash. She might even come back to him, old tart.

Out of the blue, came a rapturous burst of applause, from the auditorium by the sounds of it. Adams smiled to himself, downed the dregs of his glass, threw off the neck towel, and went out into the dimly lit corridor. No sign of life. The applause had stopped. He tiptoed along to backstage, around the sidelines. The stage and auditorium were in darkness, except for one spotlight that shone down on a high stool placed a little way onto side stage. He jolted happily as once again fake applause piped loudly out of the speakers, ringing out to the far rows of empty stalls.

"Okay," he said, hands up in surrender, "I give up." He climbed onto the stool. "Interesting, Rod. Do your worst." He placed his hands on his knees and waited.

A second brighter spot went poof, throwing its mighty light down on a black umbrella tilted backwards toward him center stage, concealing something. The umbrella was comically huge, its spikes scraping the boards, so he could only guess who or what might be behind there. This was more like it.

Dooby-do-do, dooby-dooby-do-dooby...

Singin' in the Rain. Spot on. He fucking adored Gene Kelly. He'd known deep down Thurlow would come through, the sly fox. The umbrella began to twirl and rise. Two smooth, freckly little legs clad in the cutest patent tap-shoes he'd ever seen jumped neatly into position. She bowed, and the edge of a green gingham dress and a crop of curly red hair popped tantalizingly into view.

Da-da-da-da…

Her slender legs were as light in the dance as Shirley Temple's, his absolute favorite. Her shoes clickety-clacked in perfect timing. Where did Rod dig them up? It was usually the families loaning them out for big bucks, but not families who could afford the kind of coaching this one must've had. A regular little Annie Astaire.

He clapped frantically, overjoyed. "Bravo! Bravo! What a little star we are. Twinkle, twinkle, darling."

Dooby-do-do, dooby-dooby-do-dooby...

There was a sharp zoop sound like a needle being ripped roughly off a vinyl record. The music paused. The little tapstress paused, too, marching on the spot—clack clack clack, pacing in readiness. Adams glanced around, confused.

Music blasted out at mega volume—Adams grasped the stool, almost losing his balance—and the little girl's feet burst back into action, tapping like crazy. It was the Mint-Royale remix, and deafening. He covered his ears. He hated the Mint fucking Royale remix, and even worse, it was speeding up by the second. Crazy shakes.

"Have some taste, Mr. Thurlow, please. You'll wear her out," he shouted into the racket.

Lights boomed on all over the place, flashing like fireworks on New Year's Eve. Adams screwed up his face. Not fun. This misjudgment would cost Thurlow his tights. Through the flash of darting spotlights he scanned around the stage, seeing whom he might catch hiding, then wished he hadn't. Something struck and chilled him to the core of his gut. The P.A. system that linked into the speakers was cold, its plugs out on the deck. No connections anywhere were hooked up. And still that tacky melody, those lights, blasted out at him, faster yet.

The woodpecker chip of her tap shoes drew Adam's attention back to the child, whose legs were moving at an impossible speed, a rapid blur. A sense of unreality washed over him and he wondered for a second if he wasn't actually laid pissed back in his dressing room dreaming this up.

Then, just as shockingly as it'd started, the music stopped.

"Jesus Christ almighty," he gasped, hand on heart.

As the silence hit, so the legs beneath the brolly snapped apart with a bang, then stood prone, perfectly still. The bang was on account of the great big dirty hobnail boots that now graced Annie's feet. Unblinking, hardly breathing, Adams scanned higher. The slender legs had somehow increased in girth to rugby-sized hairy stumps. And though Adams was telling himself in an internally panicked voice that this was some nasty but very clever trick, he nearly flaked out when the umbrella began to rise again. The thing with its back to him, coming gradually into view, was a box-shaped, solid hunk of muscle. Short in stature, but then, as Adams watched on, he swore the fucker was growing; the clown-pants version of the green gingham dress, complete with Elizabethan collar and Disney bows, was expanding along with it. One big bull of a head sat atop that collar, its dolly curls transformed to a rusty pan scourer. And as if that wasn't enough to nail him to his stool, the arm holding the brolly was stretching impossibly out of proportion—an E.T. arm—the other arm, coming into view, gripped something—a thick wooden handle. Its head rotated Adam's way. The profile was right out of the most gruesome of the Grimm brothers' nightmares. One dark eye settled on Adams. Its flabby lips drew back into a leer, revealing blackened teeth. There was a sudden almighty thwack as the emerging arm swung out to lodge the blade of a long woodsman's axe into the floorboards. With a shrill shriek, Adams and his stool went crashing to the floor in a comedy twosome; there he froze behind its inadequate cover. Her—*its*—axe-hand flexed out one meaty finger at a time, and cocking its head, released a gravelly sigh, "Aaahhh," as if waking to spy breakfast on the dresser, then a chilling omen. "He's be*hind* you!"

That guttural rasp had Adams scrambling to his feet and racing back to the exit door—that was now locked. He rattled it frantically. Nothing gave. When he turned to look back, only the spotlight center stage remained on. The umbrella sat abandoned there, clicking lazily spoke-to-spoke. Adams felt his way along the wall, scrutinizing each crack in the side blinds for the hideous dwarf girl.

"What do you want?" he shouted. "There's money in the safe. I know the combination."

All crap. Any takings were long gone, but if he could just buy some time. He strained his eyes to see past the spotlight into the wings opposite. Something huge was apparent there—an ogre in a green gingham shirt. What was this— some warped version of the fucking A-Team? The gleaming axe blade rested lovingly in the big man's hand. His fingers tickled its cold steal.

"Help!" Adams yelled. Somebody had to be around. There was always somebody. "Help me!"

Darting for the ladder side-stage—there was a gangway two levels up with a door out to the upper circle—he clambered monkey-like into the dark heavens, past the first platform, almost losing his grip before the second. For a few moments, he flailed one-handed from a rung, just managing to swing back. As he regained purchase, the air around him seemed to shift in waves, as if combed through by a vast fan. Then his spirits rose. He could hear somebody overhead. "Help!" he yelled again. Of course, the caretaker would've heard the disturbance. Adams scuttled like a rat fresh out of a trap up onto the lighting platform that would lead him out, but halfway along was blinded by a sudden spotlight. He stepped back, watching, waiting. Nothing moved up ahead. He could still go forward. Then something brushed his ankle and he gaped down in horror. A rope-loop was tightening around his ankle. He tried stepping out of it but at the same time, something came swinging at his head. The ballast clipped him just enough to send him flailing over the side rail. He roared through the fall until his breath was stolen by the rope's sharp tug back, then he was swinging upended between two platforms, his spare leg doing the can-can.

A flash of movement below. Something heading his way fast. The whole, towering structure rattled in its wake. In all the oscillating, Adams could only catch glimpses. The thing on the platform beneath him, with its vile, beaky-nosed goblin face, seemed now to be sporting some kind of stiff cape that stood proud of its shoulders. As it approached, it grinned up at him, raising the axe as if to swipe a blow. Adams laughed, jittery yet triumphant. The dumb bastard'd have to be twice the size again to reach high enough to have a shot. Adams doubled upwards as his swaying steadied. He was fit for his age; he'd haul himself back up. He could do it. And he'd still be ahead.

That buffing movement filled the air again. The sheer force of it knocked Adams for six and sent him swinging afresh.

"He's be*hind* you!" That voice, which, oddly enough, *was* behind him, cracked into hysterical laughter.

Adams twirled to face the unspeakable beast hovering in the spotlight, but a spit away, its silver, grey wings fluttering majestically like the ornamentation of some grotesque God. All the fight Adams had conjured up abandoned him. His jaw went slack as he swooned into the pull of the rope, which curved him mercifully away, so the glint of the oncoming axe sparkled only in his peripheral vision.

Jerry the caretaker rattled the door to back-stage, but it wasn't locked as he'd expected—it gave with a good push. He'd ignored the shouting at first, thinking it was late rehearsals or some such thing, but then the screams started, and then that horrible gargling that turned his spine to ice. The crew who worked here weren't that good.

"Who is that?" he shouted, stepping cautiously on stage. "I know someone's up there! Come down now. I've already called the police!" he lied.

All lights were out but for one spot beaming down on an umbrella center stage that was getting rained on heavily. Again came that hacking sound that made Jerry recall The Falklands, when they got ambushed on the bridge—the day he learned the difference between the sound a bullet makes hitting metal, wood or earth, to that terrible sound of metal punching through flesh. The stuff raining down was red. Blood red. Jerry was by now too petrified to go back and even flick on a light switch.

This being the theater, even the caretaker had a good sense of timing. Jerry flicked on and trained his flashlight upward at the precise moment something came spinning from above to bounce heavily off the umbrella and finally roll to a stop at his feet. From its resting point, Adrian Adam's slack-jawed, blood-streaked head stared up at him. He looked happy enough; a wide smile had been hacked across his jaw. In a fit of panic he'd never admit to after the event, Jerry swung a foot back and booted Adam's dead old head downstage, transfixed as it lollopped away—the wide eyes playing now-you-see-me now-you-don't—before he tore out of the theater in arm-waving hysteria.

Had the seats been occupied, he would have brought the house down.

CHAPTER TWENTY-SEVEN

A few days following his visit to the prison, Fionn walked into his new church to find DI Beena Ryan sitting in the front pews.

He went and sat beside the detective, who was quietly inspecting the décor.

"It's not such a load of pomp and ceremony as it used to be," he said. "We haven't got the cash to keep all that up. People aren't so impressed nowadays anyway. They'd be more impressed if we got a plasma TV installed."

"Well, go for it. Get them watching the footy round *here* on Saturday afternoons, instead of festering down the pub."

"It's a thought. Only I'm a bit of a pub-goer myself. What's your religion, Ms. Ryan? Any?"

"My mum's Sikh. My dad's an agnostic librarian."

"That does sound a bit like a religion."

"It does a bit. Which leaves me somewhere between the two, I suppose. I've always loved joining in the ceremonies, Diwali especially, with my mum's family. So does my dad. But then, I like Christmas as well. If anything, I'm more like my dad, I suppose, in that none of it means that much to me, not any more. Are your mum and dad both Catholic?"

"They were. I've lost them both, I'm afraid. My father was devoutly religious. I don't know what it would have taken for him to doubt God. He never did, no matter what."

"Maybe if he'd joined the police force. I've known a lot of devoutly religious people come into the force. But then you see too much; things you thought you knew all about, thing's you've studied in theory, only it's different looking it square in the face. No matter how faithful you think you are, sooner or later you'll doubt there's a God."

"I have to say, I can understand that."

"There are some questions I want to ask you, Fionn, but I'm finding it difficult."

"Why so?"

She looked him in the eye. "Because usually, when I ask a question, I have a pretty good idea what the answer's going to be."

"I recognized that in you the first time I saw you. Not the least bit intimidating."

She nodded, smiling easily, the most relaxed he'd seen her. "Detective Gaunt came to talk to you a couple of days ago?"

"Yes, I'm really warming to him."

"Very funny. So, he and Detective Ramsay talked to you about Ben Hunter, about your visit to the prison?"

"Yes. I was the only person who got to visit that day. They told me that."

"And while you were there, Hunter drank a cup of tea, and later ate a meal, after not touching a bite since his arrest. Quite a development that. What did you talk about? I know you've said already, but indulge me."

"I asked him to stay alive, however he might. I told him I was sorry I hadn't been to see him sooner. We discussed…our religious beliefs."

"His wife committed suicide, didn't she? She never identified the man who raped her, although she did report the crime. We'd nothing to go on. Do you think Ben might've known who it was?"

"No. Nobody knew. I suspect Anita might have, but she wouldn't say. She was scared, even with Ben to protect her. She must've thought that if she kept quiet, shoved it to the back of her mind, that she could carry on."

DI Ryan took a long swig from a bottle of water. "There's a reporter who's done a lot of research into our local history," she said. "All that stuff *we* don't get the time to do properly."

"Carl Wilson. Yes I know."

"He's shown me evidence that, year on year, for hundreds of years, this area has suffered a higher suicide rate than what are considered to be the worst black spots in the UK. Don't you think that's strange?"

Fionn realized he was biting his thumbnail, an old bad habit. "It is strange."

"Some things aren't easily explained, are they? I remember once, as a kid, playing Ouija board—well, pushing a glass around a circle of cut-out letters with a couple of mates while the grown-ups were out of the house. We were about thirteen. We thought it was just a bit of a giggle. We invented this ghost between us, Emily I think we dubbed her, and went off round this big old house my mate lived in, hunting for clues about her, collaborating to keep up the suspense. We kept, y'know, pushing stuff over, flicking pictures off the walls and that, when we thought the others weren't looking, and even though we all knew it was a pretending game we worked ourselves up into a right giddy old state, I can tell you. We ended up in my mate's front room, giggling hysterically, letting off girly screams at every little noise. It only took seconds for the mood to shift—the lights all went out. At the same time, the patio doors crashed open so violently all the glass shattered against the outside walls. Moments later of course, my best mate's parents only go and walk in, don't they? To the tune of us screaming the place down, cowering behind the couch—not girly screams anymore either: verge of death screams—and to the crunch of broken glass under their shoes.

"We were all grounded for a bloody month. Served us right. Fact is, we didn't know what we were messing with. I mean, those patio doors opened outwards; any wind that could have blown them open had to've come from inside the room. It's strange, but one thing I got a very strong feeling about, was that at that moment her parents walked in on that scene, something, I don't know what, but something was having a right good old laugh at our expense. We'd had our bit of fun, now it was having *its* fun. Other things happened after that, in that house. It lasted about six months: radios would switch on at three in the morning; you could hear something running up and down the stairs really fast, banging into walls. We'd invited something in you see, and once you've done that, it's not always so simple as just politely asking it to leave.

"Are you alright, Fionn?"

He was sitting forward, head in hands, suddenly pale and breathless. "Sorry. Yes, I'm okay. I will be."

"Not sleeping well?"

He sat upright, wiping a sleeve along his brow. "Actually." He laughed. "Now you mention it, I'm sleeping better than I have for ages. Sorry, Ms. Ryan. It's getting late. There's afternoon service soon. You are welcome to stay."

Beena Ryan stood, ready to leave. "That's okay, but thanks for the invitation." She walked toward the doors then turned back. "You do know, Fionn, that whatever you tell me won't hold up in court, so you might as well just trust me."

He shifted uneasily but said nothing.

"I suppose you've heard about Adrian Adam's murder?" she asked. "Though I think to call it an execution would be more apt. Well, they found Ben Hunter's fingerprints at the scene." Finally, she had his full attention. "Oh, but don't worry. You see, as evidence goes, that won't hold up in court either. Because—here's the strange thing—out of five digits in each hand print, only two of them match Hunter's. The other prints are someone else's. We don't know whose. Not easy to explain, is it?"

"You will know." Appolyn had said. And so he did.

Every day, Fionn scanned the newspapers for signs of the cold-blooded retribution that had doomed Adams. There were obvious hallmarks, and then things that'd troubled Ben. There was the African dictator who had awarded himself the honorary title of "God's chief protagonist on earth", who, acting as such through a near twenty-year reign, had subjected many thousands of his citizens to what he deemed to be "Divine judgment"; basically bloody-murder. Here was a fly in the global ointment whom the CIA had dubbed "untouchable" on account of so many failed attempts by themselves and others to terminate his reign; who was discovered early one morning, along with his four most prominent henchmen, in the lavish courtyard of his palace, crucified upside-down on vast wooden crosses hammered deep into the ground—a single snip to the side of the neck having allowed each would-be-disciple to bleed ever-so-slowly to death.

There was the fifty-seven-year-old Texan oil-magnate, whose national bank had proudly announced to its board members—as revealed in a leaked paper, mid-recession—that it held the nationwide record for evicting mortgage defaulters from their mainly very basic homes; who, while evading charges for fraudulent practice on a massive scale, had accepted an annual bonus of over five million dollars, very noticeably at tax-payers' expense; who was, one bright May evening, seen hurled screaming for a whole mile across Chicago's skyline, having been catapulted from within his penthouse office suite through a ten-foot-high dollar sign carved out of his panoramic window pane. One ground-level eyewitness described how the ill-fated billionaire had spun "like a rag-doll out of a dog's jaws," his body finally coming to rest in a dumpster downtown—a highly calculated shot. A later story: the dollar sign carving was so faultless and drew so much attention that one of the bank's remaining board members thought it prudent to offer the pane for auction at Christie's. Other more fearful members, and the bank's lawyers, advised strongly against it. After forensics came up with nothing other than to say the carving had likely been the work of some revolutionary nut in possession of a very high-spec laser, the pane was sent away to an anonymous site for recycling.

Across three European countries over a dozen members of what transpired to be an elite pedophile ring—among them a magistrate, a bishop, a police captain, a seventies rock-star and a prominent female politician—were found with their heads melted into their shattered computer screens. The hard drives of the same machines held enough evidence to have linked and convicted the ring a thousand times over. On the back of that turn-up, over two hundred additional arrests were swiftly made. Some highly organized vigilante group was suspected, the executions having all occurred within the space of two hours. A person working alone could hardly have achieved this, one Spanish newspaper riskily speculated, unless that person were in possession of super-human powers; and with that speculation the writer, in the body of the same article, flirted with the term "Malakh"—or "Malach" of Jewish mythology—believed by many to be "the dark side of God". As further stories and sightings of a dark-winged and fearsome angel-like creature continued to pour into press offices around the globe—often following acts of extreme reprisal—reports went from flirting with to stating a Malakh's existence.

People began to watch the skies…and hide their goings-on.

While it pained Fionn to be glad of the distance between him and Ben, at least he felt *they* had moved on, had far bigger spots to squeeze off the face of the earth than anything Rokerville had left to offer. As Ben had promised, the people around here could get back to some kind of normality, safe from the wrath their own priest had conspired to bring down on their heads.

CHAPTER TWENTY-EIGHT

Early that summer, a stretch of rubbled ground opened up at the foot of the moor where the former Saint Luke's Church had stood. Within the wire fencing only the gnarled oak tree remained standing, protected despite the developers' objections. A positive spin was achieved by then incorporating it into their picture postcard perspective of an ideal world—where every occupant owned a Juliet balcony but where nobody would step a foot outside onto their own land to grow so much as a sprig of rosemary. The standard apartment block shown in the poster would be erected before anybody could blink, let alone muster up the energy to articulate why they felt they should object. There'd been a whisper of protest locally in response to the desecration of graves and removal of historical stones. The bishop had registered the usual protestations while knowing full well that the church authorities wanted the site relocated. The fact was, there had been no burials in Saint Luke's cemetery for over a century, because no one wanted their loved ones buried there, and with no descendents of the long-dead still around to offer resistance, the graves were no more sacrosanct than the concrete shops a few streets down the estate, also scheduled for flattening.

Late one warm, breezy afternoon, Fionn jogged up to the cleared site. Hanging his fingers through the fencing, he caught his breath and took in the view. A whole new aspect had opened up beyond where churches of centuries had stood, one he'd not been able to appreciate through the protectively-meshed stained-glass windows of Saint Luke's. Even from the rabbit-hutch rooms of a modern apartment, Fionn supposed it would be a nice outlook for whoever moved in here. In recent years, the scattering of caves up around Beggar's Rock had served as hideouts for druggies and boozers. Since Ben's one-man stand, all that had changed. The council and volunteers locally had even made efforts to shift some of the accumulated rubbish from the stretch of moor that bordered Rokerville. It was fast becoming the picnic spot it used to be: a calmly idyllic setting. You might believe there was a future here if you just kept looking out that way, never looked back.

When Fionn's eye found Beggar's Rock his heart gave a lurch, yet he wasn't that surprised to see the hooded figure up there looking back his way. He'd somehow expected this. Skirting the wire fencing, he caught his breath and headed for the summit of the moors. As he approached Beggar's Rock, he saw the figure had moved and was entering one of the caves where the rock jutted out, but when he reached the cave, no movement was apparent.

"Callum!" he shouted into the darkness. "Cal!" Only the echo of his own voice came back, ridiculing his trust in his own eyes. He searched the cave as far as he could stand, then, finding nothing, went outside and mounted the rock. Up there Fionn stood alone, looking back toward the estate, the wind snatching his breath.

"*Help us, Father.*" He spun around at the pained cry of a thousand voices.

"Who is that?" he called. But there was nothing more to hear.

Something routed his attention that way, the opposite direction to Rokerville, where about a mile away the city spiraled into ever tightening circles. On the near edge stood the neighborhood Rokerville residents had long-ago dubbed "Millionaires' or Toffs' Hill", a small concentration of *Haves* that served as a negative magnet for the *Have-nots* of the estate. Fionn recalled Ami's description of one particular resident: he of the white-palace down there, the gangster, Coxer. Fionn'd never noticed till now just how stringently the house was defended: blast lights at every angle, security cameras, the electric fencing that ran full-square stood well above the already high walls. Not the dwelling of somebody happy. God alone could name that man's fear. One biblical quote sprung to Fionn's mind. "Live by the sword: die by the sword". It was only a matter of time.

*

…decomposed and mutilated body of a young woman found at Beacon Quarry on the outskirts of the city yesterday has been identified as that of the missing girl, Kelly Atkins. An autopsy revealed traces of tranquillizing drugs in her system and evidence of a serious sexual assault at the time of her death. The actual cause of death is believed to have been asphyxiation. Mother of a baby daughter, Kelly was reported missing on Saint Valentine's Day earlier this year. Evidence suggests that the attacker may have returned to the location of Kelly's body on later occasions. The quarry is a popular beauty spot for ramblers and dog

walkers. A website and incident desk has been set up and police are appealing for witnesses...

Kelly's pale, prematurely haggard face gazed out of the TV screen, pleading her case: I was just a girl, grown too old too fast, to be finally tossed unceremoniously on life's scrap heap. "Sorry, Kelly," Fionn whispered. "Whatever it was we did, for good or bad, it was too late for you, wasn't it? And I'm sorry because I cannot ask that you be avenged; cannot wish it, nor pray for it, not to bring about the return of a wrath the whole world shudders at. I'm so sorry. You sleep tight now, you hear?" With his thumb, he drew a cross on the forehead of the face on the screen. "Be at peace, child."

CHAPTER TWENTY-NINE

It was the twenty-fourth year in the life of Andrea Maynard, one she'd sworn to herself last New Year's Eve would deliver a change for the better. No such delivery was forthcoming as yet; every parcel that turned up was a far weightier bundle of woe than the last. Here she was, early evening, with her third black eye of the year so far, legging it up the A616 out of town, having bought a stupid pasty that'd left her fifty pence short of the bus-fare, heading for Holmdale, not even sure how much further she'd have to walk—except one sign a way back had said four miles. It already felt like she'd covered that distance twice over. Every muscle in her spindly legs stood proud. The backpack she'd hastily thrown together with a few bits of clothing and toiletries, increasingly felt lagged with bricks. She was already considering dumping some of the heavier items: the spare pair of trainers for a start off. They were fucked anyway, like everything Andrea called "her wardrobe". She'd been forbidden to spend any decent money in ages. And anyway, her dad might offer to buy her some new ones; he had to be better off now. Not that she would ask, but when he saw how little she'd escaped with, he'd surely want to help out. He hadn't been a great dad, but he had been a kind one when he was around, otherwise she wouldn't be daft enough to trail all this way.

She'd only been about five when her dad brought her out here for the day. The last time she'd been here in fact. But rounding a long bend, Andrea started to feel a familiarity in the views. The June nights were lighter, longer, but it was a misty, overcast day; still, the shape of the valley beyond the tree-lined road was clearly defined by the lights first dropping into a clustered bank then scattering up the hills beyond. Feeling she'd broken the back of the journey, she allowed herself a sit down on a low stone wall, heaving off the baggage for a while. An old Escort bearing go-faster stripes and a boatload of rampant cock blared its horn at her as it roared away from the village toward town. Signs were mimed through the back window indicating the occupants' enthusiasm to *well do her* if they'd time to stop. Andrea was too knackered to even give them the finger. This is why she hadn't hitchhiked. She pulled the trainers out of the rucksack, inspected the soles in comparison to the ones she had on, then chucked them over the wall behind.

Sitting there, looking down at the village lights, she tried to picture the kind of house her dad would be living in now. It wouldn't be anything like her mum's had been, all clean and modern. Her dad would be more traditional. He'd probably kept the old china cabinet that'd belonged to her grandma Maynard, with some of the ornamental animals still in it; there'd be an open fire burning, especially on dull days like this, and a dining table with a cloth on it, and he'd have a proper tea pot with a woolly cosy to keep the brew piping hot. Her stomach groaned at that last thought; it could be hours before she got as far as that cupper. She'd probably make a start in any shops that were still open—*Rick Maynard? Oh, everybody knows Richard, love, he's the local handyman, helped my old man build a shed, did a grand job*—and if that came to nothing she'd move onto the pubs. Any pub landlord would know him. If she was being realistic instead of dreaming like always, that's where she'd start. Andrea searched through her jeans pockets and counted out her change. One pound forty-four pence. No address, no photo—her mum'd cut him out of all the photos, so she'd inherited albums full of pictures with a man shaped hole between the rest of the family. She could remember what he looked like, sort of, but from twelve years ago—half a life ago—when they'd met for a burger in town. Then nothing. What a fucking daft idea, heading for the back of beyond without money. But what choice did she have? Neil had all the money padlocked away, that's what it had come to, and the slightest whiff of trouble, like today, and her debit card got locked up as well, so she couldn't even put petrol in the car, not even to get to work. This latest absence would be the last chance. Tomorrow they'd replace her. There'd be no interest in why she'd not shown. It was a Pound Shop with a rapid staff turnover—they wanted reliable staff, not somebody's sob story.

A van rattled past—another horn blast. Andrea wearily hauled on the backpack and set back off in the same direction, keeping her head down. It wasn't just the lechers, the rain'd started. She zipped her leather jacket up to the neck and stuffed her hands down deep into the pockets. She had to keep positive, keep going. This wasn't just about escaping. A stable family member was the only way she'd get the kids back, after Neil. Her dad was the closest thing to stable she could muster. She needed to crack on, start with the pubs.

Maybe some nice fella would buy her a drink. Some nice, friendly old chap, not out for a fast bit of fanny. She'd just sit and have a quiet drink while the locals talked amongst themselves about her predicament, then some old gal who knew the village inside-out would plop herself down at the table, smile, and say, "You're Richard's daughter, aren't you, sweetheart? I can see it around the eyes." There'd be phone calls, and he'd come stumbling in all emotional at the sight of her, and she'd be fed and tucked up in a warm bed by ten o'clock. All the catching up that needed doing could be done tomorrow, after she'd had a well-needed rest.

That little cluster of lights looked all the prettier for those thoughts and Andrea's heart did a little dance. Her pace picked up momentum for a short spurt, then slowed again with the dreaded realization that failure in her mission meant sleeping rough again, at least for tonight. "Not that, please, God," she whispered. She stood by the curb on the hill that dropped down to the village, her hair plastered to her skull by the now battering rain. Across the road not far ahead, two dim lights glared toward her like watching eyes. She could make out the boxy shape of a van, like a caravanette, with just the sidelights on. As she set off again in that direction, the idling engine stopped. Automatically, her senses went on full alert. She could see somebody moving around inside there, going into the back through a gap between the front seats, then returning to the driver's seat. The person sitting in there held two things: something square shaped, and something with steam rising from it that clung to the inner windscreen, obscuring the man's face. A light in the rear of the vehicle revealed shelves stacked up to the roof with what looked like books. Closer now, Andrea could see the man was probably in his late thirties, quite handsome in a geeky kind of way, his light brown hair neatly slicked back and side parted. He was wearing a crisp white shirt and blue tie. The man noticed Andrea peering in as she approached and raised his cup with a friendly smile before returning to his reading. She hesitated, observing him through the passenger window, but mostly focused on the steaming cup in his hand. The way the van was facing meant he'd just left the village. In his sort of job, you'd get to know a lot of local people—not that she recalled her dad as any great reader of books—but somebody who did read books might know her dad. The man looked up again and saw her hesitation. At first, his expression was quizzical, then he relaxed, and with a curious, crooked little smile raised a flask that'd been tucked down beside his seat, shaking it from side to side—an invitation.

Fuck the pubs, she decided. There'd only be trouble. A car passed between them, headlights blaring, shocking and blinding her for a second, but reassuring her that this spot was pretty close to a busy residential area. And Christ, was she dying for a cupper. Cold rain dripped from Andrea's nose as she nodded her acceptance to the man inside the nice warm van. Then carefully she looked both ways, like her mum'd always told her, and crossed the road toward him.

CHAPTER THIRTY

Following a bleak run of storms, late June ushered in a kinder light, the type to inspire longing and promise hope—a new beginning. The high-spiritedness of fledgling birdsong flittered from the hawthorns that bordered the allotments when, early one Saturday morning, Fionn took a stroll down there to see what might be salvaged. Beena Ryan had been right. The project had been an asset to the community, and could be again. Prior to the events of February there'd been a two year waiting list for even the smallest stretch of fertile land; during March, the council couldn't give it away.

Approaching the plots, he heard an echoed chopping that he recognized as axe on wood. It was Ben that cut everybody's wood around here, and for a mad moment he had the strongest inkling that it must be Ben he was about to see. His pace down the hill from the church steps picked up speed, his heart divided by dread and yearning.

The council had replaced any fire-damaged fencing. Thick foliage obscured the view from the lane but Fionn could make out movement through fleeting gaps a few fences down, an arm rising and falling. The hacking grew sharper. He could see now that Ben's plot was still in a poor state, with charred crops left to rot and the battered shed haphazardly boarded up. The noise was coming from the adjoining plot. As Fionn reached the fence, it stopped.

She stood there over a pile of dry logs in the midst of the remains of blackened winter vegetation, her hands pressed into the small of her back. A wood axe sat lodged in what was left of the dead stump by her feet. Fionn realized that it was the stump from Ben's plot; the log he used to rest on and smoke. Ami stretched her neck one direction then the other and in doing so caught sight of Fionn by the neighboring fence.

"How-do, mate," she beamed. "How long you been peepin' over there?"

"Hi, Amelia. Sorry, I was a little taken aback to see you."

"Ami, dog—I mean, Father. And I have that effect on people. What can you do?"

"Looks like you've been hard at it a while over there. Need a hand?"

Her slim arms were taut and sinewy, her hair shorter and slicked back, the bobbles binned. She'd grown up, just like that.

"Nah, it's okay," she said. "We're trying to save money on the boiler, that's all. Got rid of the gas fire and put in an old stove. Dad had the chimney all brushed out. This'll stock up for September. It'll 've dried out some more by then."

"Thinking ahead, eh?"

"Someone's got to." Ami glanced down a little guiltily at the hacked up stump on the ground, gave a shrug of regret. "I figured if I'd asked him, he would've said 'use it'."

"You're right. He would've said exactly that."

"Dad won't step a foot down here now—treatin' the place like an enemy. I reckon he's lost his grip."

"It might seem that way, Ami, but things'll turn around, eventually. I mean, look at you. Your dad's maybe finding it difficult to keep up the pace. What's happening with school these days?"

She shrugged. "My tutor says I'm ahead—the school gave me tutorials in my own space, set me homework an' that. Plus, dad's paying for home schoolin'. Doing extra hours on the buses to pay for it. Doesn't want me goin' back, he says. Me, I reckon I could handle it, but like I say, his grip's gone slack. I can't be arsed wiv battling him all the time." She paused. "I suppose you heard about Kelly?" she asked.

"Yes I did. I'm sorry."

"I knew she was dead, the moment she dropped out of sight. She was like, the maddest smack-head on the planet at one time, y'know, but soon as that baby came along—she was pulling it together, wasn't goin' no place without that kid. Except where she's gone." For a spell, the two of them stared blankly at nothing. Ami was the first to snap out of that. "Hey, come look at this, though, Father."

Underfoot, Louis's allotment was an ugly kind of crisp, mulchy underneath, seared by February's violent fire then bogged by heavy rain. Ami led him toward a particularly blackened patch, and crouching down brushed aside the remnants of charred plant life.

"Look. Look here. What about that then?"

Where the mulch was parted there stood a proud green shoot. The two of them just squatted there a while, staring. A simple miracle, not hard to explain, just hard not to wonder at in such a scene of apparent devastation.

"They're all over," she said. "New babies. Just have a look

anywhere. Aren't they just so sweet? I'm off up to get dad's rake in a bit, see what else is hiding away under all this fallout."

"Fair brings a tear to the eye, doesn't it? I swear, we could bring on that nuclear holocaust, or whatever catastrophe man can make, it'd all come back regardless, lush and new, like this little fellow."

"Sometimes I think the world'd be better off without us, Father."

"Fionn." He patted her on the back. "Would you just listen to us couple of wet blankets, on a day like this one. Tell you what, Ami, I'm about to take your lead." He stood up. "Wait here a sec. Give me a lend of your axe, Ami."

He went back round to Ben's allotment and, jamming in the axe blade, prized the boards off the shed door. "Like you say," he shouted, coming out with a roll of gardening sacks, a hoe and two rakes which he passed over to Ami. "Ben'd be wanting all this put to good use." He went in again for plant food and a hose. Feeling invigorated, he hopped the fence back. Ami had a helpless giggling fit, then she took a rake and they both set to work with little more said. Quickly delegating a patch for the dead scrub, they raked toward it, and stripped down to vests they continued like Wild West pilgrims for the next hour. With the charring finally bagged up, the two stood back by the gate, stunned at the life they'd unearthed. They locked eyes and smiled: a fine day's work done.

Putting the bags out for collecting, Fionn noticed that by then other allotments were being quietly tended. It was heart-warming to see people filtering back.

"Glad to see it won't go to rot, after all that's happened," he commented, mainly to himself, then had an urge to slap himself in the head. "Sorry, Ami. I wasn't thinking. You, of all people, had the right to let it."

"Nothing doin'," she said firmly. "I've put the word out. I don't want people acting like my dad, treating this place like some kind of memorial for my lost innocence an' all that crap. Don't look shocked, Fionn. I mean it. If I can move on, so can everybody."

Fionn lightly gripped her shoulder. This, he assured himself, was why the human race always survived the blasts thrown at it. "Well, job's a good 'n'," he said. "I'm so glad I saw you today, Ami."

"Why today?"

"I dunno. Some days more than others, you need a sign, something to help you to keep believing there's a future worth aiming for. So thanks. I'm proud of you." He wanted to ruffle her hair but resisted. "Well, I'd best be making tracks—leave you to it—go gouge the dirt out the old fingernails, or Lin won't let me touch anything holy. But any time I can chip in here, just give me a shout, okay? And if you want me to talk to your dad, you know? Informally. Anything I can do, just say."

"Actually," she said, "since you mention it, there is one thing you can do, for yourself more than me, but it would make me feel better." She took a while to add, "There's someone I think you should meet."

*

Scrubbing his nails over the sink, Fionn caught a glimpse of something disturbing reflected back at him through the bathroom mirror. Did everybody see it? That shadow of guilt that darkened his every expression; the kind that sits stupidly on your face when the police stop your car for that brake light you know is out, but will claim you have no inkling of.

Before showering, he turned on the radio for the hourly news, now more an obsession than the prayers, which seemed increasingly futile. There was always something.

…In the wake of a United Nations report into the scale of African Aid being diverted into the hands of corrupt militia, several prominent warlords, said to be from across three neighboring war-torn regions, have been found either dead, or wandering close to death, deep in the Sahara desert. The men, first stripped of their clothing by a captor one delirious survivor described as "God's darkness", were abandoned with neither food nor water. The only two survivors, so far, are suffering from severe dehydration and UVA burns. It is unknown how many more still remain unfound. Rescue attempts continue…

Fionn's movements grinded to a stop as the next article came through. Under the warm shower spray, cold blood flooded in and numbed his face.

…West Yorkshire police have expressed concern over the whereabouts of twenty-three-year-old Andrea Maynard, who was last seen walking along the A616 on the fifth of June. It is believed she may have been heading for Holmdale, where her estranged father had resided up until his death last year. Sources say that Andrea had been suffering from severe depression since her two young children had been taken into care. Her husband has appealed for her safe return. The police are staging a reconstruction of her last known movements and are urging any further witnesses who might have seen her that day, to come forward…

With water trickling past his unblinking eyes, Fionn turned off the shower and stood in naked silence. He recalled the denial he'd voiced to Kelly Atkins, that she would not be avenged, that he could not bid the return of the thing he'd helped bring into existence. But now, here was Andrea, who might not have had to suffer the same fate had he acted sooner. All guilt aside, Fionn faced his demons head on, closed his eyes, and quietly wished for whatever Ben was these days to get his arse back here and sort this one out.

CHAPTER THIRTY-ONE

To the west, as the sun sank back casting a bronze arc behind him, the part of it that was Ben Hunter sat high up on the cold rock of Mount Lebanon, gazing down over the Kadisha valley to picturesque Bcharre and north eastwards toward distant Tripoli. A real hawk's vision was something to behold. Down there, on a prominent city wall, the heads of six men, chief agitators on both sides, sat lodged on spikes, dripping out a caution to others.

Ben hadn't felt this fully conscious and possessed of himself in a long time. The one named "Zwerg", the dark protector, the one who fancied himself as a comedian—if he didn't know better, Ben would have thought that little guy'd been watching the Marx Brothers for the last five hundred years—he was the one who liked to take over in a fight. Fights were what that dude'd been waiting for, psyching himself up for all this time. But Ben was strong, too. That's why he was here, he guessed, a part of all this, surveying the world as the sun took a rest. His situation becoming clearer, if not one hundred percent. So this wasn't what he'd thought at first. But so what? That mattered less than he could've imagined. Between the three of them, they were getting the job done, more of a job than anyone else was bothering to do. The Bible might have promised an Armageddon, a big old clean up, and yep, we could all wait around a lifetime of Christmases for that to happen, while in the meantime millions more innocents would cop for the shitty end of some greedy bastard's stick. No. The change was now. And it would be sizeable enough for the whole world to witness.

Since the first melt, every transformation had become less tricky, as if each element of the gathering entity's cells had gained some level of recognition, a commonality, to the point where Ben no longer anticipated the changes coming. Things happened faster, cleaner, fused more readily. There was always pain, no denying it, but that was only right; such power should never come without pain. He suspected the Zwerg even enjoyed it.

There was so much more still to do. With the rumor of their presence spreading, a world full of anguished voices cried out to the skies. Depictions of their being materialized, etched on skyscrapers and cliffsides in every land. Ben was reminded of the Bat-signal radiating into the skies over Gotham, the distress call, the cry for help. Yet with each approaching dawn, he felt the Zwerg inexplicably pulling them backwards. Appolyn was the thinker, the receiver, and she was holding something back from Ben, something he couldn't get to, but he suspected that was to do with the memories he'd accessed, perhaps by accident, during the trauma of that first melt. He still had those pictures at the ready; could play it all back like a scene selection. Was her cruel murder the making of a saint? There was that crowd of jeering faces, viewed by the Zwerg through the fierceness of living flames, the sudden terror of those onlookers as he berated them. But these were things Ben didn't want to think too much about. He suspected it would come to no good.

The last thing he wanted was for the mission to stop, or be diverted even for a second, but Appolyn stirred restlessly now and was torn. He felt it. He sensed her goodness being tainted by a bitterness he didn't understand. Even the Zwerg didn't lie. But they weren't speaking the truth either, and to his mind that was just as bad. He felt her thoughts returning to a mutual friend. There'd been pleas from home; calls for their return. Fionn would be the excuse, if he ever joined those pleas. Maybe he had already. They'd tapped into him somehow. Fionn had an eye on the world; he cared more than most. That had been important at the start. But Ben couldn't see why that mattered now; now they were out in the world. No, he would keep things on track as long as he could, even though the pull of his other two parts was irresistible, especially as he loved half that number deeply now, as his own flesh and blood. The Zwerg he would drop off at the tip tomorrow if it wasn't for the man's commitment to her protection, his freakish strength, and an executioner's single-mindedness in seeing each task through to its ultimate conclusion. And there was something else to that part of their number: an ability, whether gift or curse, to see ahead in time, to predict events concerning them. Only this gift, too, was compromised by the Zwerg's obsessive lust for vengeance; that personal score he needed to settle, which clouded his foresight, a score that Ben couldn't allow to be followed through. Not yet, or maybe ever.

The faces Ben had loved before were fading gradually. It made no sense for him to go back and stir up all that emotion. And, as if to seal his determination, one aspect of the future that was becoming clearer to all of them, was that there would be danger in returning to England, to the place of their origins. Some inkling was forming a cloudy picture in the Zwerg's crystal ball; his *ankh*; that all-seeing part of his mind's eye: a vision of some mean old mama, who was of a mind to go buy herself a gun and shoot their collective arse the fuck out of the sky.

CHAPTER THIRTY-TWO

Fionn took the morning paper and a cup of tea into his booth just before ten, expecting the usual low Saturday morning turnout. But he'd barely been in there a couple of minutes when a heavy bottom rattled the seat next door. He put the tea quietly down and went through the formalities.

"Morning, Father."

"What have you to confess, sister?"

There was a heavy sigh, no doubt accompanied by the roll of eyeballs. "I have to confess, Father Malloy, that I married a right wanker." Her accent was strong northern Irish. A vaguely familiar voice—not a regular—and one too fast and furious to be easily interrupted. "Excuse my French, but I swear he hates our guts with every ounce of his petty little soul."

"Hates who? Your family? The church?"

"He has these go-faster gloves, with the checkered stripe over the top—you know the type? And believe-you-me they work. I truly dread the thought of going out anywhere with him lately. Even the shopping—and I love shopping. Only, I don't drive myself, you know, so what am I to do, get the effing bus? Sure, we all come into the world imperfect and then life twists us up along the way…"

"True words…"

"… and it's rarely great, is it, your average working class upbringing? But his family—I can't tell you what his dad was like: an evil man. Forgive me, Father, but I'm glad the effer's dead and buried, cremated though he was."

"What is it you wish to confess exactly, sister?"

"I'm afraid, Father. I might make light of it, but I am… I'm afraid of the man I chose to marry. But yet ashamed to be afraid, if you get my drift, because I don't even respect him, not any more. Truth be told, he's a pathetic pig."

"Has he hit you?"

"No. Not hitting, not me. It's more the way he makes me feel."

"Well, fear is not a sin."

"Isn't loathing, though, towards a husband? I *can* confess I won't be a wife to him any more, not in…that way. He's cruel, see. I mean, I'm no teenager now, and he'll say things like, 'Can you make it tighter?' I mean, what a thing to say, in the act. I says to him, 'Who do you think you're on here, Derren Brown?' I don't know, at times he seems not so bad, then it's like something snaps in him. I don't know what exactly—it could be many things—but I see it happen, him going over the edge, all set for a rant. And it's got worse since his dad passed on, like he's taken over the mission."

"What mission?"

"A campaign of hate."

"You say he hates *us*. Who are you speaking of?"

"All of us, Father. Womankind. The female of the species."

From there on she covered the same ground, until after

twenty minutes Fionn suggested she pop around for a less formal chat some time, give him a chance to consider what she'd confided, though his instincts told him that, with the brunt of it off her chest, she probably wouldn't bother.

After that, things went quiet. He was about to call it a day when he heard somebody approaching the booths, almost creeping. Inside, the person slowly turned to face the grid between them. Sitting sideways as he was, Fionn could still distinguish the bulky shape to be that of a man. Something wasn't right about him, something in the proximity, the breathing, a toxic and weighty element that hung in the air like rubber-smoke. Fionn felt glared at.

The voice, deep and cynical, was somehow unexpected and rocked Fionn a little in his seat.

"She's been in here blabbin', has she? Don't tell me. I already know." The man was chewing something, something minty by the smell of it; even his chewing was angry. The accent was broad Yorkshire, not a young man.

"She dun't know when to shurrup, that's her problem."

"And what's your problem, Mr.?"

"My problem?" He laughed without humor. "Where do I start? Let's see, shall we start with all you sanctimonious cunts tellin' the rest of us how to live our lives—when you're not fiddlin' wi' little nippers, that is." He broke for the priest's response but none came. Fionn was listening, intently. "Or shall we get onto the state of this sewer you lot call a neighborhood, eh? Like pigs wallowin' in yer own filth. I'm sick…" He spat. "…of hearing about the shock of what happened to them poor lasses. Shock my arse! What do they expect, this lot, raisin' their girls like whores and their lads like dogs? That lot were just dogs out on t' common doing what dogs do best. Don't talk to me about shock; all them young tarts made up to t' nines, dolled up like prossies after a fast fiver, swankin' around t'streets till all hours—lads bayin' out the windows, fiddling wi' their dribbly little dicks. Don't tell me it's the state of society today. It's parents. Stupid mothers, not doin' the basic job that's theirs to do. Just poppin' out kid after kid like stray dogs, fuckin' dumb bitches."

"What have you to confess, brother?"

This time it was the man who started, as if while ranting away to himself in a closed room, somebody had walked in unexpectedly and interrupted him.

"Confess? Me? *Nowt.*"

"But I've heard your confession before, brother, have I not?" Fionn felt a mild tremble infecting his own voice.

"Fuck off!" There was a violent thud as the man punched the wooden partition between them. "You shut your mouth, priest. Shut it! Understand?"

"It's been a long time. Is there something more you need to confess? Or to the same?"

There was a clattering as the man stormed out like a loose bull. Fionn got to his feet a little shakily but was out in the church in time to glimpse the back of the man heading out of it: medium height, chunky, a tradesman maybe, late fifties, grey black hair, the neck beneath blazing like a ham on boil.

Moments later, Mrs. Chuk walked in from outside puffing and blowing, brushing her arm. "Gracious me, almost took me down the steps with him. How rude."

Fionn swallowed hard. "Do you know him, Lin? Who was that?"

Both went to the doors and witnessed an old silver Mercedes speeding away from the green up into the estate. "It's Cloda Bullimore's husband—Terrence they call him. She used to be a good practicing Catholic, did Cloda, but she's gone flakey on the faith, Father Fionn. No big surprise with a bloke like that breathing down your neck full time."

"I need you to do me a favor, Lin," Fionn told her. "I have to be somewhere and it's important. There's somebody I can't let down right now. I want you to give Cloda Bullimore a ring, warn her that her husband followed her here and that he's probably on his way home right now. Can you find her number okay?"

Lin was already on the move. "I'll get it sorted, don't you worry. You get off, Father. Leave this to me. You don't need worry yourself about the likes of him."

But Fionn *was* worried about the likes of Terrence Bullimore. It'd been years, and now, after all this time, he could finally put a name to that voice.

CHAPTER THIRTY-THREE

Raz ascended the wooden staircase with quiet apprehension. Bright daylight outside and he could barely make out the next step ahead. It was like every blind in the place had been drawn down and nailed to the window frames. Beside the inert creepiness of the dark house, there'd been the phone call; Raz disliked any phone call that insisted he "come alone" to any place. Lately, Stanley Coxer was like some humongous firework with a spark lingering halfway up its very short fuse. His behavior was growing weirder by the day. Now Raz came to think about it, it'd been a whole lot of days since the last time anybody so much as clocked the man, maybe a couple of weeks even. He hadn't thought about it much up until now because—even though he'd never admit it to Mumpy, who harped on like some old lady re the riskiness of cuddlin' up too close with Coxer—deep down Raz was relieved to've been allowed some time out. For once, Mumpy tagging along right now would be no bad thing. Raz had to ask himself why a high-flyer who practically shat cash would buy such a huge pad and then whittle his living quarters down to just one speck of it. What was he scared of? No doubt, he'd sacked-off the cleaning service as well; everything was well dirty: dust caked everywhere, toilets rotting, garbage scattered all over.

Raz reached the door up the three short steps and knocked lightly. "Mr. Coxer? It's me, Mr. Razool." He wanted to add *"your friend"* by way of reassurance, but that sounded creepy enough in his head, so he kept it there. "Will I be comin' in?"

No answer. The dogs yapped behind the door. The man was in there all right. Those little beasties were invariably where Stanley was.

"I'm coming in then, Mr. Coxer."

Raz used his key off the set. He'd almost succumbed to a smile when he'd got those off of the boss—nobody else had the full set—but right now they felt like the keys to his own personal prison. Two steps in and the rank odor sent him reeling out of the room, almost falling back down the steps. He had to suppress his gag reflex before taking a swift breather and braving it back in, this time holding his T-shirt up to his face. The two shit-smeared pugs did their standard battle charge then just scuttered around his feet, whelping pitifully. Their dishes sat a little way in, empty, no water even. To the right, the master bathroom door stood open. It smelled like the loo had been well-splashed but not flushed in days. What the holy-fuck was up with this man? Splotches of doggy-doos and piss puddles riddled the floor amid chewed-up biscuit wrappers and empty tins: beans, soup, dog chow, clearly whatever supplies he'd had stocked up. One of the dogs had blood caked around its muzzle, no doubt from foraging in a spent can.

"Mr. Coxer!" Raz coughed. "It's me, boss. Raz. Mr. Razool. *Your friend.*" It had to be done.

A faint human whimpering came from the far side of the room, behind the white leather couch parked under one of the blacked out windows. Stuff was piled along the back of it—books and things—securing a blanket stretched between there and the windowsill, where more books secured the other end. Raz flicked the light switch on but nothing happened. The bulbs were out. He could see that now. Removed from every socket.

He went slowly toward the couch. "It's okay, boss, just chill, just me comin' over." But Raz wasn't chilled. He was wishing he hadn't left his fucking gun under the car seat.

Weak flashlight spilled out from under the blanket; unsteady light. Raz stood by the couch's end, staring down into the gap between it and the window wall, trying to mask his disgust for the hunched, unkempt figure sitting quivering down there, gripping a torch in one hand and pointing a twelve-bore out from the other. Stanley's face was frozen in terror; one gooey eye twitched out a steady rhythm; a right optical-orgasm. Raz lowered the T-shirt from his face, his sights trained away from the two dark funnels of the rifle's muzzle, into the twitching eyes of the seated man. Loathing aside, he was fully aware that he could die at any moment.

"Mr. Coxer. It's okay. You can put the gun down. It's just me. I come just like you said."

"Alone?" Coxer howled back, the vaulted ceilings echoing his fevered pitch.

"Just me. Just like you said, boss."

"I need more food. My doggies need walkies and poop-poops! Nobody helps around here anymore!"

As calm as he could, Raz leaned forward. "That's what I'm here for, yeah, boss? Whatever you need. Now, come on. Give." Gently he eased the rifle from Coxer's grip, reached aside and laid it on the couch. "Just tell me what you need an' I'll sort it, okay?"

Coxer gripped himself in the rifle's absence, shaking violently, the flashlight monstering his already crazed features. "They're coming for me," he screeched. "They want to get me!"

"Nobody's after you, boss. And anyways, I'm here now."

"Oh, you don't know. You have no idea. You haven't seen my dreams. You may well be in this room." Stanley punched a finger at his temple. "But you're not in here with me. Are you?"

Raz couldn't imagine a worse place to be. Clearly, a chance needed taking here. He crouched down before the deranged man, maintaining the standard blank expression. "So what?" he said. "So what if they wants to get you, whoever 'they' is. You don't go out like this. This is not how men like us go down—cowering in a baby tent covered with pooh."

Coxer's quaking steadied. An expression like his own sat at the boundaries of his face waiting to close in. "That's a-awfully cheeky of you," he grinned. "I still have a long sharp knife about my person."

"I'm your friend," Raz assured. "And I ain't gunner see you take a skid like this, boss. So stab me if you fink that's the best option you got." Raz shrugged. "It'll just be more mess to clean up. And like you say, nobody's helpin' no more. So it'll be your mess to sort, won't it?"

Stanley broke into a fit of hysterics. "Oh, you are funny, young man. A fucking hoot! You're my absolute favorite, you know."

"Sweet, boss. Now come on…up. Stand up." Raz offered a hand, helping Coxer to as straight a posture as the man could achieve, which was still pretty bent. "Now, let's get you cleaned up nice, boss, yeah? And no more talk of being got at. Any fucker gets any place close to you while Raz is on watch, gets a payload from this baby." With Stanley on one arm, he picked up the rifle, flexing his sinewy arms. "Make no mistake."

CHAPTER THIRTY-FOUR

By Saturday afternoon, it was over seventy degrees. Driving not being his strongpoint, especially among such hostile competition, Fionn took the bus in with Ami. The Square was heaving with life, mostly life in its early stages, which made Fionn feel old and conspicuous by collar. He never used to feel that way about the uniform. Once he'd felt proud to wear it.

"I'm not sure what you're expecting from this, Ami," he said on the bus.

"They're not all the same. Not all about celebs and gossip an' shit. I trust him. A lot of his work's concerned with us, with Rokerville. I want to understand. Don't you?"

He nodded reluctantly. "Even though they say 'ignorance is bliss'. Yes I do."

"He campaigned with MIND, on the back of all the suicides, to get more healthcare support for the mentally ill round here." Ami shrugged. "Most of it's been pulled now, like. With the spending cuts, an' all."

"I didn't know the man was involved in that campaign, I have to admit."

"This ain't just about what happened to me, Fionn. I wasn't good mates with Callum. Straight up, I thought he was a bit of a spaz, like everybody." A look of regret passed between them. "But I felt well sorry for him when the gang was right up in his face, picking on his mum and dad an' that. There've been loads like him, Carl says. Good kids, just...opting out young."

"You couldn't have stopped that, you know."

"I know." A little later, she added, "He won't say, but Carl knows something about Ben. I miss him."

"Me, too. But would you ever want to see Ben come back?"

She shrugged. "Whatever goes down, I know he'd never hurt me."

Fionn would have liked to say the same, but all of a sudden, in the face of his own question, he wasn't so sure.

Carl Wilson sat outside one of the café-bars, a battered leather satchel at his feet. Regardless of the heat, he wore a raincoat, one he'd probably had for twenty years plus, by the looks of it. He reminded Fionn a bit of his uncle Michael: a bit tatty, a big broad smiling face and masses of grey frizzy hair that went mostly upwards like candy floss; not paparazzi by any long shot, but a risk somehow. Fionn felt that strongly.

Carl stood as they approached, an eager hand outstretched to grasp his. "Father Malloy, grand to meet you at last. And Amelia..."

"Easy now. Ami. Please, dog."

"Well, lovely to see you again, Ami. What can I get for you, sweetheart?"

"You really don't think I'm hangin' out here wiv two old codgers like yous?"

The two men shared a laugh and the ice was cracked if not broken.

"So, you taking yourself off shopping, young lady?" Fionn asked. "Who'll see me home on the bus?"

"Not shopping exactly." Ami looked coy. "I'm meeting someone, actually, if you must know."

Her eyes locked on that "someone" as she said it, walking toward them across the square: a tall, lean lad who looked of Indian decent, wearing a checkered shirt and faded jeans, smart with it. Good skin. Not from the estate, Fionn quickly gauged.

"So, you can chop logs, and now you have a boyfriend," he remarked. "What else don't I know?"

She took the lad's arm and wrapped it comfortably over her shoulder. "Plenty, sunshine. Fionn, this is Deepak—Deepak, this is Fionn, my telephone to God."

"I've been called worse."

Fionn offered a hand, which the boy shook saying, "Hi'.

"Carl you've met. Well, we'll see yous both around then. See you, Carl."

Carl raised a friendly hand. Fionn felt strangely put out that this reporter had met the boyfriend first, and the two men stood looking awkwardly across a small metallic table for a while after the kids had left.

"So, beer or lager, Father?" Carl ventured.

*

"She's a strong young woman," Carl commented a few sips into his pint. "She'll see all this trouble out."

"I hope so," Fionn said. "You're a historian, Mr. Wilson? Besides the reporting. That right?"

"Call me Carl. I'm writing a book, on the lines of how regional history has impacted on the present. Lessons unlearned and all that. All will out!" He waved an arm dramatically around the crowd. "If anyone can be bothered reading about it. It won't outsell Jordan's latest biography, put it that way, but there's a fair bit of intrigue, which I'll enlarge on later. It's a good city we live in. It used to be great, at the top of rungs, ladder-wise. All down to hard-working people and a fair few sheep."

"Yes. Wool was big. Now they all want Lycra."

"They do indeed. I don't blame them."

Fionn sipped at his beer but it was going down like guzzled chips. "I have to say, Carl, I'm not quite sure why I'm here. How I can help with your research?" he asked.

Carl nodded solemnly and smiled, as if he were expecting resistance. "There are certain dark aspects to the history," he said. "The worst having happened in what is now your parish, Father. I wanted to get the…religious view, if you like—bounce a few ideas around. For instance, there was a plague hit the area very hard. Nothing unusual in itself. Plagues happen sporadically throughout British history. Only this bout, around the mid-sixteenth century, was predicted."

"By who?"

"Somebody very odd, so the records have it. A monk who'd settled here, from Germany I believe. A very repugnant individual. He was executed. The proddies were baying for his blood already, so he made it worth their while, committed mass murder. More than a dozen men in one night; a right old killing machine, he was." Carl took a drink and sat back. "But I'll let you read about all that," he added, taking a large manila envelope from his satchel and placing it on the table. "Luckily, that whole episode was recorded. I've even updated the text, so it's easier for you to read. Have a gander when you've got a minute."

"It all sounds interesting," Fionn said. "But I'm still not sure what it is you want from me."

Carl gave him a broad smile. "Oh, you'll work it out, Father. You're a smart lad."

They sat in silence again, taking in the sights but unavoidably returning to the growing tension between them.

"You remind me a bit of a policeman," Fionn said. "Allowing a man all the silence he needs to incriminate himself."

"The statement of a guilty man, some might say." Carl opened his hands. "But so far, as incriminations go, who the hell listens to me? During introductions at the last director's meeting my editor extended my address to 'Carl Wilson, local witch-hunter and general crack-pot'. So there you have it. But can I ask you something, Father?"

"Fionn."

"Can I ask you, Fionn, have you ever been bitten by a bug that gets into your system and won't let up?"

"Yes, I suppose I have."

"So you'll know the feeling. For me, the bug bit many years ago. At first, it was looking into my own family's history—and this was before the internet, mind. It grew pretty much into an obsession from there. My ancestors, Catholics themselves, settled in your parish when the old Saint Luke's was fairly new, during the reign of King James, when things had calmed down a bit religiously. The original church, that of Saint Agnes, had been sacked by protestant marauders in the days of good old Henry, around the Pilgrimage of Grace." He noticed Fionn flinch, and tapped the manila envelope between them. "That's when all this trouble started. The more I uncovered, the more my efforts were concentrated on developments in the parish since. I believe I raised a question there?"

"You said Saint Agnes? I've…heard of her. Do you know where she was interred?"

"Yes, I do as a matter of fact. Her ashes were removed to Canterbury during The Pilgrimage."

Fionn fell silent; so the ashes in the phial he'd taken to Ben in prison—who's the hell were those? He knew without asking that he'd find out.

"…it's not just suicides," Carl was saying. "But violent deaths generally. No suicide rate, over centuries, anywhere, is higher than in your parish, Fionn. Many of the victims, prior to death, have spoken of 'being called' to the point of insanity, by an agent of God, they supposed."

"But you don't buy that?" The porcelain perfection of Appolyn's face flooded his mind's eye.

"For years, I didn't know what to believe. But the evidence kept stacking up. Now, yes, I do believe that some supernatural presence has taken root in the parish. Some part of this presence may even think it is good—perhaps it started off good at heart. But not a saint. I believe it's contaminated—corrupted, by the very nature of its existence."

"What do you mean 'by nature of its existence'?"

"Do you remember the story of Moses?" Carl asked. "The exodus from Egyptian bondage?"

"Yes, of course."

"Poor old Moses, eh? After wandering the wilderness for over forty years, getting the Ten Commandments sorted, keeping those wayward Hebrews on the straight and narrow, he himself was denied passage into the Promised Land…"

"…For taking credit for the flowing waters at Meribath-kadesh, for in doing so, he attributed the power of God's hand to his own."

For the first time since they'd met, Carl looked deeply serious. "God doesn't share power, son, not with mere mortals. Where supernatural power is sought and gained by men, by whatever ritual, the door that's opened won't lead to God."

It was getting harder for Fionn to look Carl in the eye. "So why all the suicides? What would something evil want with the likes of young Callum?"

"They say if you open a void, something will rush to fill it. I believe that a void was opened up here a long time ago, and that what filled it needs to recruit souls, harvest them if you like. The first recorded suicide is in that envelope, Fionn: a good man, amongst many of his time who were not. Like young Callum, you might say. And, I suppose, the more worthy souls the Devil suspends in Purgatory, the less God has to work with."

"I'm not sure I want to read what's in there," Fionn said.

"Denial's a powerful remedy for reality. But this isn't just about the past. That plague that was predicted hit in the mid-sixteenth century. Many of its victims can be traced back to one event. The one in that envelope. An event that happened right where Saint Luke's stood. Entire family lines died out. The only lines that did survive might well have been allowed to for a purpose. Something's coming for them. That was a promise. Another prediction."

"I don't know what to think anymore." Fionn pushed his hair back from his face, suddenly feeling stared at from all angles of the busy square.

Two people did happen to be looking his way, and

approaching at a casual pace, two people he quickly recognized, as did Carl Wilson, who smiled and nodded as they reached the table.

"Detective Inspector Ryan," he greeted warmly. "And your joke-cracking sidekick... I forget his name."

"Detective Gaunt," Fionn offered.

CHAPTER THIRTY-FIVE

"Very interesting," Beena Ryan slapped the envelope down on the desk in front of Fionn. "This man certainly does his homework, doesn't he? Ancient history though. Is any of this relevant to our friend, Ben Hunter's disappearing act?"

"I don't know. I haven't read it. You took it off me before I had a chance."

"What else were you talking about, you and Wilson?"

"He wanted a 'religious view', he said, on some of the research he's done around Saint Luke's parish. I wasn't much use, I don't think."

"How's Amelia? I noticed you came into town together."

"All that time, you were watching? Well, she seems okay. All the outward signs say she's mending. How can you really know?"

"You can't. Time will tell. You can pray for her, though, can't you?"

"Yes. Of course. I do."

"Well." Beena sat on the edge of the desk facing the chair he sat on. "It's nice to see you, Fionn, but you really didn't have to come along. It's Wilson we want to talk to. It's him we were watching."

"Why?"

She blew a little laugh down her nose.

"Well, am I okay to take this?" Fionn picked up the envelope.

"It is yours. Can I take a copy, though? I'd like to give it a thorough once-over."

"I don't see the harm."

"So why are you here, Fionn?"

"I insisted on coming because, well, I was going to ring you. There's something I need to talk to you about. Something I heard in confession today."

"Tricky one. What?"

"A man's voice. One I recognized from a few years ago, not long after Ben's wife, Anita, committed suicide. What he said back then…concerned her."

"Did he confess to the rape?"

"Not confess exactly. It was more like a gloat, to taunt me almost. I'd say he hates the church, among other things. Basically, back then, he said something about Anita, something intimate, about her body, that only somebody who knew her sexually could know. It stuck with me terribly, because he seemed pleased, proud, to 've caused her death. Though he didn't admit to forcing her."

"'Intimate things' doesn't do it, Fionn. You have to tell me what he said."

"She was very naturally pretty, Anita. Didn't need make-up, didn't bother with fashion and all that. So Ben was a bit shocked when she went and got a tattoo. He confessed he was angry about it at first. It was a hawk, like his nickname."

"Where abouts on her body?"

"Under her knicker-line at the front. Just a miniature. You could tell he got to like the idea, that it was just for him. He said you wouldn't notice it even if she wore a bikini."

"The man you describe could have been a lover. An angry one maybe—say if she'd dumped him. Maybe he'd seen the tattoo that way."

"No. No, Beena. You had to see them together, Ben and Anita, it's a rare thing I know, but they were actually in love. They could shut out a football crowd and only see each other. There were no lovers on either side. I'd stake my life on it."

"Who tattooed her?"

"A place off the estate, run by a lesbian couple. She'd made a point of telling him that, so he didn't have to picture any man getting that close up."

"Did you see the man back then after this... confession?"

"Like I say, he didn't confess exactly, but I knew he was the one. I was waiting for him to straight out admit it when things went quiet. I went round to confront him, but the box was empty. I asked around but didn't find anything out. I didn't tell Ben, of course. What was the point? I never saw the man, or heard his voice again, till today. Lin saw him on his way out. She knows him."

Beena folded her arms. "And?"

"His name's Terrence Bullimore." Fionn was shaking, enraged. "And I know where he lives."

"I'm going to have to ask you to stay away from him, Fionn. You understand? We both know what you're like. You're no good to your flock banged up for assault. You did the right thing in telling me."

"What'll you do?"

"I need to think. I'll get the file out, certainly, have a look. See if there's anything that ties Bullimore in, see if we've anything else on him. There have been others. Unsolved cases. But this is a difficult one."

"I'll testify."

"Even so, in the absence of an out-and-out confession— and from what you've described of him so far, that's not likely—we're scuppered; the only first-hand witness, the victim, is dead."

PART FOUR

A Beginning

CHAPTER THIRTY-SIX

Evidence presented to the High Sheriff of Yorkshire: translated extracts from the personal journals of the monk, Hexter, also referred to as "Zwerg"; him found to be in hiding at The Church of Saint Agnes on the moor.

In times gone by, would I not have further curved my backbone for the inflated estimation of mankind? No more. The diffidence of youth absurdly diverted my thinking. Throughout my sojourns in France, did I master the arts of trickery as practiced by the folk sorcerers and spell-makers of the southern regions. And here, on my arrival and in the solitude of the monastery at York, I quietly perfected my art. Mere pleasantries of magic—that I might charm those hearts I so repelled on sight. In the market square did I perform such conjuries for those boorish numps: a dainty bloom plucked from a maiden's hair, a mouse from the pocket of a child, a coin from behind a fellow's ear. On my travels, such fellows later found themselves lighter of the same, for I did inwardly curse the greedy then as I do now. But my hand was slight and the visions lifted the spirits of my audience. How I craved their mute-faced adorations.

On notice of these activities, my master at York expressed the strongest disapproval, but nevertheless I had grown tired of such frivolities. Yet in time, when the townsfolk rose against us all, so that we were bound to flee, it had come to suit their purpose to dredge the past and so dub me "Warlock". My bitterness was such that I would have their fickle eyes. With my brothers, did I hurry myself from the presence of those simpletons and on to the aid of those rebelling at Richmond, and though the fight was fierce, it did not weary me like some. Indeed was I heartened by it. It is not the fight that afears me; not the swords of men, but the heart of humankind itself, that which barely palpates in sight of the persecution of innocent souls; that heart whose vast number succumbs easily to the wiles of the rich and empowered, those who would rape the land of common peoples, claiming its flower for their own.

*

Here now do I rest at Saint Agnes, a building of ancient invention, too frail to outlast the weather on this bleak moor; already her walls crumble. Two others accompanied me, one of them Matthew, pierced through the gut, whose health now spirals each day towards God's mercy. Our sanctuary is with a reverend, namely Mark, who has held this church through many troubles. The king's good intentions towards our treasured brother Robert Aske were, as many suspected, a ruse. Likewise, promises made to those awaiting safe return to their homelands—those urged to come forward in order to speak of progress, of peace—amounted to a goblet of water in the seas.

Word of late has it that the priory at Esholt, in the absence of any profitable annuity, is to be sacked. We hear tell of others from far and wide scrambling for refuge. Our sustenance is low and local sympathies are on the wane. Brother Mark prays and keeps good heart, but I see the mettle of these people, that which lurks behind the eyes, what treachery infects the heart of them; that they would see us rot for a suckle on the teet that is the approval of him in the king's favor.

*

What man could be so accursed of God and live? So repugnant of form as to spirit the night-terrors into the chambers of babes, to be shunned by the lowest emaciated dog of a street-beggar? What onlooker with his sight fully intact would gaze upon this squat, deformed stature, this face that is surely Satan's own jest, but while suppressing a sardonic smile? What woman would feel aught than at best a female's modest charity?

Am I not sufficiently blighted, without God should confront this, the countenance of his most lowly toad, with that of an angel? One whose serenity and sheer perfection would rival the star encrusted winter skies; who now, for my sins, has constant presence here at Saint Agnes' chapel. Since her arrival, and that of one other from Esholt, I have observed this sister Appolyn in her dealings, that though slight with hunger she would surrender her last crust of bread to another's stomach, even though it be fuller than her own. A graceful spirit so pure and chaste as to damn the thoughts of men. And yet while my heart would not reach her soul but with infinite blessings, my evil mind ravages and consumes the image of her; I would own every part of her being, would lock her away from the unworthy eyes of men. There are no vows of silence here—such things are futility—and yet she seldom speaks, her quiet thoughts still flying heavenward to a God who has evidently abandoned this, our earthly plight. Of her few chosen words, those to me are seldom in aught but mocking: "Why so nimble in your step, my brother?" she whispers, though having the mercy not to turn, to condemn me with a look, as much she would be entitled, when once again I fail in concealing my presence about her. In her few adult years, no doubt she has seen the love of men fall across her path many times. She does not invite it. And what kind of jester would I be to invest hope in such a fantastic thing? Since her ascendance from the priory I fail to sleep, and do supplicate myself in heartfelt prayer through each long hour of night; even bleed the veins of my wrists for riddance of this venom. And still, each morning the fever runs more rampant in me, so that I fear increasingly for my sanity.

*

Since the execution of Aske at York, none are safe. Henry has eyes everywhere—eyes that bore through walls and into souls, planting every imagined evil in passing. Those whose number harked in glory of The Pilgrimage now whisper, isolated, broken, huddled in cellars. Undoubtedly, this, our refuge, will fall, as have so many. I regret that it is my presence here that invites the fury of the King's followers. My name is known to them and my blood, of an alien nation, is, as such, deemed of little worth. Yet, in spite of my pleas, none of this number here will surrender to secular life; that is sworn; and thus one outcome is assured, for all. God forgive me, but it would pain me no more than has this accursed life to die. But then what of sister Appolyn? To see her innocence imposed upon by but one malicious hand would condemn my soul to an eternity of tormented unrest.

Prayer is but dust with no breeze to lift it. It is with this pen I do swear to protect her I adore from the onslaught of the aggressors, with my life. Yet even as I sit and write this, my oath to her, the words glare back at me in derision. For truly, it is my own presence about her I must reckon with. This war in me is fiercer than those that rage across the battlefields of hell. I fear that before I flee this wretched world for the pit of Hades, I will pay the devil for a taste of my angel.

Testimony of Thomas John Alcott, Personal servant to Samuel Liddle, Thirtieth July 1537

Following the hanging of Robert Aske at York some days past, a hue and cry was sounded by order of the high sheriff of Yorkshire, declaring that, at the king's behest, "a good number" from every village and town that hath partaken in the rebellion should be "rounded up and publicly hung, drawn and quartered" for crimes of treason. A riotous mood infected the region in the wake of these declarations, and a band of freemen—obliged to take up arms under instruction of two long-standing watchmen: namely the landowner, Coxteth, who by then had forcibly reclaimed monastic lands purchased in defiance of the rebels, and one other, namely my master Liddle, a farmer of sound wealth and note, also founder of the tannery—went out in pursuit with intent to uncover three men known to have participated in a muster at Richmond; chiefly the monk Hexter, he of Germanic strain, who stands accused also of acts of heresy and witchcraft and of inciting local hostilities. Our instruction was that those collaborating to conceal this monk were to be forcibly arrested and taken for trial and sentencing at the leisure of the mayor, aldermen and sheriff of the city.

Seventy strong, we left the city afore sunset and presently stormed the outlying church of Saint Agnes, situated on the westerly moor, where it was rumored him-thus named, and others in the region, who locally had bolstered up the rebellion so-called "The Pilgrimage", lay in hiding. A number among the mob, though generally unruly, were in morbid fear of this monk, Hexter; him Luther's followers had formerly dubbed "Zwerg" or goblin, on account of some peculiarity of form, for this one was known to readily employ extreme violence in the face of conflict. Local dwellers added to the gathering hysteria with claims that this monk had performed illicit dark rites in nearby caves, that evidence of unholy offerings had been unturned, that he was indeed a sorcerer; a warlock, dedicated to the Devil himself.

One man of Hexter's brotherhood was found to be dead outside the church, covered, but not decently buried. Our men sealed off the cellars while those above ground were apprehended. Only five souls, two nuns among them, were found to remain within the immediate walls of the church, all of them close to starvation. None struggled against their captors and were hastily bound at the wrists, but as feared, the one named Zwerg was absent. When the cellars were accessed, a passage leading out to the moor was uncovered. Disorder swiftly ensued.

Some of Coxteth's number, having previously encountered this fellow in a skirmish, grew frantic, charging raucously about the area, waving weaponry, upsiding every stone that might conceal the fugitive. Many among my master Liddle's company followed suit and all fanned out chaotically. In the confusion that followed, several stragglers of both parties were soon found mortally injured, brutally hacked about the neck, laid dead or dying from blood loss. None around had seen an assailant in their midst, though in the days that followed, some men confessed with reluctance to having been bewildered by an apparition. Each spoke of it the same—in that they had, at intervals, caught sight of a dog lurking in the darkness, which, while darting about in a frenzy, appeared to have no head, only a blooded stump where the head had once sat; and yet before their eyes the thing stayed up and pacing, seeming to track their every movement. Dwellers of the village later gave word that a similar dog in breed and color—the hunting hound of a local farmer—was indeed found decapitated the following day.

The assaulted members of our troupe were terribly mutilated, the most horrific aspect of the corpses being in their expressions. By most likely the blow of an axe, hideously gaping smiles had been hacked into the faces of the men, as though their killer wished to send them out in fits of merriment.

As a sudden high tide washes in, so a black fear enveloped the crowd. Our numbers regrouped and banded together, observing each flank of our mass. Cries of vengeance rang out. When next I looked, I saw with dismay that the five Catholics apprehended from inside Saint Agnes' chapel were hanging, still alive, by the neck, from a young oak in the church grounds. I had wanted no part of such a deed, only to apprehend these few, and yet it was done, and speedily. Our elected leaders took pride as the instigators of this, and showed no mercy. For the younger of the two nuns—one close in age to my own daughter just recently wed—

death approached at a cruel pace. For the sake of her youth and frail beauty, many of us had pitied her greatly from the onset of the siege. I begged now that those few still intent on this lawless act must let her down. At least three of these souls were no party to murder. They were innocent. Liddle, my master, struck me for my outcry, proclaiming, "Those who oppose the king's wishes shall surely join these traitors in the grip of the noose." I did fear for my safety, having not seen my master, usually a studious and quiet man, of such a brutally determined mind, yet I protested still; that the weight of the maid was nothing but to bring about her death in extreme suffering. It is my testimony that I did then rush forward through the mob, striking blows where needs be, and unable to reverse her fate, did sling my weight on the ankles of the maid, not allowing my own feet to brush the ground beneath.

I did not watch it. They say her face darkened and she passed forthwith.

Further testimony of Thomas John Alcott, Fifteenth August 1537

I regret to say, that since that night previously accounted for and these further events I am bound to describe, I shall swear not that I am sound-of-mind, only that I will speak the truth as I believe it to be.

Twelve men dead in the space of an hour, brutally slain. A massacre such as I have never witnessed the like. Then two more butchered before first light, each in the same way. How could it be that one man alone could wreak such havoc? As though God himself, or the Devil more like, had endowed this goblin with the force and speed of storm-winds. It was agreed by all, that no man would leave the moor until this Zwerg was found and brought to justice. That first day, however, we kept close proximity, with no attempt to widen our search until reinforcements could be mustered. While we toiled in the heat to bury our own, Coxteth, a wild eyed man—prone himself, in my view, to acts of lunacy—decreed that the bodies of the Catholics would remain hanging, to peel in the sun like fetid fruit if needs be; that such an outrage would surely draw out that last, most wanted, of their number.

In this matter, he was proved correct.

The ensuing search was intense. Many men, good Lutherans some, came from as far afield as Keighley by the second night. Their number soon amounted to two hundred strong. Considering the village could accommodate very few and with the nights mild, most camped out on the moor, with a watch set up in each direction facing outward. All were vigilant. Yet from under our noses, he took her. Defying our very eyes, he did creep in and cut her down; at dawn the first day of August did we not wake to find the body count at the oak to be four. Overnight the corpse of the young nun had been spirited away. The crows were by then hard at work with those unfortunates left to their appetites.

The search resumed in earnest and before noon, a small party of us were alerted by an elder woman of the village to a spot on the moor where she had seen glimmers of a fire burning in the night. Those of us present ventured forth, armed with cleavers; one man of Coxteth's employ carried a pistol. In the distance, we spied a formation of rocks. The exact direction we followed at the old woman's instruction led us to the openings of a cluster of caves.

We approached stealthily. It was myself and one other, the young tanner named Fuller—whose testimony is also written—who took a certain entranceway and eventually happened upon the sight that will burden me until death, and perhaps beyond.

As we ventured deeper into the cavern, the space before us opened out and light was apparent all around but the like of which I have never seen before: not bright as daylight or kindly as candlelight, but rather a dull and green hue, such as one would expect a stink to emanate from. The aroma that dominated the enclosure, however, was that of a kindling fire and the pleasantness of meat in the roasting. From somewhere ahead came sounds of chanting; how many voices met our ears we could not say atween us, but that one was evident above all: a harsh croak we took to be that of the monk. Sworn to see this through, our feet shifted us forward until we could move no more.

The chanting had ceased, though I cannot say when. He whom we sought stirred not on account of our presence. It is my belief that he even wished to be found, having committed the final deed he had set out to execute. In a clearing of flattened earth sat the monk, Hexter the Zwerg, hooded, cross-legged, his form horribly at odds with humanity; a rough-hewn boulder in sack-cloth. So gently did he rock to-and-fro over that small fire—while gorging veraciously—that one might have thought it a babe he cradled. But it was no living thing he embraced. In an instant, the smell that had seemed so enticing filled us with sickening revulsion. For between the monk and where we stood there lay spread the body of the nun, stripped of her gowns, her silver hair fanned out, her naked feet pointing to the fire, toward the monk, her arms extended like those of the crucified deity, her face somehow young, as if life had not fled her but within the hour. Her head, hands, and feet marked the extremities of a circle drawn around her in blood, undoubtedly her own. Within the circle were etched in blood, also in charcoal, what I know from learned books to be demonic symbols—my own father being a seeker of witches and student of their dark practices: one etching, an Ankh, symbolizing mythical eternal life and rebirth, was clearly scribed, as was the All-seeing eye of a pyramid, representing spiritual sight, inner vision, and higher knowledge. Other signs of alchemy were drawn, also a bat, and in each section, a fallen angel, such as are requested by men rather than sent forth by God, whose character is marked by the blackened wing. In each hand of the nun was placed a slaughtered beast, one a falcon, the other a snake of the field; each dealt with in the same manner as the maid: their chests hacked open, their hearts gouged out; the same organs which— barely cooked in the timid flame—now filled the champing mouth of that monster before us; the bristles of his chin hung with bloody tendrils of flesh.

I will state here that the Zwerg sat alone, that the end to the cave was visible behind his position and no other way in or out was feasible, other than that which we had entered through, so I can offer no explanation as to the voices that chanted in unison with Hexter, but that our ears witnessed a riot of them.

As we made to bring an end to this atrocity, the murky light we had observed on our approach concentrated thickly about our persons. My companion clutched at rocks, then he let out a sound, I thought at first, of extreme shock as his legs began to fail. But when I reached to secure him I saw that the flesh about the back of his neck was indented, as if clasped by fingers of an invisible hand, one that urged him down and forward to his knees. Spittle hung from his gaping mouth. I myself then felt something that I do not wish to speak of at length, except to state that it was not human and did press at me also, even beneath my lower garments, most intimately, doubtless with an aim to weaken my purpose. This, however, only served to hasten me. I shouted my alert to others searching close by. My cries were strained, but those who had set out in our company were by chance close at hand and came swiftly.

Fuller and I regained our strength and resolve and thus our group advanced, to no obvious perturbance, I have to say, on the part of that hideous goblin. The axe he had wielded for certain at Coxteth and Liddle's men, and which had rent apart the corpse of the maid, sat idly by him. No attempt was made to raise the weapon in his defense to avoid arrest. He only laughed—a hollow rasp from the gut—the vilest sound I ever heard uttered, as we dragged him into daylight, still swallowing down the last remnants of his lurid feast.

Burning the Zwerg could not be postponed. Statements would be put to the sheriff. Even those of us who regretted the former act of our masters bore no objection to this. The body of the nun must burn also, it was deemed, for who could know the outcome of such a demonic ritual as her body had been subjected to. No man present could fail to observe the absence of rigor in her limbs, the fresh, comely appearance of her flesh, even to desire it. For decency's sake, we swathed her corpse in cloth before securing it to the stake the monk was now heavily bound to, for despite his strange stature no man doubted his might.

As the torch bearers went forward, Coxteth casually mounted the pyre, dehooding the Zwerg so all could view the extent of his curse. I must say Coxteth took great pleasure in this.

"See here the devil's own," he announced, before stepping down to safer ground. "And question not our actions this day."

The crowd shrunk back at the Zwerg's grotesqueness: the brittle nest of hair, the dark, heavy brows that capped such deep-set eyes as only fury dwelt in. Each feature seemed dragged out of proportion: the nose bulbous, the cheeks pocked and swollen as rancid apples, the bloated lips curling back to reveal teeth rotted to the core. Had I not witnessed the scene in the cave first hand, compassion may have compelled me to pray for such a blighted individual. But prayers for a soul so surely doomed, without hope of redemption, could only bring offence to God.

Coxteth and Liddle stood forward of their troupes as the flames took hold, each throwing into the fire the monk's tokens: from Coxteth the falcon, from Liddle the snake. The monk's eyes widened as his feet began to burn. He gripped the hands of the dead maid strapped close by his.

"It is our good fortune," Coxteth boasted with cheer as the rising flames faltered. "That a fair wind blows this day." He now focused his cruel gaze on the agonized, squealing face of the monk. "That we may see this abomination of Satan burn slowly."

"And to such a merry dance," my master Liddle offered, more mirthful than I had never seen the like, watching the flames sear the legs of that strange being struggling against the ropes that held him fast. It struck me then, as at the hanging of the Catholics, how little I knew my master, a man who had impressed me by knowledge and charm. But though his countenance might appear one of gentle handsomeness, beneath this guise there clearly dwelt an appetite for brutality.

"Dance, demon, dance!" he goaded, and, to my horror, mimicked the

howling of that man half charred yet half alive before us. Some in the crowd laughed along; others flinched, as I.

For my part, I had never witnessed a burning, nor would I wish to again. I covered my nose to the stench, and would have covered my ears to those dreadful screams, had they not suddenly, abruptly ceased. And, in the face of God and all there present as his witnesses, did those cries not turn to shrill cackles of laughter. Reality, as we knew it, had shifted in its boundaries; the scene we were next to observe would outrival the absurdity of the chanting and the strange mist I had come upon in the cave. The whole position of the monk relaxed, as if those flames eating his very being merely caressed him with tenderness. And, while the fire advanced, bubbling and popping his flesh to the neck, Hexter swung his cold gaze about the crowd, seeming, impossibly, to settle on each man in turn, to meet each fearful eye and scorn it. Equally, his proclamation penetrated each and every ear, a message delivered to us in faultless English—though it be known he spoke little outside his own Germanic tongue.

"Die in pain, ye who jeer, ye who hath trampled the innocent under hoof aside the bad. All the forces of hell shall unleash on you. Die in a sea of agonies! Your offspring also shall see plague, shall witness your number fall to it—shall perish in the wake of its ravening hunger."

The smile had fled my master's face; no pleasure would return to it that day or I suspect ever after. Something was occurring, an illusion perhaps—as with the specter of the headless hound—in that, as the body of the maid behind him slumped and withered in the flame, the face of the Zwerg did somehow soften and become youthful, as if he were absorbing her beauty as his own flesh. Then the eyes of it fell fixed upon Coxteth and Liddle who stood frozen in their positions, conspicuously forward of the crowd.

"Cursed be yours, this day and here on in." This was delivered forth as a duet: his own voice and what one could only take to be that of a maid. "Who will survive only to fester in shadows awaiting vengeance!

Your pitiful lines shall dribble forth from the single most evil thoughts harbored in your heads." To Coxteth, he added, "Ye, oh instigator of the weak! Whose offspring shall scurry as the termite, hiding neath stones, afeared even at the light of day; who will bore his sordidness into ever-smaller holes. Cursed be yours! And thine." This to Liddle, who outwardly flinched, "Fated by you to squirm belly-down as the rat of effluent streams, to exist among men, though no man is he; doomed to lap his tongue in the very pit of humanity, to gorge his appetites on the eyelids of sleeping babes—from here on in will yours degenerate into its filth, until your tormentors return with a vengeance and your piteous seed be obliterated! And thus, with a wailing of agonies, will ye both know your end!"

With that final word, the wind dropped, and as if hell itself had opened up its gate in answer, a gust of flame burst upward from beneath the stake, fiercely enveloping all above. The monk made not another sound, only gripped tight the hands of the young woman bound to him in death, whose beauty I had watched disintegrate and reappear in his own features. Many averted their eyes, afraid that Satan himself might rise to bathe in the inferno. Those who could not resist, as I, will likewise swear, that as we continued to observe the form melting amidst the raging flame, it did appear to transform, to sprout huge wings, then the next moment, to adopt the leanness and thrashing manner of a snake. That which had begun its destruction as two human beings and two beasts was now, by our foolish making, one shifting entity.

*

Those brave enough, kept the fire constant for two days and two nights, stoking the cinders with dry kindling until nothing remained save the dust of their bones. Its unholy ashes, to the last fleck, we sealed tight into an urn, then similarly a casket retrieved from within the church, interring all deep within the earth neath the shadow of the oak tree, now mercifully unburdened of the corpses that had hung there. Following the interring of the casket, four nominated men remained stationed at the spot, alert, in turn, for a further four days, lest, we feared, something might break loose from the soil, so dreadful was the beast we'd witnessed born.

The elected four reported no such occurrence, only having experienced extreme night terrors; each related a vision of his own imminent death. No doubt induced by the sleeplessness that even those of us far away from that place experienced at length.

Personal writings of Thomas John Alcott, prior to his death late September 1537

Following my testimony, I am returned home to my wife and four children, but in these past weeks, have found no solace in their company and less yet in mine own.

Word has it that a band of souls, entire families, infants and all, came peaceably and in unison to the local sheriff from the priory village of those nuns put to death at the behest, not of the king, but of those two previously named watchmen, whose names I will scribe no more, one of them a master I will serve no more, both of whom now stand pardoned. This party of villagers I make mention of, unaware of the futility of their endeavors, came to plea in earnest, for clemency on behalf of the two nuns, in particular the younger nun whom they knew as Appolyn, a girl of Scandinavian descent, who had dwelt among them and shown them unquestioning charity, assisting their every ill, not least, demonstrating boundless love for every child in her midst. Their cries of despair at her cruel execution were heard in the farthest streets of the township.

When the fire on the moor had died, the ashes of the dead interred, and the mood at Saint Agnes' church steadied, those two watchmen, despite all and still bent on violence, did have me flogged for my insubordination at the hanging of the Catholics.

What sleep the good Lord now affords me is blighted by haunting. I cannot say nightmares, for her whose spirit comes to plague me is too vivid to be founded in my imaginings alone. I never did hear the voice of the maid, her condemned at the oak, but in that unholy duet with Hexter from the flames, and yet I know it to be her who doth supplicate me constantly, calling each nightfall, pleading aid which I must not be tempted to minister, for to do so I would be damned. And to do so I must return there. And I wouldst rather die than be summoned back to that place.

CHAPTER THIRTY-SEVEN

The Sheer-Craft Kitchen warehouse staff knocked off mid-afternoon Fridays—if the boss wasn't around, that was. The boss liked to keep them chatting. If they got bored of the golf-talk, started sneaking off, he'd quickly revert to football, so they'd be helpless to resist. Today though, he'd been picked up early and taken out by his missus to some health club she'd signed them both up for as a birthday surprise. He'd be bubbling the cheese off his bollocks in a nice Jacuzzi right about now. Shaun Dodds, a.k.a. Doodler, the forklift truck driver, had a few loads left to shift so he ended up the last to leave. He didn't mind. It was good downtime to think, and recently his mind had turned to romance. Even after the loads were done, he utilized some packing card to doodle a unicorn jumping a love-heart. A present. He locked up about quarter to three and posted the spare keys back through the door as always.

Doodler hesitated before getting into his Micra. Biting his lip in a bit of a quandary, he took out his cell phone and speed-dialed Tracey. As he did, it occurred to him it was probably a bit soon to be putting her on speed-dial and he wondered if, when she answered, there'd be any way of her telling he'd committed to that. It was her voicemail he got. "Shit," he muttered, then. "Er, hi, Trace, it's me, Shaun Dodds—Doodler. Er, just to check we're on for tonight— still okay… for that? And, er, give us a ring back. My number's…aw, you have it, don't you? So…see you tonight then, babe. Bye." He pressed end-call and reeled off a barrage of "*shit shit shits*" to himself. He hated leaving messages on the spot like that. He was crap at it—had probably given her second thoughts she wasn't having up till that. He'd felt dead-good ten minutes ago, like he was on a promise for tonight. All the signs 'd been pointing in that direction. On the way home from the pub, passing through the Granger-Belt Industrial Estate last Wednesday night, she'd held his cock while he took a piss. That was always a good sign. It'd taken some talking her into, mind—Tracey was a good lass—but she copped a hold of it in the end. He'd been too mortal to get a boner anyway, and was so chuffed at seeing her hand on him that he'd guided the spray to slash her name through the grime of the New-Pin Cleaning Co's security shutters. There'd not been enough bottled up for the "ey" on the end of Tracey, so he'd just done an "i" instead. But, to his credit, he did manage to dot it.

Doodler was still deep in Tracey-world, half a leg into his car when an elbow came down full-force between his shoulder blades. The wind knocked out of him and he fell back to land arse first on the gritty tarmac. Next, a fist-blow to one ear, with the added impact of the other ear ricocheting off the car; the combo almost deafened him, then he was dragged up to his feet and pressed by the scruff of the neck against the rear car-door.

Glaring up close was Rambo Bullimore, his head red as a

bell-end on a whorehouse spree.

"What the fuck? Get off me, ye mad bastard," Doodler protested.

"Think yer fuckin' funny, don't you, kiddo? You and yer nasty little spray-can effigies everywhere anyone looks," Bullimore hissed.

Doodler's response was all but choked off by the force of the grip on his neck. "What you fuckin' on about now?" His eyes began to water under the pressure.

"That offensive graffiti on the Loadin' bay wall. You mucky lot, jokin' about it in front of Jean an' all, when you know how she worships Her Majesty."

Bullimore's old silver Merc was sitting there round the side of reception, tucked in. Why hadn't Doodler noticed that when he came out? This latest fracas had been building for a while.

"It weren't me got Jean to come down, you fuckin' nutter," Doodler coughed out. "That were Adams's idea of a joke. Go get *him*, why don't you?"

"Yeah." Bullimore shifted positions, pressing a forearm against the kid's neck, slapping his forehead with the freed hand. "But it was you, you smart little twat, as drew it on there, wasn't it? Eh? It's always you, you worthless little runt. Couldn't hack it at art college so you have to go bugging the rest of us with yer dirty little daubings."

"It's not that dirty. The boss has muckier pictures up in his office. You do."

"Wills givin' it to Kate doggy style? Not dirty? Wi' them big smilin' toothy grins you think's funny an' all. It's disgustin', and disrespectful—especially comin' from the likes of a worthless little punk like you."

That "punk" jibe would normally have creased Doodler

up—Bullimore just so fancied himself as Dirty Harry or Rambo or Mr. T or any of those macho fucks—but right now he was all out of laughs. He pushed out full force, loosening the old man's grip, his own face blazing.

"Aye, I am little aren't I?" he yelled. "That's why I'm here and not Adams, isn't it, hard-man? You know what Adams reckons? He says you need that massive motor to make up for your mingy little nob."

"That right, is it?" Bullimore's breathing took on an ominous weight. With seemingly little effort, he forced Doodler back against the car, holding him steady while he fumbled with his own flies. "Well, let's have a look, shall we? Let's have a look see what's what."

Doodler went limp, his downcast eyes wide, the color draining from his face. "No, don't," he pleaded. "I didn't mean it, mate. Please stop."

Bullimore gave a snide little laugh. "Oh, relax. *Relax*, silly little boy." He backed away, hands up, shaking his head. "Do you really think if I were queer I'd be getting me knobbler out for some spotty oik like you? Nah. I think not." He ruffled the lad's hair. "Numpty." Then walked off toward his car, smiling back at intervals, but mainly to himself, as if the two of them 'd just shared a joke.

Doodler stood rubbing his neck. "Fuckin' nutter," he mumbled again. Then louder, "It's been proper shite since you came 'ere. Why don't you fuck off back to B&Q? Or better still, back to Paddy-land wi' yer missus. Fuckin' nutter."

Seconds later Terrence Bullimore's Mercedes-Benz, Class 220 E Saloon, screeched past him, the horn blaring out Dixieland: *Papa-da-da-papa papa da-da-da!* Rambo Bullimore gave Doodles a comradely salute as he passed. That was the sort of thing he did all the time.

CHAPTER THIRTY-EIGHT

Terrence Bullimore took the scenic route home. His mother was visiting for the day, keeping Cloda busy, for once. He was in no rush to join the tumult of the witches' coven; plus, he was getting a nice buzz from the altercation with young Shaun Dodds; that'd been long overdue. A steady drive would be just the ticket now, let off the last of the steam before teatime. So from the warehouse, Terrence drove up City Road and linked onto the moors at Toffs' Hill past the golf course. Once over the top, he could veer back toward town then take a left-hand down into the Butcher's Arms car park. A good few hours might pass before he'd have to tolerate two sets of hurt, accusing looks.

With heavy summer rains coming and going and the recent muggy heat, the roads were still on the slippery side. He'd had his tires changed as always before winter 'd kicked in, and had checked the treads on a monthly basis since. Any fool whose standards didn't meet up had better just watch out for him coming.

Between bouts of drizzle, the sun broke through, bouncing off the wet roads in dazzling shafts. As the altitude escalated, strong winds rattled the car. He clicked on the sidelights, as was the law in such changeable conditions. As he eased up to the T-junction to turn left onto the upper moor, a grubby looking yellow Mini idled past with one sidelight out. Despite the weather, the driver's side window was right down with hair billowing out all over the place. A cocky little blonde. No doubt with her trance music on full blast, irritating the shit out of everyone she passed. Another car was approaching after the Mini but Bullimore slipped out between the two, causing the oncoming car to skid a tad. Its driver beeped the horn and flashed in protest but then slowed off, leaving ample distance. Pussy.

The Mini slowed from fifty down to around forty as Terrence roared up to the back end of her, edging in so close that from behind it might appear as though the Merc were being towed along by the tiny car. A filthy car, Terrence observed with some irritation. Weather aside, it probably hadn't seen a carwash in a year. Her back window wiper was only dragging the dirt around. Frustratingly, this meant Terrence couldn't get a decent look at the face through her internal mirror; just a rosy blur in amongst the flying hair. He made a bet with himself that she was pretty, though. Not too cool with it, mind, her head darting about comically, like they do when they get worried—silly bitch. He only wanted a peek at her. Not as if there was time for much else, unless she was offering.

A pale, slender arm extended from her window, waving him past while she slowed down further still. Terrence stayed put; passing on by wasn't the plan. Then she made a bad move—she went and touched the brakes. That flash of red light had Terrence blasting the horn in a pleasant little fury. It was a good horn, a veritable bull-call. Next, his own window was down in the hope that she'd catch the bellowed-out pearl of wisdom.

"Stay at home if you've nowhere to get to, you daft bint!"

It was then he twigged what the root of her panic was. Inside the smeared rear windscreen wavered one of those *Baby-on-Board* signs. Glaring intently through the grime he could make out a chubby little shape wriggling about in one of those carriers that goes backwards in the passenger seat to face mum, although he was pretty sure, nowadays, they were supposed to be in the back. So she liked breaking the rules, eh? Terrence felt a rush of something extremely unpleasant. If he could have backed off at that point he would have, and felt better for it—something he would recognize later when he looked her in the face—but the compulsion to carry on was by then unstoppable. The fact was if you were willing to take them, babies could prove the perfect hostage. This trumped-up little missy could either quit pissing about and speed up to a satisfactory pace or pull in properly and let him go past or, last choice, get good and carved up. If her and baby ended up stuck in a ditch, well so be it. It'd present the perfect opportunity for her to get the good talking to she deserved.

She slammed her brakes on.

Terrence growled, genuinely astounded, just managing to swerve out and around her driver's side back end. "You've a bloody baby in there, you nutter!" he yelled, almost alongside her window. He could see the road ahead was clear, right up to a right bend in the far distance. But then, if the cunt didn't have the audacity to speed up again.

"What the hell? You mad cow!"

The car behind had backed right off, staying well out of it.

Silver blonde hair lashed the Mini's rooftop as she pulled a fast-forward. So she wanted a race, eh? Okeydokey. Terrence hit the button to the passenger side window, ready to bless her with a few choice words of wisdom before applying his superior acceleration to get in front of her; once past, he'd slam *his* brakes full on. Fair's fair. The young woman stiffened as Terrence drew alongside, her sights trained ahead in the standard lame effort to ignore him, her unruly hair obscuring the features he was now intent on getting a look at. He glanced briefly ahead—still clear—then leaned her way. "Hey—you, love—oy! Don't you think you should learn to fuckin' drive—" The remainder of the slur stuck in his throat like unchewed cake. Something in the motor wasn't right. For a start, the thing that wriggled and thrashed over in the baby carrier was not a baby at all. No human baby at any rate. Unless some hallucinogenic dope had been slipped into Terrence's lunchtime cupper, the thing he was looking at, all wrapped up in newspaper and writhing against the strap that secured it, was a small pig.

"What fucking weird shit…?" Terrence began as their speeds synchronized, but again ran dry, as in response the Mini's driver was turning her head to deliver the face he'd been so longing to see. His first idea was that she was wearing one of those fencing masks, the meshed type that covers the entire face, so that was why, amid the blown blonde locks, her face was a seamless, featureless oval. Continued scrutiny, however, told him that what he was looking at wasn't anything synthetic; it was solid, pulsating, living flesh. And as he remained transfixed, the fleshy oval tilted back, stretching open. A fist-sized black chasm where a mouth should have been, gaped open and let out a hybrid shriek: somewhere between a fox on-heat and an air-raid siren.

The pig in the baby-seat wriggled frantically. But by then

another sound was blasting out at Terrence, this time from ahead. A horn.

Bright light blinded him as he whipped his gaze away from the circus inside the Mini to the imminent horror ahead. A truck, full-beam flashing, was braking out of the bend—only yards away. No amount of superior brake-power on the Merc's part could prevent a collision. Bullimore's car was hit face-on then plowed backwards in a flurry of sparks, toward a now stationery line of proceeding cars, the occupants of which were out and hurdling fences, away from the oncoming carnage. Terrence, his legs now in bits, was still alive and screaming fit to birth a pig himself when the truck took a leap and crunched him under-wheel. Within a few short seconds he was granted something close to his dearest wish—that he should come back as a Ferrari—by being welded as one into the car he'd considered to be the next best thing.

CHAPTER THIRTY-NINE

"So Thomas Alcott was the first recorded suicide—the good man you spoke of?"

"Who is this speaking?"

"Come on, Carl."

"Young Father Malloy, I'm guessing. Nice to hear from you."

"The long arm of the law couldn't hold you indefinitely, then? I feel so much more streetwise for hanging out with you, Carl. Can I ask what they're after you for?"

"Oh, everybody wants a piece of me, Fionn. So you read the documentation I gave you?"

"More than once. Where'd you get all this information?"

"Oh, I've loads of it, son. Piles of stuff between then and now on top of what you've read. I suppose I'm in the process of honing it down to something people can get to grips with. But to answer your first question: yes, Thomas was the first death I'd call consequential, down to the ritual that took place. The headstone would have been too weather-worn to be discernible, but Thomas Alcott's would have been one of the stones moved from the graveyard up yonder; erected back when it was the church of Saint Agnes."

"How long did it take him to go, once the nightmares started?"

"A matter of weeks. He was already troubled, clearly, from the events he'd witnessed. The others, those recorded by the sheriff as having been at Saint Agnes, their names have been wiped out, exactly as foretold by Hexter. There was plague. Whole families died out. Apart, that is, from those of the ringleaders, Coxteth and Liddle."

"And?"

"One I know of. The other…I'm still tracking down. I'll let you know."

"Maybe we should let *them* know."

"Let them know what? What would I tell them exactly? 'Hey, fellas, check out the old family tree; note how you're the last flimsy little twig on it, oh, and, according to prophesy, your days in the sun are numbered.' Believe you me, Fionn, if you knew Coxteth's heir, and I do have the misfortune to 've had dealings with him, you wouldn't bother anyway. That aspect of the prophesy's been met to the extreme. This man, Coxer, is a parasitic maggot, alright."

"Him. I do know of him. His house is the big white one across the moor."

"The money side of town…. Are you still there, Fionn?"

"Carl. I've done something terrible. I've been a fool."

"Really? Are you ringing to confess to me? This is all a bit confusing."

"Please, listen."

"Okay, I will. But shall I tell you something first, Father? Earlier the same day Ben Hunter went missing, I'd made an appointment to see the chaplain at the prison, really to see what I could find out about your friend, Hunter. After the massacre on Rokerville, I had a strong sense of something kicking off, something beyond the ordinary. I never got past security, but I did see you go in. You're quite a striking young man, Fionn. Not a face easily forgotten. I know it was you who helped Hunter, somehow. Don't you think, after all these years of grilling folk I can't spot a man with a guilty conscience? You don't have to tell me what it was you did. It doesn't matter now. But if you care to tell me, it won't go any further, I'll give you my word on that."

"Just…tell me again. Saint Agnes, what happened to her body? Her ashes?"

"I checked again, since you asked. They're interred down at Winchester Cathedral."

"I still can't believe she lied. Not out-and-out like that."

"Is she as pretty as they paint her?"

"Not just pretty. She's perfection. You'd go mad, Carl."

"Not me, son. Women aren't my weakness. I'm more your Brad man than your Angelina."

"Maybe so, but it's not a sexual thing, I mean, man or woman, she literally drives you insane. Won't let you be. Won't allow you to dismiss her."

"You're not the only one it's driven crackers. Do you think because you joined the priesthood you're some kind of superhero? The priest you replaced at short notice—what happened to him?"

"I attended the funeral but I didn't know him. I was told it was a heart attack."

"It was. He was forty-three. And not the first one to go that way prematurely at Saint Luke's. Other priests are among the suicides over the years. You stood up pretty well."

"I don't want letting off the hook."

"Whether that's the case or not; whether you played your

part or not, these events were predicted, like the plague that hit those freemen and their families. It had to happen."

"Why now? Why did it push so hard?"

"It would've felt at risk, with the church going, the cemetery; but maybe it was just its time to shine. By my calculations, counting all possible deaths linked to the parish, Callum Heslop made a thousand; the thousandth soul up for grabs."

"Poor Callum. I see him in dreams. Sometimes…in broad daylight. Sometimes all of them, I think."

"What do you get from them? What do you pick up?"

"Their fear; desperation. Appolyn did say it was their time. A thousand souls! But then why take Ben along?"

"You'd have to tell me more about Ben."

"Ben was…*is* one in a million."

"Well, that's why him. A human element was vital, of course. Look, Fionn, there's no point dwelling on what's passed. It's surely better to act on what you know now. You know that whatever it is that powers that thing is corrupt, and dangerous. And you know it'll be back."

"Yes, it will. I've even wanted it. But what can I do?"

"It knows you. You can get close to it. You can destroy it."

"I wouldn't have thought it could be destroyed so easily. Don't you read the papers?"

"It *has* a human element."

"Ben? God, no, Carl. I can't even think of it."

"Somebody has to."

"Do they? Isn't enough of it—isn't the larger part of it good, at least with Ben in the mix? Appolyn was a good human being once. Isn't this Malakh just fighting for the justice we've all been hoping for? Wishing for? Isn't this what the world wants: some fucking…action at last?"

"A real-live avenging angel? Ha, but the part of it that's good, or believes it can be, *that* isn't the part that'll take over, not once it's back on its own patch, on its own mission. The person that performed Satanic rituals to bring the entity into being, this Zwerg—he's the one that'll always hold the power. I bet you, all he's up to now is getting your mate on-side, like he did with *her* once upon a time. Then, believe you me, once he's got what he wants, all hell 'll let loose. The source of its power is evil, Fionn. And, the thing is, if you don't go looking for *it*, it'll likely come looking for *you*. You're connected to it; that makes you a risk. It'll have sensed your regrets already."

"In a way I still wish I didn't have regrets. Those women, girls, who are being murdered on our doorstep. That could be stopped. You might think me crazy. But Ben was my closest friend, and if he's coming back, then part of me is still happy. I can't help that. I love the man. I'd trust him with my life. I want to see him again, Carl, that's God's honest truth."

"You know what I wish, Fionn? That this was one of those video phones, so you could see me shaking my head here. Fionn, seriously, if you've summoned it back, you just take my advice: you get your hands on a loaded gun and you keep it by your bedside, and in a handy pocket by day, every day. Because, I'm telling you now, the thing that's coming back, it isn't your friend any more. It's not Ben Hunter."

CHAPTER FORTY

"I couldn't have stopped. I tried. That poor feller. I saw his face. I could still see his face when he went under. He...burst open. I don't know what the hell his car was doing out there. I mean, it shouldn't have been, not so near a bend, not on a narrow road like that—*Jesus*—but it's not like I can lay blame on the poor bloke now, is it? What good would that do? What happened to him, no bugger deserves that."

Rory Speck was crying again. So far, it had taken over an hour to make this much progress. Detective Inspector Ryan and Detective Gaunt sat by his hospital bed, patiently awaiting the full story. Road Traffic Collision was not their department but Gaunt had heard something; something odd one of the eyewitnesses had told traffic police at the scene. Then the system had coughed up the victim's name, one of mutual interest. So here they were.

"We can come back later, Mr. Speck," Beena Ryan suggested. "If you feel you need a rest."

"No." He wiped his eyes on his pajama sleeve. "No. I'd rather get it out of the way. Just promise me I won't have to tell it ten times over again, after you've done."

"There might be the odd detail RTCD need to check back on," Gaunt confirmed. "But we'll do our best to keep it minimal, Mr. Speck. Tell us about the other car, the one Terrence Bullimore's Mercedes was overtaking. You said it was a yellow Mini?"

"Yeah, bad condition, really battered, filthy, like someone might have gone and dragged it off a tip and jump-started it."

"And the driver? Or any passengers?"

"I thought there was just a woman at first. A skinny thing, blonde, didn't see her all that well, and then there was a baby seat next to her. You know, that sort of a one as turns backwards? Thank Jesus that wasn't in the Merc." Rory's eyes betrayed his mind running that as a film clip he'd no wish to view. "God, no, not that. Fuck, no."

Gaunt waited for the vision to subside. "But then you saw somebody else in there, did you, Mr. Speck? You said there was somebody else, besides mum and baby, in the yellow Mini?"

"Not exactly, no. Not at first glance—and I'm talking glances here. But, like, there must have been a feller in there, maybe laid down in the back asleep or summat, because he was the one who drove off after. I don't get how, though—I would've noticed someone that size in there. Admitting, it was all over so fast. But he was massive, this bloke, a right tree trunk."

"Describe him again."

"Tall, about six-five, musclely like a weight-lifter, sandy blond hair. Didn't really see his face from that distance away, where I seen him, once he was out of the car, like. But it looked weird, his face, kind of…jellified, burnt maybe. I probably wasn't seeing things right by then. Sorry."

"If I can just skip back from there," Beena Ryan said. "So,

your lorry set alight, and you were pulled free? That's when you saw this tall man get out of the vehicle?"

"People from the other cars, yeah, a real good bunch; they came and pulled me out. Then the truck went up. Bang!"

"And the yellow Mini was where by this time?"

"Where it had stopped, about fifty, sixty yards down the road past the accident, just parked there, like whoever was in it was just sat watching. Then—"

"Sorry, where were you at this point?" Beena checked.

"Laid on the verge—my legs, y'know—I was facing the truck, but across the road from it, so I could see past the bonfire—that man at the bottom of it, cooking, Jesus Christ…"

"Take your time, Mr. Speck."

"…but I could see past all that, to the Mini. There was lots of people round me, y'know, trying to help. But when they separated a bit, well then I sees this massive great bloke standing by the old Mini, facing us. Just standing with his head hung, sad, like."

"Carry on," Beena urged.

"It's daft."

"It's okay. Really. Go on."

"Well, I don't know if that little woman who was driving the car at first were stood behind him or what. It doesn't make sense, 'cause she wouldn't be that tall. But it was like—shit…okay—like his own arms were hanging by his sides, right? But then there's a woman's arms as well, sort of wrapped around him, like they were growing out of his armpits."

"Go on, Rory. I'm listening."

He laughed but not happily. "Well, there was one arm resting across his chest and then another was reaching up, sort of cradling that melted face, like your mum would, like your wife would, if you needed a cry."

"I see. Then what?"

"Let me think. Well, the next time I get a clear look, the big feller's getting into the driver's seat—just him, no woman there as I could see anymore. He didn't look back, not once, just climbs in and pulls the car away real quiet, real slow, and drives off, away from the fire, like nothing had happened— just trundled off along the moor."

Mrs. Speck came in and requested that the detectives leave her and her husband alone. He'd had enough for one day. There was the detail of the number plate, that every witness so far had described as dirt smeared and unreadable, but when Beena Ryan turned back she decided that detail could wait. They'd never find the car, she was sure of that, and Rory Speck was all done for now, like his wife had said—the wife who now cradled him in her arms as he quietly wept, one hand gently cradling his face.

CHAPTER FORTY-ONE

"Oy, hold it right there, you two! Get your fucking feet wiped!" Mrs. Copeland was outside Stanley's office door, playing hostess in her own unique style. "You're not at home now. That's a good bit of Axminster in there. Go on—wipe."

Inside, Stanley Coxer sat waiting with Raz close by. He'd taken to keeping Mr. Razool on a tight leash. One couldn't trust too many people in this game, but the lad seemed like a genuine sort, if not a little serious by nature. Loyal though, almost as good as getting a new dog. So Stanley spoiled him accordingly. Not with chocky-bickies, but an even more humongous wall-mounted HD TV set in the crash pad at the house, not to mention a brand spanking new four-wheel-drive for the rounds, and snatch on tap, of course. There was always some banged-up con's bewer needing a top-up on the Income Support and Stanley liked to try them out before passing them along to the punters. So Raz got his cut of all that. It didn't hurt to divvy up the booty, not amongst friends.

In the company of young Raz, Stanley found himself

enjoying life more, almost like the good old days, keeping his hand in the running of the business. Today he'd even left Booboo and Wilby back at the house. He and Raz had been passing the time doing coke and web-porn until the city-based delivery boys showed up with last night's takings. A shipment was due in at the warehouse in a matter of hours and Stanley made it a rule to be well out of the way by such times.

Mrs. Copeland finally ushered Mumpy and some other pond-life into the office.

She patted Stanley's hand. "You alright, my darling? Let me know if you want owt. I'll be right outside. You hear?"

"Thank you. You're like a mummy to me, Iris."

She left the four men alone. It amused Stanley to see the hurt looks of betrayal on Mumpy's face these days, whenever he clocked darling Raz. Comical.

"Takings down still, Mumps?" Raz asked.

Mumpy shrugged, giving him the Elvis lip until Stanley cracked into hysterics. Confusion then clouded the lad's sultry expression. "Pickin' up," he responded finally.

The Bubba who'd come in with Mumpy, another of the standard tattoo-necked white batch, hung back by the door while monies were exchanged.

Bravely addressing Stanley directly, Mumpy said, "Someone's askin' for a shooter, offerin' top-whack."

Stanley shrugged. "And so?"

"It's for vis old lady he knows, right?" He threw a thumb back over his shoulder at his track-suited tag-along. "Off of v old manor."

"And *so?*"

"Well, do we do v business, or what? She is like…old."

"Old, is she? Well I don't know. Shall we call Mrs.

Copeland in and ask her opinion on the matter?"

"No. Don't."

Stanley sighed, sitting back in his chair, elbows on the rests, fingers splayed and pressed together at the tips forming a miniature steeple. "Do you know what diversity means, Mumpy?" He ventured.

Mumpy looked upwards, as if for inspiration. "Ur, it means... everybody's v same."

"No, no, no. It means, dear fellow, everybody is diff-er-ent. It reminds us that our darling nation is formed of many facets. Our glorious land is a body, if you like, where all of these facets come together as arms, legs, heart, and head, all working in unison. Therefore, if we dis-crim-in-ate against race, gender, sexual orientation, age etcetera, etcetera, then we sever a vital member of that body and are effectively crippled, dragging along our own weight. To recap and be plain, Mumpetty—because I see you're looking rather more discombobulated than usual—di-ver-si-ty means that *all people,* be they black, white, gay, straight, young, old, boys, girls, or circus clowns, may well be different to one another but are all, nevertheless, entitled to the *same* opportunities. *And so?"*

"So... sell va old lady v shooter?"

"Bang on." Stanley slapped the desk. "By George, he's got it! Take the damned loot and give Mrs. Miggins a nice forty-five, extending our best cordialities."

Iris Copeland gave a light knock and put her head around the office door. "I've had a call, lovey. Those dumb truckers, or a word that rhymes with truckers, are running a bit early. You'd best make tracks, eh? Leave 'em to me and your young man there, eh?"

Raz nodded his agreement and stayed put.

"Right, ho." Stanley was on his feet, a little irritated at that announcement. "Now are we finished here, sweethearts?" he asked the two young men still dawdling in the background. "Can daddy go about his business? Yes? Thank you and good-bye."

CHAPTER FORTY-TWO

Her footfall echoed off the church steps like an announcement to the township. Inside, the church was in semi-darkness. He was sitting slouched in the pews midway in, one arm along the wooden back. None of the usual, "Hello, Ms Ryan,", only those eyes, narrowed, lustrous and expectant. Her heartbeat jumped up in her throat. Nothing needed saying. She went to him, cupped his darkly stubbled chin; so much softer than she'd imagined. He slunk down, pelvis jutting: an invitation. She straddled him, his head fell back, and they kissed, hard, open, and ready. Her clit pressed against that perfect pole of flesh; she felt the measure of him and the lust in her mouth tasted of hot metal. She fumbled with the black gear which undid easily, like pantomime clothes. Her hand slid under his loosened belt, eagerly fumbling, already knowing how good he would feel in her, how he'd hold her hips captive until she felt the sweet agony of his force. She looked him in the eyes but found no want there, only scrutiny; suddenly she wasn't the woman he was about to fuck, but some germ under a microscope. As her heart lurched, her hand closed on something: not a smooth cock, but a podgy, sweaty little hand, that seized hers, dragged her down, down toward a shark-sized mouth that was opening at the core of him. "No," she screamed. "Let me go!" But her captured arm was already sizzling in its acid gut, her head half inside its meaty yawn. Then the teeth snapped shut.

Beena awoke wide-eyed around half past four in the afternoon, panting herself back to the real world, certain that if the mind had corners, something nasty had just looked around them all.

She turned onto her side, away from the snorting mound beside her. A painful aching swelled in her abdomen. The cramps were always worse the first twenty-four hours—the horniness the same—but though the purpose of this latest interlude had been romantic, all she wanted now, after the accidental and oddly disturbing nap, was to clean up and make tracks. She tiptoed to the bathroom, which she noted with annoyance hadn't been treated to so much as a once-over since her last visit. The period was a heavy one. She flushed away the wasted tampon and sealed the blood-laden towel tightly into a sanitary bag, before burying it halfway down the waste-bin. This kind of thing still felt awkward here. She showered quickly, that same old urge to get out a.s.a.p. driving each of her actions faster toward the door. Before five o'clock, her coat was on.

"You not staying for a bite?"

"James." She hesitated, turning back. "You made me jump."

"Glad I still can."

"I was trying not to disturb you. I set the alarm so you'd get back in on time."

He smiled, breathing heavily, easing himself up against the

headboard.

"I said I'd have a bite to eat with dad," she reminded him. "We don't want to go back in together anyway, do we?"

"Don't we? It's been nearly a year."

"Still."

Gaunt pushed down the sheets, displaying a long, twitching erection. "Come back to bed for a bit. It's still early."

"Tempting," she smiled awkwardly, suffering a flashback of shark's teeth. "But I've got the cramps pretty bad. So, no, I'll get off."

He pulled the sheets up again and sat forward, arms on knees. "Off to pay your pet priest a visit, are you? I saw a note in your schedule."

"That's intrusive. And why say it like that? You know, if you didn't jump into sensitive situations with your big size-ten boots first, you'd be able to come along with me, wouldn't you?"

"I don't like him."

"And don't we know it. I suspect it's mutual. That's why he's not likely to open up if you're there with me." Beena went back to the bed and kissed him, resisting the ensuing enthusiasm on his part. "I'm seeing dad first, anyway. We'll catch up when I'm feeling a bit better," she said. "Grab a bite at lunchtime tomorrow, maybe."

"Why not when we've done with work tonight?"

"Could get late for me. Something's coming. I can feel it. Bullimore was no straightforward road accident. That run-in he had with Fionn Malloy is connected to it, I'm sure. So by the time I've had a visit with my 'pet priest' as you call him, I might well have more work to do."

*

Though his paid hours had been reduced, Charles Ryan always stayed at the library until everything was in order for the following day. So it was a quick tea and sandwich with his daughter in the café opposite before he walked back over for a last tidy up.

"I'll come in," Beena said, 'if that's okay. Pick up that archived stuff of Carl Wilson's if you've dug that out for me."

"Yes I have, love. Come on downstairs."

There were a couple of articles from the nineties more focused on reported hauntings around Saint Luke's parish than on the suicides. Again, Wilson claimed, reported rates of sightings were noticeably higher than elsewhere. Though most were of individual apparitions around the graveyard, one Rokerville resident, who had lived in the same house opposite the church for thirty years, gave an account of seeing a whole crowd of shadowy specters wandering around the moor one night, as if having lost their way to an ethereal football match.

Her dad shouted an offer of coffee partway through her reading and she almost jumped out of her seat. Shortly after he'd gone off to prepare that, Beena felt an even deeper chill in her blood. Although nothing seemed to move, something made her look up. Facing where she was seated, a man stood leaning on the service counter, staring directly at her. She got the feeling he'd been staring at her the whole time she'd been sitting there, and the funny thing was, when she gave him as good back, he didn't back off with any sense of being caught, just carried right on gawping.

"Hello," she said flatly. "Did you want something?"

He smiled, straightening up. In a weird way he was quite

good looking. Late thirtyish maybe, but with that slick, sterile smartness one associates with doorstep Mormons: side-parted hair combed neatly away from the type of polished skin that's never suffered the standard aggravations of fags, booze, or likely any drug stronger than aspirin.

"Do I want something? Well I'm not quite sure," he said coolly. "Let me guess. You must be Charles's daughter."

"Sorry, do I know you?"

"Perhaps, if the opportunity presents itself. One might say, I'm a port in a storm."

"And what's that supposed to mean?"

Without responding, except to raise an eyebrow, the man picked up a box of books, which had been sitting on the counter, then turned to leave.

Beena got the feeling she'd been given a riddle by this oddball, although about what, she couldn't imagine. Charles came in with two steaming cups of tea and shouted over cheerfully, "You can pick up the rest next week, Don. I'll put them aside for you, once they're back in."

The man called Don gave the strangest little laugh, like a song, and as he turned to press a hip against the door out to the rear car park, his eye settled again on Beena. This bloke had absolutely no shame. Either that or he was an out-and-out bloody psycho.

"Who the hell was that?" Beena asked incredulously.

"Donald?" Charles Ryan said. "Aw, he's a good lad is Donald. Very thorough in his work, and a bit of a charmer." He picked up and smacked his daughter's hand. "You could do worse."

"Thanks a *bunch*, Dad."

While Beena printed off Wilson's articles, she kept one eye on this Donald character as he loaded his box of books into the back of a white library van. Before shutting the back doors, he selected something from the box to take with him into the front. Still wearing the snide smirk, he gave Beena a wave.

"Cheeky get," she mouthed at him.

Donald's smile never wavered as he climbed into his van, placed his flask on the passenger seat, and reversed out of the car park, giving her a last lingering look as he went.

At the exit to the main road, Donald paused, leaning forward, checking the windscreen then the skies, wondering if those ominous clouds might bring a welcome spate of rain.

*

Fionn sat isle-side in the pews, deep in thought, scribbling notes into a small black jotter. Mrs. Chuk was busy cleaning around the altar. What with the noise from the vacuum cleaner and all the concentrating that was going on, Fionn failed to hear Beena Ryan walk into Saint Luke's.

Beena's stomach turned over in a sickeningly pleasant way as once again she experienced a flashback of that afternoon's dream. Approaching him, her first thought was to cough, clear her throat, anything that would discreetly alert him to her presence without startling him, or making her feel like some stalker hovering over him. She didn't cough. For a while, she just watched him work, his smooth hand lightly holding the pen, his dark unruly hair hanging forward, brushing the bridge of his nose. It occurred to her then that should he turn around, how could he know whether she'd been standing there for a minute or for hours? Then she cleared her throat, turning a little pink in the face, surprised at how predatory she felt around him all of a sudden. She might've laid the blame on James, for putting ideas in her head, but really, the "typical woman" chanting chauvinists were spot-on, this was just like her: she couldn't have him, so she wanted him.

The vacuuming stopped, as if on cue.

"Father Fionn."

His head turned quite lazily. She was waiting for that first response, first look, what was there in the eyes: a twitch, the turn of a mouth that would tell her how much he already knew without being told. Fionn broke into an easy smile, as if he'd just woken from a nap to find his mother passing him a cup of tea. She felt uneasy face-on, and it wasn't because he knew anything. The expression on his face assured her he clearly did not.

"Beena. How are you? Have a seat. I was off with the fairies there."

"Are you busy?"

"Well it's all very exciting tonight. We're showing a DVD on the new translation of The Mass, in about an hour. Finding it hard to concentrate, if I'm honest." His smile slipped.

"Well I won't keep you long," she said, sliding in beside him. "I just thought I'd better let you know about something—something that concerns you, since it was you who brought it to my attention."

His face dropped to the extent that she wondered what exactly it was he was expecting to hear. "What is it? Who is it?"

"Terrence Bullimore. He's dead. A road traffic accident. A really nasty one."

"Right." His head turned back to his notebook, not really seeing it, absorbing what she'd just said. "Right."

"What exactly were you expecting to hear?"

"I don't know exactly."

"Has anybody else said anything about Bullimore?"

"No. Nothing to me anyway. Did he cause it? The accident?"

"Why do you ask that?"

He shook his head, tapping the pen on the book, distracted. "Oh, I don't know. The little I learned of him, he seemed the type who'd drive at fifty past a primary school."

"Yeah, he was that alright. Was there something else?"

"You came to see me, Ms. Ryan, remember?"

"Yes, I know, but something's worrying you. Tell me what's on your mind. I might be able to help." There it was. Right there in the eyes. Something he wasn't saying. "Come on, Fionn."

"Just...are you sure it was an accident?"

She shrugged. "Why? What do you think it was?"

Something in Fionn Malloy's expression turned hard and cold. After a while, he placed his book down on the seat, and without further looking her in the eye, said, "I think I'd best go see Cloda Bullimore. See how she's taking this. I'll see you later."

Beena watched him walk away, then got up and left.

CHAPTER FORTY-THREE

Despite meticulous planning, the shipment—which less than two weeks prior, had left Afghanistan via the silk-route: up through central Asia then on to Russia—pulled up outside the roller-shuttered doors of Copelands' warehouse three hours earlier than agreed; only a matter of minutes after the boss had taken off, minus the latest sidekick Iris was now lumbered with. Iris Copeland only hoped to God Stanley hadn't seen that truck rolling in while he was still in the vicinity. He'd go bloody spare. And nine times out of ten when Stanley Coxer went spare, somebody got bat-whacked into next Friday.

Raz guided in the reversing lorry until it was safely in the loading bay. Two young Russian guys climbed out in a languid fashion. Gun in hand, Iris Copeland gave them a grand old dressing down about the cock-up time-wise. One, in his limited English, protested, "I no understand, lady. No need of gun. Please. Check load. We go. All is good." Raz was already on the truck, totting up. It was a risky situation; Iris's regular crew was otherwise detained on account of a police raid on a night-club she had shares in. It was clean, but the boys were still a good hour off the all-clear. Even so, after much ear bending and a random sampling of the merchandise, Iris handed over the drivers' cut, plus the keys to a pool car parked outside. Once they had the money, their muffled English perked up. "Take a chill-pill, lady," the less vocal one sneered as they ducked under the half-closed roller shutter.

"This is all bullshit," the first said. "England: shit. But for London. London is good. In London, one girl, two thousand pound a night."

"Each night?"

"Every night. One girl, two thousand pounds."

Their mumbled career aspirations trailed off as they got in the pool-car and shut the doors. The engine fired and they pulled away.

"I'm wasting me breath on cocks like that," Iris grumbled as Raz pulled down the roller-doors. "Don't know what's with all these newcomers lately. Ignorant twats." She waved the gun. "I'd 'ave shot the cocks off 'em if I'd a silencer on this."

Raz checked his texts. "The boys'll be on their way in ten, Mrs. C."

"Give 'em another ring any road," Iris croaked, sucking a fag lit from the end of the last one. "Tell 'em to get a move on. And stick t' kettle on. I'm parched."

They were sitting in the office with the door open, Iris supping tea, when Raz's nostrils began twitching bunny-style. "You smell smoke?"

"It's me, ye big bell-end."

"No. It's not you, Mrs. C. It's not cig smoke. Smell that. See?"

Iris killed her fag and they went back out into the

warehouse. All the lights were out. Raz was about to flick a switch but Iris slapped his hand.

"Soz," he said. "Yeah, might be the lecci. Don't smell like 'lectrics though, that."

"Did *you* switch these lights off, Razool?"

"No. Why, didn't you?" The color drained from Raz's face.

They moved to where the shelves opened out. With razor-cut eyes, Iris peered into the dark chasm of the storage facility with the loading-bay beyond. "No. I did fucking not turn them off." She spat. She spied a crack of light just past the truck. The loading bay doors were open again, enough for a football to roll under. "You 'ave to be fucking kiddin' me," Iris hissed. "If them bastards have come back I'll..."

"I locked it. I swear," Raz whispered.

"Well it's open now, and summat's burnin' in 'ere. And if that shipment goes up we might as well go up with it, sunshine. There's a torch in my desk. Go fetch it. I'll wait here."

Raz went off and came back with the flashlight switched on. The beam wasn't brilliant; the batteries were low. He panned it around the warehouse. The smell was getting stronger, coming from somewhere down the far end where the truck sat unguarded.

"Give us that." Iris snatched the torch. "Get your arse over there."

"I smell petrol."

"Ten out of ten. Nah, shut up," she wheezed. "Somebody's in 'ere. You go round left. I'll meet you at the van. Don't dawdle."

As was getting to be his habit, Raz'd left his gun in the car again. He pulled a blade from the holster on his calf and set off around the shelving units. With the drivers gone, Iris 'd locked her gun back in the safe. She was debating whether to go get it when she heard what sounded like a kid giggling somewhere ahead. She walked toward it, swinging the flashlight, pausing to pick up one of the cheap garden rakes she had shipped in from Asia for twenty pence a piece to sell on for a quid. Not surprisingly, there was no weight to it. Nothing she peddled high-street-wise had weight. But these forks were good and sharp; they had that going for them at least. It'd jab a prying little eye out easy enough.

She moved a little less cautiously toward the loading bay but then jumped hard. Something darted through the flashlight, heading around the truck's hood to the other side, something with a right rocket up its arse.

"Razool!" she barked. "Behind the truck. Go!"

No answer. The little whippersnapper started beating on the van: *boom, boom!*

"So you wanner play games, do you, you little fucker," Iris snarled. She swung the light at the back of the truck, just catching sight of a small figure in some kind of cloak ducking back out of sight. "Why tonight, of fucking all nights? Get yersen out here, brat! Kid or not, I'll 'ave yer. I'll jab yer sassy little eyes out and roast 'em for supper. Out here, now!"

Girlish chuckling echoed around the warehouse beams, only with a smoker's hack in it to rival Iris's own, almost aping her. Well this wee fucker had now earned herself a cute little scar to take through puberty.

The smell of fumes was suddenly stinging.

"Raz! Stop pissin' about and get your arse over here," Iris yelled panicked, running for the truck with the three pronged fork out ahead of her like a bayonet. On the one hand she imagined the evil she'd readily inflict on this joker—she'd dealt with many a joker in her time—but on the other hand, she checked out that inviting shaft of light at the base of the roller-shutters, that crack of the outside world, that she might roll through Indiana Jones style with the express intention of legging it to Barbados for the next ten years. That thought dissolved as she stopped dead, sucking back a breath sharp enough to cut her throat. That cloaked joker was standing right there by the hood, facing her. A kid? The flashlight's beam had drained to a flicker but, fuck, that was some gimpy looking kid. Iris gave the flashlight a rattle and her eyes bugged wide as the batteries kicked out a last dying surge, lighting up the thing: the fugly dwarf-kid with its five-o'clock-shadow, with its pretty kilt and Wellies under the cloak, pulling a bloated pet-lip, waving bye-byes.

"I'll kill you," Iris bluffed, stabbing the air.

In a freak-baby voice, it sang a little song: "*Bye bye, bargain basement lady. Bye bye fwom the vewy heart . Better leap for life, Milady—or booom! You'll light up like a fart.*" Its dark eye reflected a flicker of light behind Iris. Then with a grin and a wave, it split faster than a whippet on Es.

Iris's nostrils filled with acrid smoke. For a moment, she was stapled to the spot by a fit of violent sneezing but managed to swing the flashlight around just in time to clock the source of the problem: a cartoon length fuse had been lit and had just reached a smoldering, petrol-drenched rag sticking out of the fuel pipe of the truck. Iris turned to flee the same instant the rag popped into a live flame. The thought that went through her mind in that split second was that having come over from Hull the truck'd probably been running on fumes when the drivers'd pulled in. She was wrong about that: the tank held over fifty liters and, trundling over at an idle pace, barely half had gone. A spark ignited what was left while Iris was still in smelling distance. The tank blew with a deafening boom showering the warehouse with truck shrapnel and the neat white load it had contained; the place looked like Santa's grotto after a stag party.

A good chunk of Iris Copeland, still alight from the blast, landed in a batch of counterfeit Barbie outfits from Korea. The garden fork with her severed hand still latched on was propelled at such velocity that it lodged with a zing into the breezeblock wall of the loading bay. Iris been right about that: those cheap old forks were good and sharp.

*

Raz stumbled dazed into his four-by-four and shot the bolts. Getting from the warehouse to there was all a blank; that face in there that had set him off running, *that* was clear as day. For one mad moment, he pulled out his mobile to punch 999, then he remembered just who he was, who he worked for, and what exactly the emergency services would find behind the bulged and shredded roller shutters. He could see something lodged in the debris down there, as if in a last bid to wheedle its way out to freedom: a blackened head, still smoking where her hair had been, and cut into the front of what had been the old bag's face, a big red gash of a grin. Another blast and the roof was raining down in sheets. Flames crackled up into the evening sky. The place was a tinderbox. Not far up the road was another one. Raz rolled the Shogun up to the pool-car with the two charred Russians still crackling away nicely inside, the cocky banter replaced by cruel flames spilling from their mouths. Another blast as the car's petrol tank caught.

No 999 calls would be necessary. Raz made his own

contribution to the smoldering stink by ripping the Shogun's tires up to eighty in ten seconds flat.

CHAPTER FORTY-FOUR

Raz's cell phone screen buzzed with some kind of weird green static shit, maybe from the heat, but he knew too well if he didn't find some way to let Stanley know what'd gone down here, more heads than Iris's would roll. He shook his phone only to get back a fizzling complaint. "Shit!" he bawled, then caught sight of himself in the rearview and realized why it was hurting so much to frown; his face was scarlet and dotted with rising blisters. The left section of his hair where the sculpting had been was blitzed, the Scarface eyebrow likewise. "Oh, Jesus. Fuck," he groaned. How could he not have known how badly he was hurt? It was the goblin thing, poncing his brain out, and that something else that'd flown up and out of the furnace like it was immune: some huge, dark-winged fucker like they'd drawn in the newspapers—like they said, cause it couldn't be photographed—but like most, Raz'd thought all of that prize shite. Like that vigilante man busting out of the nick, something the authorities were spreading about to put the shits up people like them, or like Mump'd put it: a right old conspiracy feery.

Not so, it seemed.

The Jag collection dominated Coxer's expansive ground-floor garage, but all the classics were in there: the ranks of Bentley, Porsche, and Lamborghini lined the whitewashed walls. It occurred to Raz as he tucked the Shogun in along the back that he would have preferred something sleeker, less macho-camp than the four-by-four. But Stanley Coxer wasn't the kind of guy who checked your preferences, more the kind of guy who made assumptions about you then pleased himself acting on them. If he liked you.

Heading for the first floor, double-checking every lock and bolt behind him, Raz calculated how many times of late he'd promised himself out of this crap before it got too late to run. Too many times. Sure, on the face of it things had chilled since Stanley's big hissy-fit; business was zigzagging back up the chart, but the paranoia here in the Coxer camp had been quietly gathering, concealing its mass like cockroaches behind the Hocknies and art-deco carvings, just waiting to spill out into the first blade of darkness. And now this. Raz stopped by the bathroom to splash cold water on his face; it sizzled. He roared at the mirror. "No! Not now! I want out!" At twenty-four, he wasn't exactly proud to be on the dead end of two marriages, especially the last one; he'd meant those vows. In hindsight, he could have made either work with a bit more effort and a lot less fist. And right now he'd rather be back in the thick of the domestic grief, nappies and all, than palpitating to keep up with the boss's appetites, knocking the back out of any old crack-whore that got slung under his cock. Or hare-tailing it from some livid beast-man.

The handset in the crash pad was full of the same fuzzy static nonsense as his mobile. He picked up the TV remote and flicked on the big-screen. That was working fine. Maybe the satellites were down all over. He needed to cool it, just chill till the boss showed. Until then, there was fuck-all he could do. Trembling in shock and agony, he perched on the edge of the couch and switched to Comedy Central, where the latest rerun of *Friends* was showing. This was good. This is what he'd choose to chill down to if no fucker was sitting over him playing judge and jury. So it had been on fifty thousand times, but the girls remained fit and the guys were funny, especially Joey; all-in-all a good combo; all you need from telly. He sat back a little, one frazzled ear trained on the automatic gates outside. An episode had just started. There was some English dude Raz recognized from the Harry Potter films playing a movie actor in a First World War flick with Joey. They had on the old dowdy brown gear. Raz was no big reader but he liked to read about the wars, especially the First World War, The Great War they called it; about the hardship down in those trenches; how you could never get clean or dry or get decent chow; how you could see your brother or your best bud blown to chunks a girl's spit away; how when those boys took a bullet it would be their mums they cried out for with the last breath in them. Raz wasn't convinced on that score; the mind would automatically jump to the place where it most wanted to be; it would be the bewer's picture in the breast pocket, not the mum's old mush; some tasty lady waiting in the sidelines, that they might never've even gotten a finger into yet, it being the old days and respecting ladies and that.

The episode was nearly over when he heard Coxer enter the lobby downstairs. Something sounded wrong. Raz left the program running, listening intently for the familiar sounds. Stanley Coxer coming up the stairs tonight, though, seemed starkly at odds with the usual routine. For instance, Stanley liked to sing on an ascent, the kind of singing your dad does—good and loud—to inform you of his approach, in case you're smoking, or summoning up the jizz-genie with a good rub on the old langer-lamp. No such song-making was apparent. In fact, what was heading up the stairs didn't sound much like Stanley at all. Not unless he was barefoot and scraping the walls either side of him with a bunch of Freddie Kruger knives while whispering some weird voodoo to himself.

Wearing a catatonic expression, Raz slunk down into the couch, visualizing how invisible he could make himself seem from the open doorway behind. Within the room, only the TV gave off a little light. And now, the brighter light from the landing was gradually being swallowed up as something the size of or bigger than the doorway reached it; then it just seemed to stand there. Maybe Raz really was invisible. The adverts came on—he sat through them with glazed eyes—then came the next scene. The guys were sitting in the coffee shop, Central Perk. Phoebe said something cute and Chandler shot it down in flames. Behind Raz something hacked out a chuckle; not a pretty sound. So the spook was a comedy fan, too. It came as a shock to Raz that he couldn't move when he most needed to—like someone had pumped a heavy dose of Ket into his thigh. Then another shock: in his stone-cold terror he found that the face infiltrating his mind's eye wasn't that of his last wife Shana, who he'd always considered to be the love of his life, nor was it the beauty from Subway he'd been pursuing for weeks—it was the face of his mother that smiled down on him, as if he were laid suckling at the breast. And as the dark mass enveloped him, it was her name he whimpered.

CHAPTER FORTY-FIVE

Stanley eased the Aston Martin V12 Vantage up to the wrought iron security gates. The first floor of the house was lit up like Christmas; the boy was either getting a tad extravagant or he was afraid of the dark. That irked Stanley a bit, as did the thought of having to get all the way out of the car just to get into the grounds because the remote had been on the blink for God knows how long because the usual guard had proved somewhat untrustworthy. So much so that Stanley had felt the necessity to remind the scoundrel of the downside of electricity, by having a rather large fellow lower a live drill into his Jacuzzi.

Perhaps Raz could fix the gate. He'd fixed the kettle.

The moon was on the waning side of full, but bright enough to cast eerie shadows around the sculptures in the grounds. Stanley liked that. He preferred the dark hours. Far easier to sneak up on people, as he might sneak up on Raz after switching all the lights off. At the wall plate, he manually punched in the security code, but instead of the smooth whirr of the advanced mechanics he'd paid good money for gliding into action, there came a grinding chunk as the gates scraped barely a meter apart.

"Fuck-a-doodle-do," Stanley mused. "What now? What indeed?"

Hands in pockets, he looked around nonplussed, for who might happen along to sort this out. The next house was a good walk away, and the people who lived there hated his guts. Nothing and nobody was likely to happen here. He took out his mobile, which read *LOW BATT* and blipped its protest when he punched the call button; then it went flat.

"Raaazzz!" he yelled toward the house, eyes bulging fit to pop. Again, nothing happened. "You fucking coked-up, vacuous chav! Help Stanleeey!"

He hurled the phone and lunged forward, bare-fistedly gripping and pushing the gates in a fair old frenzy. There was grating movement, but in the end the gates only sprung closer together, so he could no longer even squeeze through bodily.

"Y*ooouuuu…* useless fucking articles," he growled. Spittle frothed onto his chin.

This wasn't good. This latest prank of the devil was the sort of thing he had to cast behind himself. He stepped back, and after a few deep breaths shook it out, just like the doctor ordered—from the top of the head to the tips of the fingers. Wibble wobble, shake shake. "Aaahhh," he let out a sigh, his shoulders allowing his neck its former length. All better. Then he calmly climbed back into the V12, fired up the engine, and drove with steady but determined thrust at the gates. There was much heaving and cracking and the inevitable shattering of headlights, but the gates gradually gave way, allowing a now relaxed and smiling Stanley to scrape on through with chips of Tungsten silver paint flying to the four corners of the grounds.

"There," he congratulated himself. "Where there's a will

there's a way."

Piles of aggregate, decking planks, and expensive ornamentation still cluttered the grounds. Now approaching September, the landscaping that Stanley had commissioned to begin in the spring was still on hold due to shoddy workmanship and various other disagreements that might yet end in a healthy round of gunfire. The auto-lights worked okay though, and clicked on in sequence as the injured V12 lolloped up the graveled driveway toward the garage. On remote command, the shutters rolled up like butter; more like it. As Stanley was about to drive in, something overhead clicked off the moonlight. He stuck his head out of the car window. The sky was clear as day. Lights began flickering on inside the ground floor—Stanley's personal car-showroom. One could never have enough space for toys. He turned and reversed the V12 into its slot as the shutters were gliding to a close before him, and was momentarily reminded of the house on the street where he grew up—which the neighbors referred to as "the red house"—that Stanley had passed most every day of his childhood, yet never noticing, only after many years, that the house actually *was* painted red. Just as looking out now he could clearly see, mounted on a pedestal alongside the driveway, a life-sized statuette of an angel with authentic outstretched wings; a rather beautiful thing that made him wonder just how many times he had driven past it without due note. He didn't even remember ordering it. But then, he didn't remember a lot of things. Stanley's thoughts, of late, were increasingly like cottage cheese, sliding off the bread at the least tilt.

*

Raz's door was open with the TV blasting. *Scrubs* repeats for ever more. Good old J.D. monologuing on what a bummer it is having to tell people they're about to die. "Turn it up a bit, Raz, dear," Stanley bellowed as he passed the door. "They can't quite hear it in Boston Spa." No reply. He backtracked, popping his head around the doorframe. The boy was napping on the couch, his head slumped forward on his chest. What Stanley would give for somebody who could but for a day keep up the pace. "Sleep tight," he quipped. "Pretty little faggot."

Along the landing, Stanley closed his door on the rant of TV ads, although he didn't really mind. There was something reassuring about having noise about the place, almost like having children. Which reminded him of another commotion he should be hearing.

"Wilby, Booboo!" He clapped his knees mid-crouch, scanning his rooms, ready to catch the first doggy to fly his way. "Come to daddy-kins."

Nothing. Stanley's smile expired. Would his every plea go unheeded tonight? He took off his jacket, slinging it aside Travolta style. It landed on nothing, just went skidding through the dog hairs and pee-soaked puppy-pads scattered across the boards—Raz's bright idea.

"Here, my babies," he tried again. "Time for cuddles."

The pugs ate shit if it was on the go, yet their dishes sat untouched. Very odd. There came a whimpering, a duet. Stanley knelt, peering beneath the couch over by the windows. Two sets of beady red eyes stared back out. Both of them were under there, flat as rugs, chins between paws.

"Aw, what's the matter, my chuchi-faces? Tummy bugs, is it? Aw, come to daddy then. Daddy's going to get a big bubbly bath. Doesn't Wilby want a nice bubbly bath with daddy?"

The dogs were hardly looking at him, more past him, into the hollowed-out ceiling-space. He turned to see what the Dickens was spooking them. The ceiling was vaulted with exposed beams. It'd been two floors originally but Stanley preferred height and space. No hiding places. The room was dimly lit but, clearly, there was not so much as a spider up there. Drama queens the pair of them.

"Suit yourselves," he grumbled. "No doubt you'll make an appearance when the cookies do." He went into the adjoining suite, left the door ajar, and turned on the bath taps, singing, "My heart belongs to *Daddee*". Booboo's favorite.

A vintage Bordeaux and a squidgy Marmite-tub sat on the windowsill alongside the gun holster with the .38 in. Stanley flicked on the whirlpool and still in tuneful mood sang, "God save our graaaacious queen," to the sentry-like rise of his prick, which arrived a whole glowing helmet clear of the froth. "Wilberforce!" he reached for the Marmite. "Come to daddy. Daddy's got a tweet for Wilby. Come and be my favowite."

Raz's TV went off.

"Nighty, night," Stanley called, then jolted violently—the Marmite jar was launched across the room, Bordeaux infused bathwater splashed out over the white floor tiles, his wine glass followed, shattering on impact. "What the fucking creeping Jesus?" Stanley bellowed.

Halfway up the crack of the door that stood open toward him, a dark eye peered in. As his own widening eye fixed on it, the lower lid flickered upwards, in amusement.

Stanley leapt from the tub, his first instinct to grab for the cricket bat he'd left parked by the bidet. It wasn't there. He then realized that his bare feet had absorbed a few sizeable chunks of the broken wineglass. "Oops. Ow. Shit!" He stumbled backwards, perching on the bath's edge, and pulled out the shards he could grip. The tiled floor had become a pool of blood and wine. "Shit-a-brick!" he yelled. He looked back at the crack in the door. The eye had vanished.

Pistol in hand, Stanley toweled himself off and hobbled into the living room leaving thick slivers of blood across the white surfaces as he went; his hair, superbigged by the steam, capped his crazed expression. He paused a little way in, taken aback by the sight of another bath in the scene before him: the tin bath, which he kept at the warehouse for special occasions, was sitting right there under the beams. He limped his way to the door that opened onto the landing. The corridor stretching ahead was now in darkness but for some kind of light issuing from Raz's pad, a very dim, greenish light that seemed to Stanley to be nonelectrical.

"Mr. Razool!" he shouted sternly. "Would you mind coming in here for a seccie, please?" He stood at his own door, waiting. "Why am I repeatedly ignored this evening? Get your rank Paki arse down here, you waste-of-space wide-boy!"

That got a response, but not from a voice he recognized as that of Mr. Razool. In fact, it sounded like a veritable symphony of voices in the room down there; whispering, cackling, conspiring by the sounds of it, in on a joke Stanley wasn't party to. The next noise made him point the .38 a little shakily ahead. Oversized toddler footsteps clomped their way out of Raz's room. Marionette style, it was the legs, in high stride, that came out first. Then, there he stood. An obscene miracle: the sagging puppet of his dear young friend, held upright on invisible strings, the bloody, half-burned head clinging on by the mere thread of its spine. And as Stanley's heart flew into a fit of palpitations, the insolent corpse began to shake it out, from its lolling head to the tip of its graying-brown fingers. Wibble wobble—shake shake. Tatters of soggy brain slopped about the floorboards.

Stanley counted down from ten then calmly closed the door between him and it. In the center of the room, his cricket bat now stood leaning against the tin bath. So, it liked games. Fine and dandy. Stanley Coxer was no fool; if his number was up, at least it might be fun, he might get in a few nice swipes to send this demon limping away. He placed the pistol on the bureau by the door, walked to the center of the room, and picked up his bat.

"Party time!" he bellowed with a howl of laughter. "Who's balloon am I to pop first? Come on then. Let's have you." The place was silent apart from his own echoing hysterics and the labored panting of the two little dogs firmly rooted under the couch. Stanley circled the room, exhilarated, whacking at invisible flies. "Come out, come out, for a bottle of stout!" When he turned back, somebody was sitting in the tin tub: a naked girl, hunched forward with her back to him, a luxuriant mound of soft silvery hair hung down about her pretty knees.

Stanley, bat gripped firmly in hand, walked over to the bath.

"Hello," he said. "Nice of you to pop in, dear. You look awfully like my last meal."

She giggled, peering coyly up through strands of silken hair.

"Top notch," Stanley praised, raising the bat in both hands. "Now I wouldn't normally, as a rule, crack open the skull of such a delicate and pretty young lady—normally I do nicer things to pretty young ladies—only, I do get a slight sense here of *nothing to lose…*" He felt betrayed by the tremble in his voice, that twitch of an eye. He didn't want to care about dying, yet he found he did, and no way was he going out without a major tantrum. "So I'm afraid," he continued, "if you don't stand up and face uncle Stanley like a brave girl, tell me what the giddy-aunt-fanny is the deal here, then I am bound to bring my willow down on your sweet little spine. Now stand. Face me!"

She screeched horribly, her head craned backwards as if tugged by the hair. Stanley jumped back, watching with morbid fascination. So delicate a face, even in its agonized state; she began panting, as if in labor. Something was moving, swelling beneath the flesh of her back. The skin around the shoulder blades began to rip. Something twitched out.

"My lord," Stanley gasped. "Whatever next?"

The girl ascended, lifted by some invisible force, her arms beckoning the heavens as two vast black wings unfurled from her tiny frame. Her breathing steadied and she turned her head to smile sweetly over one wing at Stanley. Giddy on the experience, he smiled back. "Now there's a trick," he complimented. "We should sell tickets." He raised his bat and with brute force swung at the fairy's torso, but like a rubber band it simply twanged out of range, then faster than his eye could track she went fluttering upwards like a great moth, veering back over his head and out of sight. Stanley turned in aimless circles, scanning every nook of the ceilings, every piece of furniture. "Little angel," he squealed. "Come to Stanley. Come and play. I won't pull your pigtails. *Promise.*" He stepped back, spontaneously kicking out as something snagged his lower leg. And there she was again, crouched behind him. Little imp. Her pale breasts were Stanley's undoing, a momentary distraction while she slid the knot in snug against his ankle. His last attempt to whack her was so pathetic he had to laugh. He'd lost the will. She was already up in the beams, tossing the slack of the rope over the central joist, then in a reverse flurry of wings, down she came, tug, tug, tugging. She could not possibly possess such strength, and yet up Stanley went with an almighty roar, his towel dropping free as he came to an abrupt stop, dangling head down high over the tin tub, blood pumping from his torn feet.

"Okay. I saw yours, so you have to see mine. Fair dos." Stanley just couldn't help himself; still turning by his ankle in a narrowing arc he broke into a fit of giggling hysterics, "Weeee," he screamed. Then burped. "Oh, oh, that wine's coming up." The contents of his stomach sprayed out as far as the white couches. "That'll stain. Ahem. Excuse me," he blurted wetly, seeking out the naughty angel, wondering how impressed she must be by his ample dong. "Can we get on with this?" Mid swing, it was a little child he caught sight of, standing right beneath him, her back to the tin bath, her curly head down, a bit lost. Instinctively, he covered his parts.

"Ahem! Excuse me, young missy," he demanded. "Who let *you* in? It's like ruddy McDonalds in here tonight. Are you with the strange bat-lady?" She shook her coppery head. How utterly cute. It occurred to Stanley then—and he was astounded it hadn't before—that *red house* thing all over again—that for the five thousand or so women he'd fucked royally there hadn't been one paternity claim. Not one. Now there never would be. Not for him. Hard as it was to shake that thought away, he needed to return to the business at hand. Blood from his glassed feet ran all the way down to his neck. "Excuse me, little miss curly-top," he called down. "In a bit of a fix here, you might have noticed." His cell phone sat on charge on the bureau close to the door. "Be a sweetie, will you, and pass me that phone. There, on the desk. Ooh, or better still, get the gun—but do be careful with that." He waved a hand. "Off you go. Tootle along."

The little girl complied, treading graceful little Welly-booted steps over to the desk, and, for a few short moments, Stanley allowed himself sight of a reprieve. What a silly sausage he was. He already knew this kid. Had seen her before. Seen *it* before. In so many nightmares. And no, of course she wasn't getting the phone, or his gun. Something of her own was now leaning up against the wall by the bureau; a long handled axe, sizeable enough to take down telegraph poles. The imp-thing picked it up, stroked the gleaming blade, recently sharpened by the looks of it, and turned around with a grating chuckle.

The usual wisecracks failed to surface. Stanley's own chuckles had all dried up.

The hideous goblin face tilted. "So we meet again, termite," it rasped.

"I'm sure I've not had the pleasure," Stanley wailed. "This is clearly a case of mistaken identity. I demand to see my brief. I've done bad things, I'll grant you that. I am a bad, bad man." He waved a finger. "But I won't be blamed for something I didn't do!" Yet all the while he pleaded his case, Stanley was getting flashbacks of their faces; oh those faces: that of the innocent maid going up on a rope, the dwarf's bubbling in flames. It might have been stored way down in his psyche, far away from the everyday thoughts of petty rivalries and fast cars and fine wines and Marmite licks in bubbly baths, but it had only ever been waiting to resurface, to finally be acknowledged.

"Now wilt thy line be stamped out," it pronounced, its dark brows colliding. "Scurry no more." It broke into a run and leapt toward Stanley, swinging back the axe.

"I'm too high, numbskull," he jeered. He was right. The first blow merely chipped his temple. "Ow, ow, that fucking hurt," he laughed bitterly, streaked and dripping with blood. "Get on with it, troll!" Blood sloshed around the awaiting tin bath. Stanley's heart hollowed as sounds of distressed yelping filled the air. The pugs had crawled to the perimeter of their hiding place and were watching him go out, so terribly slowly. "Don't look, babies," he begged, starting to sob. The monster loomed over them, glaring down, then back at Stanley, cruel amusement behind its mock-petulance. Those vile flabby lips.

"No! Not them. I have sinned, I confess. They have not."

"There is a trick I know with dogs. See how they run, free of the weight of their idiot heads."

"But they are innocent. Innocent! Please let them be," Stanley wailed. "True, I know you, Malakh, I confess it. My bloodline played its part in your making. I beg you, finish me. Just me."

"Hexter," a girl's voice from within the goblin whispered it. "Enough."

Something in the vile face relented. Its expression softened. There was, it seemed, an unspoken pact between its elements. To his short-lived relief, a near-by Persian rug was snatched up and thrown over the pugs' vantage point. Then without further ado, the kilted trickster, now huge and chunky as well as sinfully ugly, trotted back to the door, turned, and with a salute and click of a heel, ran like Rudisha into an impossibly high vault, lopping off Coxer's head in one.

CHAPTER FORTY-SIX

Fionn awoke in his church, notebook in lap, as when Beena Ryan had dropped by to tell him about the fate of Terrence Bullimore, except, but for the moonlight creeping in, the place was in darkness. His pen clattered to the floor and rolled away as he sat upright. Was this even the same day? There was a sense of timelessness, a feeling that he might have been slumped there for weeks—gone unnoticed by passing congregations. Was he a ghost? Had he given up and died? All those times he'd struggled awake from the nightmares, or was sure he'd been dreaming when in fact he was up and wandering around; is that what this was? There was a familiar feeling, of a gathering presence close by. He turned to look up the dark void between the seating, to the doors and narthex beyond. Nobody was there; nobody that he could see. Yet that dark space contained breathing, the beating of hearts, and the pained whisperings of souls caught in the firing line of some unfathomable power struggle.

Fionn stood, unafraid, and turned to face them. It seemed strange to talk into an empty space—like ringing home and hearing your own voice message talking back. But he sensed the urgency here, and taking a deep breath addressed the throng. "Some of you I know," he said. "Most of you I do not, but I do know *of* you. I know of your plight, and I swear now I will do whatever I can to help you. As God is my witness, I will make amends for what part I have played in prolonging your suffering."

His attention was diverted; something nearby was changing hue, gaining light. His eyes drifted reluctantly to the notepad which lay open on the pew where he'd left it, bearing writing not his own, that now glowed luminous green on the page. What was scrawled there was the statement of one indifferent to the feelings of others. It read, *Either you are with us, Priest, or you are against us.*

A further swelling of light turned his sights to the main doors up ahead. Through every gap in the framework a bright green fog seeped in, contaminating the air. Fionn knew he was locked in a nightmare, but one as much a threat as a solid punch in the face in the light of day.

"No!" he shouted. "This is God's house. You have no place here!"

From within the stagnant-pond breath there rang a gaggle of laughter, polluting the sanctuary of the church with its evil stink. The panic Fionn now felt was not his alone. There was an unseen scattering, as in an earthquake zone; terrified souls darting every which way for cover, for home, wherever that may be. The clearing occurred in an instant, then Fionn stood alone with that pea-soup fog lapping toward his feet.

Failing a frantic attempt to rouse himself, he knew he had to move fast. He ran for the altar and cupped his hands into the font. As he hurried toward the back door which would take him through to the rectory, whispering voices as old and gnarled as dinosaur bones cackled close behind, scheming each torturous act they might visit. *"Wait for us, Priest,"* the voices scorned. *"Cast down thy robes and dance in our midst. We know thee well. We like thy taste."* Fionn scattered holy water over the threshold and frame of the door, then slammed it shut behind him. There had been a lock but his dreaming mind robbed him of it. Watching, waiting, he backed slowly toward his bedroom door, thinking ahead, *If the waters fail, as with poisonous gas I'll use sheets to stifle every nick that might permit entry, then sit out these horrors until morning, or the soonest I can wake.* The door to the church was steaming now, vaporizing the holy waters. Soon it would be alight; it could not be stopped.

"No," Fionn moaned. He rattled the bedroom door. It was jammed. He threw his weight against it. The door swung inwards and he plummeted into nothingness; only a deep empty blackness met and enveloped him. His guts went on tumble dry. He was nowhere. This is what nowhere felt like. And as he pinwheeled into the endless depths of his fearful mind the only coherent thought to console him was that, this time, the evil force that had first assaulted him in the old church, that which held at its mercy the souls of the dead of his parish, was fearful, too.

CHAPTER FORTY-SEVEN

Inside the mansion of the man at the top of her most-wanted list, there were two firsts for Beena Ryan. One, it was the first time she'd seen this particular man's face minus the unshakably gloating expression; that grin now hacked widely into it didn't paint a happy picture at all. Stanley Coxer held DI Ryan's gaze for longer than she wished. She'd seen a lot in her fifteen years in CID, but the bulgy-eyed severed head floating in a tin bath brimming with its own blood was the second first that day. The scene smacked of an abattoir.

"Execution," Dolcie from forensics concluded. "No doubt about that. I don't envy you the task of narrowing down the suspect list for this particular fellow, DI Ryan. Wasn't exactly popular, was he? But, I suppose, at least this has to be a one-off."

Beena looked up at the blood-smeared corpse roped up by one ankle, its other leg flailing loose like an obscene chicken wing, a single axe blow, this time, having cut clean through the neck.

"A one-off? No. "Afraid not. There are some photos back at base, of almost exactly the same crime scene. Happened about four months ago. Not around here, mind you. Down London. Do you remember the Adrian Adams case, the execution in the theater? The details of that one were never made public, for obvious reasons, as you might gather, but some not so obvious reasons as well." She nodded at the bathroom door. "We've lifted a few full sets of fingerprints from around the door frames. Make sure and have a good look at them, Dolcie. You'll be surprised at what you find. I guarantee it."

Beena went out to the landing where the body of the younger victim was now covered, ready for bagging up. James Gaunt was leaning against the wall, a little pug dog under each arm, pretending he didn't want his face licked.

"You look flat out," she said.

"It's a dirty job but someone has to do it."

"I'll have one of the officers drop them off at the shelter." She put a hand out to stroke one of the dogs but Gaunt pulled away.

"No. No need. I'll drop 'em off at me mum's. Be quicker than doing the paperwork. They can stay at mine, just for a couple of nights, till we can sort something else out; something more permanent."

"You sure about that?" Beena smirked. "Never had you down as an animal lover."

"Well, maybe you don't know me as well as you think."

"Maybe not." She conceded, nodding. "Well, if you don't mind having them, I suppose it'll be okay. Not like they'll be penning statements as to what happened here."

"I don't mind at all, like I said." James gave Beena a look over his shoulder as he walked toward the stairs. "It'll be company for me, won't it?"

PART FIVE

Endings

CHAPTER FORTY-EIGHT

Fionn was in no doubt that they were back. This was their…its home, after all; where it was born; its longstanding link with mortality. And after the vision he'd suffered, he had to face the possibility that what Carl Wilson had said could be right; Ben couldn't possibly be the man he'd known and trusted. How could he be? The few short months since his marriage into the entity had seen the world shaken up like a Gin-fizz. And if the root of its power truly was evil then that shake-up could turn its attention on anybody who got in its way. There could only be so much time for Fionn to act.

He tried calling Beena first, something he'd put off for too long, but all her numbers were on answer mode. Clearly, she was being kept busy. It was almost midday, a darkly clouded September day. Carl wasn't answering his mobile either and hadn't called in to the press office yet. In order to keep the promise he'd made, Fionn needed something from the reporter, details only he would have. He got the Micra out of the garage. Rain poured down in sheets. The little car still ran okay for fifteen years old, but as Hawk'd often said, "Just as well you took that vow of celibacy, mate—you'll be pulling no pussy in that"—the everyday kind of recollection that seemed painfully unreal now.

On his way up through the estate, he drove past the Johnstons' house. Amelia was heading out of the garden and flagged him down. He opened the passenger side window and she leaned in with her umbrella hooked over the car roof. In the harsh light he noticed for the first time the depth of scarring on her face—one track running through the delicate flesh of her eyelid—and found it hard to smile.

"Father Fionn, I was goin' to come down and see you. Where you off to?"

"To see our friend, Carl, if I can track him down."

"I'd come along with you, say hi, but…" Ami looked uptight. "What's goin' down, Father? I know somefink is, right, and I'm sick to death of being treated like a little kid. Dad, Joe—everyone—they've all gone well-weird. Won't talk to me, even around me. What's happening?"

"Well, you're right, Ami. Something is going on. But…before I say it, believe me, this isn't just a cop-out, but I really can't talk right now either. Just promise me you'll lay low till I get back, okay? We'll talk later."

"Lay low? What the hell? Just tell me what's going on. How long can it take?"

"You'd be surprised. I promise we will talk later, Ami. Come down to Saint Luke's in a couple of hours. Actually, I'll pick you up on my way back. But…just for now, stay indoors. Promise me you'll do that."

"No I won't promise anything. In fact, I'll go running round the estate wavin' my arms round footy-fan style if you don't come clean with me. What is it, Fionn?"

"Just…" He couldn't think quite how to put it. "Just, if

you see Hawk, you stay away from him, Ami. Well away."

Her face became grave. "Don't say that. I want to see Ben. If he's here I want to see him. I could help talk some sense into him."

Fionn came as close to stern as was in his nature. "Go inside, Ami," he said. "I'm not kidding. Go on in."

Without another word, she turned and walked back into the house. Fionn drove on, gutted to deal with her like that, but having voiced his greatest concern, also feeling that his mission might be more urgent than he'd been prepared to admit to himself.

*

Carl Wilson's flat was on the outskirts of the estate, a leafy glade developed by the council in the eighties and kept free since of the kind of troublesome elements who might undo such efforts. Carl's flat was on the middle floor of a three-story council block. His contact details had been in with the lengthy history lesson, along with a note to call around for a cupper and a chat any time, meaning Fionn didn't feel too conspicuous when a tiny old lady, who said she "loves a feller in uniform, especially the handsome ones", let him into the lobby downstairs.

There was no answer at Carl's door. He might have just left for the office, but Fionn was getting bad vibes. After a short wait, he tried the door. It was locked. The door of the utility room to his right, separate from the main flat, stood open. The washing machine was mid cycle, churning the laundry on soak, meaning Carl couldn't have been gone for that long. Fionn was considering going to track him down at the newspaper's head office when he felt wetness in his palm.

Turning his hand over he saw blood. Carl's front door was brick red, so Fionn hadn't noticed right away, but blood was splattered all over the place; he was standing in a pool of it. A thinning trail led into the utility room. The heavy, repetitive clunk inside there now numbed Fionn's spine. He went in cautiously, scanning around, but nothing looked that out of the ordinary. A black brogue lay on the floor, its lace missing, and a small dark object was sticking out from under the washing machine. Fionn crouched and slid it out. It was a handgun. The washer's barrel turned over, quietly whirred, then the water sloshed to a stop. Through the glass oval before him Fionn stared in at what looked like a drowned poodle—a mass of hair sitting on the water's surface. But as the water stilled and the hair settled he realized he was looking at white flesh beneath it: a forehead. The barrel went over three times, stopped again, then the crimson water began to drain away, and Fionn gaped in mute shock at the dead face of Carl Wilson, his head severed just under the chin; his own shoelace had been utilized to sew his mouth tight shut.

And while Fionn crouched there, paralyzed, the cycle went on spin.

CHAPTER FORTY-NINE

It was going to be a long day, inevitably followed by an even longer night. DI Ryan had Wilson's computer transported back to the station. Something in there had to tell her where this thing was headed next, who its next target was. It was time to stop keeping up and start pre-empting it. The idea that it had targets was at least less disturbing than the prospect of it letting loose at random. From what she'd witnessed of its work so far, that was unthinkable.

It was after four when she came out onto the landing. Fionn stood by the stairwell, staring blankly through the shifting throng of constabulary and forensics.

"I've wanted to tell you," he said to her. "I caused all this. I wished for it to happen."

"Great. Well you'd better come with me," she said. "Tell me once-and-for-all whatever it is you've bloody done."

*

Carl Wilson's hard drive sat on the desk. A young officer who Beena addressed as Steven brought tea and sandwiches into her office. Once Steven was out of the room, Fionn drank a little tea then continued where he'd left off.

"At first, I thought it was a saint I'd unearthed…the ashes of a saint. A miracle. Because, I suppose, we needed a miracle on Rokerville so badly. I would say I never doubted her, but in truth, I did. There was something…unangelic about her, certainly around her. I was just desperate to believe. I wanted to see angels, to believe that things could change—all the injustices—I wanted to change things." He sat forward, head down. Now he looked up at her.

"Are you going to charge me?"

She sat back, frowning. "With what exactly?"

"I don't know."

"What have I got on you?"

He shrugged. "Desecrating a grave. Smuggling substances into the prison. At least."

She shook her head. "I can't make you feel better this way, Fionn. Much as you'd like me to. Do you see me taping any of this? We're in here alone." She almost laughed. "It was a condemned grave, now a grave no more. And what you took into the nick for Hunter wasn't exactly a class-A substance; in fact I wouldn't know how to classify it. I've no proof you did squat. You wouldn't be the first nutter to come in here with some ripping yarn cooked up in a fit of guilty conscience. No. I reread the history. That's not evidence either. If what you say is true then you're going to have to make the peace with your God. My Super, Ms. Osbourne, who happens to be God around here, insists anything of this nature stays firmly off the record. Anything resembling the mystical, supernatural, whatever… We're under orders. If there's no law to cover it, or better yet—to solve it, then we're not interested."

"How can you be ordered not to be interested?"

"To show an interest. To act on it. We just deal with the crime in the wake of it all. That's our job. Any voodoo is your lot's department. So, unless you can tell me who this thing's got it in for next, I think we can safely call it a day here." She tapped Wilson's computer. "Hopefully this'll cough up what I really need to know." She reached down and plugged in the hard drive then hooked up the screen.

"Whoever's next I don't know. The Malakh—the Zwerg—swore vengeance on two men, or at least the eventual end of their family lines."

"Number one—Coxer? I don't know why I'm asking you. Like I say, I read the history on this myself. I just find it all hard to swallow."

"Did he have any living relatives? This Coxer?"

"Strangely, no. We've looked at that before. No family, no kids we know of. And for somebody who'd dip it in a bowl of rice pudding if it had its legs akimbo, that has to be saying something. He might well 've been sterile."

"Maybe he was."

"So, following the end-of-line prediction, the second man may be childless, too. I don't believe it's a woman. Those men who stood and watched it suffer, it's them it wants; that image in reverse." She wiggled the mouse as Carl's computer warmed up. A little hourglass told her to be patient. "Off the top of your head, Father, how did it describe Liddle? What was his particular curse?"

"He'd be the lowest of the low—'*feasting off the eyelids of babies*' was the bit that stuck with me, but probably more a metaphorical than a literal slur."

"You're right, but some metaphor. It's what rats used to do in the slums, preying on the weak and helpless. There was a term '*Rat of effluent streams*', and '*The lowest of the low*'."

Something clicked in her eyes. "This might well be someone we want as much as your angel friend does."

"Names change over time," Fionn pointed out. "If Carl hasn't managed to dig it up yet, this person might not be so easy to track down."

"Well, we'll see. I'm a bit of a detective myself, you know." As the computer finally buzzed to life, she started on the sandwiches. Noting his reaction she said, "You get used to eating on days like these. Otherwise you'd drop."

"Beena," he said. "Can you tell me now why you were after Carl?"

"We had a tip off he'd purchased a gun. We got a wealth of info courtesy of our friend Kelvin Goddard—damage limitation for him—once we had him banged up. He's out by the way. On probation. I've warned Amelia. Shit!" She'd just opened a file marked *Family Tree*. "There are about a thousand different family lines here. Liddle Liddle Liddle," she parroted as she scanned down the list. "Come on! Ah, here he is. No, fuck it—'scuse me—there's six or seven at least."

"No Christian name for Liddle appears in the account of the ordeal. It may 've been a big family. Any sons or cousins would've been in the same trade, looked more or less the same on paper."

"Well, it's a start." She clicked open the first document. "More than I had yesterday."

"Could I ask you for something else?"

Beena was engrossed, hardly paying attention. "Fire away."

"When you opened the document files, there was a sub-folder marked *Recorded Suicides*. Could I have a print-out of that?"

"What do you want it for?"

"I need to say a prayer, for the victims. I need their full names."

"Names? All of them?" She looked up at him aghast for a second. "You are aware it'll be centuries' worth? You're going to say a prayer for each and every one?"

"Yes."

She shook her head but backtracked and did what he requested. Fionn had been hoping for a simple list. He was handed a thick wad of pages, names yes, but in the body of a more in-depth text.

"I'm trusting you," she said. "Not that I've cause to. Just tell me none of that information goes any further than your prayer mat."

"It won't, I promise." Fionn packed the pages together and rose to leave. "Thanks," he said. "I'll leave you to it then."

Beena was back glued to the computer screen. "You can stay if you want to, if there's anything more you think you should tell me…that might help."

"No," he said. "I was supposed to see Amelia at Saint Luke's hours ago. I made her a promise. I need to call her at least." He added, "By the way, the voodoo department won't be my department for much longer. I'm leaving the priesthood. I've already requested a meeting with the bishop. I think it's time to throw in the towel."

Without flinching or even looking up, she said. "You're right there. I think it probably is."

"Right. Well, bye then."

Beena swung around to say something further but as she did, the door opened without a knock and James Gaunt walked in, a lollypop protruding from his mouth and a corresponding lump in one cheek. Behind him in reception, two officers were trying to hold up a thick-necked, spotty young man who was collapsing through their grip, crying like a smacked toddler. At first Fionn thought he was drunk, but it didn't really come across like that. "Not my Raz," the lad wept bitterly. "Not my man. Not my *main man.*" And down he went again.

Gaunt retracted his lolly, clicking the door shut with a smirk. "They've more chance of standing up a johnny-full of jisum."

He looked blankly at Fionn, who nodded, offering a weak smile before quietly taking his leave.

CHAPTER FIFTY

At around ten that night, James Gaunt wrapped up as much of his end of the Stanley Coxer business as was possible for the time being, then it was over to his mum and dad's for a quick bite, pick up the new lodgers and shoot off home.

While accepting that dogs were no substitute for a woman, by midnight Gaunt was thoroughly enjoying his first night with the two little pugs around. When it came time to turn in, they had this crazy ten minutes where they had an almighty scrap under the bedclothes—better than anything on TV. His mum 'd taken to them straight off, so there'd be no problem with daycare. He told her he was thinking about keeping them, to test out her reaction, but in his mind he'd already committed to it, so luckily her reaction wasn't a bad one. Sure, they were dirty little buggers, and the next woman would probably be just like the rest of them, too fussy for her own good. But then if a woman was going to balk about a bit of a mess, she might as well balk about a lot of one. That or crack on and tidy it up herself.

The misgivings came at three in the morning when the

whimpering kicked off. Heavily dazed from the exhaustion of the day, James patted around the bed. "It's okay, scamps," he croaked huskily. "Nightmare's over—get back off to sleep." But the dogs weren't on the bed. The collywobbles were coming from under it. "Aw, fuck this," he groaned, then reminded himself how traumatized they must be. Back when he joined the force, he started out in the dog-training unit. The unit manager, Graham Ellery, who lived on the estate where all the trouble happened, had topped himself one night: whiskey and downers; no note, no nothing. The old spaniel that 'd been his work buddy near on ten years just about did the same, refused to eat or drink till it was decided it would be kinder to just put it out of its misery. It wasn't as if James didn't know the score. Around this time one night previous, these two pups were witnesses to the butchery of their own alpha-male.

James forced the quilt off and hung over the window side of the bed, a space just big enough for a small dresser unit alongside. By the streetlight shining through the thin curtains he could make out the two of them cowering under there, tiny tails wiggling back toward him. "Hey," he coaxed, clicking his fingers, "Come on back up then. It's okay."

The dogs backed toward his waiting hands, lapping and yelping nervously, but at the same time were intent on the gap at the opposite side of the bed that looked out into the expanse of the studio flat. James caught a flash glimpse of why. He sucked in a sharp breath and threw himself back onto the bed then laid there pinned to it, like shifting an inch might drop him out of the sky. Hanging over the side, he'd seen something python-sized slithering along the floor, heading toward the bathroom. It certainly looked like a python, only with a human head on the neck end. Even while

James reassured himself that in his extreme tiredness he must be experiencing some weird hallucination, a thudding came from inside there. The pugs started yapping like fuck. James sat up and pressed his back against the velour headboard, suddenly very aware of his nakedness. What the hell *was* that? He eased his weight slowly to that side of the bed and glanced over the edge. He could see nothing on the floor, but still was not inclined to put a foot down. If there was ever a moment when a hand would whip out from under the bed and grab your ankle, this was it. Something else…the bathroom door now stood ajar. The light in there wasn't on, yet a dull glow radiated out into the bedroom, slicing the atmosphere in sharp lines, like a cinema projector. James couldn't see inside but could hear rustling, like paper being rummaged through; no effort to even muffle the racket was apparent.

"Who's that?" he shouted. "Get the fuck out of there! I'm armed." A bluff.

By the time he turned thirty, James Gaunt had come to accept that he was something of a bastard, renouncing any delusions he'd ever harbored of himself as the noble hero. But he'd always thought himself a brave man, one who'd walk toward a loaded gun if he saw any chance of disarming an assailant. But right now, right here in his own home, listening to that thing in there breathe its ancient, rasping breath—a thing that seemed not to give a flying fuck about his presence—he found all he could do was watch and wait. The bin lid crashed shut and, as the bathroom door creaked open wider, James adopted shallow breathing, immobility, aiming for invisibility; playing dead in the hope of evading death. He wanted only to close his eyes, to wait for whatever it was to do whatever it was going to do. Just let it happen, hope it was quick; he'd had a good innings. But then he'd seen the plight of Coxer. No way had that been quick. He opened his eyes, ready to face it, then watched incredulously as Beena Ryan walked out of the bathroom. Clearly, though, some caricatured version of Beena he was making up as the nightmare persisted. A noticeably shorter and stockier Beena for a start, and wearing clothes that lacked clear lines, as if they'd been drawn on. She hesitated passing him, pulled at her knickers, shuffled her bottom, and pulled an icky face.

"Smacks of Gazpacho soup," she croaked in a chain smoker's voice, complete with a Bronx twang that sat somewhere between Bugs Bunny and that of the old schnozzola, Jimmy Durante. "If you're gonna soyve up mush, soyve it hot, for pity's sake. Yuk!"

The dogs had fallen silent, tucked well away out of sight. Lucky them.

Every hair on James Gaunt's body stood taut as the cartoon Beena turned her head toward him and smiled, her mouth a rotten black slash in the darkness, her eyes the cold, silver-black of ball-bearings; one of which now gave him the cruelest little wink. "Better close dem peepers, baby." She had reached the bed. "Diss might hoyt."

CHAPTER FIFTY-ONE

Jet started up around two-thirty in the morning, even earlier than usual, barking at shadows, barking at fuck-all. Paula Ellis, his sole owner of late, willed herself to sleep through the first ten minutes of it then leapt up in a fury and slapped the blasted hound. This shouldn't be her problem, and wouldn't be for much longer. Paula couldn't pay the rent all on her own, so it'd be back down to her dad's, and he was even less a dog-lover than she was. If no one took the mutt off her hands soon, it'd be turfed out on the moors.

Jet cowered under hand. He'd need a piss now no doubt. Probably a dump. And there'd be no more of that in the flat. At least her and Rob 'd managed to get a ground floor one that had access to the communal grounds out back, meaning when Jet crapped in the middle of the night there was no nosy twat about to watch Paula not bother clearing it up. Why should she? She'd never asked for a dog in the first place, let alone asked to be lumbered with it after Rob pissed off with the latest tangoed tart from Facebook. The dog was a staffy-lab cross, young enough to be well-crackers and big enough with it to drag her off like a spare tail. Paula was a

size fourteen but weak with it. She'd walked Jet out the once.
Never again.

"Gerron wiy it, sharpish," Paula growled, letting Jet out via
the back patio doors. It was blowing a gale outside, whipping
her dressing gown up around her knees, threatening to whip
the doors right off the hinges if she wasn't careful. She held
tight onto the handle while the dog trundled out, wagging his
whole body, looking back, hankering for the hug he'd never
get from her. Half a dozen steep concrete steps led down to
what was, after a week's non-stop rain, a churned up mud
bath. Once the dog was down there, Paula shut the doors and
switched on a small lamp at the back of the living room,
mindful not to shine too much of a spotlight on Jet's doings
in case the barking roused some nosey git who might see a
small turd as a crime heinous enough to warrant a thousand
quid penalty.

Beyond the apartment grounds, it was just moorland for a
good two miles. No onlookers there. It was pitch black
outside and Jet fit right in; one thing he did right. In the dim
lamplight, Paula spread newspapers from the patio doors
inwards to catch the thick of the muck he'd drag back in, for
what it was worth. Between Rob's lame-arsed DIY efforts
and Jet's collage of busy paw prints, she'd not get her bond
back in a million years. But she liked the flat clean, as clean as
she could have it, so she overlapped plenty of newspaper.

A bustle of movement outside caught Paula's attention.
Oddly, beyond the wall of the grounds there looked to be a
whole bunch of people wandering about, pacing aimlessly
back and forth. Hard to see who they were. Some looked like
they were in fancy dress; outfits from Dick's-days. *But it was
the middle of the night. What the fuck were folk playing at, throwing
fancy dress parties around in the middle of the night?* Things 'd really

quieted down since that Hawk bloke went on the rampage. Any gang activities had snuck underground, so even if you knew it went on, you didn't have to watch it going on under your nose. But now this. Funny thing was, there looked to be a mix of ages, some really old people, nothing like your regular party crowd. One bloke, all blacked up like a miner, had something heavy looking wrapped around his neck, trailing off behind him. Something clinking. His head looked half twisted off his shoulders—all wrong, all crooked. Paula shuddered and crept up to the glass doors as the blackness of the moor swallowed the man, but not before she saw it was a chain trailing behind him. She jerked back. *How sick can you get?*

Jet suddenly darted by outside, bouncing pin-ball style off the steps on the way toward a tall hooded boy who'd managed to get into the grounds and was squatting down, holding out his arms. No gangster type by any stretch—far too square—what with the tatty parka and the kind of drainpipe jeans her dad would wear on a big night at the snooker club. Paula snapped the lock on anyway. Fuck the dog. He looked happy enough. Her phone was on charge in the kitchenette. She backed toward it, keeping one eye outside. Jet was up in the lad's arms, giddily licking the face inside the hood. Something about that coat was familiar. Paula reached back and dragged at the charger wire until the plug clanked out of the wall and across the worktop.

Jet and his new friend seemed to pause, looking her way. The parka stood too far proud of the lad's face for her to make out any more than a mish-mash of obscured features. But something told her she definitely knew this person. Paula speed-dialed her dad, she thought, but got her friend Donna's answer service. She looked down and did it right this time, but all that came back at her was static fuzz.

Down at the foot of the steps, Jet started to bark like crazy. He was alone. Paula peered out. The wandering weirdos had just vanished. Probably gone up to Beggars' Rock to get even more shit-faced. She opened one door just enough for Jet to scamper in, but before she could pull it closed a gust of wind whipped inside and swiped the door outward with such ferocity that Paula was hurled screaming through the night air, clearing the steps to land a belly-flop in the mud below.

For a few minutes, she just sat there winded and sobbing from the shock, her shoulder length hair clotted around a face that looked all set for a bout of guerrilla warfare. Up in the flat, Jet was again bounding around in a fit of excitement, mucky paws and all. Paula wiped the mud from her eyes and got up, crawled up the steps, and shut and locked the doors behind her. Slumping down on the newspapers, she eased a clay-laden dressing gown off her shoulders. Under it, her nightie wasn't so bad. With two wet thuds, the slippers came off next.

Jet went silent. Little twat knew what was good for him. No way was she in any mood for antics now. Scanning about she saw he was lying within the entrance of the kitchenette, staring intently across the room to where a huge weeping-fig plant, courtesy of Rob's idiot mother, covered almost the entire wall. Paula followed the dog's sight line and jolted so hard her teeth nipped her tongue. She gripped her mouth, pressing back blood and an onslaught of petrified gasps. Somebody was standing in there amongst the leaves. As calmly as possible she forced herself to her feet, her eye fixed on the legs extending from the thicket of foliage—drainpipe jeans. She edged past the kitchenette toward the corridor that led to the front door. Her dad's house was only two streets down the estate. She'd get out the door and leg it there, barefoot or not.

The gangly figure started to weep, his horribly scabbed hands pressing up against his shrouded face.

"What d' you want?" Paula pleaded, frozen by the doorway. "I've got nowt. No money. No cards, wiy owt on 'em any road. Tek the telly, for fuck's sake. Tek owt what you want, just ger out."

The boy shook his head from side to side, sobbing harder.

"Look. I can't help you, love. Whatever's up. I've trouble comin' out of me ears. You can't stop 'ere. Go down to t' church. They 'ave to help you there."

His head shook violently now, his sobs turning to agonized cries.

"You'll 'ave to do," she shouted. "You can't stay 'ere."

His tormented howling nearly shook the walls. The hands came away, allowing lamplight to creep under the hood, and as it did Paula stood muted, staring into a face that had no more stable a construction than a spilt bag of chicken innards. And somehow, more shockingly, embedded deep in the mess of him was a mangled up pair of glasses, one wiry end creating a tent effect in the parka's hood.

Amongst the mangle of cracked chin bone, the flesh parted. "I can't get in there!" he protested wetly. "They won't let me!"

That's when her panicked mind skipped back to Rokerville Comprehensive, to realize who this was. "I'm so sorry, Cal," she said. Her heart steadied a little and she found the strength to start moving again, as far away from him as she could get. "I can't help you, mate. I can't."

CHAPTER FIFTY-TWO

Sometime after four in the morning, Alan Ellis answered his front door to a daughter he barely recognized: one half dressed, mudded up to the eyeballs and shocked into a state of speechlessness, the likes of which he'd never witnessed in all his days. "Who's done this to you, love?" he demanded. "Him? I'll 'ave that dirty little fucker by the torrs if he's laid so much as a finger..." His rant died off as he caught sight of the bright flickering at the summit of Rokerville Avenue. The oak tree in the apartment grounds, that'd stood in the churchyard of Saint Luke's, surviving centuries of sun and storm, was fully alight and crackling out its death throes. Inside the apartment block, lights popped on in fast succession. The whole complex seemed aglow in a subdued kind of way, floodlit from behind by the kind of haze you'd expect to find hanging over nuclear waste dumps. And perched on top of it all, up on the ridge of the roof, like some hideous gargoyle surveying its castle-keep, stood the Malakh, its rust-stubbled face twisted contemptuously beyond humanity, its dark wings a-flicker at the ready.

Rokerville's residents were out of their homes and streaming down the hill into a broadening torrent that led to one door. Although generally there was an understanding of a common cause and a collective need, some stepped up the pace as it dawned on them that there'd be a hell of a queue with all this competition. Fionn Malloy heard the pounding before it even started. It was in his head, a battering ram that went off before dawn. So when the first ones arrived in person, he was ready.

Kelvin Goddard had been out on probation for a fortnight, which had turned out to be the most sinfully boring two weeks of his entire life. His dad might as well keep him on a leash. One slip up and Kelvin 'd be straight back in On-License, which would be no bad thing as far as he was concerned, he'd learned more in that few months' bang-up than in the whole of his piss-poor existence up to it. So when Kelvin heard the commotion outside and looked out to see Louis Johnston chasing his cigarette down the street, his two lads and the squealing slut in tow—how much better did *she* look on her back, begging for mercy—his thoughts turned to arising opportunities. He checked the bedroom next door. His dad was well out of it. After his half bottle of Bell's, the old fart 'd kip through a twister.

Louis Johnston's Astra might've born all the right signs— *Neighborhood Watch*, *Alarm fitted*, *Key code sound system*, *Immobilizer*, all that crap—but Kelvin had been watching the Johnston's little routine long enough to know the alarm was fucked, making the uncoded stereo fair game. Plus, he'd watched Louis disable the immobilizer about a year back, the first time it kicked in and proved a bit of a hassle. Louis and his family were barely out of sight before Kelvin was outside their car with his newly acquired metal file. One swift pump and the lock popped just like he'd been told it would. Kelvin stood back, smirking, chuffed as Mickey Mouse in a cheese factory. This was the start of everything he'd ever wanted for himself. There 'd be no nine-to-five minimum-wage slave-drivers telling him what the fuck to do. He'd show these fucking losers around here, looking down their nosy beaks at him like they wouldn't 've dared to a year back. Cars were just a start—cheap, easy meat. Prime steaks would follow. He had clued-up mates now who had buyers on tap, all lined up and waiting.

As Kelvin's fingers closed around the door handle, a dark cloud loomed. Yet more rain. This was why, as soon as there was quids aplenty in the bank, he was fucking off to Benidorm.

A mighty whoop discharged directly above him and Kelvin looked up just in time to see the flash of a silver blade amid the monster's vast wingspan.

"Three strikes and yeeerout!" The Malakh roared earthwards.

The axe came at him so fast it was all a blur, and Kelvin Goddard stumbled backward, staring in disbelieving horror at the white-boned, bloody nub of his right wrist. The fingers of his severed hand still twitched around the handle of the Johnston's car door. Then the winged police-angel took-off as fast as it had arrived. The initial shock subsided, the agony kicked in, and Kelvin sat down hard on the pavement, gripping his spurting wrist, screaming fit to wake the dead—those dead that weren't already awake.

*

"I can't help you."

Fionn stood before them all, his back to the altar, and, finally, to the God he'd usurped by his actions. He was dressed in jeans and a T-shirt. The shirt had a cat's smiling face meowing out of the front of it. Under the scrutiny of his former congregation he began to wish he'd put more thought into what he'd thrown on.

"You have to help us, Father. You have to take our confessions," Louis begged. "It's Armageddon. It's here. We 'ave to confess our sins."

Fionn ran his gaze over the multitude of pleading faces. Those who already understood and accepted his conviction had settled down into the pews to tremble quietly into the new morning, one that might bring their streets a reprieve. But outside the sirens blared.

It was Amelia who stepped forward to face Fionn directly.

"Why won't you do this for us, mate? What's goin' on? We need you now."

Louis looked away in shame, as did his son, Joe, both knowing they'd played their parts; both sure of what the man who'd served them as priest was about to say.

"I cannot hear your confessions, Ami, because I caused this." Fionn had struggled to find his voice but now spoke loud enough for all to hear. "I brought this down on you all. I am a greater sinner than any of you. Your confessions will only be wasted on me. I wished for this, and I contrived to cause it. And now, before I can face a single one of you again, I have to stop it."

The disbelief on Ami's face turned his gut to concrete. Louis sat down heavily, his head dropping into his hands. Without another word, Fionn turned and walked back to the vestry, where he locked the door. He made a call to Lin, who like most people was up and alert, and told her to stay home, to hole herself in, and to answer the door to no one. Then he went to the back room, where he'd harbored the Malakh's ashes all those months ago, months that now seemed like years, and took Carl's handgun from the top drawer of the filing cabinet where he'd hidden it, slid the weapon into his belt, and covered it over with the smiling cat.

*

Rain spattered the windows of the studio flat. As dim morning light filtered into his bedroom, James Gaunt came around in crumpled contortions up among the pillows, the pugs welded in close to his belly in fitful sleep. He wasn't one hundred percent clear on what had happened to him, except that his jaw felt like it'd chanced into the path of a wrecking ball.

"Jesus Christ," he groaned. "That was the fucking worst..." He wasn't sure what of.

It took a while for him to swing his legs round and plant his feet down on the floor. Even then, he checked under the bed. For what? Was he losing it? This level of crazy didn't happen yet. Not to him. His drained mind struggled back to the last thing he remembered before blacking out, but when the scene replayed he wished he could forget the fucker: first there'd been a kiss, like being pie-faced with a plateful of rotting fish, then her beef-chunk arm 'd swung back, pain like a lightning bolt shot through his head, then morning.

James went stiffly to the bathroom and found himself stepping through the scattered contents of the waste bin that'd been dragged across the floor. So it had happened. Or could he have sleep-walked through here, done this to himself? Was he that sick and tired of life? The dogs could've done it though. That made more sense.

As he reached the dribble-end of a piss, James lifted one foot to peel off something that'd stuck to the sole of it. On doing so, he experienced an instant knee-jerk revulsion common to men. His farewell drops strayed around the toilet seat as he struggled with the paper, the remnants of a sanitary bag welded to him by the stale blood clotted around its torn insides. "Aw, yak!" he grimaced, tossing it aside. James felt relieved, if not a bit confused, that the actual contents of the sanitary bag never did turn up.

CHAPTER FIFTY-THREE

Discarded beer cans and bottles littered the cave's entrance. Cruising in on a low glide, The Malakh, in the shape of a narrow-winged Zwerg, swung back his blood-stained axe hub and swiped a blow through a stack of cans, sending them ricocheting off the walls like hollow bullets. In the voice of TV commentator, Ray Hudson, he bellowed, "Well if *that* wasn't a bravado goal, my son, I don't know what is!" He bounce-rolled all the way to the cave's back wall, finally landing upside-down against the rocks. "Couldn't have put it better myself, Ray," his Gary Lineker whole-heartedly agreed. "It's been a good, long while since I've seen a semi this impressive."

Hexter the Zwerg melted down and reformed the right way up. He was lazy that way.

The moodometer was on the upswing; one big fat fish, namely Coxer, down, one more yet to be fried and savored at length, plus however many tiddlers needed battering along the way. Hexter slumped back while the chuckles steadied. "Boy, oh boy, oh boy. There ain't no rest for the wicked," he hollered, good old Brooklyn-style—his favorite twang in the whole wide world—for the benefit of anyone close to the surface and in need of good cheer. "Ha ha. Phew, some big night, eh, gang? Roll on judgment day. Fuck that—roll on this morning!" He stretched his broad, hairy little legs out from under the sackcloth monk's robe and locked both hands behind his head. "Aaahhh, home-stinky-home. It don't got no five stars, but it's my crib."

The litter was an accumulation of years' worth of teenaged revelries. But there'd be no comebacks on that score, not from here on in. A view from the cave's entrance to the new apartments down at the brink of the township saw their subjects languishing in a healthy dose of devil's breath. That was as close as any sucker 'd dare come now. They'd got the message, alright. Nobody meddled on the Malakh's watch.

And speaking of meddling, there was that little matter of a priest turned turncoat to tango with. But even the hint of an idea as to how had the big old dumb gardener struggling up with a Pierrot face on. In fact, even as the thought took form, there came a rumble of discontent, admittedly getting feebler by the day. "Okay, okay." Hex slapped his boulder belly. "Can it, Titshmarsh! What a fella has to do ta earn a bitta peace in this God-forsaken hovel. Jeees."

So, for now, that one could go on ice. Another day or two on the home turf—a good old resurge of power—should see the third man soaked up nicely. This little act had started out a duet and would stay that way. Besides, the priest was nobody important, a redundant messenger boy. The reporter who wound him up would do for now. Boy-oh-boy had the Zwerg got that blabber-mouth's case sewn up; don't he just got that old schmuck in a spin, ha ha. Nobody but nobody wangles a shooter with the express intent of taking a pop at the Malakh. An example had been made.

"Hey, Appi. Appi, Appolyn," the little man pestered, poking about himself. "Coming out for a date?" He pulled a giant box of Smarties from his sleeve and rattled it. "Treats on me."

With delicate grace, a slim arm extended forward from under his own, honked his nose, and slapped him in the head.

"Ow! Ouch! What was that for, baby? Well if I ain't Valentino pardon my foibles. Hey, ain't that what a cat coughs up in the Bronx?" He thumped his chest. "Ahem, hack! Boy-oh-boy, here comes another foible—get it? *Foy-ball!* Ha ha."

A finger poked him in the eye.

"Ow, yikes!" He made a grab for her arm but it dodged quickly behind him, yanking his head back by the wiry tuft up top, while another hand emerged to paddle his face east to west. "Ow, ow, owee!" He gnashed his rotten teeth at her but she was too fast. "Cut it out. Ha ha—ooohhh no!" The nails dug into his ribs, tickling hard. He wriggled like an electric eel on charge. "Okay, I give in. I give in. Stop already!"

Her arms retreated. The wings tucked in for the night. The Zwerg pulled open his robe and kissed the face of Appolyn as it rose from his left shoulder, and as it gradually merged toward his own he did his best rendition of Old Blue Eyes "Under My Skin".

"Yes, Hex. Don't I know it."

"What can I say? That vow of silence way-back-when did my box in."

"You broke all your vows."

"Again—what can I say?"

"Be still a while, won't you."

He saluted his diminishing head. "Nighty night then, honey-bunch," he crooned. "Keep him sweet."

Appolyn's head took over centrally. From the shoulder opposing Hexter's absorption, Ben was rising—his damp face a sickening yellow—until the body that had flown in was half Ben's own, half Appolyn's, except for a stubborn clump of red frizz blanketing the naked chest. Old Zwerg didn't like to be left out. Ben cradled his right side, his other half, his angel, gently resting his head on hers, his breathing weak.

"I used to come up here all the time. Used to climb those rocks out there with me mates. But I don't remember who with now—some lad with specs on, an' another who was always ribbin' him about it. Jamie somebody. It hurts just to remember. Just to remember who I am half the time. I'm so damned knackered."

"You've worked hard," she soothed. "You can rest now. Recharge. Leave things to us for a while."

"So, that lad down there, just nickin' a motor. That's where we're at now is it?"

"It's a phase."

"And the lad at Coxteth's place an' all. So young."

"Is youth in itself an excuse for the inhumanity they showed to others? Your memory fails you, Ben. Do you not remember how your mission began?"

"I do remember that. These latest, they were bad lads, I know, but there was a change ahead for that lad at Coxteth's. There was a chance for that one, I felt it. A solid discontentment with the ways he'd fallen into. There was a dream of something better up ahead."

"He made choices. We made the example. End of... Please, let us not quarrel, my Hawk. Don't doubt us now. Hexter's anger is distraction enough. He's not seeing things clearly."

"I heard—his Ankh's gone skewiff."

Appolyn laughed gently, cradling and rocking her larger half. "Let him have his moment. It'll be over soon enough, then there'll be more time for us."

"I promised we'd stay away from 'ere. No matter what."

"I know you did, Ben, but don't forget you have been avenged. You and your wife. Before we can continue our mission, we must be, too. We *must*. Completely so. We had to come back. As did you, for Anita."

"I just don't know anymore. I can't think straight."

Appolyn cupped his face. "Then don't think." She kissed him. "My dearest, sweetest, Hawk."

"Hey! I'm still here, y'know." the Zwerg quipped up from Ben's larynx.

"And you can stick around," she hissed into his fuzzy mesh of chest-hair. "But for pity's sake, shut the fuck up. We sleep, then back to business."

CHAPTER FIFTY-FOUR

No sleep. With the promotion five years previous came an average seven a.m. start, but Beena Ryan could generally get by on four or five hours sleep a night. Now, sitting in the car outside her house at eight a.m. following not a blink of shut-eye, she felt exhausted; tugged two ways. Emotional dilemma was her weakness, the W in her SWOT that she'd never own up to at interviews. Departmental matters she could snap through her fingers, but then there were people. There was the matter she'd turned up in Wilson's files that, if the trail was accurate, might at some point throw her father in the path of risk. Then there'd been that message from Amelia Johnston. Apart from the Rokerville estate deteriorating into a general war zone overnight, Fionn Malloy was now no good to anybody remaining there, having thrown in the towel about as fast as he'd said it. Beena felt bad about that. She'd meant to take back her response to some degree but had missed the moment, then never called him to put it right. Despite her own agnosticism, his failure in his basic duty as a man of God had enraged her; it'd felt personal, which was always a mistake.

Her aching head tossed a coin and she made tracks toward the city library. The rush-hour traffic kicked in by the outskirts, rendering the dual carriageway a virtual parking lot. The library phone was on auto-answer till nine and her dad, as usual, wasn't answering his mobile. She'd wasted her time getting him the damned thing. The first time she tested it, on the standard ring-vibrate, they'd been sitting just across the room from each other. She actually *told* him she was about to try it out, then watched him throw it in the air like a fully activated mini Hadron-Collider. Anyway, she considered, it would be better to try explain things face to face. After radioing Gaunt to meet her there, she stuck on the siren and barged her way through the metal sea.

The main doors were unlocked when she arrived but Charles Ryan wasn't at his familiar post at the front desk. Only half the library's lights were on and a fresh autumn storm gathered outside, casting imposing shadows through the high Victorian sashes.

"Dad?" she called in the reserved tone people adopt in libraries, even empty ones, as the place appeared. Her heart thudded hard. "Dad?" Her voice echoed. "It's me." She suddenly didn't want to announce her name aloud. Suddenly she felt very alone. Why wasn't Gaunt here yet?

There was a crash somewhere below. Beena went to the staircase that led down to the basement, trying not to think too hard about what caused the noise, but at the same time acutely aware of the sound her heels made on the linoleum floor; she might as well have brought the siren in. As she descended the stairs, she thought about Carl Wilson. Even if they had found that gun the tip-off said he'd purchased from

Coxer, she doubted it would have been used in some random drive-by shooting. Carl wasn't the type to cause trouble for ordinary people. Carl's whole life had been a fight for justice for ordinary people. Watching the campaign of the Malakh had been no different for Beena Ryan than for most people—even though she'd seen far more of the evidence of its existence than most—there was still that same combination of unreality, mingled with a quiet, if not shameful swelling of gratitude. For when it came to lopping off bad-guys' heads, that black-winged avenger was something of a people-pleaser: greedy extortionists, pedophiles, rapists, mass-murdering dictators, all being the collective public's idea of prime targets for the Malakh's particular brand of coldblooded justice. But what Beena realized now, as she reached the basement, was that Superintendent Osbourne did have a point back when she looked at its face caught on that prison camera. Ordinary people might have plenty to fear, too; you could wind up with your head on the block simply for disapproving, or worse— opposing the beast; or perhaps by just being in the wrong place at the wrong time, like her dad was now. Armed or not, Carl Wilson had been terrified by his discoveries. Finding him that way—not that different to the way they'd found Coxer— had felt obscene. Carl Wilson was no bad man. Beena's father was no bad man either; he just happened to be here, now, on the Malakh's predicted route. And as Beena entered the basement, now filled with a real sense of urgency, something else about the photos from the seg block came back to her, another detail the Malakh's adulating public had been spared: that cold black eye, glaring out through the bars, at anyone who dared to challenge it.

There was movement among the shelves not far away.

Shuffling. As she rounded a gondola end bearing every work ever written by Stephen King, complete with eerily animated depictions, her dad dropped his second pile of books that day so far.

"Shit!" she blasted, startling herself even more than him. "Sorry, Dad. But God…switch on your bloody mobile for once, will you? I needed to talk to you. Urgently. I had a good mind to send a squad car round. That certainly would've made you jump, wouldn't it?"

Charles Ryan took and patted her hand. "Don't be silly, Been, they've enough to do, those squadies. You can talk to me now, can't you? Shall we have a cupper?"

As always, her face slipped helplessly into a sixteen-year-old's smirk, complete with rolling eyes and shaking head. "I've no time for tea, Dad. Listen to me, will you? There'll be a couple of officers arriving here shortly, whether you like it or not. You need to lock all the doors and windows till they get here. I'll help you."

"The windows are intruder-proof, lovey, unless they're going to fly in. What on earth's the matter, Beenie? You look washed out. You could do with an iron supplement."

"I'm fine, Dad. Really. Come on, let's get this done." As they carried out a quick check of the windows, which on first glance looked painted shut, Beena asked, "You know your mobile van-man? What's his name?"

"Donald?"

"Yes, Donald. What's his full name?"

"Little. Donald Little."

"Yep, that's what came up when I checked. Look, it might sound daft to you, but I believe somebody's after him. Somebody very dangerous."

"Oh cripes. How extraordinary. Such a nice, quiet young

man, Don is, as well. Is it drugs?"

"What makes you say that?"

"It's always the quiet ones, isn't it?"

"Well, not this time. Come on, keep going, Dad." She urged him toward the main doors upstairs. "We need to secure this place, firmly, till backup arrives. What time does Liddle get here? … I mean Little."

"He only needs call here twice a week, and today's not one of his days, I'm afraid. He'll be out and about as always."

"Oh crap. Any idea where he's heading now?"

A squad car pulled up outside as they reached the doors. Beena speed-dialed James Gaunt as her father went to check Donald's Rota. James's phone was busy. She texted over the location. He'd just have to catch her up.

CHAPTER FIFTY-FIVE

Donald Little paid a visit to the nature reserve on the way to his first book-stop, a fresh pair of latex gloves pushed deep inside his trouser pocket. He passed a couple in their sixties out walking two Labradors, holding hands and chatting about a summer holiday they'd enjoyed at somebody's villa in Corsica—their daughter's by the sound of it. The choice of the great Gracie Fields, Corsica, he recollected. He concluded that, despite an overrunning of the types that troubled him, the world still held plenty to smile about—plenty of the types worth smiling at. So Donald did so, raising a smooth, manicured hand to the old dears before strolling on. Another fifty meters along the path, he veered up a sharp grassy bank to a copse of trees. There were two barbed-wire fences to negotiate at the summit then he was into the sheep territories that another old couple, who he'd chatted to on the moors recently, had made mention of, in terms of, "Where was one to walk dogs these days without the risk of them getting shot at by over-zealous gamekeepers?" The advantage of all that, as Donald had mused, was that sheep territories were indeed by-and-large *dog proof*, an essential aspect of "hide-the-corpse" because it was dogs that tended to "go seek".

Once he reached the tree-shaded spot, Donald rolled on the gloves with surgical precision. Squatting down, he shifted back the perimeter of anchoring rocks then pushed back the layers of debris that covered the Fire-block rubber sheeting he'd wrapped her in, which was getting harder to *un*wrap each visit. It was hard to say what compelled him back to this particular kill, except that overall he'd enjoyed this skinny little tart better than anything else that had flaked out on its back in his van. Even the smell didn't bother him anymore; even on those hot days when the putrification was at its worst. He didn't mind. It was a good smell, of victory over temptation. And although he hadn't in fact resisted temptation in this case, he had at least put the beast to bed for a while. Unfortunately, even tightly bundled in the rubber, there wasn't that much left of her now. Not much more damage he could do. Barely a patch of the blackening flesh remained unpunctured. With her fully exposed, Donald looked down with mounting regret, knowing it was high time to let her go and move on to pastures new.

*

The mobile librarian had barely driven a mile when it seemed that once again God had read his thoughts and thrown in his path the next viper of seduction; at times he was unsure whether indeed God was friend or foe. Temptation seemed to fly so fast into his path these days. Right away, he recognized the make and model of her car. Until recently, he'd kept a low profile watching her get in and out of it. But now here she was, flashing him down on this same stretch of road where Andrea Maynard, a few months earlier, had succumbed to the contents of his flask. He eased the van to a halt, smiling at that thought, and watched keenly through his wing mirror as the sexy detective stopped her car behind him and stepped out. As he tracked those pretty legs to his door it occurred to him that were he someone else, were he a weaker man, he might have feared that her appearance meant his number was up. But Donald shunned fear. Also, it looked like the half-breed was alone. What could she hope to do? Even if she meant business, which, judging by her expression of amiable disquiet, couldn't be any business resulting from the slightest inkling of his goings on.

"Thank God," she said as his window slid down. "Thank God I caught you, Mr. Little."

Donald frowned. "I'm a believer, Miss Ryan. Could we perhaps not bandy the Lord's name about so lightly?"

She blushed a little. He liked that.

"Sorry about that, Mr. Little, but this is no light matter at all. There's something I need to talk to you about, urgently. You may well be in danger. The best thing would be for you to come back to the station with me right away."

"Right now, Detective Inspector? Are you sure it's quite so urgent? A lot of people depend on me, you know. Good people."

Her eyes seemed to twinkle, to smile. Were that not extremely attractive, Donald may have considered it a little odd. He glanced down at the bulge in his pocket—the discarded gloves in their tidy little ball. A little soiled but the last pair he had on him unfortunately. They would do.

"I have to say, it's about as urgent as it gets. My colleague's on his way." She checked the time on her cell phone. "He's been chasing my tail all morning but if he's not landed here in the next five minutes, we'd best just go."

He studied her tail end as she gazed off down the road. Even under the dowdy raincoat, he could tell it was a shapely tail, the kind you could really dig your nails into. Donald swallowed hard. This could be a long morning. At least he'd made sure, as always, to store a clean shirt and freshly pressed pair of slacks in the van. Dark clouds were gathering. Thunder rattled overhead. Donald watched Beena Ryan swipe the first drops of rainfall from her face. It was a smooth, crème-caramel face, if not quite so pretty as he'd remembered from her visits to the library.

"Fancy a nice Twinings, Ms. Ryan? While we're waiting for…?"

"My colleague, Detective Gaunt."

"Yes. Well hop in."

The heavens opened at his very suggestion. His whole life had been choreographed this way.

CHAPTER FIFTY-SIX

Donald watched her sip the tea from the spare beaker he kept in the back for such opportune occasions. Her lips were full and pink, free of the unnecessary tarnish of lipstick. Sadly, a whisper of dark hair overshadowed the upper lip, the downside of girls of Asian descent, he always thought. The upside, of course, were the Sophia-Loren-esque almond-tilt eyes. Growing sleepy now.

She was wearing a plain shift-dress under the Mac, so neutral as to be almost colorless, and low heeled shoes. The sensible type. A pity really. So many sillier girls were more deserving. But then, she was here.

"How is the brew, my dear?"

"Very nice, thanks," she answered groggily. Her thick dark lashes grazed her cheeks. She struggled to push herself upright. "Sorry," she said. "Not much sleep last night. None, in fact. Heavy week all round. *Come on James.*" The van faced uphill. She checked the wing mirror for traffic heading their way from the city. The road was quiet.

Donald had noted that, with the acquired caution of the legally minded, Ryan had observed his every move while pouring the tea, had watched him take a sip of his own before she touched hers. He was of a mind that every girl should have the sense to take similar precautions. For that reason, he always had the spare beaker ready laced with Ketomine.

"So what is it you wanted to discuss with me, Detective Inspector?" As he spoke, he casually turned the key in the ignition and slipped the van into first gear. A mile ahead, there was an abandoned factory. That's where they'd conclude this conversation.

"I can't remember exactly," she croaked, strangely ignoring the move he'd made. Playing it brave no doubt. She lacked the strength by now to play it any other way. Her head nodded chestward then snapped back upright.

The van rolled steadily ahead. "So tell me about this colleague of yours." Donald eyed her over greedily.

"James? He's a good friend." She yawned. "He'll be here any minute. You'll see."

"A good buddy, eh? I bet you get up to all sorts, don't you?"

The van entered the grounds of what was once a thriving woolen mill. Donald backed the van into a cluster of sycamores inside the factory wall, then switched off the engine. Ryan's head lolled helplessly back against the seat rest, her eyes darted around in confusion. He slid one arm along the back of her seat, while his other hand eased the remains of the tea from her grip.

"Let me relieve you of that first little burden, my petite eastern princess," he soothed. "A few more burdens along the way and you'll need worry no more about all those leery little boys back at the office."

The eyes were still open, still there with him, though the body was as limp as over-boiled spaghetti. The best possible combination.

"Sthtop it," she spluttered, a dribble of saliva trickling from her mouth.

"Oh look, the half-wit protests. Like father like daughter. How quaint." He wiggled her head by the chin. "Come on, Mrs. Police-Lady, don't give up so fast. Fight it. Come on. Talk to me a little longer. Tell me all about your good friend, the dick-tective." As he spoke, he pushed her dress up and with his free hand fumbled under the passenger seat to the hidden pocket where he kept the tools. The long carving knife came to hand first. Sheer luck. "Tell me all about those antics you get up to after hours, in your grubby little downtown station." The back edge of the knife caught on the underside of the seat. Donald leaned down and gave it a wiggle. For a moment, it wouldn't budge. In his impatience, he yanked it hard, tearing through the upholstery. When his attention returned to Beena Ryan's face his whole insides shifted like quicksand. She was smiling at him, like an idiot. Did she not comprehend by now the gravity of what was about to happen to her? His shocked reaction had her grinning wider still, offering him a glimpse of some thoroughly unbrushed teeth. He lifted the knife so she could see, but by then she was far more intent on answering his questions.

"Yeah, okay, I'll spill da beans, Don," she rasped. "Jimmy's a hoot. Ya wanna see him in the buff, sunshine. Boy, what a tushy! What a totem-pole! But don't he just like to stick it to dem goyls." She sat bolt upright. "Oh *boy*, don't he just." The meaty thighs he'd unveiled moments earlier rose up as she gripped the seat's edge and rutted. "Hey, baby, take a memo!" And she really wasn't that petite at all. "A long one. And take it where da sun don't shine, ha ha haaa!" And that 'tash on her lip wasn't ladylike either. More ten o'clock shadow than five. She cocked her head. "In fact, Don, I'd say I needs me a new squeeze. Wadaya say?"

Donald Little recoiled, the knife he'd raised a motionless glint midair. His eyes locked on those before him—black as rats'—as the thing grabbed his knife-hand firmly by the wrist, seized his face and puckered up. "Kissy kissy time."

"Those eyes. Pure evil! Satan's eyes!" Donald shrieked. "Get ye hence!"

"Well, excuse me, Mr. Bookworm. How's dis?" In super-fast motion, it fluttered an instant set of dolly-long eyelashes. "Dat float ya boat, huh? Dat honk ya horn, honey-bunch? Well whoopee! Now drop da formalities—let's play *hide da bookmark*!"

The mossy mouth smashed wetly into Donald's. The tongue slid in deep. He struggled in vain, gagging against the invasion, his eyes wide with shock. The strength of the thing was unreal, and the stink—the carcass he'd just reburied was potpourri by comparison. He stopped bothering to push her away; he reached up over his head to transfer the knife from his shackled hand. In his panic, he grabbed the blade, slashing his palm wide open, his muffled scream choked out by the monster detective's slimy tongue tunneling deeper. He grasped the handle, raised the knife high, and thrust its point down between the neck and shoulder of the thing that held him. A myriad of incensed voices roared out of its gaping mouth as it drew back. Blood splashed the inner windscreen as Donald yanked the knife out with an adept killer twist, then he squirmed for the door and spilled out onto the cracked wet concrete of the factory car park like a newborn calf.

Donald shuffled back then, for a while, didn't move.

Behind the blood-smeared windshield, all was still and silent. A steady stream of rain plastered Donald's ever-neat hair untidily to his face. Clutching the knife's handle tight into his gashed hand, he stood up and backed slowly away, his eyes intently facing the windshield. He had not been ready for this, hadn't made his peace. He'd dreamt of it so often, yet he'd not been ready. Because, he reasoned, he hadn't needed to be ready, this really was not his time. Because, as he'd suspected, this supposed destroyer could actually be destroyed. Its strength meant nothing. It was naught but pitiful flesh and blood.

A clap of thunder resonated throughout the surrounding valley just as the rear doors of the library van exploded outwards with a bang. Donald halted, maneuvering the knife in both hands so that the blade pointed upwards, to where it would come at him from. The rear of the van was out of his view, almost against the trees. The Malakh seemed to wait the longest time before its dark wings flicked out, then it was fast as light, in an instant up on the van's roof facing Donald, panting, bleeding heavily. To some extent it was still Ryan, only fused with a hulking great mono-browed caveman. That day he'd stared at her, enjoyed her awkwardness across the library, he'd detected a hint of outrage in that face. What glared down on him now, rendered that kitten-like by comparison. Now she—it—looked extremely cross indeed.

Donald thrust his trusty blade into the sky, his face defiant as ever. In response, the Malakh swung its axe, flipping it hand-to-hand, winding the handle through its big sausage fingers with the synchronized ease of a slick-chic twirling baton. A final treat—the chopper went spinning high in the air, faster than a jet-propeller blade, to land neatly between the two hands of the monster, who had adopted the stance of attacker, and whose attention was firmly fixed back on Donald. "Aaaahhhh," it crooned. Then it was airborne. Overshadowing his position, it stemmed the rain like a vast umbrella. Donald kept his sights on its heart—to strike a blow it must raise its arms—for while Donald Little might have found it convenient to play the square most of his life, he'd never lightly accepted a single blow to his person. At school, he'd broken the arm of the first scumbag who'd aimed one. After that, they'd left him alone to become invisible again. Invisibility had been a good ally, but speed was his closest; he was faster than this big dumb ape could possibly guess. And he could jump, high. But even as these thoughts calculated the odds in his favor, he was watching the Malakh's arms extend out beyond its wingspan.

"No!" he protested furiously. "That's cheating! That's not fair!"

It roared laughter, bending in the long comic arms to plant a fist on each side of its bulky waist, then with a patronizing series of nods it pronounced, "Well, Don, let's just think about what is and isn't fair!" Its look was quizzical. "Let's talk about Kelly." Its arms went up, hands meeting once more around the axe's handle, close to the end for a better swing. The first blow neatly sheared off Little's upraised hands, so neatly that they landed together, palm up behind him, to cushion his head as he fell astonished to the concrete. The knife they'd clasped skittered away. Donald's high-pitched squeals of agonized fury echoed off the walls of the empty factory and out around the valley. The Malakh landed astride him. "Fair?" a young woman's voice cried out of it. "Was Andrea Maynard fair? Skinny, knocked-out little Andrea?" She chopped down into his groin, neatly severing the root of Donald's lifelong anxieties. "Was Kelly fair?" Chop! The

Malakh was deaf to his screams. "Like a fair fight, do you, Donny boy?" The beast hopped back. With the hands and cock out of the way, the axe rose and fell more methodically—beginning at the feet, avoiding deep blows to vital organs, or any region that might make this one quick.

In the long minutes that followed, while Donald Little could still think straight, he prayed to his God, his absolute and ultimate betrayer, that the wicked angel would finish him quicker, or at least take his eyes, so that he wouldn't have to watch as chunks of his favorite person in the whole world went flying off without him.

CHAPTER FIFTY-SEVEN

Through the branches of molting roadside sycamores, DI Beena Ryan watched slack-jawed as the honey-monster Beena Ryan flew off into the clouds; heading home, she gauged. James had recounted the previous night's events at his apartment—the upturned bin; the bloodstained empty bag. If it could do that, with just a swatch of secondhand blood, then there'd be no stopping its progress. It could be anybody. Anything.

She and Gaunt stood at the roadside by the abandoned car, the same make, model, and fake number plate as Beena's own. A quick check had told them Little hadn't turned up at his scheduled stop. And now there was the Malakh's presence. Altogether, this didn't look good. She radioed down to have the road closed.

"It came from in there." James pointed up the road toward the old wool mill. "Did you see the blood dripping off it?"

"Yeah. I'd say it's been clipped," Beena commented, staring off into the sky. "From the way it was lurching. Not that that's likely to stop it."

"What next?" Gaunt asked.

"Get forensics down here. Get some samples of that blood off the road, see what's it's made of."

The storm had passed and the autumn sun had set to work on reclaiming the waters. From the passenger seat of Detective Gaunt's car, DI Ryan sat dumbfounded, surveying the crime scene from where they'd stopped abruptly just inside the rusty iron gates of the factory grounds. Any further and they'd risk contaminating the crime scene, because it was so very extensive. Body parts were scattered almost the length and breadth of the parking lot. Most of the spilled blood was concentrated around the center, where what was left of a man's body remained on display: basically, a torso with hacked back stumps and a gorge where the groin had been. The head was still attached.

"Not exactly hallmark, this one," Gaunt said. "Shite almighty."

Ryan got out of the car first. Gaunt followed, pale-faced. She instructed the uniformed back up to keep their positions behind the perimeter. The library van sat parked to the left of the gate, backed up toward the trees, its ruptured back doors clung loosely to their hinges. The two moved cautiously forward, Gaunt getting ahead now, ranting urgently into his radio for the paramedics to get a move on, for what it was worth. He stopped close to the mutilated corpse, looking down into the face, its eyes wide open.

"It's him," Beena said. "It's Donald Little. Fuck! That's that then."

"Looks like it wanted to make this one last," Gaunt said. "Why the hell?" He squatted, carefully reaching forward to bring the lids down over those eyes, then jumped up sharply, backing away. "Jesus Christ!" he gasped, clapping a hand to his own mouth.

"Stay there, I said!" Beena demanded, stretching a hand back to the officers absent-mindedly drifting forward of the police-line. Maybe it was something about the scene, or seeing a real-live avenging-angel in the flesh, but a sense of frenzy, of hysteria almost, was closing in on the gathered party. People she knew to be sane and reliable were acting plain weird.

"His fuckin' eyes moved," Gaunt blurted.

Worse followed. A shallow moan gargled through the thick blood lodged in the throat of the butchered man. He was trying to speak. The stump of his severed right arm rose feebly up toward them, as if he was unaware there was no hand left for them to take hold of.

"God, no..." Gaunt whispered.

"Just go get something to tie on him," Beena snapped. "To put tourniquets on him...Go!"

Gathering all her strength, for the first time since starting the job, Beena Ryan struggled to hold on to the contents of her stomach. She rested one knee down in the mincemeat surrounding what was left of the man—a man she'd once taken an instant dislike to, not that it mattered now—and placed a hand gently on his chest. She might have been going for an Oscar when she assured him, "It's alright. We're going to help you." All she meant was they'd do as much as they could.

Gaunt had removed his belt and was on his way back toward Beena with three more he'd collected when a young female officer caught their attention. She'd hopped over the dry stone wall and was peering into the open back of the library van.

"What the hell are you doing?" Gaunt shouted. "Get back

over there!"

"There's something in here, sir," the WPC shouted back. "I think it's a body." She moved in toward the van, out of their sight.

"Careful!" Beena shouted. "Don't touch anything."

The sputtering of the mutilated man grew frantic.

"It's a body, Ma'am. Looks like it was a girl!" The young woman appeared again, holding something, despite the order. A card of some kind. "There's knives and stuff in here." She stopped speaking and stumbled back to the wall, which she virtually collapsed over, hurling violently.

Even from where she knelt, Beena realized then she could smell it, too. Her line of vision focused in on something hanging out of the back of the van—rubber sheeting of some kind—and some stuff coming off it, what appeared at first glance to be a thick brown liquid dripping away, but what she soon realized was a trail of bugs of every species practically running a river out of there. At the wall, another PC relieved the first of the card in her hand. Others were comforting her, staring mutely over the wall into the van.

"What is it?" Beena shouted.

"Driver's license, Ma'am. It'd been placed in her hand." He held it up. "It's Andrea Maynard. It's that young lass that went missing."

Four belts hung redundantly at James Gaunt's side as any progress forward on his part ceased forthwith. Beena withdrew the hand she'd offered in comfort, stood up, and stepped back to watch coldly on as Donald Little gargled out a bitter farewell to a world that would miss him like a royal dose of the clap.

CHAPTER FIFTY-EIGHT

Though the department was swamped with calls, Beena Ryan made a mental note to return Amelia Johnston's call before the day was out; even if she couldn't get over there right away, she could at least keep a tab on Rokerville through Ami. SFOs had been stationed around the estate since Kelvin Goddard's bloody castigation, but it seemed the longer a unit was in there the harder it was to keep in contact. There was something in the air itself, some sort of idiot gas, that got thicker the closer you came to the Malakh's lair. Gaunt had spent hours trawling through film footage to back up the morning's report, but any attempts to film the Malakh had come out the same—a static fuzz. Even through its boldest antics it seemed intent on maintaining its mythical status.

Many had fled the estate. The Johnstons were staying put at home. Out of everybody, Amelia seemed to be the one keeping a clear head, as if surviving her own personal trauma had rendered her immune to the chaos. Fionn Malloy was no longer contactable. Beena had to wonder what an AWOL priest does after resurrecting a lethal entity then quitting the cloth. She couldn't think too much about it, but suspected he might well have done a bunk altogether.

*

Fionn Malloy had been taught that when you die, your soul is judged and sent forth to one of three places: Heaven, Hell or Purgatory. Purgatory was never clearly defined in the scriptures or other writings, only presented as a kind of halfway house where sins were purged until souls were fit to reapply for their places with God. In light of recent events, it seemed to Fionn that this halfway house, for many, meant being trapped here on earth. Or held forcibly.

For the last time, Fionn arranged his vestments neatly on the bed before dressing, as was necessary in order to perform the essential Mass. He'd read of an old Padre in Italy who had done the same for a host of tormented spirits under similar circumstances, where there had been disturbances through evil rituals and abnormally high occurrences of unexplained deaths; where effectively, victims had been seduced into Purgatory and denied their Last Rites. The old Roman priest had professed that after performing such a mass—focused on the plea of Saint Gertrude, to free those souls whose essence the earthbound demons sucked on—the evil spirits that had blighted his parish were rendered powerless and thus forced to return to their source: back to Hell. Exorcising evil spirits was tricky business, one the church shied away from, perhaps because it had proven so disastrous so many times throughout history. The Mass was one other possible way. But one not in itself without risk.

*

Amelia Johnston perched on her wide windowsill with the lights out as the sun began to sink over the moors. Unlike others on the estate, she was keeping watch. She looked again at her dad's car parked down by a path still streaked with the blood that no amount of rain would wash away, that had stained the pavement as far as the Smith's gate four doors down. Neither her dad nor any of the neighbors had bothered trying to clean it up. After all, how much more blood would spill before this was over? If it would ever be over. Something undeniable was building in the very atmosphere of Rokerville.

Amelia turned the Post-it note through her fingers, the one with the number on, wondering what she could say that was news, that would give her an excuse to get DI Ryan over here. They needed to find Fionn. Amelia ran over and over in her mind what he'd said. "I caused it, and before I can face a single one of you again, I have to stop it." Before she made up her mind what to do, Fionn Malloy had walked up the hill on the other side of the avenue, all done up ready for Mass. That couldn't be right. By the time Ami opened the window and called to him, he was out of earshot, or so deep in thought he failed to hear. She quickly punched in Beena's number. Voicemail picked up again. Ami sent a text headed *urgent!*—at least that would be picked up at some point—then crept downstairs to get her coat.

*

The ornamental railings fronting the apartments' landscaped parking area looked punched out, *as if by an almighty hand*. Two armed police officers sat on the hood of their patrol car close by the ruptured gates, both staring off into space, happy enough, as if they'd had a tip-off that Santa was coming early, riding the skies of Rokerville complete with whinnying reindeer. Fionn had witnessed a similar duo further down the hill and was reminded of the guard in the prison chapel the day he visited Ben Hunter. *Don't think about Ben,* he cautioned himself. *Don't connect to them through thought. Not now.*

On approaching the red brick structure, it was hard to tell that the building was new. A tinge like old, dank moss infected it, seeping into every crack, adding fifty years to its appearance overnight. As Fionn passed the mound of dead charcoal that had been the oak tree, a breeze whipped up, spraying his lower garments with ash. Instinctively he looked up to the roof. Nothing was up there. It was just a breeze.

Along the building's front, doors left wide open from residents fleeing the previous night's disturbances clicked and banged as the wind explored each space behind them. Along to the left, about where his church had stood, Fionn found the ground floor flat marked *16,* the one Alan Ellis's daughter had escaped from. He stepped inside, immediately feeling a draft hit his face. Glancing down the corridor through the living area, he noticed that the back doors were also wide open. As he stepped forward, the one behind him slammed shut. The air stilled but at the same time gathered weight. He kept going. In the living room, a small lamp was still on at the back of the room. Fionn knelt by it and opened the book of Latin Mass. Outside, past the open doors, the blackness of the moors seemed endless, but as he began to speak, to read, to prey, the crowd slowly gathered. He did not allow their numbers to distract him, and so he continued. Soon they were mounting the steps, and to his left a large pot plant rustled.

CHAPTER FIFTY-NINE

"Eternal Father, I offer Thee the Most Precious Blood of Thy Divine Son, Jesus, in union with the masses said throughout the world today, for all the holy souls in Purgatory, for sinners everywhere, for sinners in the universal church; those within my own home and of my family. Amen."

The ensuing chorus of muffled sobs tortured him, not least that closest by, coming from the tall boy who hid his face, or the lack of one, beneath a fur-lined hood. The weight in the air was their fear; a collective dread that the priest would be stopped. Fionn continued, his voice trembling.

"Oh my Jesus, forgive us our sins; save us from the fires of hell. Lead all souls to heaven, especially those in most need of Thy mercy. And console the souls in Purgatory, especially those most abandoned."

Doors slammed loudly in the surrounding flats. Something touched his neck. Pressing in.

"May all the souls in Purgatory be with you today, O Lord. Amen."

And moving down his back. Nails digging in. Fionn

continued.

"Eternal Father, I offer You all my prayers, works, joys, sufferings, and merits. And I also offer You the body and blood soul and divinity of Your dearly beloved son, our Lord Jesus Christ. And I also offer you the bitter passion, agonizing death, holy wounds, and precious blood of our Lord Jesus Christ. And I also offer you the Holy Name, Holy Face, sacred heart, and divine mercy of our Lord Jesus Christ."

The hooded boy emerged from the cover of the weeping fig tree and, head bowed, knelt down before his priest. Many figures who had hesitated on the steps outside entered the room to kneel likewise. Fionn now stood, unfurling the seemingly endless list of names he had spent the previous night and day compiling.

The back of his robes ripped open. The probing fingers nipped him violently, clawed at the flesh of his back. He barely flinched.

"Eternal Father I ask four things in union with all the masses that are being said this day throughout the whole world, and also in union with all the crosses and sufferings of all mankind this day throughout the world. Firstly, to expiate all the sins that all the holy souls in Purgatory committed during each and every day of their whole life. Secondly, to purify all the good that all the holy souls in Purgatory did poorly during each and every day of their whole life. Thirdly, to supply for all the good that all the holy souls in Purgatory ought to have done and that they neglected to do during each and every day of their whole life. Fourthly, for relief and deliverance for all the holy souls in Purgatory. Amen."

A united "Amen" resonated out to the moor. With its swell, the punishment to the priest's flesh ceased instantaneously. Silent tears tracked his face. Clearing his throat, allowing his voice a renewed strength, he continued, "And I beg you, Eternal Father…" He allowed the weight of the list to fall free. "…to please grant to me through the prayers and intercessions of all the holy souls in Purgatory— the following favors." Standing taller than he'd ever felt, he read the first, most urgent in his thoughts, "Take Callum George Heslop…"

The figure in the parka rose to his feet. And as a soft, silver light enveloped him, the obscuring hood disintegrated before Fionn's eyes, revealing a face perfectly whole. For a brief moment, Callum looked overjoyed to see him, as if he'd been blind up to that moment. But soon other things, beyond where the priest stood, in his small human capacity, appeared to Callum, things of another world, that turned his smile up as far as it could go, like the kid had just witnessed the most amazing trick in the circus. Then the light that swathed him imploded, and Callum Heslop was gone.

Fionn allowed himself to weep briefly before gathering his senses, then backtracked to the list's beginning, as it had begun in September 1537, "Lord, take thy servant, Thomas John Alcott…" A man in Tudor clothing stood up, smiled beautifully, and soon left likewise. A queue was forming outside, orderly, patient, a sense of calm filtering through. Father Malloy stepped up the pace. God willing, a thousand names would go tonight.

"And take Anne Winston, Peter Cryer, Amie Stirling…" and on he went.

*

Some of the later faces he recognized from archived

photographs. Others he knew. Then he spotted an unmistakable face among the throng of shadows. So slight and demure; typical of her to shrink back in a crowd. Her name wasn't due but he sensed this needed doing quickly. "Dear Lord, take Anita Jane Hunter..."

The wife of his friend stood up shyly, her face saddened at first, cursed by an awareness that he'd hoped wasn't with the dead. She'd lost her man, they both had, but as the warm light wrapped her soul in unspeakable joy, she had to press her knuckles to her lips to stifle a giggle, and soon her essence diminished to a sparkle in the night.

She knew, Fionn thought, *that she was leaving Ben behind, forever. Like my own, his soul is doomed.* And with that glimmer of a thought his guard was down. A gust of wind stormed like a vandal through the apartment, cracking open every door, ultimately concentrating into a boulder-fist that gut-punched Fionn to the back wall.

*

The corresponding text from DI Ryan told Amelia to wait at home where it was safe, until she could get over there. By that time, Ami had already searched through ten apartments. Number sixteen didn't feel any different from the others, except that she had to push the unlocked door quite hard to open it, like someone was behind it, barring her way. It was at precisely the moment she entered the living room that something hurled Fionn through the air and slammed him violently against the wall close by. She screamed in shock, steadying herself on the doorframe. Fionn slid down, gasping for breath, shattering the table lamp on his way, shrouding the place in sudden darkness. Ami could just make him out, crumpled there against the wall, groaning in pain, but couldn't move to help. Her legs were useless.

"Father Malloy," she cried, unsure of why she was being so official, except that he was in the uniform. "Sorry, I can't move."

Fionn held out a firm hand, silently indicating she shouldn't try to. She hesitated, unsure. He pressed a finger to his lips, begging her compliance. As her eyes adjusted to the darkness Fionn struggled back to his feet, took a few deep breaths, then swiftly resumed his former position, and his reading. "Lord, take Fathers Peter O'Brien and James Galloway..."

Ami slid down the doorframe until she sat on the carpet, as speechless as she'd ever been. She watched in awe as the two named men, dressed like Fionn in priests' clothing, stood up from amongst a dark, patiently waiting crowd that Ami had failed to notice till now, and in a shower of the kindest light imaginable, took their leave for some place better than Rokerville.

Ami remained there, rooted to the spot, her sleeve-swaddled hands pressing back each tiny cheer that fought to escape her open mouth, as the process went on into the night.

CHAPTER SIXTY

The entity snapped awake at three a.m. with a creeping feeling that its grave had been trampled over. It woke unaware that its bulk was in mid-melt, leaving the face featureless apart from the bloodshot eyes, the lower lids of which hung slack like a bloodhound's. The previous day's wounding had taken its toll, and now, compounding the agony, it felt an inexplicable weakness, a sapping of its immense strength. There came, in the following minutes, the realization of an absence, abandonment, that the source of their power, the wealth of it accumulated over centuries, had sunk back to the depths.

They were alone.

The Zwerg was incensed. No way was Hex about to lay low for the next five hundred years waiting for another thousand schmucks to put out the necessary essence. Whatever ritual had been undertaken to cause this damage would get reversed, and quick! Extracting pointless confessions—no fucker was getting let off—had proved one of the fun parts of its campaign; the art of torture was practiced and perfected.

Appolyn instinctively knew she should be the one present at the surface. At least initially. The Zwerg was the enforcer, yes, but she, Appolyn, was the negotiator, the springer of traps where traps were prudent. As for Hawk, poor Ben, he wasn't much of anything now. Practically sucked dry. That's what Hexter did to everything. He was too greedy.

Appolyn adopted the form that was familiar to the messenger—that of an angel.

At the cave's opening, she surveyed her condition. Holding out one slender arm, she immediately recognized that none of her former glow was evident. In those few hours of rest—a respite crucial to their restoration—her aura had faded to an earthly dullness. What's more, the mending had been ineffective. No wound should persist, only melt away. Drawing a hand up to the nape of her neck, she was able to fit two fingers deep into the gaping wound the weasel Liddle had inflicted; withdrawing them she observed fresh blood. At least the blade had failed to penetrate Ben's essence which, while it remained vital, was the only part of their entity that could be destroyed, dragging the rest of them with it: the reason, though it pained her, that she was prepared to see him dissolved. Her face darkened upon looking down at the structure that had been erected on the church grounds, their birthplace. All that work. So much time for just a butterfly's day in the sun. Her formerly resplendent wings hung like the dirty grey blankets of beggars. Even so, they must now carry her, while they could, to face their betrayer, to reverse their fate.

The priest was still present there, she was sure of that as she drifted downwind. The place he had returned to was at the point where his altar had stood, where she had first tempted him. He might well die there this day. The Zwerg wanted it badly now. If their fortunes proved irreversible then he could have him. The sin the priest had committed against his God was surely unforgiveable; he would be bound to Earth. Perfect justice: having robbed them of a multitude of souls, his soul would be the first of the new line that would replenish their strengths.

*

Fionn sat on the cold steps, waiting. Once the final spirit had passed, he'd pleaded with Amelia to go home and wait for him there. She hadn't been gone long when Fionn felt it wake up.

His link to the Malakh had been closer than he'd wished to realize, for now its anger registered hard. Strangely, sitting there gazing out to the moorland, the damp wind whipping his face, he felt at peace. Even in the face of death. Even a death that held no promise of a reprieve. Before now, whenever he'd imagined the future, he'd seen something to aim for, seen himself somewhere. Now he saw nothing. But that was okay. He'd made his peace with God. If he was to die tonight then so be it. He had nothing left to fight for. But even as he told himself that, he knew he would fight.

*

The armed patrol officers stationed around the estate were suddenly alert, as though the sleeping sickness weighing down their energies had gradually lifted as night approached dawn. Beena Ryan pulled in by the patrol car parked outside the apartment block. That ugly green haze had lifted from the scene; she was Dorothy walking into the land of Oz.

Something radical had happened here.

"Has anything gone off tonight, that you've noticed?" she asked the officers.

"Sorry, Ma'am," the older man said. "I can fill you in on about the last hour or two, but that's all. Some old lady went in one of the flats a bit ago."

"Went inside the block? What for?"

"For her medication, she said…" The older officer looked embarrassed admitting it. "Didn't see the harm, but…"

"She wasn't that old," the younger officer interjected. "Probably forties at most. She just looked older. Smoker's face. Booze an' all, I'll bet."

"Anyway," the other shook his head, as if all that was of no consequence. "Sorry. Nothing else I can tell you. That young-un's been waiting for you a while. She wouldn't talk to us. Same old, same old. Shall I wake her up, Ma'am?"

Beena walked over and looked into the back seat of the squad car where Ami was slumped, one side of her tired, damp face pressed against the window. "I'll do it," she said. "I'd better do. She's the only one who knows what Father Malloy's been up to." She went around to the other rear door, leaned in, and gave Ami a little shake. "And by all accounts," she added, helping Ami out of the car, "he's been up to something."

*

Far from the perfect being he'd kept in mind, the waif of a girl flying limply toward him more resembled a pretty Nosferatu. One side of her neck had been gouged open and blood drenched the length of her mock-angel robe. Her grey, drained expression held none of the serenity that had formerly convinced him of the presence of a heavenly host.

She landed with somewhat forced grace a short distance from the foot of the steps of Number 16, where Fionn now stood, halfway up, ready. His eye was diverted momentarily from her pallid face to the mud that clung heavily to the hem of her gown—somehow final confirmation of her imperfection.

She smiled weakly. "I should not wish to see you again, Priest, yet it is good to see you."

"I am afraid, Appolyn, that I cannot say the same."

"You believed in our cause," she said softly.

"The term 'hood-winked' springs to mind."

"Miracles are not from God alone, dear Priest. You helped work a miracle. Please, stay true. Reverse what you have done, support our mission, and live on."

Fionn shrugged. "Can't say I'm that bothered to."

She stepped forward, her smile withering. "Reverse it anyhow."

"It's not possible. Even if I wanted to."

"You can curse God, deny Him, and He, in turn, will deny your prayer."

Fionn laughed out loud. "Sure. Whatever you say, Appolyn. Only you out-and-out lied to me once before, if I remember rightly. The Ashes of Saint Agnes, my eye. You're all self, self, self, girl."

Rage uglied her face as she moved closer.

Fionn drew Carl Wilson's gun from his robes and raised it in line with her head. "Stay down there," he ordered. "We can talk well enough from where we stand."

A familiar mocking tainted her expression as she observed the beginnings of a quiver in his hand.

"Of course you realize," she said, "that Ben is in here with us?" She stepped closer still. Fionn held the gun steady, knocking off the safety catch. She hesitated, smiling cruelly, then took another step. He was reminded of a game he'd played as a boy—*What time is it, Mr. Wolf?* Where each approaching step, for any fool not alert enough, might lead to *Dinner time!*

"I don't believe he's there anymore. I don't believe he's anywhere." Fionn's voice faltered treacherously. "I felt him die. Like I felt my father die, like I felt my mother die. I don't believe anything you say anymore."

"He is here with us," she assured. Her throat rippled. "Fionn," Ben's voice called, but it wasn't quite Ben's voice, more like a close impression. "Please," it begged. "She can help me." Then calmly, in her own tone, she agreed, "I can help him. And we can go on. We can do so much good together. We have so much left to accomplish: everything you wished for."

Trembling with doubt, Fionn lowered the gun. "By feeding on the misery of others? Is that what you want, Ben? If that really was you? Is that what you want? To suck the life out of the living?"

"Address me alone," she ordered.

"Okay, angel. Carl Wilson was a good man. He'd done no wrong. He was innocent, and you bloody lot murdered him. Just because he got in your way, because you didn't like him. Because you're no more perfect than the next psychopath. The power that kept you going was evil, and now it's gone. And I'm glad of it."

"Last chance, Priest!" Appolyn stiffened at Hexter's intrusion, suppressing his impatience. "Your gun is useless," her voice returned. "Take back your prayer or die."

"Okay, I'll die. But first, just tell me," he said. "Before you go, Appolyn—because I know the other fellow's dying to make some spectacular entrance. Who are you? Do you even remember? Do you remember that you were once good? How much you were loved? Hexter has corrupted you."

She laughed, almost tiredly. "Ah, you think we are opposed. Not so. I exist because of him. I am Hexter the Zwerg, and he is me. And what of being loved? What good is love to the dead? Only power matters in this world. Men showed me no mercy, and I shall spend eternity showing them no better. So your damage is done." She sneered. "We will recover. We have waited this long. And then what of you? Do you imagine yourself forgiven now, holy man? Remember what the Lord spaketh unto Moses, his most faithful, who turned his face but for an instant. 'You may view the land at a distance, but you yourself shall never enter that land which I am giving to the Israelites.'"

Once again, she had casually invaded the archives of his mind. Fionn's guard fell flat, and in that instant she took off, soaring over his head, and as her wings clouded him, her face altered, the mouth stretching out to an unsightly grimace. Her shape changed, bulked out. Having witnessed such a transformation before, he leapt from the steps to get some distance between him and it. Struggling through the cloggy mud, Fionn rose, turning to face it.

"*Dinner time!*" the Malakh sang.

The thing that'd landed up there on the top step certainly looked hungry, though it might have been drooling with rage judging by the clash of heavy brows. Like a steam train accelerating, livid breaths chuffed out of it clouding the cool air. The eyes were snake-like, its fingers talons, its body the hairy chunk of a wild boar. Silvery blackened fangs packed its flabby jaws. The glimpse Fionn 'd caught of it in dreams had been a teacup poodle by comparison. This is what it was hiding from the cameras: barely a trace of humanity remained.

Staying fixed on the Malakh's position, Fionn tried to ease backwards, but his feet had lodged deep in the mud. That's when he realized he was no longer holding the gun.

CHAPTER SIXTY-ONE

The two armed patrol officers followed DI Ryan, who in turn followed closely behind the young girl, who led them along the ground floor level to apartment sixteen. The front door was closed.

"It's this one," Ami said. "He was in here, I swear. There were loads of spirits, and he was sending them away, like...back to God. I swear."

"Well, I don't know about that," Beena said. "But whatever he's up to he's bound to be annoying somebody, or something." She tried the door. It was UPVC paneling then a beveled glass window at eye level. She could make out nothing beyond it. The place was in darkness. She rattled the door again. "It's locked. Looks like it's on a Yale. He must've dropped the latch."

"He wouldn't 've done that," Ami protested. "It's not like he's got anything to hide. Anyway, I was the last one to come out, and I didn't drop the latch."

"Well it's locked now, love." Beena smacked the door in frustration. "You stay here, okay. We'll have to go round, lads. Ami...just go get back in the car for now."

"No way," Ami protested. "I'm coming. I know the quick way round the back."

"Hold on a minute," the older officer said to the other one. "Isn't this the one that old lady went into?"

"She wasn't that old. Like I said. But, yeah. I'm pretty sure it was this same one."

"And she's not come out again?" Beena confirmed. "Well, maybe *she* locked it. Great. Right, lads, go get whatever you've got in the car to bust this door in. Ami, what's the quickest way round? Show me."

*

Hearing the apartment's front door rattling seemed to Fionn like a world away. The thing standing above him never flinched at it, didn't so much as glance behind. There was no fear there, only seething hatred. He looked frantically around the mud and caught sight of the gun's nozzle sticking up a little way off to his right.

"Tut tut tut. Naughty, naughty," the Malakh croaked in tuneful Irish twang, wagging a claw. "Don't make me come down there, pretty boy. I'll eat your face off for breakfast, so I will."

Ignoring that, Fionn lunged for the gun, his muddy robes skewing his balance. In the same split second, the Malakh sprang forth, talons hooked at the ready. Fionn's hand seized purchase on the weapon. As he stood to fire, the Malakh took its first swipe with ease, ripping five scarlet stripes into Fionn's chest. He yelped in agony, managing to right himself, but it was hovering above him at an angle he couldn't raise a hand to without those claws getting in another rip. The Malakh flapped its huge wings and Fionn fell backwards, firing off a shot. The blast echoed off the apartments' walls and out to the moors. The bullet had passed straight through the beast. In a mock girl's tone it screamed, then guffawed laughter, beginning a tantalizing descent toward its quarry. Fionn struggled weakly in the mire, one hand pressed to his torn, bleeding chest. "Forgive me, Lord!" he cried into the empty skies beyond the monster. Out of the blue, the Malakh roared in extreme protest, for real this time; unwillingly it was retreating back toward the steps, kicking and twisting like a puppet enraged at its own treacherous strings.

Fionn struggled to his knees. The gun hung slackly in his hand. He raised it, taking aim, but hesitated. The Malakh's wings were retreating, its frame softening and at the same time, elongating like a giant strand of yellowy chewing gum. And as the head reformed, the eyes that emerged were unmistakably human. The mouth, overshadowed by a hooked nose, managed a smile.

"Ben," Fionn gasped. For a minute, he laughed uncontrollably.

The big man, drenched in a slick of cold sweat, stumbled backwards to sit on the steps. "How-do, mate," he said. "Long time, no see."

"Ben." It was all he could say.

When his father had passed away, Fionn made it all the way back to Ireland in time to say good-bye, but then had been resting in his hotel room when it actually happened; he'd felt it happen. Earlier that day, in his hospital bed, his dad 'd seemed twice as old and at the same time half the man Fionn 'd known. What had remained there in the bed, all yellowed and dulled by morphine, was barely there at all. That's how Ben looked to Fionn now.

"Do it, Fionn," Ben said. He somehow found the strength

to stand.

Fionn went cold, realizing what he meant. "No, Ben. When I fired the shot before, I believed you weren't there, Ben. I believed you dead. So don't ask me to do it now."

Ben nodded to the gun. "This is the only way. It has to be me takes it, and you know it."

"I can't."

Ben shook his head. "A bloody wuss to the end, aren't you?" He smiled. Even that seemed to tire him. "I wasn't asleep," he said. "I let them sleep, kept them down, because I felt what you were doin'. Jobs a good'n, Father. Good lad."

Fionn nodded, crying quietly. Ben was right. He was a wuss. He couldn't bear this.

"So did you see my girl? Did you see Anita off?"

"Yep. She's gone." Fionn managed to get up on his feet. He wiped a dirty sleeve over his face. "It looked amazing. I wish you could've seen..." He stopped.

Ben let out a long breath. "It's okay. I know I can't be with her. Good job, though. But it's not the last job on the agenda, is it?"

"Don't ask me again. It's not possible."

"Fionn, he'll be back. *It'll* be back. I'm too tired to fight it; *them*, if I'm honest. I didn't want to believe evil of her. Same as you didn't. But she wants me gone. Between them, they'll see me gone. You know that, don't you? You said yerself. I'm already dead. As good as, any road. You felt that because it's true. I'm just about eaten up, mate, and once that's done, no bullet 'll make a dent in these two."

"There must be another way."

"No, mate. There is no other way. Sorry." Ben straightened as well as he could. "Raise the gun," he said. "Like you had it. Come on. Good lad."

Fionn raised his arm but his hand rattled uncontrollably. Like an opposing magnet, his finger felt pushed from the trigger. "Nooo, God," he protested.

A shot blasted and Ben's throat exploded outwards. Fionn staggered back, unsure of quite what had happened. Ben's eyes widened briefly, he coughed once, twice, then dropped, his spine severed at the neck. For an awful moment, his body seemed to leave his head behind, then he came crashing down the steps, finally coming to rest on his back in the mud. Up where he'd stood, within the frame of the apartment's open doorway, stood Shirley Monk, mother of Xbox and Monkey. Half triumphant, half crazed, she roared like a lioness as Ben tumbled away, the gun she'd purchased from Coxer's goons stretched out in her white knuckled grasp.

"Ben!" a girl's voice cried out repeatedly from the near distance. Ami almost lost her trainers clambering through the churned up mud. She fell to her knees by Ben Hunter and took his dead face into her lap. "Don't go, Ben, not yet," she begged. "Don't go, Hawk. We all know you're sorry for what you did. It's okay, you don't 'ave to die. You're a good man, Ben. You're good. Don't leave us. We didn't even say good-bye."

Beena, who'd been chasing her in a vain effort to protect her from the scene, arrived by her side. "Let him go, Ami, love. It's over. He's gone." She put a hand on the girl's shoulder. "Get that bloody weapon off of her," she yelled up at the two officers, who'd busted in through the apartment's front door and were fast approaching Shirley Monk. The two complied, restraining the woman, who now gaped dismayed down at the priest standing alone in the grounds. Beyond the man she'd shot dead, Fionn Malloy was struggling to maintain his footing. He swayed. "Nooo," she screamed. "Sweet Jesus, no!" She struggled to free an arm long enough to cross her soul. "I didn't mean to, I swear!" She was quickly seized again. "I'm sorry, Father."

Beena's attention turned to Fionn and, like the others present, she stared at him in mute confusion.

Fionn had felt the pain, and strangely, had heard it—a sharp thump dulled on impact by the unbearable sight of his friend's execution. Now he was struggling to see at all. His vision was clouding; the world before him, the people in it, whose names were slipping from mind like love notes on a breeze—all of them, everything, swam in a scarlet lake. His hand seemed to rise of its own accord to trace the source of the pain, his fingers carefully tapping their way up his face until they met with the solid metal nub of the bullet that had passed through Ben Hunter and now protruded from his own forehead.

"Aw no," Ami protested from where she knelt. "Not you." She raised her eyes to the sky. "Not him, God!" she shouted furiously. "Not after what he did here. You're not bein' fair."

Fionn swayed. Beena and Ami reached him together, each receiving his weight by the crook of an arm, as Fionn Malloy dropped quietly out of the end of his own nightmare.

CHAPTER SIXTY-TWO

Louis Johnston turned up at the hospital waiting room about six that evening and led Ami, still caked in mud, away for a shower and some necessary sleep. Fourteen hours and still no news. Beena Ryan kept away until the following day. She was directed to Intensive Care, where Fionn remained on life support, more bandage and tubing than man, the eyes below the bandages blackened with trauma, his breathing assisted. It didn't look good. Beena stood over him, unaware of time passing. She found herself watching the thick layer of black stubble concentrated around his lower face, imagining she was seeing it grow; as if it still growing meant he was still working.

Dr. Suleiman invited the detective into her office.

"I doubt he'll be able to talk to you for a while," she said. "In fact it may not happen at all. Did he witness something important?"

"Yes. Very important, but, if I'm honest, I'm here more as a friend." It felt strange saying it though. They hadn't been friends, not really. But she knew if they'd met at school, with everything ahead of them, they would have been good friends. Still would be. "Is he likely to recover?"

"His temporal lobe is damaged. That's not fixable, Ms. Ryan. We have done all we can. Now we can only wait to see how he responds to treatment. Does he have family? They should be told."

Beena took a while to focus on the latter part of what the doctor had just said. "I think…well, I know, his parents are both gone. I understand he has a wider family in Ireland—an uncle, some cousins. Some of his parishioners, the Johnstons, I believe they're in contact with his family. Getting back to what you first said, Dr. Suleiman, when you say the brain damage is *not fixable*, do you mean there's no possible future?"

"He may have one, but not the same one he had two days ago; his memory, short term, will be problematic. He won't be able to process received information to the same capacity. This will affect his behavior, though to what extent we can't say as yet. I have no crystal ball, Detective Inspector. As I told you, we can only wait and see. Now, you say you are a friend? Could you take his things, please. His priest's garments. They are very torn and dirty. We can't deal with them here."

It wasn't so much a request as an instruction. As the doctor spoke, she had casually picked up a black plastic sack containing what remained of Fionn Malloy's history, the life he'd lived, the man he had been, and thrust it at Beena Ryan.

Beena's hands remained firmly in her lap. "I'm sorry," she said. "I can't take that."

The doctor looked put-out and only nodded as Beena rose and left the ward, surprised by the depth of her grief, and determining not to return, at least for a few days. If at all.

*

A week later, Ami Johnston was on the phone to the station. It was about four in the afternoon. DI Ryan sat with Detective Gaunt in her office. They'd read the autopsy report for Hunter and there was nothing to suggest that anything out of the ordinary had ever happened to him. No abnormalities. Every blood cell tested matched Hunter's medical records; every fingerprint was his own. With a distraught sister waiting to bury the man, there seemed no reason not to just let him go.

Beena took the call, aware that James Gaunt was listening closely.

"Detective Inspector Ryan speaking."

"Hi. I'm at the hospital. I thought you might have been back before now." Ami sounded irritated. "Thought I'd ring you anyway, let you know what's happening."

"Sorry, I've been busy, Ami. Any news?"

"He asked for you, by your first name."

"What? When?"

"He has been doing for a couple of days now. Says he has something to tell you."

"Ami, how is that possible? Is there a doctor around I can speak to?"

"Trust me. I'm not stupid. I know what he said, and he said that it's you he wants to speak to. Just get down 'ere, will you?" Ami hung up.

*

The hospital was roughly the same era as the city library, mid Victorian, not quite so much in need of repair, but stuffy, airless. Beena paused on the fourth floor landing before entering the ward. The nights were drawing in, getting colder.

An old sash window, bolted shut, looked down on the lamp-lit parking lot. She checked the position of Gaunt's car, reassured by his presence even though she'd derided him as a stalker for insisting he come. He was slouched reading a paperback by the car's interior light, unaware of her watching from above.

Amelia sat texting by Fionn's bedside in a room off the main ward, similar to that Beena had first seen Ami in, after the gang attack that triggered the avalanche of events she'd felt helpless to stop, or even slow the progress of since. Next to Ami, quietly reading the Evening Post sat the tall young man Ami had met in the city center the day they followed Wilson. From the corridor, Fionn's bed was only partly in sight. Beena hesitated, noticing a young doctor working at the computer system behind the desk, and went to speak to him first. She showed her badge, not so much because this was official business, but because it always got her where she wanted to be a lot quicker than if she simply asked.

"I'm here to see Fionn Malloy. Are you familiar with his progress?"

"Yes. Quite amazing, I have to say." The doctor looked up briefly. "He must be very strong."

"And he's talking?"

"I believe so."

"Rambling talking, or making sense?"

"I would suggest you go in and talk to him, Detective Inspector. See for yourself."

That, she realized, was precisely what she was avoiding.

Ami stood up as Beena entered. "Do you mind, Deep," she said.

Deepak, the boyfriend stood, kissed her on the head, gave a nod to the detective, and left. Ami sat back down. Beena sat on the edge of the bed.

"You'll be in trouble with Staff Nurse," Ami told her.

"Trouble's my middle name," Beena said, then realized how corny that must sound to a teenager. "How is he then?" She looked at the man lightly sleeping in the bed she was perched on and suddenly felt awkward about the proximity.

Apart from the bandaging and some flimsy pajama bottoms, Fionn lay naked, the sheets crumpled down around his knees. For someone who'd been severely mauled and shot in the head, at the threshold of death's door only a week before, he looked remarkably well, like someone who'd been working out, his lean body appearing taut and energized.

"He seems a lot better, but…do you think he'll be forgiven?" Ami asked. "He said he caused it all. I can't believe it."

"I don't know about all that, Ami."

"You didn't see what he did. It was amazing."

"Then he must've patched things up with his God, mustn't he?"

"I hope so." Ami smiled and nodded. "I really do." Fionn stirred. "Look, I'm gunner go, leave you to it," she said. "Bye for now. And thanks for coming."

"Okay. Bye." Beena watched her go, thinking when it came to the majority of kids on Rokerville, the bad press was unjustified. When she turned back, she got a start. Fionn Malloy stared directly at her. For a moment, she swore her heartbeat was audible through her open mouth. She considered moving off the bed, making a remark about hospital rules, but then stayed put.

"Hi," she said. "Remember me?" It was a serious question.

"Hi." His voice was barely a croak. "Course I do. You're Beena. You like Christmas."

"I do." There was a glass of juice with a straw on his table. Supporting the back of his head, she fed him a long drink. Nobody she knew had ever been this sick, but this felt easy, at least now that he was awake, less like she was intruding.

"That better now?"

"Thanks." He smiled warmly. "I'm trying to remember what I was thinking earlier," he said. "It seemed important."

"Is there any need to rush? You've got a good long rest ahead of you, Fionn. I'm sure whatever it is 'll come back to you. Anyway, it's good to see you back in the land of the living."

"Is that where I am?"

She shrugged. "Yes."

"I keep thinking there's somewhere I need to go."

"Where could that possibly be? You need rest, that's all."

"I feel fine."

"Ami said there was something you wanted to tell me, that's why I came. But I should've come anyway." Her eyes dropped. "I wanted to say something, as well, Fionn. That is, I'm sorry I was tough on you before, when you spoke about giving up the priesthood." She placed a hand gently on his. "But I do think you were right. Too much has happened."

Something flickered on in his eyes, as if the dimmer switch had been down but suddenly dialed up to full. The hand she covered turned over and gripped hers.

"Don't beat yourself up about it." He grinned. "With the uniform down the Swanee, we can date. Right?"

She didn't like the way he was looking at her. Something about his eyes wasn't right. This must be the kind of shift in behavior Dr. Suleiman spoke of. Beena eased her hand from his grip. "Steady on now, Fionn. It's rest you need, remember."

He ran a hand over the muscles of one taut arm, scrutinizing his own condition as if it were something he'd just purchased. "There's no rest for the wicked, honey."

Beena stood up, her back stiffening.

"Going somewhere?" he asked.

"I'll come back tomorrow," she assured him, patting the hand she'd ditched, maintaining a smile. "Perhaps by then you'll remember what it was you wanted to tell me."

He eased back against the pillows, placing both hands behind his head. She couldn't help thinking how much that should hurt, yet his expression was cool, blasé even. His eyes dropped to her hemline. "You once thought I was sizing up your legs," he said. "Well I am now."

"I'll be on my way then," she said. "If that's all you've got to say."

As she reached the door he shouted hoarsely, "Beena, stop, please. Wait."

She turned slowly and there, as if he'd never left, was the man she'd chatted easily with in his church, about her own family, about his life in Galway, who she really wished she'd had a chance to get to know better. "What is it, Fionn?"

"I'm sorry," he said. "I couldn't save the world. There was no red cape, not for me. Please, tell Amelia, I'm sorry, so very, very sorry."

*

Beena all but fell into Gaunt's car then hung forward, forehead on the dash, her chest heaving back the controlled breaths of a woman in the second stages of labor.

"What the fuck?" Gaunt yelled. "What's going on? What's happened? Has he died or what? Say something, for God's sake." He punched himself back against the seat. "I bloody knew it! How long 've you been in this game for, eh? Don't you know by now you don't get attached? You don't get involved."

"It's not that, James," she said, finding some level of order in herself. She sat up straight, staring ahead. "Something's not right. I keep thinking back to what Suleiman said about his condition, but even so, something's badly wrong."

"Do you want me to go talk to this doctor woman?"

Beena's face felt starved of blood. "I've a feeling that won't do any good now."

"Well, what is it that's wrong? Explain it to me."

"His eyes."

"Describe his eyes."

"It wasn't for long, but they changed. They were like…"

"Like what?"

"Like the picture, from seg block: cold and black."

Before he realized it, she was out of the car and heading back toward the hospital's main entrance.

She'd reached the fourth floor by the time Gaunt caught up to her. A young nurse sat behind the ward desk. "Visiting's over for the day," she advised them as they rushed in. "Sorry."

Gaunt flashed his badge, too burnt out to explain.

"Where's the doctor who was here before?" Beena asked. "I need a quick word."

"Sorry, he's gone off for the night. Can I be of any help?"

"The man who's in that room." Beena showed her badge. "Fionn Malloy. I want to discuss his case in more detail. It's urgent."

"Oh, I think he's been moved, Inspector," the nurse said, getting up. "I do know who you mean, though. I met him yesterday." She frowned. "Yes. Bit of a one, him. But they must have moved him from there, probably onto the ward."

"That's not possible," Beena said. "I was here fifteen minutes ago, in there with him."

"Well, I checked in there about five minutes ago myself," the nurse assured her, heading for the room. The door was closed. "Because there was a right racket in there, screaming, like someone being burnt alive, but when I checked, she was fine."

"She?"

"The young woman in bed in there." The nurse pushed the door open and stood staring blankly into the small enclosed space, as did the two detectives pressing past her. The sheets were back, the bed empty. "Oh, she must have wandered off for a coffee or something. Sorry. They do that sometimes. You can't turn your back. Give me a minute, though, I'll look up your Mr. Malloy, see where he's got to. Oh, wait…" The nurse backtracked to the name-card on the door, which read *Fionn Malloy*. "That can't be right."

Beena exited the room, folding back onto the corridor wall. Slowly she said, "Could you describe this young woman to me, please. In detail."

The nurse shrugged. "Well, quite distinctive looking, actually: pure looking, if that makes sense; really pretty, young, petite, this thick silvery blonde hair, but natural sort of blonde, quite rare, that. Can't say she looked that sick, really. She was positively glowing."

"Wait a minute. Oh, Christ!" Beena's eyes widened on a sudden inkling. "James, come with me, now!" she shouted.

She hastened back out through the double doors to the landing, followed by her colleague. A detail that had barely registered when she'd returned to the ward now chilled her spine: a strong draft, in a virtually draft-proof building.

Beena Ryan went to the wide-open sash window, its bolts hung loose, snapped back like ring-pulls on a coke-can. James Gaunt was close behind her, looking agitatedly about himself, ducking low, as if expecting a slap to rain down out of thin air.

Hands clasped to the wooden frame, Beena leaned out, gazing with silent awe at the sheer vastness of the night sky.

THE END

ABOUT THE AUTHOR

Janine-Langley Wood has been writing since childhood. At around age nine, she cut her teeth on horror reading, sneaking the Pan Books of Horror off her auntie's bookshelves. She teaches creative writing to students ranging from prison inmates to foundation degree level writers. The gothic thriller Damned Rite, a haunting supernatural thriller with a vigilante killer twist, came from her interest in the horror within.

If you enjoyed reading this, I would be grateful if you would support my work by posting a review where you purchased this book. I read every review personally so I can get your feedback and make my writing even better.

Thank you again for your support!
Janine

Please visit Janine online
http://janinewood2012.wix.com/janine-langleywood
http://janinewood2012.wix.com/melt---horror-novel
http://janinewood2012.wordpress.com/2014/10/02/vigilant
es-in-the-21st-century-3/
https://www.facebook.com/janinelangley.wood
https://twitter.com/wood_melt
https://www.linkedin.com/profile/view?id=239826938&trk
=nav_responsive_tab_profile

Lightning Source UK Ltd.
Milton Keynes UK
UKOW07f1806030215

245628UK00003B/3/P